CORPUS CALVIN

Praise for 2015 Lambda Literary Award Finalist *Calvin's Head*

"A very chilling and intense story…This author has a fresh, exciting, and slightly disturbing voice that should be heard. I recommend *Calvin's Head* to anyone who enjoys thrillers, and to anyone who wants to take a step outside of their comfort zone."—*Prism Book Alliance*

"*Calvin's Head* is an 'in the moment' psychological thriller that thrusts you right into the middle of the insanity…There is indeed a head, there's murder, there's sexual tension, there's manipulation, deception, and obsession in a gay relationship… plus, there's a dog named Calvin!"—*Boys, Bears & Scares*

"*Calvin's Head* is a solid psychological thriller…told from three equally essential points of view. I enjoyed this trip into the mind of a serial killer with some serious identity issues." —*The Novel Approach*

"Equal parts screwball comedy and suspenseful thriller, full of twists and turns—both in plot and locales…but the pièce de résistance is allowing a point of view for the dog Calvin, a unique technique that gives this novel its heart."—*Chelsea Station*

"An enjoyable thriller, perfect for a sunny summer afternoon in Vondelpark…it's actually a dark thriller that keeps the reader engrossed in the plot and wanting more."—*DutchNews.nl*

"There is a sense in the book that anything could happen…It's hard to compare *Calvin's Head* to any other book I've read. This is entirely a good thing and I'll definitely be reading more from this writer."—*Crimepieces*

By the Author

Calvin's Head

Corpus Calvin

Visit us at www.boldstrokesbooks.com

CORPUS CALVIN

by

David Swatling

2022

CORPUS CALVIN
© 2022 BY DAVID SWATLING. ALL RIGHTS RESERVED.

ISBN 13: 978-1-62639-428-5

THIS TRADE PAPERBACK ORIGINAL IS PUBLISHED BY
BOLD STROKES BOOKS, INC.
P.O. BOX 249
VALLEY FALLS, NY 12185

FIRST EDITION: NOVEMBER 2022

CREDITS
EDITORS: GREG HERREN AND STACIA SEAMAN
PRODUCTION DESIGN: STACIA SEAMAN
COVER DESIGN BY JEANINE HENNING

Acknowledgments

When I started this book in 2014, I never imagined it would take eight years to finish. Life presented some challenges—not of the literary variety—impossible to ignore. Be that as it may, I'm fortunate to have so many friends and colleagues who kept me focused on the glimmer of light at the end of the tunnel—even as I stood alone in the dark, unable to move.

First and foremost, I owe a huge debt of gratitude to BSB publisher Len Barot and senior editor Sandy Lowe for their support and patience; Greg Herren and Stacia Seaman for their deft editorial skill; Jeanine Henning for her evocative cover art; Ruth, Cindy, and the whole BSB family who attend to everything else and make an author's dream come true.

This book only exists due to the openhearted generosity of Joanne Jacaruso, longtime friend and owner of the Inn at Whitefield, my personal summer writer's retreat. Her stories about the Inn, as well as those shared by staff and local customers, inspired the fictional history of Cloverkist. I'm also grateful to my brother Steven for his expertise in all things paranormal, and to my sister Kathy, whose work with autistic children provided invaluable insight.

The Amsterdam Genre Writing Group read early chapters, and their enthusiasm was crucial at the start. And I couldn't ask for more thoughtful feedback from my beta readers: Tori Egherman, Karen Kao, Nicci Robinson, and Hiram Ed Taylor.

Master classes and workshops along the way with authors such as Megan Abbott, Dorothy Allison, Donna Minkowitz, and Nina Siegal were especially beneficial during the long dry spells. Also, the encouragement from creative writer friends played a significant role in keeping me afloat—whether they knew it or not. Annamaria Alfieri, Nancy Bilyeau, Tom Cardamone, Jameson Currier, Meredith Doench, Martha Hawley, Patrick E. Horrigan, Dawn Ius, Greg Lawson, Kate McCamy, Laura McHugh, Jon Michaelsen, Mindy Ran, Marcel

Snyders, Victoria Villaseñor, and the late great George Isherwood—to name just a few.

The New Hampshire Historical Societies of Jackson, Littleton, and Whitefield all provided important details for the story I would not have found elsewhere. For additional research, I relied upon the following primary sources:

- *Historical Relics of the White Mountains* by John H. Spaulding (1855)
- *The History of the Civil War in America* by John S.C. Abbott (1863/1866)
- *Memoranda During the War* by Walt Whitman (1875)
- *Thirteenth Regiment of New Hampshire Volunteer Infantry in the War of the Rebellion: A Diary Covering Three Years and a Day* by S. Millet Thompson (1888)

I strove for historical authenticity, but in the words of Lieutenant Thompson: "The writer assumes all responsibilities, and takes to himself all the blame that may attach for any inadvertences occurring in the book."

For Joanne

"I could hardly believe that any considerable number of persons exist among us, who give credence to accounts of spectres and disembodied spirits appearing among the dead;—yet there are many such people, especially in our country places."

—Walt Whitman, "The Child-Ghost"

1864

Doxey smelled smoke before he saw fire. Like as always. Moze said that was his special gift. He weren't smart like Moze but he knew the difference between open-air campfires, wood fires for baking bread, and the smithy's coal fire. He could tell what was burning, how fast it was burning, could even tell how far away it was burning. It weren't nothing he never learned. Just something he always knew. Moze said someday Doxey would join the fire brigade. Someday he would be the most famous fire chief in the whole wide world. Songs would be sung to praise his name, for he would save the lives of many. Mayhaps. But his special gift didn't save Moze.

It were those damn puppies what killed Moze.

The kitchen chimney kept the secret room in the tower warm, sometimes too warm. Narrow as it was, there weren't no window, so Moze had pried off a section of wood siding in the corner. During the day they kept the opening stuffed with burlap sacks. When darkness fell they pulled them out to let in fresh air. Doxey liked to stand at the hole in the wall and imagine what lay beyond the barn across the yard, beyond the woods behind the barn, beyond the trail to Possum Pond. Across the border was Canada, Moze said, where fugitive slaves became freedmen. But Doxey and Moze weren't going to no Canada. Mister Ben said they could stay put right here on Corporal Quimby's farm. The war would be over soon, Mister Ben said, and they would be freedmen of New Hampshire.

Doxey liked New Hampshire, even though it was cold, colder than he ever knew in his ten years of life. And the cold brought snow, soft white flakes that floated down from the clouds and covered the frozen earth, more beautiful than endless fields of cotton. Moonbeams bounced off the snow, and the tall trees behind the barn glittered like magic.

Doxey took a long deep breath of the cold air. Snowflakes tickled his nostrils, made him smile. Until he caught the faint stinging scent of smoke. It held no sharpness of tobacco, no tang of pine pitch. It was full of the sweetness of hay.

The barn. Doxey and Moze had helped fill the loft with hay, enough to last the long winter a-comin'. The red barn stood tall against the snow-covered ground. He saw no sign of flames, but his nose never lied. Before he could figure out what to do, he saw the wide barn door was slightly ajar. A shadow emerged through the opening and slunk low across the yard. Cassie, holding one of her squirming pups in her mouth, disappeared under the wagon by the edge of the woods. A moment later she raced back, paused by the door for a nervous bark, and ran inside.

Moze had took Doxey to see the nine puppies after they were born. "Too young to play with," Moze warned. But they visited the puppies every day. Cassie knew what Doxey knew. Those pups were in danger. Fire in the barn.

"Wake up, Moze," Doxey said, shaking his arm. Even before his brother had a chance to wipe the sleep from his eyes, Doxey pulled him up and half dragged him to the makeshift window.

"Look, Moze, look. I smell smoke. Cassie, too. Look." Cassie reemerged from the barn, holding another pup by the scruff of its neck.

"I don't see nothing. Are you sure, Dox?"

"Yes. Cassie knows, too. Look." Again, Cassie darted from underneath the wagon, ran across the snow, and scurried into the dark of the barn. No hesitation this time. That's when they saw the first flash of orange flame lick a windowpane near the rear of the building.

"Damnation." Doxey never heard Moze swear an oath against God before, and it scared him. "You stay right here, no matter what. I'll be back as soon as I help Cassie get the pups safe. Wait for me right here. Understand?"

Doxey nodded as his brother slid down the rope ladder hanging alongside the chimney.

"Wait for me, you hear?" yelled Moze as he jumped to the floor and took off through the empty kitchen and outside into the swirling snow.

Doxey watched him run toward the barn as Cassie came out with her third puppy. Moze tried to stop her, but she dodged around him and headed straight for the wagon. Moze pulled the barn door open wide and for the first time Doxey saw smoke. It billowed out and surrounded his brother. Moze waved his arms and pulled his shirt over his mouth and nose. He hunkered down and rushed inside, Cassie barking close behind.

Doxey held his breath like Moze had to. He reckoned it was a long time, too long. As he had to give up and suck in air, Moze and the dog burst through the barn door. Cassie carried another single pup, but Moze had more than one bundled into his shirt, held close to his chest. Doxey couldn't tell how many as they tumbled out. Maybe three? Was that all of them? Doxey had lost count. His brother grabbed a length of rope that hung on the wagon. As Cassie reappeared, he hugged her around the neck and, despite her struggles, managed to tie her to the wheel. She twisted and pulled and barked in a panic, as Moze stumbled to the barn. He stopped, framed in the doorway, a silhouette against the orange glow. He looked up toward the tower and raised two fingers. Two more puppies?

"Wait for me," he yelled through the snowflakes. "Wait for me there."

And he was gone.

If Moze said wait, Doxey had to wait. No matter what.

He waited as Cassie barked from under the wagon, barked for Moze to save her puppies. He waited as the fire snaked its devilish tentacles across the roof of the barn. He waited as the weathervane tottered and tipped and tumbled down down down. He waited as a burning figure staggered outside, threw itself to the ground, and rolled rolled rolled in the snow, screaming.

Doxey could not tell who that burning man was, his eyes so full of smoky tears. But he knew it was not his brother.

Moze never left that barn. Doxey smelled him.

PART I: CLOVERKIST, 1995

"Thou orb aloft full-dazzling! thou hot October noon!
...prepare my lengthening shadows, prepare my starry nights."
—Walt Whitman

CHAPTER ONE

I. CALVIN

thin air lapping / breathing gulping
sniffing scenting something burning
tree leafs falling / watching drifting
sniffing scenting something wilder
ranker danker here&gone

II. DEKKER

Mountains on fire. Steep slopes on both sides of the Notch blazed with the vibrant colors of Van Gogh's autumnal palette. Cadmium orange and yellow ochre, Venetian red and manganese violet, burnt sienna and rose madder. Nature's deciduous tapestry woven together with viridian green swaths of abundant firs. I'd forgotten how much I missed New England's fall foliage.

Nearly a decade had passed since I flew off to Amsterdam, where one season blended into another, year after year, with little discernible difference. I couldn't shake the feeling I was returning home. Odd, when I remembered the sense of displacement surrounding my final months at Camden College. Friends disappearing, suffering meltdowns, dying. Crazy times. Who wouldn't want to hightail it out of there? Crazier still how much the past six months had in common with those last weeks of college. Except for the homelessness. And the murders.

Don't go there, Dekker.

I was determined to look forward, make a fresh start, forget the past. Damn difficult with so many cemeteries dotting the countryside along the way, wearing the foliage like a colorful shroud. I lost count of how many we'd passed so far. Too many. I had enough graveyard memories for one lifetime—from the one next to the farm where I grew up to those I left behind in Amsterdam. I didn't want to think about cemeteries. Not now, not ever.

Right on cue, Calvin leaned toward me from his seat and licked my neck. He always knew when a mood change was in order. He'd been unusually subdued during the drive from Boston. Probably due, in equal parts, to the drugs I gave him for the transatlantic flight and the ensuing sensory overload provided by a new continent of sights, sounds, and scents. Not to mention his overexcitement at the airport yesterday.

I knew he'd be pissed when I finally set him free from the travel crate. He'd never experienced confinement, and I knew he'd perceive it as some sort of undeserved punishment. Rather than let him out inside the terminal and risk a hostile showdown amid crowds of weary travelers, I waited until we were in the parking lot. He gave a low warning growl as I opened the cage and stepped back. He didn't move.

In my own time, asshole.

He emerged slowly, unsteadily, probably due to the drugs, plus hours in cramped quarters. I also recognized a familiar caution in his movement. He looked around, deliberately ignoring me, and gave his body a massive shake. He groaned with an exaggerated yawn and, without warning, jumped up against me, planting his front paws on my chest, and growled his litany of complaints nose to nose.

Once he'd given me a sufficient scolding, I introduced him to Jax and all was forgiven. Tail-wagging for joy, Calvin wasn't bothered that a roomier new Jeep Wrangler had replaced our old Suzuki Samurai. As far as Cal was concerned, Jax was more a concept than a name, a word for adventures soon-to-come. He retrieved his shaggy companion Blue Bear from the crate, leapt into the back of the Jeep, and we were good to go.

I had booked a room at Motel 6 in Braintree, just south of Boston. There we could catch I-93, which would take us all the way through New Hampshire to the village of Cloverkist, on the northernmost edge of the White Mountains. Best to have a good night's sleep before making an early start. That would give us plenty of time for Calvin's necessary sniff-and-piss stops, and we would arrive by early afternoon. A chaotic family of four had taken their time checking in as we waited, the two young girls fawning over Calvin, seriously testing his patience. He didn't have much experience interacting with kids, and his woeful eyes spoke volumes.

How much of this do I have to endure?

I had turned away so he would not catch my smirk and pretended to be engrossed in a bulletin board crammed with notices hawking local tourist activities and upcoming events. One in particular caught my eye.

"Full Moon Psychic Medium Workshop. Are you Clairvoyant, Clairaudient, or Clairsentient? Reginald Masters can help you explore your potential to communicate with the Other Side. Two Full Moon Days—October 7 & 8. Only $350, including a one-night stay at Motel 6."

Thank God we had arrived before the place crawled with those mental nutcases—during a full moon to boot. I didn't go in for any of that crap but could imagine the madhouse energy flying around when a devoted faction desperate to believe gathered in one spot. Sartre was right when he said hell is other people. Luckily we'd be long gone before the hellish weekend, when Motel 6 became Motel 666.

Calvin licked my neck again, more insistent this time.

"Time for another pit stop, Mr. Calvinator?"

In reply he hung his head out the window, lapping the fresh air, watching the trees and mountains fly by. We didn't have much farther to go, but one last pee break was a good idea. A sign indicated a Scenic View Rest Area in one mile. Perfect timing.

I pulled off the highway and slowed into the nearly empty parking lot. Even though it was almost peak leaf-peeping season, weekday traffic was minimal. That certainly wouldn't be the case the coming Columbus Day weekend. I hadn't taken that into consideration, with Columbus Day nonexistent on the other side of the pond. Another bit of good travel luck. As I parked the Jeep, Cal stood on his seat, his tail wagging in my face. I leaned around him and opened the passenger door so he could jump out. Before I followed suit, I grabbed his leash, though we probably wouldn't need it.

While Calvin busied himself sniffing around, marking his

newfound, newly claimed territory, I stretched my arms, shoulders, and neck and lit a cigarette. I stepped up on the low stone wall that bordered the parking area and in the distance saw the Old Man of the Mountain, his jagged granite profile chiseled against the clear blue sky. The natural outcropping was New Hampshire's state emblem, but it was widely known across the country. Nathaniel Hawthorn's short story "The Great Stone Face" was pretty much required reading during my high school years. I remembered it well, being a big fan of boy-on-a-quest stories.

A wise man never thinks of himself as the hero of his own story, I wrote as a teenager. Smart kid. What happened to him?

"Cal. You ready to go?"

He looked up briefly and, nose to the ground, zigzagged his way back to the Jeep, where he jumped into his seat. I slammed the door shut and took a last look at the rugged Old Man. That was a good word to describe New Hampshire. Rugged. I knew of no other place that called its mountain passes notches. The state motto popped into my head.

Live free or die. I even knew the rest of the quote. *Death is not the worst of evils.* Vincent van Gogh had written something similar to his brother. I hadn't made that connection before, and a tingling sensation coursed through my body.

Get in the Jeep and drive, Dekker.

Very little traffic on the highway made for smooth sailing until we exited at Littleton, a small town with classic Americana hallmarks—covered bridge, church with a tall white steeple, and even an old opera house on Main Street. It would be fun to explore, but I didn't want to stop. We took Route 116 and headed into serious North Country. The rural road twisted and turned up steep hills and down into deep valleys, a natural thrill-every-minute roller coaster with stunning mountain vistas.

Hanging his head out the window, Calvin appeared riveted by the shifting landscape, sometimes giving a bark. *Check it out, Dekker.* I'd grown up in the countryside but this region was new to me as well. I'd never seen a road sign that said *MOOSE CROSSING—Next 3 Miles.*

Route 116 became Main Street in Cloverkist. It was as if we'd turned a corner and time-traveled back to postcard-perfect Mayberry USA, circa 1960. By comparison, Littleton was downright urban.

Cloverkist was little more than a square village green with a white gazebo bandstand in the middle. A beauty salon, a pizza place, a gun shop, and a gas station were the only shops around the square. What more did anyone need? This might be more culture shock than I had bargained for.

According to my directions, our destination was approximately two miles north, and most of it looked uphill. We passed a few houses with a fair distance between them, some run-down shacks and others well-kept summer homes. Onward and upward, the road cut through nothing but trees until a small diner called Granny Stalbird's appeared on the left, along with a handful of rustic cabins along the edge of a mirror-surfaced lake. Calvin whimpered softly, scenting the water, wanting to swim.

"Not yet, buddy. Once we get settled, we'll come back. I promise."

I caught a whiff of something else I'd forgotten. Burning leaves. Nobody burned leaves in Amsterdam. Maybe it was illegal there. Strange. I had no idea. But the scent of a backyard bonfire brought back memories of a distant past. Sunny harvest afternoons on the farm, apple picking in the orchard, autumn evening hayrides, carved Halloween pumpkins. I missed more than I had realized.

The road took a sharp curve before yet another steep incline, and all at once Cloverkist Inn loomed into view at the top of the hill like something out of a Hitchcock film.

"Holy shit, Calvin. Did Bernstein move in with Norman Bates?"

III. ETHAN

We watch the Jeep stop from on top of the rock. Wheels stop turning. Hood stops breathing. Windows wide open.

We write on the air.

J-E-E-P-D-O-G.

Jeep Dog jumps. We want to jump. Jeep Dog shakes. We want to shake.

Father Rock calms us. Father Rock sways us. We sway.

A visitor. Mom says.

A friend from college. Mom says.

His name is Dekker. Mom says.

Mom never told us about Jeep Dog.
Jeep Dog raises a leg. Pees on the grass. Kicks up the grass.
We cover our mouths and laugh. We cup our ears and listen.
We write on the air.
J-E-E-P-D-O-G.

IV. DEKKER

"I'm so glad you're here, Dekker. You have no idea." Bernstein's urgent greeting, whispered into my ear and matched by the tight clasp of her arms around my body, surprised me. Had we been closer friends in college than I remembered? Or was it just a case of distance makes the heart grow fonder? Ten years and a few thousand miles was certainly enough in the distance department. But I sensed something deeper, some unnamable but profound relief she felt at my arrival, as if a heavy burden had been lifted from her shoulders. More than a little disconcerting. I wasn't sure I was up to any heavy lifting, emotionally speaking. To be honest, my immediate thought echoed one I had less than an hour ago.

Get back in the Jeep and keep driving.

Calvin interrupted the moment with a sharp bark.

"Hey. Cool your jets, Calvin," I said. "He gets a little jealous when he's not the center of attention."

Before I could figure out how to extricate myself from her clinging embrace, the crisp autumn air was pierced by a bloodcurdling scream from inside the inn. Calvin burst into a paroxysm of frantic barking. Bernstein broke free from me, a panic-stricken expression clouding her eyes. She rushed across the wraparound porch and through the double-door entryway without another word.

"Calvin, stop. Shut up."

Ignoring my command, he lunged toward the entrance. I grabbed his collar just in time to hold him back. I had no idea what was going on inside, but Calvin had clearly switched into guard dog mode. Best I directed his attention elsewhere.

"Calvin, sit. Stay. Stay with Jax. Watch Jax. Stay."

My guess he'd bonded enough with the new Jeep to do as I said proved accurate. He sat by the passenger door, softly growling and scoping out the parking lot for any potential danger. I glanced around and saw a young boy sitting motionless on a large flat rock on the grass lawn between the end of the lot and a big red barn. As I headed into the inn, I hoped he would stay put for the time being.

Directly inside the entrance was a short flight of stairs to the second floor. To the right was a doorway into a simply decorated room with tables and chairs, probably used for breakfast. To the left was a softly lit room with a reception desk, ornate fireplace, tastefully upholstered couch and armchairs. Raised voices came from that direction, farther inside.

I hurried through a wide archway, which led to a lounge boasting an antique chandelier. Off to the left, another hallway, where Bernstein knelt next to a moaning crumpled figure at the bottom of an impressive staircase. A pale, shivering teenage girl stood above them, hands gripping her face, eyes wide and tearful, mouth attempting to form intelligible words between choked sobs.

"…can't go…up there…again."

"But what happened, Amber?" Bernstein asked. "Did your sister fall?"

"Noooooooooo," the girl on the floor screamed. "Pushed… bastard…pushed me."

"Who pushed you?" When the girl didn't answer, Bernstein looked up at Amber. "Did you push your sister?"

"No…you know…who…" she managed before dissolving into a puddle of sniveling whimpers.

"Pull yourself together, Amber. Get a plastic bag from the kitchen and fill it with ice. Make it two. Now, Amber."

The girl shook her head, as if waking from a bad dream. She scooted past Bernstein and her injured sister, heading through the Chandelier Room. I must've missed the kitchen somehow.

"Can I help?" I asked.

"You'll need to carry her to my car so I can drive her to the ER. I'm afraid her ankle's broken. Maybe just a bad sprain." She gestured to a door next to the stairs. "Here in Room One. In the bathroom. Get a couple of clean towels we can wrap around the bags of ice. AMBER, MOVE YOUR ASS!"

I started toward the room she indicated, but stopped short when a loud bang sounded in the hallway. It seemed to come from upstairs. At least, that's the direction in which Bernstein looked, her face a mask of anger. Another massive bang, as if someone up in the tower was using a baseball bat on the wooden banister. Bernstein slowly rose to her feet, still staring above the ceiling, or so it appeared. A third colossal bang shook the whole building. I heard the chandelier tinkling in the next room.

"YOU FUCKING ASSHOLE. I'VE HAD IT. ENOUGH. I'M NOT GOING ANYWHERE. I TOLD YOU ALREADY. SO JUST FUCK OFF. DO YOU HEAR ME? FUCK YOU."

There was a moment of silence and then a series of loud and fast banging, accompanied by what sounded like every one of the inn's smoke detectors going off at once. And it all stopped as quickly as it had begun. The hallway was quiet again, except for the ringing in my ears. Bernstein turned to me, her face red, but the look of anger had changed to one of sad resignation.

"Should I go up there and…"

"No," she said quietly. "I'll explain later. Just get the towels, please."

As I carried the girl across the porch, Cal still stood guard by Jax. The boy had moved from the rock and sat on the ground, face-to-face with Calvin. Bernstein helped me deposit the girl as carefully as possible into the back seat of her SUV where Amber was already sitting, staring blankly out the window. I think they were both in shock. Bernstein covered the pair with a blanket and slid the side door closed.

"This is not how I planned to introduce you to Ethan," she said with a sigh.

"Ethan?"

"My son. Your dog's new best friend." She gave me a penetrating look determining whether or not it was safe to leave her child with a man she hadn't seen for ten years. I felt like I was being mentally strip-searched. I must have passed her assessment because she nodded, walked over to the boy, and squatted beside him.

"Ethan? Remember I told you a friend was coming to visit us? Well, this is Dekker. My friend from college. Remember? I want you to stay with him while I take Jade and Amber to the hospital. Okay?"

"We don't like the hospital."

"You don't have to go to the hospital. You can stay here with Dekker. Ethan, did you hear me?"

"We hear you." The boy didn't move.

"Okay. Show Dekker around. Give him the Grand Tour. Show him your rock garden. Okay, Ethan? Words, please. Ethan?"

"We'll show him." Words, but no movement.

"Okay, Ethan. I'll be back as soon as I can." She stood up and gave me a quick hug. "He doesn't say much, but he likes showing guests around. We call it the Grand Tour. I won't be long. The girls' mother is meeting me at the ER and I'll come straight back. An hour tops. And thank you, Dekker. Just—thank you." She got in the SUV and they were gone.

The boy still sat staring at Calvin, who calmly stared back.

"Um. Hi, Ethan." Nothing. "Nice to meet you." Nothing. "This is my dog, Calvin."

I didn't expect the boy to answer, so I almost missed it when he did.

"We know."

Neither the boy nor the dog moved a muscle, as if frozen in another space and time.

**From the Diary of Corporal Anson Quimby
13th New Hampshire Infantry Regiment**

June 1864

How do I begin? I am not one who has ever tried to record his thoughts with pen and paper. That is my father's talent. But until my wound heals and I can once more fight shoulder to shoulder with my comrades until that glorious day when the Confederacy is defeated and our noble country stands again United, there is little more that can be done to pass the time. And Mr. Whitman does so entreat us, supplying paper and encouraging words. He says this War is not one to be catalogued by the General's reports or the Historian's ink, but by blood and breath of the common soldier. That is how he speaks, and I know not what to make of him. They say he is a poet from New York, come to Washington in search of his wounded brother, and once found without serious injury, remains to work as a field nurse. His abilities are not of medical practices, lest horehound candies or raspberry jams be called medicine. Gifts such as these he offers on his rounds. He is kind and caring, sitting with those most grievous ill long into the night, writing letters to loved ones home for them, reading or telling stories, as a father might to an ailing son. He was such a comfort to Erastus, the fife boy who lay in the next bed and was gone this morning. Typhus, the doctors say. As many die from such as mortal battle wounds. I dread but to think on how distraught Walt must be this day. Betimes I saw him place a tender kiss upon the boy's brow once asleep, which may seem passing strange in a ward of soldiers, but could not but fail to move the coldest heart. Erastus was a fine lad, with an easy laugh before his condition became so dire. He told Walt he would play a tune for him on his fife when he felt well enough again. But the fife remained on the stand beside his bed, untouched and unplayed. It is gone now, and may it sound most strange but I hope it is buried with him. Such thought brings Ben to mind. Like Erastus, he bears not a soldier's temperament. He is an artist, and his small notebook is never far from hand, carrying it as he does in his breast pocket. Before I was carried off the field, I begged him to keep his head low and forestall unnecessary risk till my return, for I promised Mrs. Chapman I should look after her son and bring him home safe. It pains me now to think on his tears as we parted. The doctor says I am fortunate the bullet passed through my shoulder and my full recovery is guaranteed and I will return to the Regiment—& to Ben, if I am honest. I shall be so overjoyed to see him well that I may hold him close and kiss his cheek as Walt might do at such a sweet reunion. I have writ enough, mayhap too much, for my fingers cramp.

CHAPTER TWO

I. CALVIN

two boys jumping laughing running / calvin
    jumping wagging chasing
lookit dekker / one boy playing one boy
    hiding / scenting never seeing

II. DEKKER

Calvin never had much to do with children in Amsterdam, always keeping enough distance to avoid direct contact. It surprised me when he enthusiastically joined Ethan in a lively game of Follow the Leader, no encouragement from me necessary. The boy broke their staring match. He jumped up, threw his head back, and laughed raucously toward the sky, as if Cal had told him the funniest joke ever. Sudden movements normally put Calvin on high alert, with a bark or two to drive the point home. But he simply cocked his head, casting a quizzical sidelong glance in my direction.

Is this kid okay?

Before I could respond, Ethan gave Calvin a big hug, whispered something into his ear through cupped hands, and the two set off, merrily skipping along the porch toward the far end of the inn.

I shook my head as I followed them. Nothing was going as I expected, and it wasn't only Calvin's behavior. Bernstein's over-the-top welcome, whatever the hell had gone on upstairs that precipitated the girl's accident, and not least of all, leaving her odd son in my care while she rushed off to the hospital. Okay. Clearly the boy had issues with hospitals. So did I. But didn't they have ambulances in North Country? Emergency services to call? Or was it a case of *If you want something done right, do it yourself*? That's the Tessa Bernstein I remembered from Camden College. Tough, independent, resourceful. A force to be reckoned with, especially when she and Elliott had been together. Camden's power couple—until one day they weren't and everything went a bit crazy. Understatement of all time.

Calvin pulled me out of my reverie with a couple of guttural barks. As I rounded the corner of the inn's wraparound porch, I could see a small rectangular swimming pool, which had been covered for the season. A tall thick hedge—hydrangea, or maybe lilac bushes—hid it from the parking lot. Ethan squatted at one corner of the pool between two stone puppies of indeterminate breed. He patted the head of one, which playfully held the end of a water hose, while he rubbed the belly of the other, which was posed on its back. Terminally cute. Calvin crouched a couple feet away, haunches up, head low to the ground, emitting a steady snarly growl.

"Yo, Calvin. What's going on?"

He looked up at me as he stood, gave himself a big shake, and trotted over to me. A faint scent of burning leaves tickled my nostrils again.

"The puppies guard the pool," Ethan said, in a slightly rhythmic monotone. "Summer swimming only. The pool is closed. No swimming till summer." He paused and stood. "How come Calvin don't like puppies?"

This was true but the boy had no way of knowing that. He wasn't looking at me, so it took me a second to realize he was asking me a question.

"It's probably my fault. I made a big fuss over a puppy one day. Calvin got jealous, and ever since he steers clear of puppies. He's a funny dog."

"He's a funny dog," Ethan repeated. As he had done in the parking lot, he threw his head back and cackled his bizarre imitation of laughter. He cupped his hands around his mouth and announced it to the great outdoors. "HE'S A FUNNY DOG. HE'S A FUNNY DOG."

Not for the first time, I wondered if there was something wrong with the boy, something that had been diagnosed. Or was he just acting out in the presence of a stranger? Surely Bernstein would have mentioned anything serious before she ran off. As if on cue, Ethan ran down the grassy slope toward the woods. Calvin took off after him. They chased each other up and down the lawn in crisscross patterns. Calvin stopped for a quick sniff along the trees and lifted his leg to leave his mark. Ethan laughed and lifted his leg, as well. More running, more laughing. They reminded me of growing up on my grandparents' farm, with my dog, Tracey, a boy's best and only friend. From Ethan's size, I'd guess he was about eight years old, certainly no more than ten. Perfect for canine companionship. Together, he and Cal raced back up the hill to the porch steps, where Ethan collapsed dramatically to catch his breath. Calvin sat in front of him, panting happily.

"Looks like you guys gave each other a good workout."

"He's a funny dog," Ethan said with a smile and a giggle.

"How about that Grand Tour? Along the way maybe we can find some water. You both look pretty thirsty."

"We are pretty thirsty," said Ethan, nodding vigorously.

III. ETHAN

Begin at the beginning. Father Rock says. The Grand Tour must begin at the beginning.

We lead Mom's Friend Dekker along the porch to the big old double doors, as old as Cloverkist. We tell Mom's Friend Dekker that Dr. Quimby built Cloverkist in Olden Days. One hundred and fifty years ago. Cloverkist was a summerhouse. You could still see Possum Pond down the hill. People like to know these things. Mom says.

We bring Mom's Friend Dekker inside. Calvin can take a rest on the porch. He says. Stay.

We show Mom's Friend Dekker the Hunt Room. For breakfast and parties. We show him where the deer's head used to hang before Mom took it down. People don't want a dead deer watching them eat breakfast. Mom says. We thought that was funny but Mom wasn't laughing.

We take Mom's Friend Dekker through the Red Rum Room.

Reception is too boring. Mom says. We'll call this the Red Rum Room because the carpet is red and the fireplace is warm like rum. We're too young to drink rum. But we like to say Red Rum Room three times very fast.

Red Rum Room. Red Rum Boom. Bed Room Boom. The words get all mixed up trying to come out of our mouth. Slower.

Red Rum Room. Red Rum Room. Red Rum Room. Mom's Friend Dekker tries it fast.

Red Rum Room. Red Rum Boom. Red Bum Boom. We laugh when he says Bum Boom. He laughs, too.

We like Mom's Friend Dekker. He listens to everything. Not like some grownups. We show him the Chandelier Room. The chandelier was lit with candles in Olden Days. Mom says. Candles are too dangerous, so now it's electric. At night when we squint our eyes, the light bulbs look like candles. The big fireplace is piled full of wood, ready to burn when the weather gets cold. We don't need a fire in summer time. Mom says. But summer is over and soon we can make a roaring fire and toast marshmallows inside. Mom's Friend Dekker says that will be fun.

We lead Mom's Friend Dekker through the pantry full of pots and pans and boxes and cans, past the ice machine and into the kitchen. We stop and listen, but nobody is whistling. We point to our plastic cups on the high shelf. No climbing on counters. Mom says. Mom's Friend Dekker hands me one. We scoop ice from the ice-cold ice machine and run water from the little sink by the door. We like cold, cold water and drink the whole cup down in one long gulp. We find an empty Cool Whip dish under the counter. For Calvin. We run cold, cold water in the dish. Not too full or we will spill it.

We walk slow back through the pantry and the Red Rum Room. Mom's Friend Dekker opens the doors for us. Calvin is waiting. We set the Cool Whip bowl on the porch. Calvin licks the cold, cold water into his mouth with his long pink tongue. When he is done, we want to try to lick the cold, cold water, too. Mom's Friend Dekker says that's not a good idea. We think it is a good idea and almost start to stamp our feet and shout. Mom's Friend Dekker is smiling and Calvin is smiling. We smile. Smiling is better than stamping and shouting. Sometimes we need to stamp and shout. Not now. We need to finish the Grand Tour. Days are getting shorter now. Mom says.

We march Mom's Friend Dekker off the porch and onto the

sidewalk. We march alongside the Carriage House. In Olden Days before cars and trucks, horses pulled carriages. Carriages were kept in the Carriage House. Not now. The Carriage House is a restaurant for dinner only. No breakfast and no lunch in the Carriage House. Except special parties. A business breakfast is a special party. No children allowed. Mom says.

We march past the windows. They used to be doors in Olden Days. Mom says. We HONK HONK at the statue of two swans under the window box. No more flowers. Only brown leaves. HONK HONK. We stop at the entrance between the Carriage House and the Pub. The sign above says Cloverkist Inn. We show Mom's Friend Dekker the two black iron posts with horse's heads on top, where they tied up real horses in Olden Days. Calvin sniffs a post, raises his leg, and pees on the post. He's a funny dog. We raise our leg and pretend to pee on the post. Mom's Friend Dekker laughs and we laugh. Calvin laughs with his tail. We all laugh.

We march past the windows of the Pub. The Pub is for drinking and music and pub grub. We like pub grub. Closed now. No pub grub today. We march around the corner to the back door and sit on the stoop.

Sit, Calvin. Sit with us.

The dragonflies are putting on a show over the parking lot. The dragonflies zip back and forth, back and forth. The dragonflies climb high and dive, climb high and dive. The dragonflies buzz like old airplanes at the airshow. They make zigzag patterns in the sky.

IV. DEKKER

I hadn't seen anything like it since I was a child.

"When dragonflies swarm, change a'comin," my grandmother used to say when they'd cluster above the farm pond. "Take care those Devil's Darning Needles don't sew your lips and eyes shut. That's what they do to children who lie," she'd add, with a wicked grin.

I decided to keep that bit of macabre folklore to myself.

Ethan lifted his pointed fingers and appeared to conduct the orchestra of cavorting insects. Calvin sat by his side, as entranced as the boy. Perhaps he was a bit older than I'd first thought. The language he used on his tour included both simple singsong repetitions and an advanced level of understanding Cloverkist history. He was clearly intelligent and imaginative, with a keen sense of humor. But something wasn't quite right. When I stopped him from drinking out of Calvin's bowl, I caught a glimmer in his eyes that could have turned into a tantrum. Then it was gone and he flashed an innocent smile. He had certainly bonded with Calvin. Whatever his issues, no concerns on that front.

Although I hadn't seen much of the inside, Cloverkist Inn was an impressive piece of property. A low wall of rocks separated it from the road, in classic New England style. Beyond the parking lot at this end was another wide lawn, which led to a large red barn with white trim and a couple of outbuldings. The windows of the barn were boarded over. That would be the summer stock theater, which provided solid seasonal business to help Bernstein with a solid start. She hadn't gone into much detail on the phone. Only said she'd bought the inn last spring, sight unseen from where she was living in Colorado, and made the move to New Hampshire in June.

Bernstein and I had gone through some major life changes at about the same time. I'd lost the lover I thought I'd spend the rest of my life with, and to make matters worse, his Dutch family kicked me out of the home we had shared. Not to mention the fucked-up attempt to deal with my grief by falling for a guy who tried to kill me. Twice. Excuse me if I think the concept of finding closure is overrated.

When dragonflies swarm...

What I found strange, though, was how deserted the place felt. Bernstein's SUV was the only car in the lot when I drove in. The only staff around appeared to be the panic-stricken cleaning girls, and there was no sign of any guests. It was the first Monday in October, so perhaps everyone had checked out yesterday or this morning. Was the inn open only on weekends during the popular fall foliage season? Was that why Bernstein said she could use my help?

We had a lot to talk about when she returned.

The dragonflies departed and Ethan whispered into Calvin's ear again through his cupped hands. I wondered what secrets the boy was telling his new friend.

"Hey, Ethan. Shall we finish the Grand Tour?"

He nodded enthusiastically, and pointed across the parking lot. "The Red Barn Theater is where actors do shows. Summer only. No shows until summer."

"What kind of shows? Did you see any?"

"Yes. Charlie Brown went to the island and killed the vampire."

"Whoa. That sounds like a scary show."

"It was just pretend. The actors sing and dance and pretend. Charlie Brown showed us how to kill the vampire with a stake. It's a fake stake. And fake blood. Just pretend. We're not scared." It sounded as if he were still convincing himself. It also sounded like he had combined several shows into one story. I'd never heard of any musical called Charlie Brown versus the Vampire.

"What about showing me that rock garden your mom mentioned?"

"Okay. Calvin, come."

Ethan took off running, Calvin hot on his heels. They tore around a white picket fence, which enclosed a terrace area for outdoor seating, and down a path behind the inn. I jogged behind them, to not lose sight of the pair as they rounded a craggy crab apple tree by the corner of a dilapidated loading dock, which I assumed led to the kitchen. The rear side of the inn had not been as well maintained as the front. Peeled paint flaked off what looked to be original, or certainly much older clapboard siding, giving the back of the inn a mottled, derelict appearance. Window cornices were cracked, or in some cases missing altogether. A pair of French doors on the Carriage House section looked to be sealed shut. There was no time for more than a cursory glance, but it was a stark contrast to the finely decorated cozy warmth of the interior.

The lawn sloped down behind the tower end of Cloverkist, and I caught sight of Calvin's fluffy white tail as it disappeared between two bright red maple trees below the deck that surrounded the pool. Dense shrubs and bushes obstructed the view beyond the lawn area. Where the hell were they going?

"Hey, you guys, wait up," I shouted. I heard no reply and picked up speed to catch up with them. Much to my surprise, the maples provided a kind of entrance to another open lawn, or to be more precise, a square terraced field about a half acre in size. It was bordered by a low wall of rocks, same as along the road. A few rough-hewn stone steps led down to the leveled ground.

What I saw didn't make sense at first. Ethan methodically hopped, skipped, and jumped on a grassy path created by stones and rocks on each side. Calvin followed behind him, letting the boy take the lead. From the slight elevation at the top of the steps, I saw that completely contained within the field, the rings of stones created a large circular maze. In the center stood a pile of larger rocks, topped by a rectangular slab that looked like a bench, or some kind of pagan altar. Ethan hopped, skipped, and jumped in the ever-tightening concentric circles until he reached the center. He nimbly climbed atop the slab, urging Calvin to jump up with him. Cal seemed a bit hesitant, sniffing around the bottom of the pile, lifting a leg to mark his territory. Then he joined the boy in one easy leap. Ethan threw his head back, stretched his arms wide, and again laughed into the sky. When he'd done this earlier it was oddly joyful. This time it was almost sinister. He began to spin in place, slowly gathered speed, and continued to laugh. I feared he might get dizzy and fall. Calvin barked his concern and the boy stopped, facing me.

"Father Rock says begin at the beginning," he intoned. "Father Rock says this is where our story begins. You are part of our story now. The Grand Tour ends here. Welcome to Cloverkist. Father Rock says."

And for the third time on this gorgeous October day, I thought what I should actually do was get back in the Jeep with Calvin and drive, drive as fast and as far away from here as I could go.

CHAPTER THREE

I. CALVIN

resting watching two boys talking / listening voices soft&low
someone waiting lurking hiding / someone never seeing no
sniffing scenting holding bluebear / sniffing
    scenting something more
waiting watching listening something / evermore&evermore

II. DEKKER

"The death threats were the last straw," Bernstein said, wiping the sink with a sponge, as I dried the last of our dinner dishes.

"Are you serious? You got death threats from the PTA?"

"I didn't stick around long enough to find out who they were from. But oh yeah, shit got serious. At first they were your run-of-the-mill offensive letters suggesting in no uncertain terms where I could stick my little crusade. Those escalated into middle-of-the-night phone calls, with actual heavy breathing, if you can believe it. And then just before the proposition came up for a vote, the cat disappeared." She paused for a moment, very still. "Ethan loved that mangy fleabag. I didn't know what to tell him. But I knew what I'd do if I ever found out. Anyway. That's when I knew it was time to get the hell out of Dodge."

By "Dodge" she meant Boulder, Colorado. The story of why she and Ethan had moved to Cloverkist was, in a way, as dramatic as my own recent departure from Amsterdam. I understood why she'd waited until we were alone to fill me in. After dinner, Ethan had asked if he could take Calvin to his room and read him a story. I told him Cal would like that and off they trotted, giving me and Bernstein a chance to catch up.

"Why New Hampshire?"

"A fluke. I was sitting in the dentist's waiting room while Ethan got his teeth cleaned, flipping through a copy of *Country Living* magazine. As you do," she said with a smirk. "And there it was in the real estate section. 'Cloverkist Inn: 19th century Charm in the Scenic White Mountains.' I ripped out the page, called as soon as I got home, and made an offer. Sight unseen, except for the picture. A month later it was ours. Out of the frying pan and into the fire."

Classic Tessa Bernstein. At Camden she had bounded from one cause to another, fist raised and bullhorn blaring, always leading the charge. She wasn't gay, rumored lesbian liaisons in college notwithstanding, but I was not surprised she'd take on a school district, a community, or the whole fucking state over a PTA statute that banned membership for same-sex parents. But details were missing from her story. Like what had taken her to Colorado in the first place? She was from a wealthy family in Boston, if I remembered correctly. She also omitted any reference to Ethan's father. I suspected both these things might be connected to her sudden departure from Camden during our senior year. Some kind of breakdown, classmates had said. I had a feeling we were deep in civilian *don't ask, don't tell* territory. Best left for another time.

The wall phone rang and Bernstein grabbed the receiver.

"Cloverkist Inn. How may I help you?" She paused briefly. "Yeah. Hold on a minute, will you?" She held the receiver toward me with a furtive glance toward Ethan's room. "Here. I'm going to take this in the office." I took the phone and she rushed out of the apartment. The office was across the hallway at the top of the stairs that led down to the pub and the restaurant.

"I got it, Dekker. You can hang up." She was already speaking urgently to the caller before I replaced the receiver. "Dowser Duane, you gotta get your skinny ass over here ASAP. And bring the Wicca woman. He's back."

What the hell? Dowser Duane and the Wicca woman? Sounded

like some spoof rockabilly duo. Or a pair of lost *Looney Tunes* characters. But the tone in Bernstein's voice suggested nothing funny about the call. Wicca had something to do with witchcraft, and I had a vague notion what a dowser was—someone who found water with a stick. I couldn't wrap my head around any connection between the two. Did it concern the incident earlier with the two sisters? And who was back? Clearly she wasn't referring to me. As far as I knew, no one else was here. Bernstein told me she had decided to book guests only during weekends after the summer season so she could focus on home-schooling Ethan. The local school was not up to the challenge of her gifted son, she told me. Ethan was no doubt an exceptional child, but I was still trying to work out in what way. Gifted as in genius, or gifted as in special?

I looked through the doorway into his room. He'd fallen asleep, open book lying in his lap. Calvin raised his head, acknowledging my presence, but content to stay by the boy's side.

Ethan's was the largest of four compact but comfortable rooms above the pub, a self-contained apartment set apart from the rest of the inn. An efficient eat-in kitchen and a modest living room took up half of the space, with windows along the wall facing the woods behind the inn. The furnishings were simple and rustic, not exactly what I thought of as Bernstein's style. A polished wood slab coffee table, end tables made from birch logs, and a comfortable-looking couch with a crocheted granny patch afghan. The dark corner bedroom where Bernstein slept was little more than a closet.

However, Ethan's room was painted with bright colors, fitted with wood-framed bunk beds, a neatly kept desk, and shelves well stocked with books, toys, and a small aquarium housing a pair of angelfish and a few guppies. Above two windows, a long narrow poster hung on the wall giving a 360-degree panoramic view of the White Mountains, noting names and altitudes of each. Bernstein had created a safe, stimulating environment for her young son, a place where a boy could happily throw himself into a beanbag chair and read to his attentive new friend.

The fact Calvin had attached himself to Ethan so quickly, so enthusiastically, so protectively, was worth noting. When Willy got sick in Amsterdam, Cal became his constant companion, refusing even the shortest walk outside unless absolutely necessary. Later when Cal and

I were on our own, living in the jeep, he transferred his unconditional devotion to me without question, without complaint. Little did I know his protective instincts would save my life, more than once. So his behavior upon meeting Ethan set off warning bells. I just had to figure out what they meant.

I didn't think Bernstein was being deliberately vague or unforthcoming in the information department. It was more like she was being pulled in a dozen different directions at once, unable to focus on any one thing long enough to finish a sentence, much less a story. Between managing the inn, the restaurant, the pub, and Ethan, no wonder she appeared stressed, physically drawn. We were the same age, but Bernstein had always seemed older than her years, even at Camden. Thinking back, that was particularly true the last time all of us were together. Almost all.

The Honors Comparative Literature Seminar usually met outside during the golden afternoons of early October in Vermont. The plan had been to reveal and discuss our senior thesis proposals. Under normal circumstances, this would have made for a lively mix of academic debate and opportunistic entertainment. My friends' various areas of interest were as unlikely bedfellows as their actual experiences pairing off in bed, which always revolved around the center of ambiguity provided by the comparative studies of Drew Smith Elliott. What he compared to what or to whom, when or how, was a topic of endless speculation. Elliott had introduced me into this tightly knit group and Elliott was missing. His absence was the elephant on the quad no one dared acknowledge.

"Dekker, why don't you get the ball rolling," said Bernstein, nudging me with one of the weighty volumes of Proust she always carried around. She naturally took over the leadership role usually held by Elliott. They had been the intellectual golden couple on campus our freshman year. They flaunted their sexploits with open-air abandon and remained close after their calculatedly public breakup "to explore other avenues of physical and cerebral experience." Or so they fiercely maintained. Elliott's duplicity must have been killing her. She took pride in knowing everything about everyone, using her gender studies as an excuse to plumb the depths of our emotional and sexual lives with ruthless candor. She wasn't about to reveal any chinks in her own psychological armor, however.

"Okay." I didn't mind starting. My interests were no secret to anyone. "You all know I've been reading Van Gogh's letters to his brother, Theo."

"Don't you mean obsessing over them, Sweetcheeks?" Maxwell Shelly interjected, eyes wide with mock innocence. Shelly's six-foot-six-inch powerfully built frame made him look like a basketball star, but he paraded around campus like the Queen of Sheba. Performance studies gave his extravagant personality an outlet for what he called *free expression.* Everyone else referred to it as blatant exhibitionism.

"Keep a lid on it, Shelly," Bernstein admonished. "You'll get your turn. Go on, Dekker."

"Shelly's probably right," I admitted. "But I began to notice how frequently Vincent referenced specific books. He was a voracious reader from an early age and loved bookshops, even worked in one before he began painting. A lot of his still life work includes books. Some of his portraits, too. So I want to investigate the intersection between literature and his art. It's kind of vague, I know. But there are a lot of directions I could pursue. For example, did reading Zola relate somehow to his interest in painting peasants?" I had more ideas, but left it at that.

"I like it, Dekker. It has a lot of potential," said Jefferson. No surprise there. Arthur Jefferson, a pudgy and painfully shy English major with literary aspirations, spent most of his time in the library doing endless research, which we all thought was more escape than study. He'd been Elliott's roommate since freshman year, but it came as no shock to anyone that, like the rest of us, he'd been clueless about the novel his closest friend had been writing. "Would you want to do research at the Van Gogh Museum in Amsterdam?"

"Of course he needs to go to Amsterdam," Shelly screeched. "And if his dead boyfriend Vincent doesn't pan out, he could always compare Thomas De Quincey's nineteenth-century opium-eater to Dutch drug culture. Hash brownies, anyone?" He pulled a Tupperware sandwich box from his knapsack with a flourish and waved it in the air. "Made them myself this morning."

"Absolutely not," Bernstein said, a little too shrilly. The session had barely begun and she was already losing control. Shelly flashed me a self-satisfied smirk. He always enjoyed getting under Bernstein's skin, but she made an easy target today.

Not that Shelly ever considered other people's feelings when the urge to take center stage took hold.

"Don't get your panties in a twist, Bernstein. Dekker knows I'm just playin' with him." Shelly batted his eyes in my direction. "I think your idea is lovely. Why not call it Vincent's Bookshelf? There might be a book in it. People just loooove to read books about books. And while we're on the subject of books, may I go next, Madame Chairman?"

Bernstein shrugged with a sigh, indicating she didn't give a fuck.

"Well. I had planned to create a fabuloso performance thesis, but I know how tired y'all are of me paradin' my junk 'round the art department. And then last night a whole new concept burst out of my brain, full-grown like Athena from the forehead of Zeus. What I really want to explore is the performative hypocrisy of collegiate literary tropes as abused by certain anomalous authors to write best-selling so-called fiction."

Jefferson and I exchanged a brief glance and became engrossed in the fall foliage, as if we'd never seen it before. Bernstein glared at Shelly so intensely it seemed she might spontaneously combust. Or wished he would.

"Any discussion?" Shelly asked.

"You're an asshole," Bernstein hissed.

"Moi?" Shelly exclaimed in mock horror. He'd set the all too obvious trap and Bernstein had walked right into it. "I'm not the one actin' all hurt and pissed off so that everyone has to tiptoe around on eggshells. I'm not the one wallowin' in a self-pity party of one. I got the same cannibalized hatchet job treatment as anyone else and you don't see me mopin' like some abandoned puppy."

This was true. Shelly didn't give a shit that his on-again off-again liaisons with Elliott had been turned into comic literary fodder. Self-absorbed as he was, he reveled in the burlesque parody of his flamboyance, as if Elliott had faithfully recorded his performances for posterity. Factual accuracy was never an issue for Shelly. But to be fair, while the buffoonish character based on him provided the most humor in Elliott's novel, the satiric treatment of Bernstein was darker, more personal, at times unaccountably vicious. It was hard to know what angered her most—the cruel emotionally anatomical dissection of their relationship or the fact that Elliott had kept his writing life so secret from her, from all of us, that publication of the book during the summer came as a total shock.

Bernstein picked up her books and stomped off without another word.

"Oh, come on, Bernstein," Shelly shouted after her. "Can't we talk about this?"

Bernstein flipped him her middle finger without turning around. Shelly frowned, disappointed the fireworks were over before they'd begun.

"Give her a break," Jefferson said softly.

"Well, pardon the fuck out of me. So Miss Tessa's beau left her at the cotillion. What're we all supposed to do? Hide behind our fans and pretend nothin' happened? Hell, no. And don't be givin' me that look of righteous disenchantment, Master Dekker. You know you got off easy."

I did. Elliott's novel was called *(entitled)*—lowercase and in parenthesis, an obvious play on (untitled)—and had rocketed to the top of best seller lists across the country upon publication in July. Its twenty-one-year-old debut author became the darling of the glitterati. By the time we returned to school in the fall, everyone at Camden had read it and identified Elliott's blatant caricatures, primarily based on his closest friends. The most embarrassing episodes of our young lives were splashed across the pages with willful glee and apparent carelessness, an unabashed betrayal of our most private conversations, our deepest fears and vulnerabilities.

The glowing reviews made matters worse. They praised Elliott for exposing the heartless and cruel underbelly of a spoiled generation of pretentious brats, indulging in dysfunctional, albeit comic, mayhem. They admired his bravery for turning a critical eye on his hapless peers and applauded his fresh approach, his ingenious plotting, his witty repartee. And as if that wasn't enough, he didn't have the decency or the balls to return to college and explain, apologize, or God forbid, look any of us in the eye. A clear-cut case of cowardice, everyone agreed.

Not that there was time for much discussion during what turned out to be our last semester. Without Elliott our gang of five had lost its joie de vivre, and events continued to conspire against us. Shelly was diagnosed with AIDS and left for Alabama to spend his last days with the family he claimed to hate. I wondered if he might have tried to contact Elliott, perhaps through his publisher, to break the bad news. I doubted it, but never asked. Everything was happening at lightning speed. Jefferson hid out in the vast warren of library cubicles and buried himself deeper in his never-ending research. Bernstein fucked off without warning or explanation. One day she was in class, the next day she was gone. Like Shelly. Like Elliott. And ultimately like me, flying off to Amsterdam after Grandmother's death during Christmas break.

❖

Jesus. I hadn't thought about Elliott in years. When the idea of returning to New England occurred to me, it made sense to get in touch with Jefferson. Professor Jefferson now. He'd never left Camden after graduation. A couple of doctorates had assured him tenure and the academic fast track to department head. He'd invited me to come visit him and his wife, but when he mentioned Bernstein had bought an inn up in New Hampshire, something told me it might be the perfect spot to figure out what I wanted to do next. A quiet place in the mountains. How was that working out, Dekker?

One thing for sure, it was quiet. Except for the occasional passing car, the only sounds coming through the screened windows were the chirping of night insects and the rustle of dry leaves shifting in the soft breeze. I could no longer hear the faint murmur of Bernstein's voice on the phone down the hall. I peeked into Ethan's room again. The boy was still asleep.

"Stay," I whispered to Calvin. He raised an eyebrow in agreement.

I left the apartment and crossed the hallway toward the office. The light was on, the door open, and Bernstein sat motionless at the desk, her head in her hands.

"Are you okay?" I asked quietly. No response. "Bernstein?"

"No one's called me that since college," she said without moving.

"Do your friends still call you Dekker?"

"If I had friends I suppose they would. One friend used to call me Jason sometimes. But he's gone."

"Like Bernstein. She's gone, too." She looked at me, with a hint of sadness.

"I don't know," I said. "Taking on a school district, a city, a whole fucking state? That sounds like the one and only Bernstein I knew in college."

"Maybe." A half-smile broke through her melancholy. "But I'm Tessa now. Have been for a long time. Everyone calls me Tessa."

"Tessa it is, then."

"Where's Ethan? Is he sleeping?"

"In his beanbag chair."

"As usual. I'm sorry I dumped him on you today with no warning. He can be quite a handful, especially with strangers. But he likes you. I can tell."

"He likes Calvin. I'm just the guy with the dog."

"No. You're his mom's friend Dekker. And I'm a terrible friend. I meant to have the two top tower rooms ready for you, but they're a mess. I can't rent them because there's no fire escape. The girls were supposed to clean them today, but..." She heaved a deep sigh. "You can sleep in one of the rooms down the hall for tonight. I just have to get fresh linens."

"Why don't I crash on your couch? I'll help you sort out the other rooms tomorrow. Besides, I'm not sure I can part Calvin from his new best friend."

"You sure that's okay?"

"Positive. That afghan looked mighty comfy, and I'm so tired I'll fall asleep before my head hits the pillow. You must be exhausted, too."

"You have no idea," she said as she pulled herself up from the desk.

I helped get Ethan to bed, under Calvin's watchful gaze, lifting him from his beanbag chair into the bottom bunk. He mumbled something as I pulled the blanket over him, but his eyes never opened. I picked up the worn leatherbound book he'd been reading to Cal. Gold embossed letters on the cover read *Historical and Legendary Tales of the White Mountains*. I placed it on his desk as Bernstein came into the room and kissed his forehead. Again he mumbled what sounded like the same phrase.

It's okay, Moose.

"Who's Moose?" I asked.

"Moose? Oh, that's his imaginary friend." She smiled with a shrug, handed me a spare pillow, and turned to go to her room. But she stopped in the doorway and looked back over her shoulder. "At least, I hope he's imaginary."

From the Diary of Corporal Anson Quimby
13th New Hampshire Infantry Regiment

July 1864

My wound has healed. Though some soreness remains, the doctor pronounced me fit for travel. Early in the morn I shall set forth and return to my fellow soldiers, those stalwart Littleton lads of Company D. Tonight I walked beneath the dark canopy of stars, among the makeshift hospital tents. Most unfortunate, I happened upon a gruesome scene: a pile of amputated limbs being loaded onto a rough wagon. I know not where they might be taken, or how such are disposed of, and dared not disturb the two Freedmen who worked in somber silence. The task was undertaken with care and gentleness, with no regard as to whether the useless limbs belonged to brave Union soldiers or hapless Rebels. The battlefield removes all differences, and all are alike in common humanity. But if rumors passing through Camp as like a deadly fever can be believed, the same is not so for some wounded comrades who fell into Rebel hands. I've heard it told they delight in hacking and butchering our brave defenders of the flag, and would sooner cut out the hearts of damned Yankees as cut off their legs or arms. Such brutal barbarism between fellow countrymen is near impossible to imagine, much less to understand. As if to overtake such dark thoughts, the voices of angels drifted my way. The nurses, those Sisters of Mercy, often sing together to soothe the afflicted. Like us soldiers, many undertook a long and perilous journey to serve the battle wounded, sometimes against the wishes of their family. One such is Miss Sarah Low of Dover, a petite but tireless young woman, fair of face, with a determined nature. Her brother Nat serves with the 11th New Hampshire Regiment, and when she discovered I was from the 13th, she would often sit by my cot and exchange news or gossip from home. She had entreated her friends in Dover to establish a Soldiers Aid Society, and brought me a fine bottle of blackberry brandy, which the ladies sent. I thought it better handed out among the wounded, but she said, No. She urged me to carry it back to my comrades in the field, to hearten them with a taste from home. I do believe she was thinking most of her dear brother, Nat. I wandered between the tents, in hope I might find the singers and bid Miss Low farewell, were she among them. It was not to be. I did happen upon another whose kindness had touched the hearts of so many. It was Mr. Whitman, the poet who gave me paper to record my thoughts, as I do now. I saw him behind Arlington House, where countless graves were dug to bury our dead. He passed along a row of bodies, laid out for tomorrow, loosely wrapped in bloody sheets, stopped by each one with bowed head. He muttered a few words, too soft to be heard by any but the lost soul to whom he spoke, and placed the gentlest kiss upon each forehead. When he was done, he rose unsteadily to his feet, looking twenty years older than I had seen him last. Our eyes met, but without recognition on his part. His special gift was to impart a feeling of friendship on every soldier he met. I was merely one among hundreds, thousands of his Camerados, as he called us. I cannot be certain 'twas a man he saw at all. In the dim light, he looked little more than a ghost himself. But his voice was clear when he spoke the words I shall never expunge from my memory: Not a day passes, not a minute or second without a corpse. I stood frozen to the ground as he shuffled into the dark. And as always my thoughts turned to Ben. I am impatient to find him, to know that he is alive and well. There has been no news from the 13th but that they prepare for battle again and my return to service will be most welcome.

CHAPTER FOUR

I. VALRAVEN

The two red foxes sat motionless across the arroyo. Pointed ears held back, flat against their heads, in a calm submissive state. Valraven did not need the flash of heat lightning reflected in their eyes to understand. *Volpes volpes* had led him well, as always. He rarely saw them along the way but knew the animals were never far from his side, guiding him, as they had since first revealing their true nature. And his.

The clouds above the canyon shifted, flickered, without the usual attendant thunder. Valraven hoped it would not rain. His clothes, drenched with sweat after the long hike in the desert heat, had begun to dry. His skin would adapt to the gradual drop in temperature as darkness fell, unless caught in a sudden downpour, not uncommon in October. The task at hand might last until sunrise, and dry clothes could lower the risk of hypothermia. Every ounce of stamina he could muster would be necessary to endure the ordeal to come. He had prepared for months. None of his previous experiences approached the scale of what he would attempt this night.

The ancient site was well off the beaten track popular with hikers and tourists. Not another living soul in sight among the scatter of ruins. But Valraven was not alone. He raised his arms and drew in the energy of those he had met on the long journey, who supported him when his courage faltered, shared the ecstatic joy of his successes, the bitter tears of his defeats. He felt their power rising, lifting him toward the astral plane they could only dream of reaching.

Valraven had met so many dreamers and wannabe psychics, fraudulent mediums and spiritualist fakes—some well intentioned, too many others not. The old Native American Shaman had proved to be the real deal, the only one. He had pointed Valraven out in the crowd of faithful followers, fallen to his knees, and kissed the hem of Valraven's shirt, mumbling in a language Valraven had never heard. Never heard, but understood all the same. Athabaskan, he would later discover, the oldest known tongue of the oldest tribes, whose trails stretched the length of North America from Alaska to Mexico.

"You are a very old soul," the Shaman told him. "Older than the great-grandfather of my great-grandfather. You have been chosen to help the women and children who are lost. You are the chosen one. Find them and help them cross over. They have waited hundreds of years. And at last, you have come."

Tears streamed down the old man's face.

Valraven didn't know how he understood the Shaman. The shy young woman, who had been introduced as the Shaman's granddaughter, attempted to translate what her grandfather said. Valraven shook his head.

"You don't need to explain. I understand the words but I don't know how, and I have no clue what the hell he's talking about. Do you?"

The girl gave a slight shake of her head and whispered something to her grandfather. He nodded, looking deeply into Valraven's eyes. When he spoke again, his words were so soft Valraven was uncertain they'd been said aloud. But he heard them just the same.

"You are an old soul with a young gift. You have come to learn. I will teach you, if you allow me. The foxes will guide us."

On the other side of the arroyo, the two red foxes moved as one and disappeared into the lengthening shadows. Valraven took this as a sign the appointed hour drew close, when time would begin to fold in on itself and unfold again, like the pleated bellows of a concertina. The wind rose, swept around him, and gathered in tiny spirals that danced across the ground with a lone tumbleweed, danced where the Great House once stood, tall and proud. Valraven saw it for the briefest of moments, just long enough to recognize the fragment of wall that remained.

The man with a spiral.

He strode across the kiva, where the altar of human sacrifice had turned to dust, its reign of terror reduced to no more than a whispered scream across the mesa, a dark past before the time that Valraven sought. He stood before the wall and traced with his finger the rough lines carved into stone. The petroglyph felt fresher than its ten thousand years. A male figure held a spiral in his left hand, while at his right foot a canine beast appeared to growl. Never before had Valraven's precognition been so accurate, right down to the detail of the man's splayed right hand. The only thing missing was blood. He looked at his palms, but there was no trace of his recurring stigmata. Relieved, he leaned his back against the stone wall and waited.

❖

One with a lesser gift would have seen little more than a shimmer, if anything at all. When Valraven opened his eyes, the night appeared bright as day. He was deeper into the crossing-over place than ever before, as deep as it was possible to go. A gathering of women, children, and infants stared back at him, illuminated from behind by the brightest White Light.

Valraven could rarely make others understand that the souls he saw bore no resemblance to ghosts of popular culture. They were not vague transparent apparitions floating in the air, but normal-looking human beings. Only their profound sense of melancholy distinguished them from their living counterparts. With a group this large, larger than any Valraven had encountered before, the collective sadness they conveyed was almost too much to bear. But he steeled his resolve and offered himself, a vessel for their unfettered emotions. Not only grief, but also loneliness and regret, anger and fear.

"Do not be afraid. I am here to help you."

Valraven always felt uncomfortable speaking aloud to the souls, when he knew nonverbal communication worked perfectly well. But he'd learned his voice put them at ease, relaxed them. They seemed to enjoy being spoken to in death as in life. Again this proved to be the case. At his simple greeting, most of the women turned and crossed over into the White Light without hesitation. They had not needed Valraven. They simply did not desire to leave the others behind. He had seen this before. Their swift departure not only expressed complete confidence in Valraven's ability to break the death mantras of even the most damaged souls, it boosted his confidence as well.

Not that it made his job any less complicated.

The remaining women came forward, singly or in pairs. Different approaches were required, depending on individual personalities or circumstances. Some needed a stern command. Some required gentle forgiveness. Some needed to be convinced time had passed. Some required only a simple hug and they were gone. One of the children needed to feel his warm living breath on her head. Each had a story. He listened, he spoke with them, and one by one they walked into the healing White Light.

All but one. An infant. A boy born blind who had lived only a few hours. Valraven realized the sense of urgency among the women at this crossing place centered on this single child.

Every bone in Valraven's body ached, every nerve ending sent waves of pain directly to his cerebral cortex. The pressure of his brain against the skull intensified, and he felt as if he was about to explode. He used everything he had learned from the Shaman and rose above the pain, beyond it, so he could finish the work he had begun. Failure was not an option.

He pulled the infant from the darkness, which had fallen so gradually he had not noticed. The White Light had tapered into a single ray. Time was short, but he must not rush. He held the child in his arms and offered to let the boy use his eyes. Valraven didn't understand how this was done, only that he could do it. The boy pointed to the arroyo and Valraven carried him there. Water rushed through the gully, and the baby laughed as beautiful butterflies surrounded their heads. The sun broke over the horizon and birdsong filled the air. Valraven scooped a handful of muddy earth from beneath the flowing water, breathed in its musky scent, and playfully daubed it on the boy's cheeks.

Snips, and snails, and puppy dog tails.

And the child crossed over at the exact moment the pinpoint of White Light disappeared.

Valraven sank to the ground and wept. All the emotions had been left behind, gathered inside him, and it was his turn to grieve. It would take weeks or months with his craniosacral therapist to repair the damage he had suffered. If that was even possible. He didn't want to think about it. He wanted to lie down and sleep for a week, maybe more.

He struggled to his feet and turned to the kiva. The rising sun cast his shadow across the ground, directly toward the fragment of wall with the petroglyph. Two men stood before the drawn figure, obscuring it. A fireman and a soldier in formal dress uniforms from another era. Valraven was confused for a moment. And then he knew. They were not of this place, not of this time. They were messengers from beyond. The two men raised their arms and pointed behind Valraven. East. The two red foxes watched before trotting off toward the rising sun.

II. DEKKER

I didn't need to open my eyes to sense a presence in the room, watching me. I felt no fear, so I knew I wasn't sleeping. I hadn't had that recurring nightmare for some time, the dark stranger standing over my bed. I was awake but didn't want to move, not until I knew who was there waiting in the dark. I'd played this game before, a kind of voluntary sleep paralysis. If I remained motionless and kept my eyes closed, I might fall back to sleep, and the presence might be gone when I woke. Perhaps I was afraid. Perhaps I was asleep. The only way to know for certain would be to open my eyes, to face whoever waited in the dark. Did I want to know? I slowly lifted one lid, then the other. Two large eyes stared into my own, and before I fully recognized them, a flash of pink reached toward my face and licked away the last vestiges of sleep.

"Calvin. Stop."

He knows the word and, given the right tone of voice, always obeys. But I never seem to master the appropriate tenor first thing in the morning, and the wet tongue bath will continue until I sit up out of range. However, I could tell from his urgency this was more than a friendly game of Kiss and Wake-up. No surprise, since last evening he opted to watch over Ethan and skip his usual nighttime walk.

"Okay. Okay. Hold your horses. I'm getting up."

He backed off and gave an exaggerated body shake in agreement while I unwrapped myself from the warmth of the blanket and grabbed my boots. I didn't want to wake anyone, but it wasn't necessary to turn on a lamp in the early dawn light. I stole quietly through the kitchen in my socks and found Calvin waiting impatiently by the apartment door. As soon as I opened it, he slid out and led the way down the hall, tail wagging, toenails clicking on the polished hardwood floor. I tugged on my boots, gently closed the door behind me, and followed him.

The long, narrow hallway was dimly lit at the far end by a small dormer window, but the light didn't reach far. I couldn't see them yet but remembered a couple of steps about halfway down the hall, which separated the oldest part of the building from the later addition, so I made my way slowly. Partly open doors offered glimpses of the guest rooms, simply decorated in muted greens and browns with light clover-patterned wallpaper. I wondered if Bernstein had chosen the décor or if she had inherited it from the previous owner. Why had Cloverkist been put up for sale in the first place?

By the time I reached the steps there was enough diffuse light to see the rest of the way to the stairway leading to reception, the Red Rum Room, as Ethan called it. Two suitcases I'd brought in last evening were tucked in the corner where I'd left them. Calvin stood by the tall double doors, pawing the floor with growing insistence.

Gotta go. Gotta go. Gotta go.

"Okay, Calvinator. Let's go," I said as I pushed the door open.

Calvin took off along the porch and headed straight for the grass by the bushes above the pool. An autumn crispness in the air made me wish I'd grabbed my jacket. The afternoon sun upon our arrival had been much warmer. Maybe the jacket was still in the Jeep. As Calvin continued his morning business, all the busier with so much exciting new information to sniff out, I unlocked Jax and found the black leather jacket nestled behind the driver's seat. Mac's leather jacket, one of his few belongings I'd decided was worth keeping. Considering what happened to him back in Amsterdam and my subsequent errors in judgment, I didn't need too many reminders. I kept what I brought with me to a bare minimum—easy since I owned so little—with one notable exception.

The large canvas, sealed in plastic and securely wrapped in heavy brown paper, barely fit in the back of the Jeep. A good thing I decided to leave it unframed. The possibility of having to put it in storage somewhere was unthinkable. I needed it with me, all I had left of Willy, of the ten years we spent together. Ten years brought to a cruel end, which left me homeless and bereft in every way. If not for Calvin...

A bark from Calvin pulled me out of my momentary morbid reverie, unsettling a trio of large crows from the grass under the Cloverkist Inn sign. They cawed and flew across the road, landing on a rough-hewn wooden fence and watching us intently from a safe distance.

A murder of crows.

On the hill behind them, the fence bordered a neat rectangular plot of land cut into the surrounding trees. The grass was dotted with uneven lines of weathered gravestones. Just my luck. Another cemetery. Somehow I had missed it the day before. It was probably an old family burial ground, perhaps even the original owners of Cloverkist. It looked as though someone was still taking care of keeping the grass trimmed. Maybe the town looked after it. The sun began to peek over the hill and through the birch trees. The shadows of the headstones lengthened toward the road and the blackbirds swooped into the brightening sky.

Calvin barked again, which was unusual for him at this hour. Barking wasn't really his thing but we were both taking in a lot of new shit all at once, so I'd cut him some slack. I couldn't see him and assumed he was on the other side of the shrubbery. I pulled on my jacket and walked around to the steps leading to the pool.

Calvin sat on the top step, his head cocked quizzically. He emitted a soft growl and I followed his gaze to the two stone puppies on the deck. Ethan must have been playing with them because they were no longer in the same position. The one holding the hose had its front paws on the belly of the one lying on its back, a case of sibling domination. Except the scene looked more sinister than playful. Calvin barked a warning, as if telling them to play nice. I almost laughed but it was clear no one else was amused.

III. ETHAN

Write your dreams into a story. Mom says. That's funny because the dreams come from a story. Our favorite story. Always about Ethan the White Mountain Giant.

Ethan the Giant lived in Olden Days before Cloverkist was an inn.

Before Cloverkist was a farm. Before Cloverkist was even built. The Olden Days when the forest covered all the land from river to river and lake to lake and mountain to mountain.

You weren't named for Ethan the Giant. Mom says. You were named for Ethan in the Bible.

Was Ethan the Giant named for Ethan in the Bible?

Probably. Mom says.

Okay then.

Ethan the Giant was a pioneer. He built his own log cabin in the woods when nobody else lived there. The log house burned down and he built another one. He built a stone house but that was later. He had a wife and a baby boy. He hunted in the forest and shot deer and moose for food. He carried them home on his back. That's how big and strong Ethan the Giant was.

This was our dream.

Ethan the Giant was hunting on the mountain with his dog.

A black bear cub crossed the trail in front of them.

The dog chased the cub up a tree.

Ethan climbed the tree and caught the little bear. He tied the cub's mouth up with his handkerchief so he couldn't bite and led him home to the cabin.

Ethan tied the bear to a pole with a strap and made him a trough for water. His son and the cub grew up together and played in the yard and people came to see the first tame bear in the White Mountains.

But the angry man comes with his brushes. He paints away our dreams. He covers them with angry strokes of thick black paint.

Ethan the Giant cannot stop him.

The angry man wants to paint over the little boy and make him disappear.

No. No. No. No. We scream.

We wake up and the dream ends.

We get up and feed the fish in the aquarium their breakfast. Just a few sprinkles are enough.

We go to the kitchen and pour ourselves a bowl of Lucky Charms.

We pick out all the green four-leaf clovers and line them on the table in rows.

We get milk from the fridge and pour it into the bowl until the lucky charms float on top.

We wait for Mom to get toast and coffee and we eat breakfast together.

The end.

IV. DEKKER

"Just see to it they don't burn the place down," Tessa said in an exaggerated stage whisper before leaving me alone with her two strange visitors.

And there was no doubt about it. Even by rural North Country standards, Dowser Duane and his Wicca woman, Jayceen, took eccentric to a dizzying high level.

Cal and I were on the porch when they pulled into the parking lot in a beat-up, rusted-out pickup truck that looked barely roadworthy. It hiccupped to a halt and backfired smoky exhaust fumes. Calvin gave a bark, glanced my way, and offered his opinion with a soft growl.

"It's okay, pal. They're friends," I assured him, trying to assure myself as well. He gave me a doubtful look but sat silently, his floppy ears alert to the chance of mischief. I decided I'd better leave him out here when the rest of us went inside. I'd tie him up to one of the porch columns to ensure he didn't go exploring in the woods. He wouldn't like it, but I'd deal with his disapproval later.

By the time the pair got out of the truck and were headed toward the porch, Bernstein had joined us, leaving Ethan upstairs to work on one of his homeschool assignments.

"Sorry we're late, Tessa," the diminutive young man said, shaking his head. "That piece-of-junk truck is shaky as all get-out."

"I swear, Double D, once you get me home I'm not stepping foot in that death trap again," said the woman, large as the man was small. She pulled a dainty handkerchief from between her heaving breasts and wiped her high sweaty brow. "We were putt-putt-puttin' up Prospect Hill so slow a logger damn near run us right off the road. I swear, Tessa, my whole miserable life flashed before my eyes quicker than a bobcat licks his ass."

I was used to some pretty odd Dutch expressions that made no sense to me. But they were speaking English, albeit in some alternative universe. I dared not make eye contact with Tessa and risk bursting into inappropriate laughter.

"Now, calm yourself, Jayceen," said the man who reminded me of a leprechaun. "You know these things never end well if you've gotten yourself into a dither before we even start."

Jayceen nodded, closed her eyes, and took a deep breath. We all watched as she stood in the parking lot and seemed to go into a meditative state. Tessa took this opportunity to introduce me.

"Dowser Duane, this is a dear old friend from college. Jason Dekker. He just moved back here from Amsterdam and is going to help me out for a while."

"I'm pleased to make your acquaintance," Dowser Duane said with an impish grin, extending a skinny arm covered with tattoos of various mystical-looking symbols. An inky black snake curled from ankle to calf and disappeared up under his baggy cargo shorts. He shook my hand, and his grip was surprisingly strong.

"And this is my friend, Jayceen. Jayceen, this is Jason."

Jayceen was still too traumatized from her truck ride from hell, or too deep in her recovery trance, to do more than nod. Her mousy brown hair streaked with gray was pulled up into a tight bun at the top of her head. She was obviously much older than Dowser Duane, who appeared to be in his mid-twenties. Under his mop of black hair and scruffy beard, he had piercing green eyes. Kind of attractive in a backwoodsy way. I wondered if they were a couple, but it seemed unlikely.

"Do you want to start in the pub, Dowser Duane? Like last time?" Tessa asked.

"Like as not." Dowser Duane nodded.

Was I supposed to call him Dowser Duane, too? Was that any better than Double D? Maybe I could get away with not calling him anything for the time being.

"Jason will take you in through the kitchen. I've got to get back to Ethan. You know how he gets if we don't keep to his schedule."

"Tell him we said hey!"

"Will do," said Tessa. And with her whispered warning about burning the place down, she was gone.

"Um. Can you hold on a minute? I want to get something to tie up Calvin out here."

"I've got a long lead in the back of the pickup. My old Otis passed just two weeks ago. Finest bluetick coonhound I ever had the pleasure to know. Anyway, I haven't had the heart to get rid of any of his things yet. Just left the lead there where we kept it, for camping trips and such. You're welcome to it."

"I'm so sorry. But if you're sure, thank you. That would be great."

Dowser Duane nodded and, head hanging low, went to retrieve the dead dog's lead. That was an unsettling thought. In the hillside cemetery across the road, gravestones stood like sentinels, watching. Was Otis buried there? Before I could dwell on that, Jayceen came out of her daze with a sharp intake of breath, almost a stifled scream. She slowly raised her head and looked up toward the top of Cloverkist's lookout tower.

"We're coming for you," she muttered in a low voice. "You be ready now, hear?"

Dowser Duane handed me the well-worn lead and gazed up to the tower as well.

"Do what you have to do," he said. "We got time."

V. CALVIN

calvin stay
outside sitting waiting watching / dekker inside calvin out
outside waiting wanting playing / two boys inside calvin out
sniffing scenting something burning / strangers inside calvin out
squirrel running stopping looking / squirrel hiding under jax
pulling tugging collar choking / squirrel laughing under jax
squirrel running into bushes / scrabbling screeching squirrel gone
watching waiting seeing nothing / puppies gone
calvin stay

VI. DEKKER

"I learned dowsing from my daddy, who learned it from my granddaddy, who learned it from his daddy before him," Double D explained, as Jayceen pulled the items they needed to perform the cleansing from a large embroidered bag. "We Rafferty folk been dowsers long as I know."

"I thought dowsing was finding underground water with a— what's it called? Some kind of special stick." It was on the tip of my tongue but I couldn't remember.

"Yup. A divining rod. That's what my great-granddaddy used. Mostly to search out groundwater but sometimes other things. A vein of ore, maybe. Or to find out if an old burial ground was located on somebody's property. Divination, they called it. My great-granddaddy had the gift of divination, and he passed it down to his son, and on down it came to me." He took an engraved metal case from his pocket and held it reverently between his palms.

"So cleansing is a kind of divination?" I asked, still a little confused.

"Naw. Cleansing is Jayceen's thing. It's a different kind of gift, something she has to work at. But we bumped into each other one day at the farmer's market, where some hippie from over Vermont way was selling crystals. A total pack of bullshit is what he was selling, if you ask me. Right, Jayceen?"

"Hmph," she grunted. "He didn't know the difference between rose quartz and hematite. Idiot."

I knew what hematite was. Willy had worn a necklace with a hematite pendant. But now was not the time to think of Willy. Not unless I wanted to conjure a ghost of my own. Not that I believed that was possible. I didn't believe in any of this paranormal crap. But if Bernstein was convinced Cloverkist was haunted, and a cleansing would put her mind at rest, so be it.

"So Jayceen and I got to talking and we figured why not put all our eggs in one basket, so to speak. Two gifts might be better than one, right? One could strengthen the other, and vice versa. We been working together—how long now, Jayceen?"

"Since you were a tadpole," she said. She had laid out white candles, bunches of sage, and what looked to be an antique water pitcher full of sea salt, which had a hand-painted high-relief white rooster on one side.

"Anyway. It seems to be working for us. Except here. When

Tessa first arrived, she noticed right away some spirit was hanging out, messing around in the kitchen mostly. Right, Jayceen? Whistling? And throwing shit across the room?"

"Mm-hmm." She placed lit candles in the four corners of the pub. "And we caught wind of it and stopped by, offered our services. Kind of like a housewarming present. We really liked Tessa, and Ethan is a cool kid. Anyway. We did a cleansing and everything settled down just fine all summer long. But they're back, aren't they, Jayceen? We can feel 'em."

"Them?" I asked.

"I think so. Something's calling them back to Cloverkist."

"Clover-cursed, if you ask me," Jayceen muttered under her breath.

That's when it hit me. *Cloverkist.* It sounded like clover-kissed, sweet and inviting. The perfect name for an inn. But in Dutch, *kist* meant *coffin.* How could I not have thought of that before? Suddenly Cloverkist didn't sound so welcoming after all.

"Could you do us a favor, Jason, and open up all the windows? We're almost ready to start." Dowser Duane pulled a pendant on a short chain from the metal box, which he slipped back into his pocket. The pendant was smaller, but could have been hematite, like Willy's. Or maybe it was rose quartz. I didn't know the difference either.

"The pendulum is amethyst," he said as if reading my mind. "Daddy found it in Deer Hill, just over the border in Maine. Nobody much uses divining rods anymore. A pendulum can tell you a lot more than a stick of wood, if you know how to read it. And it's better for cleansing."

As I began opening windows, Jayceen lit one of the bundles of sage, filling the air with its pungent smoke. She and Double D stood back-to-back in the center of the pub. He held the crystal pendant in front of him, allowing it to swing in an ever-increasing spiral pattern while Jayceen began to hum softly, rhythmically, slowly increasing in volume as she waved the smoldering sage in a circular motion. I backed out of the room, watching from the hallway.

"Find the Light…Feel the Love…We are Joy…" sang Jayceen in an unexpectedly beautiful soprano voice. They began moving, back-to-back mirror images, in widening circles. Pendant spiraling, sage smoke swirling, Jayceen singing, her voice calm and full of warmth.

"Find the Light…Feel the Love…We are Joy…"

It was an impressive performance. I understood how someone desperate for help, someone eager to believe, could be convinced and soothed by the sincerity with which the pair executed their routine. I almost wanted to believe myself. But I remained at a safe distance, watching them as I used to watch Shelly parade naked through the college art department, always somewhat amused. Performance art seemed a little too self-conscious for me to take seriously.

"Jason, we're almost ready to move into the next room," Dowser Duane said in a low voice. "Could you open the windows and the French doors in there?"

"Find the Light…Feel the Love…We are Joy…" Jayceen continued to sing as she moved the four white candles into the corners of the dining room. I opened the large bay windows facing the parking lot, windows that were once stable entrances—if what Ethan told me was true. This was the older part of the inn, the original nineteenth-century building. I wondered if that meant there were more spirits here to cleanse. After all, it adjoined the kitchen where Tessa had supposedly experienced paranormal activity. Did she really believe all this nonsense? It didn't feel like the Bernstein I knew in college.

After Dowser Duane sprinkled sea salt from the pitcher along the doorways and windowsills in the pub, he joined Jayceen and once again they stood back-to-back, beginning the same ritual.

The second time around, the performance felt more contrived, less sincere. The novelty had worn thin and my cynical nature took over. I remembered accompanying Willy to an acupuncturist after his AIDS diagnosis when he was willing to try any kind of treatment. We were both pretty stressed out, so he suggested I try it. I asked the young Chinese practitioner if it was enough that he believed in the healing power of acupuncture or did I have to believe in it as well. I wasn't being rude. I honestly wanted to know.

"It's enough I believe," he said with a look of consternation. "But it helps if you believe, too."

No big surprise that I didn't feel any different when it was over. It didn't help Willy either.

"Find the Light…Feel the Love…We are Joy…"

Jayceen paid particular attention to the fireplace, waving the smoldering sage within the opening so smoke curled up the flue. I suppose a spirit was as likely to use a chimney as any other entryway. When I took my bags up to my new digs on the third floor earlier, I noticed all the rooms in the tower had fireplaces. Tessa couldn't rent the top floor guest rooms in the tower until an exterior fire escape was installed at the back of the building—too expensive an investment for the time being. But since I wasn't a paying guest, she figured bending the rules shouldn't be a problem. All the other rooms were fully booked for the upcoming Columbus Day weekend, peak fall foliage time.

"Find the Light...Feel the Love...We are Joy..."

Their cleansing continued into the Hunt Room. When they finished there, Dowser Duane and Jayceen moved to the kitchen, which had four doorways, including one to the loading dock. No windows. I figured they'd spend more time there since that's where most of the previous activity seemed to be focused. I couldn't quite wrap my head around a haunted kitchen.

I gave the dining room a closer look. The massive stone fireplace in the middle of the front wall, the whitewashed plaster walls with dark rough-hewn exposed beams that also spanned the ceiling, created the perfect postcard of a New England country inn. Along the back wall, brass carriage lamps were attached to the beams and between them were framed vintage photographs of the inn—in olden days, as Ethan said. Four large paintings finished off the décor, two at each end of the room.

They were original oil works, clearly all by the same artist. Somewhat dark and dusty, in need of serious restoration, they appeared to be mid-nineteenth-century American—or very clever reproductions. They reminded me of landscape paintings by the Hudson River School artists I'd studied in college. These were definitely local scenes tied together with a strong thematic style. Two were classic exterior landscapes, both in autumn, intended to be shown side by side. In one, a multicolored mountain slope dwarfed tiny dark figures of a man and his dog in the foreground. The other presented a glittering lake in a valley between two mountains. The focal point was the artist himself, a small but detailed figure seated on a flat rock in front of an easel, painting the view. It was a clever perspective, one I'd not seen before in work from this period.

The paintings at the other end of the room proved more remarkable. On first glance, they were both interiors—one a simple rustic kitchen, the other a barn filled with hay. But in each, an open door revealed the landscape beyond, outside seen from inside—like a White Mountains take on Vermeer. If the light lacked his delicacy, this artist had an eye for detail. In the farm picture, chickens pecked in the barnyard, distant blackbirds dotted in the sky. And inside the barn, two boys sat at a table. One had his back to the viewer, and the other was holding something. A book? Was he husking corn? It was hard to tell. The painting needed a careful cleaning, which could be why the boy who faced front appeared to be Black. That didn't jibe with mid-nineteenth-century New Hampshire, unless I was wrong about their origins. The landscapes could as easily be from the South but, if so, how did they get here?

"Find the Light...Feel the Love...We are Joy..."

Jayceen's voice had a different quality now. It sounded more like she was singing gospel music. Were they both mind readers, or was it simply the power of suggestion? I may not believe in this shit, but I was getting more than a little creeped out. And they'd only gone as far as the kitchen. We still had seven guest rooms above the dining room, the Red Rum Room, Chandelier Room, and the five rooms in the tower to get through. This was going to take a lot longer than I'd thought.

I glanced at my watch and wondered how Calvin was doing on the porch. He'd been out there for almost an hour. He didn't have a problem with being left alone for that long, but he wasn't used to being tied up, and the new surroundings might be disorienting. I walked through the Hunt Room into the entrance hall and poked my head out the door.

Cal was lying in the shade at the corner of the porch, nose resting between paws.

"How you doing, Mr. Calvin?"

Even if dozing, he would've heard me. The fact that he didn't move a muscle meant he was deliberately ignoring me. A ploy intended to guilt me into coming over and giving him the attention he believed he was entitled to. Golden retrievers are master manipulators, often more clever than their humans. I wasn't in the mood to let him win this round of *Who's on Top?* But I hadn't left any water for him. His bowl was up in Tessa's apartment, and I didn't want to disturb Ethan's lessons. There must be something I could use in the kitchen.

"I'm gonna get you some water. I'll be back in a minute."

The door burst open as I turned to go back inside, almost knocking me on my ass. Jayceen barreled through, red-faced and puffing like a runaway steam engine.

"Light-love-joy. Light-love-joy. Light-love-joy. Light-love-joy."

"Whoa, Jayceen. Are you okay? What's going on?"

She stumbled down the steps, stopped, and slowly shuffled around toward me. Her body twitched and trembled. Her bun had come undone, hair a static-filled halo, eyes blazed wide with terror.

"Light-love-joy. Light-love-joy...Light. Love. Joy...Light... Love...Joy..."

She was winding down like her batteries were losing their charge. Her face faded into an expressionless stare, mouth moving without words or sound. The cemetery across the road behind her was the perfect backdrop for her uncanny, almost zombielike appearance.

"Jayceen?" I wasn't sure she could hear me, but she cocked her head slightly and spoke in a low, hoarse voice.

"Tell that whiny runt to mind his own business. He has no idea what he's dealing with. He is kindling for the fire, the inferno that will rage and destroy you all. Tell that bleeding whoreson to let Cloverkist alone, lest he burn in hell with the rest of his kind."

I sensed, more than heard, Calvin get up and stand beside me, hackles raised, growling low.

If this was part of the performance, Jayceen was one heck of an actress. Her body swayed, and for a moment I thought she might collapse into a smoldering heap. A look of bewilderment crossed her face. She bent forward and dry-heaved. I half expected some demonic entity to emerge from her mouth. But when she lifted her head, drawing the handkerchief from her bosom to wipe her lips, she seemed almost normal—whatever that meant.

"Sorry about that," she said. "I'm feeling a little light-headed all of a sudden. Tell Double D I'm gonna walk on down to Granny Stalbird's and have me a big slice of banana cream pie with plenty of whipped cream on top. He can take his time. I'll call me a ride from there. Lordy, I'm hungrier than pups suckin' a bitch's tit. It was nice meetin' you. By the way, I don't think your dog likes me." She giggled, turned toward the road, and laughed her way down the hill on foot.

Good riddance, Calvin barked.

"I couldn't agree more," I said, scratching the back of his neck to let him know he could relax. "Stay put. I'm gonna get you a bowl of water and see if Double D can tell me what that was all about."

He sat, ears on high alert, as Jayceen disappeared behind the trees at a curve in the road.

I felt a discernable chill in the air as I entered Cloverkist. It was much colder than the outside temperature. I remembered seeing a large stack of firewood out back. I hoped the fireplaces were in working order for the coming weekend. I'd talk to Tessa about that later. An eerie silence enveloped the Red Rum Room.

Really, Dekker? An eerie silence? Get a grip.

That pair of country quacks had spooked me. Maybe I was more susceptible to this mumbo jumbo than I thought. Although I grew up going to church every Sunday with my grandmother, I was never what you'd call religious. I certainly didn't buy into heaven and hell or an afterlife or anything like that.

Do you think we have a soul that lives on after we're gone? Willy asked.

I don't know. I'd like to think so. I just don't know.

If there is a way, I'll tell you.

But he didn't tell me. He couldn't tell me. He was dead. And I didn't believe the dead could communicate with the living. No matter how much I wanted to.

I walked into the kitchen.

Bernstein was going to kill me. What had those two crackpots done? Yesterday it was spotlessly clean, stainless steel surfaces and appliances glimmering under bright fluorescent lights. Now it looked like a hurricane had hit. The herbs and spices had been swept off the shelves, dumped or thrown unceremoniously across counters, against walls, all over the room. The scent of burning sage was strong, but the smells of chili powder, ginger, and cinnamon, oregano, basil and tarragon all combined in an overpowering sweetness, almost gagging me. Canisters of rice and dried beans had been dumped on the floor, making it treacherous to move. Everything was dusted with white flour, hanging in the air and mixing with the sage smoke. I could hardly breathe.

In the middle of the floor, Dowser Duane sat sobbing amidst the chaos, bleeding from cuts on his face, hands, and arms. His hair was matted with blood. How could all this have happened so fast? Jayceen must have gone totally berserk to have wreaked such havoc in such a brief space of time.

I carefully made my way into the room.

"Are you okay? What did she do to you?"

Dowser Duane looked up, tears streaming from his eyes, mixing with his blood. He looked like a warrior, face painted for battle.

"Not...not Jayceen," he stuttered. "I told her...told her to run. Run for her life. It tried...tried to...to kill me...my amethyst. Where is it? Where's my amethyst?" He looked around the kitchen in a panic as he tried to stand, slipped and fell, tried to stand again. "Do you see it? It cut me. Where is it? Couldn't...could not make it...stop...hitting me... cutting me...killing me."

He wasn't making sense. I couldn't tell how badly he was hurt but knew head wounds bled profusely. If he'd been sliced with his own crystal, the cuts were probably superficial. He reeled around the kitchen, searching desperately for his beloved—and perhaps deadly—amethyst.

"It's become more powerful, too powerful for me," he said, more to himself than to me. "I need to learn more. I need help. I can't do this alone. I don't know enough. Jayceen don't know enough. We're just a couple of fools, like putty in his hand. He'll beat us to a pulp. I need to know more. I need more help. Jayceen? Is Jayceen alright? Where's Jayceen?"

"Jayceen's fine," I said. "She went for a walk to clear her head. But it's your head I'm worried about. Let me take a look, get you cleaned up a bit. I can't tell how bad you're hurt." I half expected Tessa to come running in any minute. But the apartment upstairs was at the other end of the building. Maybe I could get this fucking mess cleaned up before she came down. I didn't want her more upset and stressed out than she already was.

I ran water on some paper towels so I could clean up his face. He fidgeted and fussed, still moaning about his damn amethyst. I was right. The cuts were superficial. I got a first-aid kit I'd seen in the pantry next to the ice machine. It contained a tube of antiseptic cream that should help keep any infection at bay. When I got back to Double D, he stood staring at the wall between the walk-in fridge and the dishwasher. A short chain dangled out of a small hole. He warily took hold of the chain and pulled. His amethyst slid from the hole in the wall, caked in white plaster dust. I tried to imagine what amount of force could have embedded it like that.

"Clover-cursed. That's what Jayceen said." Dowser Duane placed his precious crystal in its rectangular metal box and snapped the lid closed.

Cloverkist, I thought. *Clover-coffin.*

From the Diary of Corporal Anson Quimby
13th New Hampshire Infantry Regiment

July 1864

We disembarked from the train not far from Camp, behind entrenchments on the Potomac. No wind chilled the balmy air, and the new moon in a cloudless sky allowed a myriad of stars to shine upon us. On such nights, with the scent of the woods unmarred by pungent stifling smoke, one almost forgets the reason we are here—the bloody battles we have fought and are yet to fight, the suffering on the fields and in Armory Square. Such is the indignity of this Secession War between North and South, brothers in arms who have taken arms against one another. Some say it will never end, but I have faith in the Leader of our Union. No finer, braver President ever lived, and I am proud to serve him. In the distance, a wild wondrous sight spread out before us. Crackling campfires between the scattered white tents lit the night bright as day. You would not imagine that tomorrow we resume battle, for the scene was joyous and happy as an afternoon picnic. I wish my mother and my father could bear witness to a night such as this. 'Twould ease their grave concerns and soothe their worried brows to know their son found moments of peace and tranquility akin to those enjoyed on White Mountain trails so close to home. As we entered Camp we were greeted with soul-stirring refrains of popular songs, some sung in simple harmony and others played by lively musical groups—a fiddle, fife, and drum, even cornet or clarinet or concertina to complete the ensemble. Men danced together with wild abandon, some under the influence of strong drink. Others cleaned their firearms, or mended their clothes by the light of the fires. Some cooked for the long march ahead tomorrow. Some sat alone writing to loved ones, wiping away an occasional tear. And when I came upon my beloved friend, sitting by the fire, his back to me, I had a chance to observe him unnoticed. He was engrossed with drawing in his notebook, ever as always. Nothing pleases Benjamin more than to draw a figure or paint a landscape. I strained to see what subject had captured his attention. Across the campfire sat two Negro boys in tattered clothes, arms around each other's shoulders, perhaps brothers, most certain fugitive slaves taking refuge with our soldiers. Ben had captured the sadness in their faces with his simple pencil. Suddenly he stopped drawing, sensing my presence behind him. He turned his head, flashed a warm smile of greeting, and returned to his picture of the two boys.

PART TWO: FULL MOON

"As if a phantom caress'd me,
I thought I was not alone, walking here by the shore…"

—Walt Whitman

CHAPTER FIVE

I. CALVIN

leafs snuffling pawing / sniffing digging
nudging faster digging / dirt flying far&far
calvin stop it / dekker shouting / *no more digging*
stopping digging no&no

grass rubbing rolling / pressing cooling
scrunching crackling crushing / earth smelling old&old
shaking scenting something / needing digging
grumbling pissing / digging no&no

II. DEKKER

Calvin didn't grasp the concept of no digging in a cemetery, same as the dunes on the Dutch coast. If a dog's instinct tells him to dig, it doesn't matter where he is or what the rules are. Consequently he was annoyed with me for telling him to stop. That made two of us who weren't having a particularly good time. But Ethan wanted to do gravestone rubbings, and Tessa had promised he could. Ethan didn't handle broken promises well.

"You don't want to be around when he has one of his meltdowns," Bernstein warned. But sisters Amber and Jade were not returning to work after their incident in the tower, so Tessa had to stay at the inn to wait for the weekend's supply deliveries and asked if I could make good on her promise to Ethan. What was I going to say? Besides, I wanted more time to get to know the boy. I had a feeling he knew more than he was letting on about the unusual activity at Cloverkist. We had to become best buddies if I was going to get it out of him.

He came well prepared, with several large sheets of thin white paper rolled up in a cardboard tube and a case of soft lead pencils—including a flat yellow carpenter's pencil, which he explained would do most of the work. I carried his gear as he marched among the old tombstones, lifting his knees high and kicking up fallen leaves.

"What about this one?" I asked.

He shook his head and continued his search. I didn't know what he was looking for, but he seemed to have a specific idea in mind. He stopped at a marker, examined it carefully with the palm of his hand, shook his head, and carried on to another, where he repeated the process.

Since I could do nothing to help, I sat on a low stone bench in the middle of a large grouping of stones bearing the name QUIMBY. Must have been a prominent family. The headstones were of considerably higher quality than most in the cemetery, some adorned with decorative crosses or urns, and one with a good-sized granite angel. Was the Quimby family the original owner of Cloverkist? I was curious. Many New England towns had local historical societies that kept records, assuming they had survived fires, floods, or other disasters. I made a mental note to check it out.

"Calvin, come," shouted Ethan.

Cal lifted his head and trotted over to the boy. Normally he'd at least glance in my direction for approval before following a command from anyone else. Evidently my Alpha status had been usurped. By a kid, no less. Ethan knelt down in the grass next to Calvin, put an arm around his neck, and whispered something into his ear. Yeah, that boy had secrets all right. Cal listened intently, motionless. In the past couple of days, the two had formed a tight bond, one I would be hard-pressed to break.

❖

I had cleared up the kitchen as best I could after Dowser Duane's fiasco, hoping Tessa wouldn't notice anything drastically amiss. When Ethan had finished his schoolwork, I asked him if he wanted to join Cal and me for a short drive down to the lake I'd seen on my way to Cloverkist. Calvin was desperate for a swim.

"You mean the pond," Ethan said. "Possum Pond."

"It looked bigger than a pond to me."

"They use lake and pond pretty interchangeably up here," Tessa explained. "In this case, I think whoever named it had a fondness for alliteration. Do you remember what alliteration is, Ethan?"

"Cloverkist. Red Rum Room. Dowser Duane. Possum Pond," he intoned. "We're done with school today."

"Yes, we are. So you can go with Dekker and Calvin."

"Possum Pond it is, then," I said. "Would you like to come?" I asked Tessa.

"We can take the trail to the pond," said Ethan, jumping up and down. "We know the way. We can show you. We like to hike around Possum Pond." He continued to jump around the room like he was on a pogo stick.

"Hold your horses, partner," Tessa said, firm hands on the boy's shoulders, calming him. "It's too late to do the whole Possum Pond loop. Remember? Days are getting—"

"Shorter." Ethan's face began to darken.

"That's right. But if Dekker and Calvin want to go for a hike, you can take them to Painter's Palette, then head down toward Granny Stalbird's. I'll meet you with the car in the parking lot out back by the pond in about an hour and a half." She looked at me. "It's a steep trail, not so bad going down, but hiking back up is a killer. You're still a smoker, right, Dekker?"

"Guilty as charged."

"You'll thank me later." She winked and turned to Ethan. "Go find your canteen and fill it up with water."

"NOT FROM THE AQUARIUM," he shouted as he bolted to his room.

"NO. NOT FROM THE AQUARIUM," Tessa shouted back. "Are you sure you don't mind taking him? I could use a break."

"Not at all. When you come down to get us, why don't I treat you to dinner at that diner. Granny's? If the food is any good."

"You don't have to do that."

"I want to. And like you said, you can use a break. When was the last time you took a late-afternoon siesta?"

"Are you kidding?" She laughed. "When Ethan was two, maybe."

"So it's settled. I'll play Boy Scout leader and you get to rest your weary bones. You said it's going to be a busy weekend, right?"

"Don't remind me."

Ethan ran back in, his canteen hanging from a shoulder strap. He held open a small knapsack. "We need snacks, too. We need snacks for Painter's Palette."

"What kind of snacks?" Tessa asked. She knew the answer.

"WE WANT PEANUT BUTTER CRACKERS," Ethan shouted.

"You know where they are. But not too many," she said, as he dropped his knapsack, pulled a chair over to the counter, and climbed onto it so he could reach the cabinet above. "You don't want to spoil your appetite. Dekker is treating us to dinner at Granny Stalbird's."

Ethan looked at us solemnly from atop the chair, packages of peanut butter crackers in each hand. "What about Calvin? No dogs in Granny Stalbird's. It's a rule."

"No worries," I said. "Calvin can wait outside and we'll bring him a doggie bag."

"Doggie bag?" Ethan scrunched his brow in concentration, as if he'd never heard the term before. "We'll bring Calvin a doggie bag." He flashed a wide grin, threw his head back, and cackled his peculiar laugh. "We'll bring Calvin a doggie bag," he repeated gleefully.

Infectious as it was, Tessa and I couldn't help but join in. Bernstein was a great mom, with an unexpected tenderness unlike the fierce advocate I'd known at Camden.

❖

"CALVIN, COME," Ethan shouted from a gravestone set apart from the rest, high on the hill.

Calvin came running out of the woods. He stopped and shot a furtive glance in my direction, knowing full well he could be in serious trouble for wandering too far off. He gave himself a nonchalant shake from head to tail and sauntered over to Ethan.

I needed to pay more attention. What if the kid had followed him and gotten lost or fallen into a ravine and broken his leg or something? Tessa would go ballistic on my ass.

Ethan was whispering in Calvin's ear again. Cal backed away from him and barked. Once. The boy barked back. Calvin cocked his head, perplexed, and replied with an uncharacteristic paroxysm of barking. Ethan knelt in front of Cal and pressed his hands against the dog's ears, soothing him with nods and unintelligible murmurs. I couldn't begin to know what was being communicated between them, but I could sense the intensity. They appeared to reach some kind of understanding. Ethan stood and they both looked at me.

"DEKKER, COME."

What the fuck?

I did not appreciate being spoken to like that by a kid—Tessa's kid or any kid. I would have to have a little chat with him about his attitude.

I picked up his satchel of grave-rubbing material and trudged up the slope. I wasn't yet used to the elevation, and combined with the uphill climb, when I reached them I was huffing and puffing like— well, like the smoker I was. I tossed aside the briefest of thoughts about quitting as I handed the bag over to Ethan.

"You know," I said, "most people don't particularly like being spoken to like a dog."

He looked at me with a blank expression and pointed to the gravestone next to him.

"This is the one we came to find," he said in a dull monotone. "We have to do this one. Right, Calvin?"

Cal wagged his tail in agreement.

Ethan pulled out the cardboard tube and carefully removed a large rolled-up sheet of thin white paper. He held the two exposed corners tightly between his fingers, and as it unfurled, a sudden gust of wind caught the lower edge of the paper. It floated upward, covering Ethan's face for a moment like a delicate rectangular shroud.

"Can you help us put the paper against the stone?" he asked. "Please. Mom says."

"Sure," I said, catching the two loose corners as they flapped in the gentle breeze. We maneuvered the sheet of paper across the weatherworn surface of the granite slab horizontally and wrapped the shorter sides around the rough edges. I held the paper in position while Ethan rummaged through his satchel and found a roll of masking tape.

He had thought of everything. When he was done, the headstone was wrapped in the paper as neatly as any birthday gift. Box of pencils in his lap, he sat cross-legged in front of the stone and stared at it intently for a moment, nodding. As he set to work, Calvin came over and settled down beside him, watching.

The pair of them looked like a scene from a Norman Rockwell calendar. October, of course. Cemetery Boy and Dog. A strong sense of déjà vu hit me. They had sat together in exactly the same position two days ago on Painter's Palette, overlooking Possum Pond.

❖

Ethan shared his peanut butter crackers with Calvin on the large flat rock. The spectacular view of the mountains on each side of the lake was breathtaking. It was surely the same landscape pictured in the painting hanging in Cloverkist's dining room. So, definitely a local artist. The more I'd thought about it, the more I was convinced the work was all by the same person.

The perfectly shaped rock "palette" extended slightly over a craggy vertical cliff face, common to the White Mountains. The trail winding down to the water was not nearly as steep as the upper path we had taken from the inn. Some sections were navigable with the help of well-worn flat stone steps, put into place a long time ago. When snack time was over, Ethan and Calvin raced down the trail. I descended with more caution, holding on to saplings and low branches to keep my balance.

The shoreline—if you could call it that—had encroached on the forest. Roots lost their ability to hold trees erect and many had toppled into the water, lying there at haphazard angles to rot. I guess this contributed to preserving the North Country ecosystem. As the trail led around the pond, other parts of the shore were swampy, dense with tall reeds and cattails. That didn't keep Cal from wading right in to cool off and quench his thirst as soon as he could. The water looked darker, muddier than when reflecting the blue sky from Painter's Palette. Clouds had moved in, blocked the sun, and the pond appeared more suited to wildlife—the kind of place to see moose in the early hours of the morning or late afternoons. Like now.

"CALVIN IS SWIMMING," Ethan shouted up to me.

"That's okay. He likes cold water," I yelled back. "But don't you even get your feet wet or your mom will have our hides."

He nodded, jumped up and down, and began to spin along the trail.

The sun broke through the clouds, and the water's surface danced with dazzling diamonds of light. Briefly blinded by the brightness, my eyes teared up. I squinted in Ethan's direction and his shimmering figure appeared to split into what looked like two boys spinning, heads thrown back, laughing, before merging into one. That's when Calvin chose to give his body a massive shake, close enough to give me a muddy shower.

"Calvin, you shitbag," I muttered, as he raced off after Ethan. A phantom-shaped shadow chased him as another cloud passed across the sun.

III. Ethan

Butcher paper works best. Mom says. We have a big roll in our room. We use it for art, too. We like art. We like drawing and painting. We like gravestone rubbing best.

We found the carpenter's pencil in the grass behind the barn where they do shows. The carpenter must have lost it. Mom says. But we can keep it. The carpenter got another one.

The carpenter's pencil works best because it is flat and the lead is soft. We can't sharpen it with a normal pencil sharpener. Mom has to use a sharp knife. We're not allowed. Mom says. Once we tried and slipped and cut our finger. We got blood all over and Mom was really mad. We let Mom sharpen the carpenter's pencil.

We begin the gravestone rubbing around the edges. Softly, softly, so we don't hurt the stone. We keep the carpenter's pencil flat. The edges are darker than the flat part of the stone. Softly, softly, the wide lead rubs the stone. We are careful not to miss a spot. The stone is bumpy in some places and the bumps are darker than the rest. It's called texture. Mom says.

Softly, softly, we get to the name. We must be careful or the butcher paper might tear and ruin the whole thing. Rubbing around the name is the hard part. The best part. The name appears like magic on the paper.

B-E-N-J-A-M-I-N

Benjamin is buried under the gravestone. He lived in Olden Days. Everyone in the cemetery lived in Olden Days.

We lived in Olden Days, too.

C-H-A-P-M-A-N

The man's name is Benjamin Chapman. We don't know who he is or why he called to us.

We know. We cannot tell. It's a secret.

Calvin doesn't like Benjamin Chapman but he can't tell us why.

Under the name is one small word. Only four letters.

D-I-E-D

Benjamin Chapman is dead. We know. Everyone in the cemetery is dead.

O-c-t-1-3-1-8-6-4

Benjamin Chapman died on October 13, 1864.

Under the date an A and an E are squished together. We write it in the air.

Æ

Mom helped us look it up at the library. Æ stands for an Olden Days word. Ævum. We write the word in the air.

Æ-v-u-m.

It means the age when you die. We rub some more.

Æ-2-3

Benjamin Chapman was twenty-three years old when he died. Twenty-three minus ten equals thirteen. Benjamin Chapman was thirteen years older than us when he died.

"How old are you, Dekker?"

"I'm thirty-three."

Thirty-three minus twenty-three is ten. Ten plus thirteen is twenty-three. Twenty-three plus ten is thirty-three. The numbers float in the air around us. Ten. Thirteen. Twenty-three. Thirty-three. We can see them. Almost touch them. We don't know what they mean.

Our fingertips are black from the carpenter's pencil. We are almost finished. We want to hurry because our fingers tingle from so much rubbing.

No. Take it slow.

Softly, softly, we rub the rest of the stone all the way to the bottom of the paper.

IV. DEKKER

I wondered why Ethan suddenly asked me my age. He'd been concentrating with such quiet intensity I started feeling uncomfortable watching over his shoulder, so I stepped away. I learned long ago from Willy that artists don't appreciate being observed while working. I gazed across the road at the inn, which defined naïve New England charm in the morning sunlight. But when I glanced over to see how far he'd gotten with the rubbing, I saw the date of death had emerged. A chill ran up my spine. What the hell was he thinking? I couldn't keep up with this kid. One minute he annoyed the shit out of me, the next he was all please-and-thank-you, and now he'd seriously creeped me out again. Maybe a cemetery visit wasn't such a good idea, especially so soon after what went down at Granny Stalbird's after our hike.

As promised, Tessa was waiting for us in the parking lot behind the diner.

"You guys look like you had a good hike," she said, smiling.

"We did," Ethan said, running to his mom and giving her a hug. "Calvin went swimming."

"I see he did."

"He did. We didn't. Dekker says."

"Dekker's a smart guy. And you're a smart guy to listen to him." She shot me a wink. "Are you hungry? You didn't eat too many peanut butter crackers, did you?"

Ethan shook his head. "No. We shared with Calvin. Did you know dogs like peanut butter crackers? Calvin loves them."

"I did not know that," she said, tousling his hair. "What are we going to have for supper?"

"Granny Stalbird's grilled cheese. Granny Stalbird's grilled cheese." He marched toward the diner in time to his chanted sandwich, Calvin at his side.

"Granny must make a mean grilled cheese," I said.

"Granny hasn't made anything in over a hundred years," Tessa said as we followed Ethan.

"A local legend?"

"So I'm told. She lived over in Jefferson. The story goes that back in 1776 she was the first woman through the Notch, the first woman to own land in North Country, the first woman to make maple sugar up here, and the first woman to learn herbal medicine from the Native Americans. Ergo, the first woman doctor in New Hampshire."

"Sounds like quite the Revolutionary Renaissance woman. You should write a book about her."

"Sure. I'll squeeze that in between running the inn and raising a ten-year-old," she said. "You can write the book. You were always the history buff. Did you ever finish your thesis on Vincent van Gogh?"

"You remember that?"

"I remember everything. It's my curse." Her lighthearted tone couldn't mask a touch of melancholy.

"My thesis took an interesting turn in Amsterdam when I met a Dutch artist named Willy Hart. I did some modeling for him, he pushed me to finish the paper, and we ended up living together for ten years."

"Ten years? That's impressive. Isn't that like seventy in gay years?"

"Woof. Woof." We laughed as we rounded the corner of the diner, where Ethan waited by the door.

"Calvin, sit," he commanded. "You have to wait outside for your doggie bag."

Cal did as he was told and Ethan marched inside.

"And what happened with your Dutch artist?" Tessa asked with a mischievous grin. "Did he trade you in for a newer model?"

"No. He died," I said without thinking.

She stopped, face stricken with a mix of shock and embarrassment. "Oh, no. Dekker, I'm so sorry. I had no idea. I didn't—"

"It's okay. I should've mentioned it before now, but we haven't had a lot of time to catch up. Go on in. I'm going to have a word with Calvin. I'll be right there. And we'll talk later. Okay?"

She nodded, gave my arm a gentle squeeze, and went inside.

I sat on the porch bench and beckoned Calvin. He came over and rested his head on my lap, sensing my mood change.

"Well, that was unexpected," I said, as I scratched his furrowed brow. I took his leash from around my neck, looped it to a bench leg, and attached it to his collar. He doesn't seem to mind, although we never used a leash in Amsterdam. If he was told to stay, he did, without question. But everything was different here. We had to be careful. Both of us.

"Stay," I said, holding up two fingers. "I'll be back in Two Minutes." Two Minutes actually meant a few minutes, not as long as Five Minutes, which meant enough time to take a nap while he waited. Dog time, like dog years, was more fluid than human time.

Granny Stalbird's was your basic all-American diner. A central U-shaped pink Formica counter with six leatherette-covered stools, additional seating at tables and booths on either end of the room. Off to one side, a screened porch with picnic tables. Tessa and Ethan sat in a booth by the window.

"He wanted to sit where he could keep an eye on Calvin," Tessa told me, as I scooted in across the table from them. She warily watched two waitresses in a heated discussion by the kitchen door. The older of the two heaved a deep sigh, picked up an order pad, and sauntered over to us, fake friendly smile carved into her face like a jack-o'-lantern. The nametag on her pink uniform blouse said Tabitha, but her attitude seemed more Nurse Ratched.

"How's my favorite flatlander today?" she bellowed, as if we were all deaf.

"Fine," said Ethan in a small voice.

"If you're not from North Country they call you a flatlander," Tessa explained. "I keep saying the White Mountains are a range of wimpy anthills compared to the Rockies. But they don't teach geography up here. Do they, Tabitha?"

"No, ma'am," she said. "If we did, there wouldn't be no time for gun safety class. Don't want anyone mistaking a flatlander for a moose." She was kidding, of course. But you couldn't miss the undertone of menace in her voice.

"So, Sweetcheeks. What'll it be today? Granny's griddlecakes with maple syrup?"

Ethan smiled and shook his head.

"Reuben on rye with Russian?"

Ethan's smile widened and his head shook harder. Obviously this was a recurring routine between them.

"You're gonna have to tell me 'cause I'm plumb outta ideas."

"GRANNY STALBIRD'S GRILLED CHEESE," Ethan shouted.

"Well, now they know up on Mt. Washington," Tabitha quipped. "One grilled cheese with chips and a pickle."

"NO PICKLE."

"No pickle. And I'll bet you want the crust cut off after it's toasted."

"Yes, please." Ethan nodded.

"I'll have the same," I said. "But leave the crust on and I'll have Ethan's pickle."

"One grilled cheese with chips and an extra pickle." She was going to charge me for the extra pickle.

Tessa ordered a Cobb salad, something I hadn't thought of in ten years.

"No bacon?" Tabitha almost sneered.

Tessa paused and raised her eyes. "Correct." She looked directly at Tabitha. "No bacon."

"Alrighty then." She flashed a satisfied smirk and started toward the kitchen.

"Oh." She stopped and turned back to us, one sassy hand on her hip. "Margery wanted to ask but she's too scared to even wait on you. Aren't you, Margery?" The other waitress fluttered off into the kitchen like a wounded butterfly. "Was Jayceen up to the inn this morning?"

"Yes, she was," Tessa said. "What about it?"

"Yeah. She came in here after, all red-faced and flustered, talking some jibber-jabber. I couldn't make heads or tails out of it. Could barely understand her enough to take her order. Then she had some kinda heart attack or something. Right where you're sittin', as a matter of fact."

"Is she all right?" I asked.

"Oh, no," Tabitha said, eyes wide in mock horror. "She's dead. Keeled over face first in her banana cream pie." She flounced into the kitchen to deliver our order.

"What happened this morning, Dekker?" Tessa asked in a hushed voice.

I glanced over at Ethan to gauge his reaction to Tabitha's gossip. He didn't appear to have heard. He was playing with his silverware, holding knife across fork in the form of a cross. A coincidence, I hoped.

"I can't stay here," Tessa said. "Have that bitch pack our food to go. Ethan, come on. We're going to wait for Dekker in the car."

"What about Calvin's doggie bag?" he asked.

"We're all going to get doggie bags," I told him. "Go with your mom. I'll be right there."

Tessa grabbed her son's hand and practically dragged him out of Granny Stalbird's.

❖

"All done," said Ethan. He knelt proudly in front of his finished handiwork, arm around Calvin's neck. He'd done a meticulous job. The engraving on the headstone had transferred perfectly to the paper, clear and easy to read. A young man named Benjamin Chapman had died on October 13, 1864, at the age of twenty-three. Killed in the Civil War and his body returned home for burial? Something else to look for at the local historical society.

"What's that?" Ethan pointed toward the bottom of the rubbing.

An unusual shape had emerged there. Two, in fact. One long and slender. Perhaps a sword or a pen? The other ovular, with a small spot near an indentation. A vague sense of recognition hovered at the edge of my consciousness. When I realized what it was, its momentary elusiveness made perfect if uneasy sense.

An artist's palette and brush had been engraved on the stone.

From the Diary of Corporal Anson Quimby
13th New Hampshire Infantry Regiment

August 1864

We have been summoned home to vote. Many Northern states have enacted legislation allowing soldiers to vote from the battlefield, but not New Hampshire. Mr. Lincoln won the state by a wide margin in his election of 1860. But they say he may lose New Hampshire if we Republican soldiers do not return to add our votes. And if our Commander-in-Chief needs us to carry out his noble mission and end this cruel War, it is our sworn duty to do what is necessary. We shall be granted two weeks' furlough. If this shall include the lengthy journey, I know not. I do know it shall bring me boundless joy to see Father and Mother again after two prolonged and treacherous years. Of greater import, I am hopeful that the trip and time away from the bloody battlefields shall bring much-needed relief to my friend, for Benjamin is in a such a sorry condition—I know not what can be done for him. The doctors here in Washington are too busy with the seriously wounded soldiers to pay heed to his troubles. I convinced an assistant surgeon, one RJ Sibald from Massachusetts, to spend some minutes with him to assess the nature of his ailment. Sibald confirmed what I suspected. There is no physical complaint to remedy, he said. He has seen many soldiers return from battle with such symptoms (extreme fatigue, heightened anxiety, constant chest pains) and has found nothing to be done that shall relieve their suffering. In some severe cases the soldiers are dismissed from duty and sent home. What becomes of them there he could not or would not say. Nor did I speak of what I knew to be the cause. When I returned to the Regiment after my recovery, I was pleased to find Ben in good spirits. Little could I comprehend that the debacle of Cold Harbor, where I sustained my injury, was like to child's play, incomparable with the battle yet to come. General Burnside's attempt to end the everlasting Siege of Petersburg by exploding a mine succeeded only in showering unparalleled chaos upon our beleaguered Battalion. I did not witness the worst atrocities, the shooting of the Negro troops trapped in the crater or the massacre afterward of those wounded and unable to flee. But what caused Benjamin to descend into wild-eyed madness was the horrific sight of Negro soldiers being bayoneted by fellow Union soldiers, themselves fearful of reprisals from the victorious Confederates. I cannot write more of those darkest of days. Were it not for the tender ministrations of Moze and Doxey, nursing Ben, spoon-feeding him when he refused to eat, watching over him night and day, even sleeping by his side—I fear my friend may not have survived the ordeal. Benjamin is an artist, not a soldier. He enlisted as he did, caught up in my fervor for the righteous cause of Freedom. His inclinations were never political, and so he had no interest in returning home to vote, not unless the two fugitive boys were allowed to accompany us to New Hampshire, a safe haven where they could grow up and live their lives as Freedmen.

CHAPTER SIX

I. VALRAVEN

What the hell was he doing in Arlington? In spite of Valraven's special relationship with the dead, he hated cemeteries. Rest in Peace, everyone said. The majority of the dead did rest in peace. They passed over and into the Light with grace and dignity. But the few who didn't, the spirits, or ghosts as most people called them, could be a royal pain in the ass. They screeched and screamed, vying for his attention. They wandered aimlessly, moaning and crying, expecting him to comfort them. They were trapped in an eternal psychic vortex of their own making. Unless they figured that out for themselves, it was only a matter of time before they dropped Down and disappeared into the underworld darkness forever. No light. No peace. Nothingness.

Very few spirits roamed between the endless rows of uniform white grave markers, making Arlington Cemetery quieter than most—if he disregarded the busloads of chattering tourists. It was easy enough for Valraven to ignore the living, even among the densest crowds, but he could spot a soul or spirit a mile away. When he saw the outline of a figure atop a hill in the distance, he instinctively knew he was about to receive an answer to the question of why he was here.

The footpaths in Arlington meandered this way and that, a haphazard maze, difficult to navigate without a map. He took longer than expected to find his way up the hill to the oldest part of the cemetery, where the first soldiers were buried during the Civil War.

A single row of modest gravestones lined a large square rose garden, once owned by the wife of Robert E. Lee, according to a plaque near the entrance.

The spirit Valraven had spotted half sat, half leaned casually against a headstone, probably his own. He appeared to be in his late twenties, a handsome young chap with disheveled dark hair, long sideburns, and a scraggly chin-beard. He wore a long belted blue jacket and lighter blue baggy trousers, a bit too short for his long outstretched legs. His boots were tattered beyond repair. Arms crossed, he gazed into the distance with an air of studied indifference.

"Howdy," Valraven said.

The spirit glanced in his direction, and then looked around to see whom else he might have spoken to.

"Are you addressing me, sir?" he asked. "You can see me?"

"Oh, yeah. I have the distinct feeling you're waiting for me."

The whisper of a smile flickered across the spirit's face. Valraven had occasionally met what he called helper-spirits. They were a different breed altogether. Not discontent with their disembodied state, they could be a useful source of information. But they were also cagey, sometimes with their own hidden agenda. Valraven decided to take an indirect approach.

"What's your name, soldier?"

"I'm no soldier," the spirit said. "RJ Sibald, assistant surgeon, at your service."

"Terribly sorry. I assumed…"

"The living usually do. Assume. I expected more from you."

"Again. Please, Mr. Sibald, accept my humble apology," Valraven groveled. Spirits enjoyed making fools of the living. But Valraven did not sense the usual callousness from this one. His taunts revealed a certain melancholy. Perhaps Valraven had misjudged him.

"I accept your humble apology," Sibald said. "But it vexes me no end that the living give so little recognition to the assistant surgeons who braved the battlefield—to save lives, not to take them."

"Is that where your life was taken? On the battlefield?"

"If but 'twere such a noble death reserved for me, I would not await you these many desolate years." He paused, staring at his boots. "For one unfortunate as I, waiting is a weary business."

Valraven began to feel Sibald's profound sadness. His spirit needed to be unburdened before he could disclose the information Valraven required. How he knows these things is always a mystery.

"RJ? May I call you RJ?"

Sibald nodded without looking up.

"What happened, RJ? Why do you punish yourself so? What mistake condemns the noble assistant surgeon to such grief?"

The wretched long-dead young man threw his head back and howled, a heart-wrenching wail of despair. His pain blazed through Valraven's veins like a red-hot scalpel's blade.

"The pills," he cried. "I took their pills. Morphine, opium, laudanum. I took them all. I could not but relieve their pain too little, and mine was too great. I knew not how else to numb the agony that lodged in my brain, in my heart, in my very bones. I took but one at first, and saved another to sleep. But could not sleep, so took another and another and more and more, until I could not work, could not sleep, could not live without them."

Sibald again threw back his head and let loose another barbaric yawp.

"Sometimes I hear them screaming still, screaming as the surgeons take their arms, take their legs, screaming as I take their pills. I deserved not to walk among the living, but was too cowardly to die. And then I met your soldier, the beautiful sensitive artist, the lost soul you seek, who had seen such abominations and suffered so and I could not help him, no, could not, would not help him. His friend took him away and I took the pills, all the pills, every last one, and I slept, slept like the dead. When I woke, if mayhap what I have become can be called awake, I was here. And here I wait."

Valraven wanted to weep from exhaustion. Assistant surgeon RJ Sibald's emotional confession drained all Valraven's energy.

Behind the spirit's spent form, a rift in the ether manifested and White Light began to bleed into blue sky. There was little time to lose. If Valraven wanted the message Sibald was destined to deliver, he needed to muster the strength to speak.

"RJ?" he rasped. "Can you hear me, RJ?"

The spirit slowly lifted his head.

"It's almost time, almost time to cross over, cross over and find eternal rest. But before you go, I need to know. Why was I summoned here? You have something to tell me, don't you, RJ? What is it?"

"Boston," the spirit whispered. "North to Boston."

The White Light began to envelop him.

"What's in Boston? It's a big fucking city, RJ. What am I supposed to find in Boston?"

"The man with the spiral will guide you...beyond Boston...The lost soul you seek...the soldier..." His body disintegrated as the White Light consumed him.

"A name, RJ. Give me a name."

"So much sadness...turned to anger...His power grows...will destroy them..." Only his face was visible, barely visible. The White Light blinded Valraven with its penetrating glare.

"Destroy who, RJ? Where? What am I supposed to do?"

"Save them...Mother, Son, Unholy Ghost...Save them...save the only begotten son..."

The White Light flickered, the fissure closed, and the spirit was gone.

Valraven collapsed onto the footpath, barely conscious, but not for long. He tried to repeat everything the spirit had said, fearful he might forget. Boston and beyond. Man with a spiral. Lost soldier. Anger. Power. Destruction.

Save the only begotten son.

Whose only begotten son?

Darkness engulfed him.

II. ETHAN

Room Thirteen is dark. We are not afraid of the dark.

We like the dark in Room Thirteen. It's our secret hideaway. Nobody knows. Not Mom.

Where have you been? Mom says. Cobwebs in our hair.

Spiders know. Nobody else.

Room Thirteen is full of things from Olden Days. We like to touch them. The wooden trunk. The lampshade with fringe. A box of rusty tools. Dusty bottles. Empty frames.

Don't touch those frames.

Who says?

Don't. We'll get in trouble.

Who says?

Don't.

We touched them before.

Before was before. Don't touch them.

Who says?

Don't.

We never argued until yesterday. Today we woke up arguing about the gravestone rubbing. We can't stop arguing.

We gotta get rid of that thing.

No we don't.

Yes we do.

That thing gonna bring trouble.

Who says?

Get rid of that thing. Throw it out the window.

We can't do that. Mom will get mad.

Moms don't know everything. Take it out back. Burn it.

We can't do that.

We gotta.

Who says?

Do it.

No.

We feel the screams coming and there is nothing we can do to stop them. We stamp our feet. We wave our arms. We throw ourselves on the floor and kick and pound. Nothing we do makes any difference. The screams come and tears pour out of our eyes.

Calvin barks. Mom runs in and holds us tight in the beanbag chair. Calvin licks our tears. Mom rocks us like a baby. The tears stop and the screams stop and we are quiet.

Can you tell me what happened? Mom says.

We can't so we don't say anything. Just keep quiet.

Ethan. Mom says. It's going to be a busy weekend. I really need you to chill.

Take a chill pill. We think it but don't say it.

Take a chill pill in Room Thirteen.

Come downstairs with me. Mom says. You can help Dekker bring in firewood before it rains. She leads us by the hand. Calvin follows us. Down the stairs and through the dining room to the kitchen. She opens the loading dock door and Calvin runs out.

Mom's Friend Dekker puts logs into boxes for rooms with fireplaces. We shake our head and run out of the kitchen. Take a chill pill. We run around the corner and through the Chandelier Room. Take a chill pill. We run into the hall and up the Tower stairs. Take a chill pill. We run all the way to the top.

Room Thirteen.

III. DEKKER

"What was that about?" I asked Tessa.

Ethan's face had appeared briefly through the screen door but before I could say good morning, he disappeared.

"He's always withdrawn after one of his meltdowns," she said from the doorway. "And he just had a doozy. He came through it quicker than usual, though. I think that may have been Calvin's influence."

"I wouldn't be surprised. Dogs have this psychoanalytical sixth sense, Calvin more so than most. And his rates aren't bad, either."

Tessa managed a smile.

"And you have no idea what causes these meltdowns?" I asked.

"I used to rack my brain trying to figure it out. Was it something I did? Something I said? Or maybe it has nothing to do with me at all. I gradually realized there was no way of knowing." She paused and shook her head. "Anyway. It is what it is." She turned back into the kitchen to deal with the morning's produce deliveries, and I turned my attention back to the woodpile.

Cloverkist was fully booked for Columbus Day weekend. The first two couples had checked in yesterday evening. Both the restaurant and pub had been surprisingly busy last night, testing the limits of her competent but minimal staff. I offered to chip in, despite my total lack of experience. She told me I'd be doing more than enough if I kept Ethan entertained and out of her hair until closing time.

I helped him mount his gravestone rubbing in an old frame he'd found somewhere, and we hung it on the wall in his room. Not what

I'd choose to have hanging in my bedroom—far from it. But Ethan was clearly pleased with his accomplishment. He'd shown no signs of distress after the shocking news about Jayceen's death, and spent the rest of the evening before bedtime reading to Calvin, as he had every night since we arrived.

I'd only been half joking to Tessa about Cal's skills as a shrink. In his inimitable canine fashion, he'd taken it upon himself to watch over Ethan. He didn't stay with me in the Tower at all, refusing to even set foot up the stairs. He slept in Ethan's room, and every morning I had to cajole him to come out for a walk while the boy slept. Maybe he didn't suffer from the jet lag waking me up much earlier than usual. His attentiveness to the kid suggested there was more to it. Their bond strengthened day by day, so I wasn't surprised to hear he'd extended his special brand of healing to Ethan. I knew firsthand how effective it could be.

"He was getting better before we moved here," she had said during our first real heart-to-heart talk, brought about in part by the unfortunate events at Granny Stalbird's. We sat on the sofa, feet up on the rustic coffee table sharing a bottle of red wine.

"I worked my ass off to keep him in regular school classes when one idiot doctor said he might be autistic. What did he know? He spent an hour with Ethan. I was with him twenty-four seven. Bullshit." She got up and peeked into Ethan's room to make sure he was asleep. She lowered her voice and continued, pacing like a polar bear, as the Dutch say. "My son is special, I told them. But not Special Ed special. He's smarter than any kid his age. Communication difficulties? He'll talk your freaking head off. Atypical perception? He sees the world a different way. Big fucking deal. At the beginning of every year I talked to his teachers. They were great. They understood what I was saying and they agreed with me. They all loved Ethan, said he was one of their favorite kids. Sure, he had his bad days. Who doesn't? But I wasn't going to let anyone stick any fucking label on him. Autism Spectrum Disorder. Asperger's Syndrome. High Functioning. No. No way. Not Ethan. Not my boy."

She paused, either to catch her breath or contain her emotion. Or both. I was afraid if I said anything conciliatory, anything at all, she might burst into tears. She'd always been incredibly passionate in college, but I never thought of her as high-strung. But we'd both gone through a shitload since our days at Camden College.

Tessa Bernstein was the smartest person I knew. She would have graduated top of our class if she hadn't left in the middle of senior year. Yet despite her high IQ, maybe she had a blind spot where Ethan was concerned. Totally understandable. Didn't we all let our emotions get in the way of our intellect once in a while? Especially when it came to matters of the heart?

"Maybe it was a mistake to leave Colorado, pull him out of school, disrupt his routine," she said. "We talked about it. We got books about New Hampshire from the library. He read about Ethan the Giant and the Old Man of the Mountains. He was excited about coming here."

"Of course he was," I said. "He still is."

Was he? I didn't really know.

"Don't beat yourself up. You did what you had to do. And maybe he needs more time to adjust. But he will."

Would he? I had no idea.

"Like you said, he's a smart kid." I was saying what I thought she wanted, needed to hear.

"He's a little boy so lonely he had to invent an imaginary friend. A little boy who has bad dreams, and not only when he sleeps. A little boy whose mom loves him but doesn't have a clue how to help him." She hesitated before saying more. "I'm going to be honest with you, Dekker. When you called and asked if you could visit, the main reason I said yes was for Ethan. I thought maybe having a guy around for a while would be good for him. I hope that doesn't freak you out."

"Of course not," I lied. "Not at all."

Once I'd filled the boxes with firewood, they were too heavy to carry more than one at a time. All five tower rooms had original working fireplaces as their only source of heat. I'd installed myself into Room Eleven, one of the rooms on the top floor, and had no intention of lugging two heavy boxes up three flights of stairs. I'd be warm enough without a roaring fire.

Tessa wasn't in the kitchen as I walked through on my way to Room One. She was probably in the laundry room washing or drying tablecloths and napkins, sheets and towels—her least favorite task, previously delegated to the sisters who swore they'd never set foot in the place again. The more I thought about those girls, the more suspicious I was of their so-called accident.

When Tessa had taken me upstairs for the first time to show me rooms Eleven and Twelve in the Tower, a Ouija board lay open on the carpeted floor of the landing between them. Tessa was furious when she saw it. She'd told the girls in no uncertain terms she didn't want them messing around with that thing in Cloverkist. She'd intended to throw it away weeks ago when it turned up in a pile of board games kept on a bookshelf in the odd lookout turret. It didn't take long to locate the heart-shaped plastic pointer, used to spell out messages from spirits on the board, cracked like it had been stepped on.

Had the girls spooked themselves and fallen in their rush to get downstairs? It seemed the likeliest explanation. But since the episode with Dowser Dan and Jayceen, I was beginning to think a more sinister force might be at work. Nothing supernatural. I still didn't believe that superstitious gobbledygook. No, something real and more dangerous. What if someone wanted the flatlanders gone, gone for good?

"Nonsense," Tessa had said when I broached the subject after another glass of wine. "They may not be the most welcoming folks, but everyone knows how important tourism is for the local economy. What would anyone have to gain if I closed up shop?"

"Maybe someone wants it for themselves?" I suggested.

"They could've bought it already. It was on the market for months before I found it—in a magazine, for fuck's sake. Nobody in North Country was interested, or could afford it if they were. I paid considerably less than the asking price—and I put out a big chunk of change to get it up to code. So if or when I sell, it's not going cheap. Haunted or not."

It was the first time she'd actually used the word *haunted*.

"You actually believe that?" I asked, trying to keep my voice neutral. "That Cloverkist is haunted?"

"Go ahead and laugh, Dekker," she said. "I know it sounds ridiculous. But I'm not so sure it matters what you believe. I've seen and heard things. I can't think of any other logical explanation."

"Like what? Tell me."

"Whistling in the kitchen," she said. "That's how it started. I was cleaning up one night, in the downstairs kitchen. Alone. We'd only been open a week or so, and business was slow. I'd let everyone go home early and was wiping down the counters when I heard whistling. Not like wind in the timbers, nothing like that. Someone was whistling a tune, the same few bars over and over again. A familiar melody, but I couldn't place it. Someone must've stayed behind, I thought. I called out, asked who was there. The only response I got was more whistling. I looked on the loading dock, in the laundry room, in the pantry. Nothing. No one. And the sound was definitely close. Once right behind me, almost in my ear. I didn't know what else to do so I shouted out. STOP. And it did. It stopped."

"I've got a feeling there's a *but* coming."

"Oh, there's a but, all right," she said. "It stopped that night. But—it came back. Only in the kitchen, and only when I was by myself. I asked each of my staff if they'd ever heard anything like it, and they all looked at me with no idea what I was talking about. I got used to it. There was nothing scary or threatening about it. It was...I don't know...friendly. Until we started to get busy, that is. Then the whistling got louder, more intense. The same familiar tune but not so friendly anymore. That's when I heard about Dowser Duane. He and Jayceen came and did their cleansing thing and—presto!—no more whistling."

"Okay," I said. "You win. I got nothin'."

"Oh, I've got more," she said with a grin. "A couple weeks later I was talking to a guest, a history teacher from New Orleans, and I told her about my whistler in the kitchen. She raised her eyebrows and said she'd done a lot of research about slavery in the South before the Civil War. She'd read that kitchen slaves were forced to whistle while they worked—to prove they weren't eating any of the food. She said Cloverkist might've been part of the Underground Railroad that helped fugitive slaves get to Canada. And maybe my whistler in the kitchen was a former slave, one that didn't make it to Canada."

As I walked through the kitchen to get the last box of firewood, I tried picturing what it looked like in the nineteenth century. Wooden smoke-stained walls instead of white plaster. Black cast iron stove, pots and pans, instead of shiny stainless steel. Dim gaslight lanterns instead of bright overhead fluorescent tubes. The image in my head matched one of the paintings in the dining room. And the other painting, the one in the barn with the two boys. Had their faces been Black?

I picked up the last box and looked around for Calvin. No sign of him, but I wasn't concerned he'd wander far. When I finished, I'd take him and Ethan for another hike around Possum Pond.

I was winded when I got upstairs to Room Three. I set the wood by the fireplace and was about to sit on the bed for a brief break when I heard a noise from above. Footsteps, a scraping sound, something falling. It must be coming from Room Twelve, the room across the hall from mine. Ethan? It had to be. I took the stairs two at a time to catch him at whatever it was he was doing. When I got to the room, it was empty. I looked in the closet, the bathroom, under the bed. Nothing. I went across the landing to my room. No Ethan there, either. He must be in the lookout tower. But it, too, was vacant, quiet as a tomb. I shuddered. If not Ethan, who—or what—made the noises I heard?

At the bottom of the stairs, Calvin sat looking up at me. Tessa must have let him in.

"You could've come up, you know," I said.

No reply necessary.

"Okay. So, where's Ethan?"

Calvin lifted his ears, but otherwise didn't budge.

"Come on," I said, coming down the carpeted steps. "Let's go find Ethan."

He didn't move a muscle, simply continuing to gaze up the stairway.

I turned to see what could have him so enrapt, and nearly leapt through the ceiling. The boy stood on the landing, silent and motionless, staring down at Calvin.

"Jesus, Ethan! You scared the crap out of me. It is totally not cool to sneak up on people like that." I waited for an apology, but he appeared to take a page from Cal's playbook.

No reply necessary.

"Where were you, anyway?"

"Room Thirteen," he said in a flat voice, not breaking eye contact with Calvin.

I was pretty sure there was no Room Thirteen in Cloverkist.

"Oh, really? And where exactly is Room Thirteen?" I asked.

"In Olden Days," he said with the faintest trace of a smile.

CHAPTER SEVEN

I. CALVIN

sniffing scenting trailing something
something large&dark&rank
stopping sniffing hackles rising
something female something young
looking listening nothing seeing
something here&there&gone

somewhere garbage smelling spreading
tickling tummy sweet&burnt
running faster finding licking
dekker shouting *calvin no*
stopping waiting sitting watching
dekker shouting *tessa yo*

II. DEKKER

"Does that mean what I think it means?" I asked. Tessa and I stood behind the inn and surveyed the mess. Black plastic garbage bags pulled from the dumpster by the edge of the woods, torn open, and contents spread in a surprisingly ordered semicircular pattern. Shredded butcher paper and large tin cans licked clean, as well as other less identifiable remnants. The sickly sweet rotten garbage smell mixed with a ranker, wilder scent. Does a bear shit in the woods?

Tessa nodded her head. "Yup. Bears."

"Bears, as in plural?"

"Mama Bear and her cub, if they're the same ones that paid us a visit in the spring," Tessa explained. "I've told Storm over and over to make sure that hatch is closed tight." Storm was her dishwasher, busboy, and general all-purpose kitchen helper. Not the sharpest knife in the rack. "But you know we were balls to the wall busy last night. When it gets too late, he gets overtired and that's when he screws up."

"Will they be back?"

"Chances are they will. In the fall their food sources are dryin' up and Mama's trying to put on as much weight as possible before she finds a cave to hibernate in for the winter. So yeah, they'll come back— at least until they figure out there's nothing more to scavenge here. In the meantime, I'd keep a close eye on him." She glanced toward Calvin. "Especially at night."

"You hear that, Mister?"

Cal gave a half-hearted bark of assent. Surely he also scented the potential danger.

"Grab a couple Dahmer bags from the laundry room," Tessa said over her shoulder, as she headed back inside to oversee the breakfast buffet. "And seal them tight to keep the delectable smells to a minimum."

"Did you say Dahmer bags? As in…"

"Oh, yeah." She laughed. "Once I got a delivery of some flimsy-ass trash bags that kept tearing open when they were too full. So I called the supplier and told them I wanted the big black heavy-duty plastic bags that Jeffrey Dahmer used to pack up his victims. Those suckers won't break open on the way to the dumpster. That was an order they'll never forget, and the name stuck. Dahmer bags."

That was the Bernstein I remembered from college. That was the Bernstein who would've scoffed at the very idea of ghosts haunting Cloverkist Inn. Her mood improved last evening as guests began checking in. Everyone was in better spirits. Ethan gave early arrivals his Grand Tour, Calvin tagging along, tail wagging. The kitchen crew cheerfully put out beautiful plates of food, the waitresses and bartender joked with their customers. The gloomy atmosphere pervading Cloverkist since I arrived on Monday had vanished.

I found the roll of Dahmer bags in the laundry room on a shelf holding cleaning supplies. All the things a murderer needed to cover his tracks. Dahmer bags were no joke when you'd been face-to-face with an actual serial killer. I began feeling light-headed, probably from all the fumes in such a small space. I reached for a shelf to steady myself, the shelf full of lighting fluid, butane canisters, boxes of matches, and cans of Sterno. All the things an arsonist needed to set a fire. Why were my thoughts spinning in that direction? Or was the room doing the spinning? I closed my eyes.

Maybe it was all me. Maybe I had brought my darkness and despair from Amsterdam. Maybe Tessa and Ethan would've been fine if I hadn't shown up. Maybe I was the catalyst, the spark that would light the fuse and implode Cloverkist. Maybe everything happening was my fault. If I were gone, maybe everyone would be better off. Maybe—

I heard Calvin barking outside. I stumbled through the wrong door and found myself in a Jacuzzi room, which I hadn't known existed. The strong smell of chlorine filled my nostrils. I couldn't breathe. I needed fresh air. I unlocked a sliding glass door to the yard, across from the back end of the pool. The stone puppies watched me from the deck. They were barking at me. No, Calvin was barking.

Disoriented, I realized the dumpster was around the corner, hidden by a high hedgerow. Calvin's barks sounded panicky, a warning. I squeezed between the building and the shrubbery. It scratched at my arms, clawed at my face. I extricated myself from the savage shrub. On the other side, Calvin stood barking at the loading dock, expecting me to come from that direction, the way I'd gone in.

"Calvin. What is it?"

Cal stopped and looked at me, puzzled.

What are you doing over there?

Good question. What the hell had just happened to me?

Calvin ran over and jumped up against my chest, knocking me down onto the grass. He held me down with his front paws and licked my face as if he hadn't seen me in months, let alone minutes.

"Okay. Okay. That's enough." But he wouldn't stop. I felt like he was licking me back to life. Maybe he was. When I finally got him off me, I sat up and he gave himself a mighty shake.

"Are we better now?" A single bark said yes.

The roll of Dahmer bags was still in my hand. Dahmer bags. Jesus, Bernstein. Too funny.

"Okay, then. Let's clean up after Mama Bear's picnic, shall we?" Calvin led the way, as usual.

III. VALRAVEN

Valraven seldom strayed far from his primitive lakefront cabin in northern Maine. When he did, he preferred staying at nondescript cheap motels like Super 8 or Best Value. They were quiet and the staff rarely asked questions. The coffee sucked, and you didn't want to inspect the mattress too carefully. None of that mattered for one night or two. This Motel 6 was perfect, right next to the Braintree stop on the MBTA Red Line.

His plan had been to check in late Friday night and head into the city early the next morning. He still didn't know what he was looking for but figured he'd begin with the historical buildings near Downtown Crossing and wander toward Beacon Hill. With what little information the unfortunate assistant surgeon RJ Sibald imparted before crossing over, this was a good place to start.

Valraven wasn't surprised when things didn't go according to plan. They rarely did with matters concerning the afterlife.

Motel 6 didn't provide breakfast, and Dunkin' Donuts down the street promised more grease than his stomach could handle first thing in the morning. The free coffee offered in the reception area would hold him until he got into the city. More people than he expected filled the room, maybe waiting for a tour bus to arrive. He sensed eager anticipation buzzing in the air. He looked more closely at the eclectic collection of characters. This was no tourist group. These folks were here for some common purpose, although he couldn't quite put his finger on what. That's when he realized not all of those gathered were living beings.

He was accustomed to the occasional spirit popping up in unlikely public places. If they sussed out his ability to see them and started harassing him, a simple *Fuck off and leave me alone* was usually enough. For several to show up in a Motel 6 lobby at the same time was strange. And none of the living seemed to be aware of their presence, despite the spirits' attempts to attract attention.

Everything clicked into place when Reginald Masters walked through the door with his small entourage. His appearance triggered a tidal wave of reverential oohs and aahs, which he acknowledged with a saintly nod as the crowd parted to let their idol pass.

Valraven recognized him. Their paths had crossed at a small conference many years ago, where most of the discussion revolved around UFOs and parapsychology. Valraven had been searching out ways to understand more about his own developing nature and abilities. He didn't learn much during his brief contact with Masters, except that they had nothing in common.

Reginald Masters was a total imposter, from his pretentious British accent and consoling smile to his rolled-up sleeves and Larry King suspenders. The epitome of a self-inflated twentieth-century snake-oil salesman, preying on the lost and the lonely, the desperate and the deluded. He charged a healthy fee for his "expertise." Valraven sat among the flock of believers as the skinny bald-headed charlatan began his two-day Full Moon Psychic Medium Workshop.

It couldn't be coincidental they were both in Braintree at the same time, in the same fleabag motel. Under a full moon, no less. Valraven must have been sent here. He had no idea why, but one thing was certain. If by some freakish twist of fate, Reginald Masters turned out to be someone's only begotten son in need of a savior? Valraven would walk out the door and let the deceitful motherfucker die.

"I want to thank each and every one of you for coming today from the deepest center of my soul." He spoke in a high-pitched, more nasal tone than Valraven remembered. "My name is Reginald Masters, but I want you to call me Reg. That's what my dear departed mum called me, calls me still. And if Reg was good enough for her, Reg is good enough for you. Because you are all every bit as important to me as my mum was when I was her one and only little boy."

Oh shit, thought Valraven. Shit on a shingle.

❖

Reg loved the sound of his own voice. He spent half the morning session sharing the highlights of his illustrious metaphysical career and providing a blowhard-by-blowhard description of what everyone could expect to experience or witness in the next two days. They would learn about telepathy, self-hypnosis, trance channeling, automatic writing, psychokinesis, and remote viewing, also known as traveling clairvoyance. Valraven had read up on all these pseudoscience practices over the years, none of which had anything to do with his particular talent. Masters couldn't possibly cover all those topics in the time allotted. He would whet their appetites and leave them hungry for more, ensuring advance reservations for his next paranormal trainings.

Reg droned on so long even the spirits lost interest and drifted off elsewhere. Valraven relieved his boredom by taking a closer look at the thirty or so participants. The majority were middle-class middle-aged women, judging from their well-groomed appearances. Two bookending the front row looked like they'd come directly from Central Casting. Dangling earrings and jangling bracelets, colorful scarves clashing with mismatched turbans, and heavy-handed makeup created an effect more clown than medium. Of the handful of men, only a scruffy youngish guy sitting alone one row in front of him seemed sincerely interested. The others wore hangdog expressions, like their wives or girlfriends had dragged them along against their will. What were the chances of them returning for the afternoon session, when there was a bar right across the road? Slim to zero, Valraven figured.

"So, are we all ready to discover our psychic potential and open ourselves to spirit?" Reg asked, arms stretched wide, face lifted upward.

Only a few softly muttered their assent. Not enough for the revival tent aspirations of Reverend Reg.

"I said, ARE YOU READY?" he thundered, startling them awake.

Oh, yes. They were ready. Valraven almost expected to hear them shout *amen* and *hallelujah*. He felt a jolt of energy surge through the room. Oh, yes. They were ready, all right.

"We'll begin with a technique to bring ourselves into an altered state of consciousness, so our mind and body is prepared to receive spirit. Now, there's no need to be afraid. Breathe in as deeply as you can. Hold it as long as possible. And let the air out slowly. When you think you're done, push out a bit more air, and then a bit more. Now, close your eyes and repeat that ten times, which will quiet the mind and allow spirit to enter."

Valraven hated standard meditation techniques. What always worked better for him was going outside and smoking a cigarette. But he went through the motions. He didn't want to stand out from the group and draw old Reg's attention. He was convinced if he was here to make contact with someone, it was *not* Reginald Masters.

Next came relaxation of the body—feet, legs, hands, arms, spine, neck, scalp, face. Then imagining the beam of bright white light coming down from above, flowing into mind and body, until it concentrated around the heart and surrounded the body with its protective shield. No one in this room saw any kind of white light, least of all Reg. Certainly not the White Light Valraven experienced on a regular basis when he helped his lost souls cross over.

"Oh, it brings me such joy and peace to feel the openness to spirit you have all achieved," Reg crooned. "The protectiveness of white light surrounds us, joins us in psychic harmony. I don't believe I've ever had a group so in tune with spirit in so short a space of time. It's as if we were destined to join forces together this weekend under the benevolent influence of the full moon, the Hunter's Moon. Did you know it's also called Travel Moon and Dying Moon? I think we travelers were indeed meant to meet and converse with those no longer living at this propitious moment in time."

Reg paused and surveyed the room, making eye contact with each member of his select group. When Reg trained his gaze on him, Valraven resisted the urge to look away. If the imposter had even the slightest bit of psychic ability, surely he would recognize Valraven. He did not.

"The Past is entombed in the Present!" Masters incanted. "With those potent words by our esteemed father of psychometry, Joseph Rhodes Buchanan, we shall begin our travels today. Now that you have opened your mind and body to spirit, two simple psychometric exercises will strengthen your clairsentience, the empathic ability to intuit information by way of your feelings. To accomplish this, you will work in pairs—and not with a friend or partner you came with. No. It's important you find someone you have never met before."

Valraven didn't have to be psychic to anticipate what was about to happen. The two overdressed women in the front row turned simultaneously in his direction, as did almost every other female present. Even unshaven and in dire need of a decent haircut, his rugged good looks made him a goddamn chick magnet. He leaned over the chair in front of him and put his hand on the shoulder of the only other single man in the room.

"I don't know about you," he said in a low voice, "but I'm a little self-conscious to expose my secrets to any of these ladies. You wanna team up?"

The guy nodded, eyes wide and clearly relieved. The husbands and boyfriends got the same idea, leaving the women to pair off with each other. While everyone got themselves rearranged, two assistants passed out small pads of paper and pencils.

Masters told them to take four separate pieces of paper and write a true fact on three of them. On the last piece they were to write an obvious lie and fold each paper in quarters so it couldn't be read. The idea was to hold each other's papers, one at a time, and determine on which the lie was written.

"It should feel different from the others," Reg said. "Take your time. This isn't a contest. Your partner will tell you whether you have it right, or if you need to shuffle them and try again. And before you start, vigorously rub your hands together to get the energy flowing."

Parlor tricks, thought Valraven as he scribbled a few words down. It didn't matter what he wrote. He'd already decided to tell his partner he'd made the right choice, whichever one he picked. The young man was so earnest and seemed to be searching for something. Valraven was oddly attracted to him in a way he'd not felt for many years. He wanted to hold the guy in his arms, but not sexually. Comfort and protect him. He could see himself doing it, holding him in his arms—oh, shit. That wasn't right, that couldn't be right.

A memory of the future. He had them all too often—usually signaling bad news. The past might be entombed in the present, but so was the future. Valraven didn't understand how this trick of psychic time travel worked, but knew it when it occurred.

"Um. This one, I think," the guy said, unfolding the square of paper. He'd taken his time making up his mind. "It says, 'Go Red Sox.' Is that the lie?"

"Yup. Sorry to say, I'm a Yankee fan." Valraven hated baseball.

"Better keep that to yourself around here," the guy said, looking around to make sure no one heard. "Your turn."

Valraven rubbed his hands together and made a show of examining each piece of paper. Telepathy wasn't his thing, so he picked one at random and unfolded it.

"Were you really born in Boston?" he asked.

"No, I wasn't. That's a lie." The guy actually blushed, like he'd never told a fib in his life "I'm Duane, by the way," he said. He held out his hand, which Valraven grasped and shook. He had a surprisingly sturdy grip for a little guy.

"Valraven. But you can call me Val." He winked and Duane giggled, blushing deeper still.

"A pleasure to meet you, Val. I think we got a pretty good connection."

"I think we do, Duane. Indeed, I think we do."

CHAPTER EIGHT

I. DEKKER

The unframed oil painting propped against the bay window in Room One mirrored the mountain view as seen from Cloverkist, the same bare peaks of granite nestled against the clouds, the nearly identical patterns of colorful fall foliage. The woods on the slope between Possum Pond and the inn had grown taller, thicker, so the pond's surface was no longer visible as in the artist's rendering. Otherwise, the picture-within-a-picture effect was extraordinary. Including the naked guy casually stretched out on the window seat, gazing at the scenery.

"No doubt about it," Gregor Arktophonos said, barely able to contain his excitement. "When I arrived last night, it was too dark to be certain. The window looked the same but I needed to see the view, the mountains. Then I saw the others in the dining room and nearly choked on my wine. More by the same artist? Was it possible? I've been staring at this all morning. And yes. Yes. I'm absolutely convinced it was painted here."

"It's amazing," Tessa said, shaking her head. "I don't know what to say."

"How long have you been trying to track it down?" I asked.

"Oh, a weekend here and there for the last couple of years. Whenever I had spare time," he said. "It became something of an obsession."

Arktophonos, assistant curator at the Boston Fine Arts Museum, looked as Greek as his name. Dark hair and Mediterranean complexion, tall, broad-shouldered, well-built, probably in his late thirties. But his accent was pure Bostonian. He'd found the painting by accident, searching for something else in the museum's catacomb of basement storage rooms. It had never been catalogued or unwrapped. It had simply been stamped "Donation" and shelved.

"Art historians dream of a discovery like this," he said.

"I don't understand," said Tessa. "What makes this painting so special?"

I wondered the same, especially considering the other works. They were all well done, if a bit naïve. But they weren't masterpieces, not on a par with early American painting from the Hudson River School, which I'd studied at Camden.

"It all depends on what I can learn about the artist. When did he paint? Did he have any formal training? From who? Some of the White Mountain School painters studied in Europe, and their work reflects European techniques of the great Masters."

"The White Mountain School?" I asked. "I never heard of that."

"You wouldn't." He frowned. "Our New England artists are greatly overshadowed by the fame and popularity of the Hudson River painters—many of whom also visited the White Mountains for its unique rugged landscape."

"I know the Hudson River School," I said.

"Dekker and I went to Camden College together," Tessa said. "Art history was his thing."

"Then you'll know the artist Thomas Cole founded the style." Arktophonos turned to me, thick black eyebrows raised in a question mark.

I nodded, with the feeling we were in for a short lecture. I hoped it would be short.

"Cole was one of the first to sketch and paint the White Mountains. He was drawn to the region in the 1830s, I believe, after the Willey tragedy made national headlines. A family of seven killed in a devastating summer mudslide. They fled in such haste, an open Bible was later found on the table in their home—untouched by the avalanche. Horrible. Anyway. A couple of years later Cole visited the site and painted a gloomy landscape of broken stumps and jagged granite under dark gathering storm clouds—a painting sadly lost, like the poor Willey family. Hawthorne based a story on the incident."

"But what has any of that got to do with this painting?" Tessa asked.

"I was getting to that," Arktophonos said. "Cole's work brought widespread attention to the White Mountains, still an untamed wilderness. Then other artists wishing to broaden their horizons flocked to the area, and first-time tourists looking for adventure began making the difficult journey north by stagecoach."

"Speaking of which, I've got an inn full of leaf-peepers who'll be adventuring elsewhere for dinner if I don't get back to the kitchen," Tessa said. "Don't get me wrong. I'd love to hear the rest, but Dekker can bring me up to speed later. Right, Dekker?"

"Sure."

"And anyway, you're booked until Monday, Mr. um—Gregor. We'll talk more in the pub tonight or tomorrow. Because I really am—interested." She nodded enthusiastically.

Don't go overboard, Bernstein.

"And Dekker? Don't forget you promised to take Ethan to Littleton. Renege on Chutters and you'll see a meltdown like no other."

"I won't forget."

"I just don't want you to get distracted." She winked as she made her escape.

"Sorry," I said. "She really does have a lot on her plate right now."

"No need to apologize. Once I get going on my favorite topic, you should see how quickly I clear out a bar."

I laughed, surprised Gregor had a sense of humor and not surprised my gaydar had kicked in with the bar comment. Yes, as Bernstein hinted so unsubtly, Gregor Arktophonos was an extremely attractive man.

"What is…Chutters?" he asked.

"A candy shop in Littleton. Supposedly has the longest candy counter in the world, or so says Mr. Guinness. Ethan is Tessa's son. He's ten, so—kid in a candy store thing."

Shut up, Dekker.

"Well, I'll let you go, then."

"Oh. No rush. He's out playing with Calvin. My dog. They're fine. We've got plenty of time." Why was I talking so fast? "I really am curious to hear more. Those paintings in the dining room caught my eye right away. But there's something about this one that's—I don't know. It draws you in."

"Emerson wrote about the ephemeral nature of beauty that shimmers in the yellow afternoons of October," Gregor said. "There's a great deal of Emerson in this painting."

"And a fair measure of his buddy Whitman, if you ask me."

"Indeed. That's another reason this could be such an exciting find. The male nude figure in American painting doesn't make an appearance of any note until Thomas Eakins in the late nineteenth century. You know *The Swimming Hole?*" He didn't wait for me to nod. "Of course you do. He portrayed the one naked male activity Victorian prudishness could accept—men skinny-dipping together. With their dog, if you look closely."

Was he flirting with me?

Was I flirting with him?

"But if this painting pre-dates the 1880s, as I'm fairly certain it does, we've found an artist unafraid to break with conventions adhered to by his contemporaries. I'd like to look at the others again—in the daylight—if that's possible."

"I don't see why not," I said. "Come on."

He didn't stop talking. I led him across the hall and through the Chandelier Room.

"Only in recent years have we begun to reevaluate the importance of the White Mountain artists. Their work went out of fashion at the turn of the twentieth century and has been virtually ignored ever since. This could be the breakthrough we've been waiting for."

Remnants of breakfast had not been removed from tables in the Hunt Room, which meant Storm hadn't shown up yet. Tessa would be furious. I was glad we didn't go through the kitchen. I began opening the wooden Venetian blinds over the windows on both sides of the dining room, letting in bright late morning sun. Gregor went straight for the paintings, examining them closely.

"The frames appear to be original," he noted. "They might tell us something. But the canvases are in dire condition. I can almost feel the layers of dust and grime that need to be removed carefully to restore them to their original condition."

I joined him as he stood in front of the barn scene with two boys.

"You see how he's depicted the exterior landscape from inside. Very clever."

"Yes. I noticed that." In fact, I felt good about my initial analysis of the paintings. There wasn't much Arktophonos mentioned that I'd missed. "What about the boys at the table? It's hard to tell, but I thought they might be Black."

"That seems highly unlikely," Gregor said. "Why would they be? Unless...We absolutely must have them cleaned. That's all there is to it."

"Once they're restored, maybe we'll find a signature."

"Oh, I know the artist's name. Or at least his surname. It's Chapman. The one I brought from Boston is signed at the very bottom edge of the painting. B. Chapman."

A storm cloud must have passed over the sun because the room became darker. The temperature dropped, like someone had turned an air conditioner on at full blast. The air thickened, making it difficult to breathe before thinning, as if sucked from the room.

"The weather changes so quickly in the mountains," Gregor said, rubbing his muscular arms vigorously with his hands. "Now, if we can just find some evidence of when Mr. Chapman painted the pictures."

"I know," I whispered.

Gregor's raised his bushy eyebrows once again.

"At least, I know when Benjamin Chapman stopped painting."

II. ETHAN

CHUTTERS. CHUTTERS. CHUTTERS.

Calvin barks behind our head.

Okay. Settle down. Both of you. Dekker says. We have to find a place to park.

Mom parks down by the covered bridge over the river. Moose-in-a-panic.

He turns the Jeep and we park by the bridge. We unbuckle our seat belt and open the door. Calvin jumps from the back and onto our lap and out the door first. We follow him.

Dekker points to a sign. The river is called the Ammonoosuc. Dekker says.

Yes. Moose-in-a-panic. We say.

Dekker laughs and puts Calvin on his leash and we march up the hill to Main Street.

Chut-ters. Chut-ters. Chut-ters.

We do our Chutters March. People passing on the sidewalk smile. We smile back.

Chut-ters. Chut-ters. Chut-ters.

Everyone likes Chutters. The only problem is too much to choose. We can't have everything. Mom says. So we make a list.

Gummy Bears and Gummy Worms.

Pop Rocks and Smarties.

Tootsie Rolls and Mary Janes.

Candy Corn and Jelly Beans.

Fudge for Mom.

Maybe Dekker will pick different candy. We can share.

Does Calvin like candy?

Candy's not good for dogs. Dekker says. Especially chocolate. Chocolate is poison for dogs. Dekker says.

No chocolate for Calvin.

Dekker ties Calvin to a parking meter in front of Chutters.

Calvin, stay.

We walk through the door and WHAM. All the smells of all the candy mix together and we breathe in the sweet air. Chutters is like Willy Wonka's Chocolate Factory in real life. We want to run up and down the aisles. Breathe in everything at the same time. Don't run. Mom says.

We show Dekker where to get the bags for candy and the plastic gloves so we don't spread germs. Some people put all their candy in one bag all mixed together. We put each kind of candy in its own bag. So Gummy Bears don't stick to Jelly Beans and Mary Janes don't taste like Tootsie Rolls.

Are Tootsie Rolls chocolate?

Yes. Dekker says.

No Tootsie Rolls for Calvin.

The hardest choice is always Jelly Beans. Chutters has way more than the 50 Official Flavors. We always want to try something new but we always end up with our favorites.

Berry Blue—never Blueberry—and Bubble Gum. Coconut and Green Apple—never Red Apple. Peach and Strawberry Jam. Tutti-Frutti and Watermelon.

Small handfuls. Mom says. Dekker has big hands. We hold the

bag open. Dekker puts a big handful of each favorite in the bag. Dekker doesn't know what Mom says. We don't tell him.

Last we get Fudge for Mom. Maple Walnut. Mom doesn't like to share Fudge.

Then I better get some for myself. Dekker says. I'll share mine with Mr. Arktophonos.

Who's that?

The man in Room One who brought the painting from the museum. Dekker says.

We watch the candy lady cut Fudge into perfect square pieces with a large sharp knife.

You know, Ethan. Dekker says. He squats down next to us. Mr. Arktophonos and I really like those paintings in the dining room. Your mom said you're the one who found them.

The sharp knife slips on a walnut and cuts the candy lady's finger. She says a bad word. Blood drips on the Fudge.

Where did you find them? Dekker says.

Room Thirteen. We didn't mean to say. Our head was full of Fudge. It just slipped out. We didn't mean to say.

We feel the scream in our belly. It wants to come out. We don't want to scream in Chutters. We stamp our feet to keep the scream inside.

What's wrong, Ethan? Dekker says. Do you need to go to the bathroom?

We shake our head and stamp our feet. The candy lady is sucking the blood out of her finger. No. No. No. We do not want to scream in Chutters.

We throw ourselves on the floor and kick and pound the carpet with our fists. The scream is trying to come out. We close our mouth tight. The scream is coming out the edges. We can't stop it. We kick and pound the carpet harder. We hear Dekker say our name. We feel his hands under our arms, picking us up. No. No. No. We are not screaming in Chutters.

Dekker carries us outside fast. We are screaming outside. Dekker says our name over and over and over.

Calvin is barking. Calvin is jumping and barking. He wants to be free. We want to be free. Our arms swing and our legs kick at the air. Dekker sits on the sidewalk and holds us tight and says our name over and over and over again. Calvin is licking our face.

We open our eyes and through our tears we watch the screams disappear up into the clouds.

III. DEKKER

It was over as quickly as it began. I wasn't sure what set him off but remembered what Tessa said about Calvin helping. I dropped the bags of candy, grabbed him, and got him out of the store as quickly as possible. Sure enough, Calvin's attention seemed to do the trick and he quieted down in my arms on the sidewalk. I ignored the troubled stares of passersby and realized what Tessa must deal with on a regular basis. Like her situation wasn't problematic enough being a Jewish flatlander. She'd told me some appalling comments the local yokels had made about meeting their "first Jew." Some probably thought she was a witch with a possessed child.

Another good reason not to subject Ethan to a North Country elementary school.

"Ethan, are you feeling a little better now?" I asked.

He nodded, although he still looked like he might burst into tears at any moment. Calvin sat snuggled close by the boy's side.

"Can you sit here with Calvin for a minute while I go back inside and pay for our candy?"

He nodded again, wiped his eyes with his sleeve, and put an arm around Cal.

The woman from the fudge counter scurried from the doorway where she'd been gawking. I headed toward her, pulling a credit card from my wallet. She finished boxing the double order of maple nut fudge while another girl weighed the bags of candy Ethan had filled.

"Your son must be a handful." I tossed my card on the counter, in no mood to chat or correct her. I stood back a few steps to watch Ethan outside the store window. He was whispering secrets in Calvin's ear.

I signed the charge slip without checking the amount, slipped the card into my pocket, and grabbed the two bags of candy.

"Good luck, sir," she sneered.

"Fuck you very much," I smiled back.

Ethan unhooked Calvin from the parking meter. Without a word he handed me the leash and took the bags of candy and fudge. We headed back to the parking lot in silence. Ethan looked at me hesitantly when we got to the Jeep.

"May we have ice cream?" he asked in a small voice. "Please?"

"Sure. If you know a place." He nodded. "Do we walk or do we drive?"

"Walk. Across the bridge."

"That old covered bridge? Will it hold all three of us at the same time? Because it's a long way down to the river and that water is lookin' mighty cold."

Ethan rolled his eyes and cracked a smile. We put the bags in the Jeep and he held out his hand for Cal's leash. As soon as it was securely in his hand, boy and dog took off at a run.

"Hey, no fair," I shouted. "I didn't know it was a race." I followed after them, and by the time I got to the bridge, they were halfway across. Ethan leaned on the railing facing north and yelled.

"MOOSE-IN-A-PANIC." He turned to the other rail facing south. "MOOSE-IN-A-PANIC." He and Cal continued to run across the bridge until they got to the far side, where they turned and headed upstream along a footpath. He seemed to know where he was going, so I didn't feel the need to keep up since I could see them clearly ahead of me.

The source of the Ammonoosuc River is Lakes of the Clouds, on the western slope of Mount Washington. I'd been reading up on it in case Ethan asked me any questions. Somewhere south of Littleton it joins up with the Connecticut River, which flows along the border between New Hampshire and Vermont, through Massachusetts and Connecticut, to the Long Island Sound. It reminded me of *Paddle-to-the-Sea*, a favorite children's book of mine. A little boy carves an Indian in a canoe, sets him adrift on one of the Great Lakes, and he travels to the ocean.

That's me in a nutshell. Paddle-to-the-Sea. Drifting where the river takes me. Part of me was beginning to consider the idea of settling somewhere. Cloverkist? I wasn't sure, but in a short space of time, I'd begun to feel the need to protect Tessa and Ethan—from what I didn't yet know.

"DEKKER, COME." Ethan waved from a bridge on the road leading to I-93, and I saw the ice cream shop up the hill on the other side. Another Norman Rockwell image sprang to mind.

"WAIT FOR ME," I shouted back. "WAIT FOR ME THERE."

Of course, they didn't wait. By the time I got to the road, they were already in front of a two-story Colonial style house, white with gray trim, which had been converted into an ice cream parlor. Ethan sat at a picnic table on the front lawn and Calvin lay in the shade beneath it. Before I could catch my breath to scold him, he pointed at a sign across the side parking lot.

"What's a Horse Cemetery?" he asked. The simple block print sign pointed toward a narrow tree-lined lane on the opposite side of the road.

"I guess it's a graveyard for horses," I said. It sounded like something from a Stephen King novel.

"Can we go there after we get ice cream?"

"Sure. Why not?" No better way to take care of a kid who just suffered a major meltdown in public than taking him for an ice cream cone and a stroll to the Horse Cemetery.

Within a small square plot just off the country lane, a wooden fence surrounded three simple gravestones. Maud, Molly, and Maggie. Two died in 1919 and the third in 1929. According to a plaque, the horses belonged to the wife of Dr. Eli Wallace. Her dying wish was for her three beloved mares to be kept together, even in death. There was an odd postscript: they'd been buried with their harnesses, saddles, feed boxes, and blankets.

"Why would the doctor do that?" Ethan asked, sitting on one of the markers, while Calvin sniffed the perimeter.

"I don't know," I told him honestly. "In ancient Egypt, the dead were buried in the pyramids with all the things they might need for their journey to the afterlife." I didn't mention that included favorite pets and servants. "But that was a long long time ago. We don't do that anymore."

Ethan sat, elbows on knees, chin between fists, brow furrowed in concentration. A soft breeze set the poplar and birch branches rustling above us, leaves floating gently to the ground. The faintest scent of burning filled the autumn air. What was the Emerson line Gregor quoted?

The yellow afternoons of October.

"Dekker? Do you think Benjamin Chapman was buried with his paints and brushes?"

A crow broke the silence with its sharp caw before I could think of an appropriate answer. Calvin looked up, barked once, and trotted to Ethan's side.

"I doubt it, Ethan. I don't think that kind of thing was done when he died. Maybe that's why they engraved them on his stone."

"Maybe that's why he's so angry," the boy whispered into Calvin's ear.

CHAPTER NINE

I. VALRAVEN

Moonlight crept across the bed through an opening between the worn blackout curtains. Unlike some, Valraven never felt the influence of a full moon. Law enforcement agencies reported a rise in crime rates, prison guards noted extreme behavior changes in inmates, and schizophrenics were especially vulnerable. There were no scientific studies to support these claims. But if unaccountable susceptibility was at the root of full-moon mythology, surely those with inklings of a psychic nature—real or imagined—were likely candidates. Valraven had a hunch this could be the case with Duane.

The young man stirred, pulled the bedspread tighter to his body. It had been a long time since Valraven had lain awake listening to the soft breathing of another beside him. He couldn't remember her name, the Shaman's granddaughter. Gender aside, the girl and this boy were two innocent peas in a pod, inexperienced and shy, yet curious and seductive. What drew them to him? Nothing he'd done deliberately, at least not that he was aware. He'd inadvertently chosen Duane to partner with during the morning session. The North Country bumpkin had been impossible to shake off once the connection was made.

They'd finished the morning with another psychometric exercise, meant to further increase their clairsentience in preparation for full and open reception of spirit. Reginald Masters told everyone to choose a small personal object, something held easily in the palm of a hand.

"A metal object works best," Masters said. "But whatever you might have on your person. A piece of jewelry, a key, or a lucky charm. Don't think about it too much. It's important to keep your mind free and your body relaxed."

"You wanna go first?" Duane asked.

Valraven pulled the generic silver key to his Squapan cabin from his pocket and handed it to Duane.

"Not very interesting," he said. "But it's all I've got except for some loose change."

"Reg said a key was okay," said Duane.

"Rub your hands like you did before," Reg instructed. "That'll get the psychic energies flowing. You might feel them start tingling this time. That's a good sign."

Valraven suppressed a smile as Duane held the key between his teeth and rubbed his hands together enthusiastically. Between how thick Reg laid on the hocus-pocus and how willingly Duane attended to every detail, it was hard work keeping a straight face. He was sorely tempted to join the men who'd take refuge in the bar after lunch. But he couldn't escape the feeling there was a reason to stay. Was this where assistant surgeon RJ had directed him?

"Now, hold the object between both hands and let it speak to you, through you. Say whatever you hear or feel out loud. If it means something, your partner can nod encouragement—but nothing more. Don't ask direct questions and don't engage in conversation. Let spirit guide you."

Duane gave Valraven the kind of wide-eyed look he might make before a bungee jump. He took a deep breath and dropped the key from his lips into his cupped hands. Almost immediately he lifted his head and a puzzled expression crossed his face. He wrinkled his nose.

"I smell pine trees." Duane frowned. "Fresh cut wood. Like up home. That can't be right."

Valraven caught his breath.

"I see a lake and a mountain and a woodshed. I hear birds singin' and crickets chirpin'. And loons callin' on the lake." He shook his head. "I'm sorry. All I'm gettin' is stuff I see every day. Nothin' special off this key. Unless…" He looked deeply into Valraven's eyes. "Does this key open a door to some place in the woods? A cabin on a lake somewhere? Someplace like where I'm from?"

Valraven nodded and Duane heaved a huge sigh of relief.

"Well, alrighty then." He grinned from ear to ear. "Let's see if there's more."

Valraven hoped not. He didn't want Duane drawing the attention of Masters, who snaked around the room, listening, watching, offering bogus encouragement. Valraven didn't want Duane blowing his cover. As much as he despised Masters, he had no taste for pointless confrontation. But he was curious what else this odd country boy might glean from his past—or his future.

It could go either way.

Duane held his cupped hands close to his chest, raised them to his nose, and inhaled deeply.

"Now I smell smoke. Like a bonfire of autumn leaves." He shook his head. "No. Not leaves. Books. I see a pile full of burning books. Oh. Oh, dear. This key is getting hot. Hotter and hotter. The books are burning. Black smoke rising in the sky. Ouch. Ouch. It's hot. Too hot. I don't know how much longer I can hold it. Ouch. It's burning my hands. Burning the books. What does it mean? I don't know what it means. Ouch. OUCH." He dropped the key. It spun across the floor until coming to rest at the feet of Reginald Masters.

Masters picked up the key and held it delicately, cautiously, between finger and thumb, like it might bite or sting. He looked from Duane to Valraven, who resisted the urge to avert his gaze. Their eyes locked onto each other. The room became silent, everyone aware something was happening, something not within their grasp.

"Yours?" Masters asked, holding the key toward Valraven. He nodded, took the key without breaking eye contact, and slipped it into his pants pocket. He could feel the key's residual warmth against his leg.

"The image of burning books—does it hold significance for you?"

"None I can think of," Valraven lied. None he would admit. Certainly not to good ol' Reg. He'd never told anyone about the books he'd thrown into the fire one drunken night at the cabin. Was that what Duane had seen?

Masters blinked, conceding the staring contest, and turned his attention back to Duane. "Let me see your hands, son," he said in a soothing voice.

Duane stretched out his arms and Valraven saw dark red welts in the center of each palm. Stigmata. No blood, but it didn't always manifest that way. Valraven knew there was no scientific explanation for the phenomenon, which he'd experienced on rare occasions. Oddly, he had no religious background. The first instance occurred shortly after the advent of his gift. It had been incredibly painful, as it clearly was for Duane. Tears streamed down the young man's cheeks.

To make matters worse, spirits picked up the psychic scent and began materializing at an alarming rate, drawn to Duane like moths to a flame. Motel 6 in Braintree seemed an unlikely geographic vortex for such activity, but spirits weren't as discerning as most believed. Neither Duane nor Masters appeared aware of the sudden convergence, even as the spirits vied for their attention. One rather gruesome case was particularly aggressive, her face spattered with what looked like thick yellow pus. Valraven guessed she'd passed recently, hadn't yet learned she could alter her postmortem appearance to a form more tolerable for the living. Her frustration grew as she poked and prodded Duane ineffectually.

"DOUBLE D," she shrieked. "DOUBLE D. KEEP AWAY FROM HIM."

Valraven thought she was referring to Masters until she trained her lifeless eyes in his direction. She was in his face—literally. Spirits were capable of nothing more disgusting. It felt like his head had been thrust into thick cold custard, the smell a vile combination of sickly sweet overripe fruit, rotten eggs, pungent sweat, and acrid smoke. Valraven tried not to gag.

GET OFF ME, he commanded wordlessly. *GET THE FUCK OFF.*

The spirit shot backward across the room with a surprised look on her face.

"Leave him be. You leave Double D outta this," she moaned before disappearing through the wall.

Masters was still examining Duane's hands.

"Is this some kind of trick, son?" asked the imposter. He wasn't used to being upstaged by a participant. "Don't lie to me, boy. Reginald Masters won't be played a fool."

Duane's lower lip quivered as he shook his head, not speaking. All color drained from his face. He looked like he might faint.

Valraven put an arm around Duane's shoulders and pulled the frightened young man gently away from Masters.

"I've got a first-aid kit in my room," he said. "Why don't we go and put some ointment on those burns?"

"Burns?" Masters hissed, his voice uncertain.

"What else?" Valraven said. "Young Duane got his psychic energy so fired up, the heat must've conducted straight into that key and burned his palms. I'll take care of Duane. You carry on with everyone else."

"I think this might be a good time to break for lunch," Masters said, attempting to take control of the situation. "We shall reconvene here at one o'clock. And don't forget to wash your hands. It's important to release any negative energy that may have accumulated…"

Valraven paid no attention to the rest of the spiel as he ushered Duane from the roomful of inquisitive eyes across the empty lobby and outside into the bright autumn sun. Duane allowed himself to be led along the sidewalk like a sleepwalking child. He leaned against the stucco wall as Valraven unlocked the door to his room. After shepherding him inside, Valraven glanced outside. They hadn't been followed by one of Masters's toadies. He locked the door and pulled the curtains closed.

"Why don't you sit on the bed," Valraven said. "You look like you're about to keel over."

Duane did what he was told. Valraven found the ointment and knelt in front of the young man.

"Let's see your hands."

Duane rested them palm upward on his legs. The marks were already fading. The salve was more of a placebo than a treatment.

"This won't hurt," he said. "It'll just feel cool." He dabbed a bit of the white cream on his fingertips and gently massaged it into the disappearing redness on Duane's rough callused skin.

"I'm so tired," Duane said. "I don't know what's goin' on. This stuff never had such a powerful effect on me. I must be gettin' old."

"This has happened before?" Valraven asked, stifling a smile. The kid looked to be in his mid-twenties.

"Oh, not this thing with my hands. Never seen that before. Plenty of other stuff. That's why I came down here. To see if I could get some help from Mr. Masters. Jayceen said I was in over my head."

"Jayceen?"

"Yes. She was my Wicca friend. We'd do dowsing and cleansing as a team. She's dead now. Since Tuesday. I think it maybe might be my fault. It was right after…" Duane's chin fell to his chest. Valraven didn't have a clue what he was talking about, but felt sorry for the little guy. Whatever was going on was taking a toll on him.

"Tell you what. Why don't you lie back and take a load off? I'll run across the road to the deli and get us a couple of meatball subs for lunch. How's that sound?"

A light snore said it all. Valraven eased Duane's head slowly to the pillows and lifted his legs onto the bed. Chances were good he'd be out longer than a short nap and wouldn't be too upset if he slept through the afternoon session of Reg's sideshow.

Valraven closed the door quietly behind him and walked across the motel parking lot. As he waited for the light to change, a couple of the medium wannabes stared at him from the other side of the road. The two women quickened their pace, heads down to avoid eye contact as they passed him on the crosswalk. Valraven had made a memorable impression. No big deal. He'd never see them again.

At least none of the living.

Inside the deli, while waiting for the meatball subs, the revolting spirit who'd invaded him in the motel conference room reappeared by his side. He ignored her presence until he realized her earlier aggression had been replaced by a familiar sadness. He knew who she must be.

"Jayceen?"

Confusion filled her face. "You know my name?"

"You're Duane's friend, aren't you?"

She nodded, almost imperceptibly. "Sorry I hurt you," she whispered. "Didn't mean harm."

"You didn't hurt me. You have to be careful how you do with the living. It takes time."

"Don't have time," she replied, agitation creeping into her voice. "Double D don't have no time, neither. You gotta get him outta there. Double D be in a steamin' cow pie of danger."

"You mean Duane?"

"Yes, sir. Duane. Double D. Take him far from that damnable place. It's gonna burn."

Jayceen vanished before Valraven could ask what she meant. A newly dead spirit had little control over its comings and goings. The fact she was able to return to him meant her message was important, despite its frustrating ambiguity.

If she could be trusted.

Spirits often messed with your head just for the hell of it, but Jayceen's concern for her friend seemed genuine.

Duane was still sound asleep when Valraven returned to the room with the subs. He sat down and took off his dusty boots. He'd been on the move for too long and was profoundly travel weary. His last encounter with Jayceen had drained what little energy he had left. He needed rest if he was to deal with whatever was to come. He wished he could conjure a memory of the future so he would be better prepared. That was impossible. Like most of his so-called gifts, those particular visions appeared unbidden. He had no more control over such manifestations than newly passed spirits like Jayceen.

Duane took up little space on the king-sized bed, leaving plenty of room for Valraven to stretch out on the other side. He hoped the young man wouldn't wake and get the wrong impression. That would be one complication too many. He closed his eyes, but it felt like he did not sleep for more than a few minutes. And yet the afternoon sun had set, replaced by the bright white light of the full moon.

II. CALVIN

watching Ethan silent sleeping / and another always waiting
both protecting Ethan dreaming / evermore&evermore
listening hearing something coming
scenting something flapping flying
squirrel swooping in&out
calvin standing softly whining
squirrel squeaking gliding gone
calvin tracking thru the kitchen / open doorway
seeing squirrel flapping flying / down the hallway
fleeing in darkness
nudging gently pushing door closed
keeping flying squirrel away
watching Ethan silent sleeping / and another always waiting
both protecting Ethan dreaming / evermore&evermore

III. DEKKER

Goddamn full moon. The shadows cast on the walls of Room One mocked my annoyance. I hadn't felt the effects so powerfully in a while. I should have recognized the signs earlier when I flirted shamelessly with the Greek from Boston. But the trip to Chutters and Ethan's meltdown distracted me. Maybe the boy was also sensitive to the lunar cycle.

Gregor Arktophonos snored into the pillow, his muscular tattooed arm resting across my chest. I wanted to leave but didn't want to wake him. If I stayed a few more minutes, he should be deeply asleep enough for me to slip out unnoticed. I examined the elaborate ink that encircled his bicep—Greek letters between two intricately linked bands.

"What does it say?" I had asked, tracing the patterns with my finger.

"If not for hope, the heart would break." His smile held a trace of melancholy, but he kissed me before I could say more. His lips were soft, his tongue tender yet insistent. I offered no resistance. It didn't matter if the moon had guided me. There was nowhere else I wanted to be. Strange I didn't see it coming. Or maybe not.

We'd returned from Littleton in the late afternoon. The two waitresses were busy setting dining tables, the bartender polishing wine glasses, and Tessa was having her own minor meltdown.

"Thank God you're back," she yelled across the dining room, emerging from the kitchen. "We're gonna be balls to the wall tonight and I could really use your help. I don't know where the fuck Storm is. He should've been here hours ago. Allison's working her ass off to get caught up on prep and I need you to get a fire going."

A metallic crash from the kitchen did not bode well. Tessa took a deep breath and knelt to give her son a kiss on his forehead, which he immediately wiped away with his sleeve.

"Ethan, honey?" Her voice softened noticeably as she spoke to him. "How 'bout you take Calvin up to your room and read him a story? Dekker's gonna give Mommy a hand with a few chores and then he'll be up to fix you hot dogs. Does that sound good?" She looked at me. "Is that all right?"

"Sure. Cal and I love hot dogs," I said to the silent boy. "We can do 'em boiled or pan-fried, however you like."

"He likes them boiled, don't you?" Still no response. "He likes them boiled." Strain was creeping back into Tessa's voice. "Ethan? Are you okay?"

He raised his arm toward his mother, holding one of the Chutters bags. "Fudge. No blood."

"Oh, thank you, sweetie," Tessa said, taking the bag, confused.

"Calvin, come." Ethan turned, marched toward the hall, and disappeared up the stairs without another word, Calvin following close behind.

"What was that all about?" Tessa asked.

"We had an interesting afternoon," I said. "I'll fill you in later. You mentioned a fire?"

"Yes. The wood-burner in the fireplace," she said, heading back to the kitchen. "There's newspaper and kindling on the loading deck. You know where the firewood is." She saw Storm had arrived before the swinging door closed behind her. "WHERE THE HELL HAVE YOU BEEN? IF WE WEREN'T SO FUCKING BUSY I'D FUCKING KILL YOU!"

Though I hadn't built a fire since Boy Scouts, it's one of those things you never forget—like riding a bike. A memory of cycling through Amsterdam with Willy flashed through my mind, but I shook it off and set to the task at hand, almost bumping into one of the flustered waitresses on my way to the loading dock. The hearty aroma of roasting meat filled the kitchen. Allison stirred two pots on the stove at the same time, and the sous chef prepped the salad station. Tessa violently chopped vegetables with a large sharp knife, while Storm slowly loaded the industrial dishwasher.

"Could you get those dishes done sometime this century, Storm?"

The loading dock was tranquil in comparison. But the rumbling of a dryer in the adjacent laundry room reminded me of the curious episode I'd experienced there, so I didn't linger. I grabbed a couple of newspapers and an armful of kindling, and opened the kitchen door. A plastic bottle spun through the air and smashed against the wall next to me with a dull thud. Allison screamed and I dropped the kindling. The top had popped off the bottle, splattering a thick creamy substance everywhere. I wiped a splotch from my cheek and tasted it.

"Ranch dressing? My favorite." I smiled. Tessa wasn't amused.

"Are you kidding me?" she shouted toward the ceiling, waving the knife in her hand. "I do NOT have time for this today. GET OUT. GET OUT. GET OUT."

No one moved.

"What are you all staring at? Back to work," she barked. "Storm, clean up that mess and get started on the burgers. Allison, your garlic cream sauce is boiling over. Janine, make a new batch of ranch. We open in half an hour, people. Move your asses!"

Everyone scurried back to whatever they were doing, almost as if nothing had happened. I wondered who they were more afraid of—a possible mischievous poltergeist or Tessa? No contest. I gathered up the kindling quickly, hotfooted back to the dining room, and had a roaring fire going in record time.

I was about to head upstairs when I felt a tap on my shoulder.

"Does room service include your fire-building abilities?" Gregor asked with a grin.

"Ha. I guess I could help you out with that a little later."

"I'm sure I can manage. I wanted to invite you to have dinner with me. I've had some thoughts about these paintings I'd like to run by you."

"Oh. I'd love to but I'm making hot dogs for Ethan. I'd ask you to join us, but he's not great with strangers and he's already had a pretty eventful day."

"Not a problem. Maybe we could meet in the pub for a nightcap?"

"Sure. Ethan usually conks out by ten, but I have a feeling he'll turn in early. Once he's asleep, I'll take Cal out for a last walk."

"So let's say ten-ish?"

"Sounds like a plan." As he turned to leave, I added, "There's a local duo playing music in the pub tonight, so that should keep you entertained if I'm late."

"I'm sure it will." He winked.

Ethan was more uncommunicative during supper than usual. I didn't want to make matters worse by pressing him too hard. Tessa left a flyer on the kitchen table about an event called Return of the Pumpkin

People in Jackson, which I assumed wasn't far away. She'd scrawled "Sunday?" across the top.

"Do you know anything about the Pumpkin People?" I asked.

He looked up from his plate and shook his head.

"Your mom thinks we'd like to go see them tomorrow."

"Pumpkin People?"

"Businesses and families in this town called Jackson put up displays with scenes from books or movies—all made with pumpkins. Sounds like it might be fun. What do you think?"

Ethan shrugged and stuffed his mouth with his hot dog, Calvin waiting patiently for his turn. Ethan held the last bite above Cal's head and dropped it neatly into his mouth. One swallow and gone.

"Maybe afterward we can make our own Pumpkin People."

"Pumpkin People," he repeated.

"Right. We could do a Pumpkin People scene from one of your books."

"Pumpkin People." His eyes took on a glassy stare. "Pumpkin People. We are the Pumpkin People." He looked like he might fall asleep at the table.

"Hey, sport. I know it's early, but you look pretty tired. How about getting into your pajamas and I'll read you a story?"

Ethan pushed his plate to the center of the table, got up from his chair, and weaved toward his room.

"Pumpkin People," he mumbled. "Pumpkin People. We are the Pumpkin People."

Calvin watched him and turned his head toward me, hoping for the last hot dog. I tossed it to him. He downed it in one gulp without chewing and trotted into Ethan's room. By the time I'd washed the dishes and wiped the table, Ethan was in the bottom bunk bed. His eyes were half-closed, almost asleep.

"Ethan the Giant," he muttered.

The only stories he ever wanted read to him were from his book of White Mountain legends. I found the worn leatherbound volume where it always was, on the floor next to his beanbag chair. I settled in, thumbed through the pages, and began reading the tale of how Ethan the Giant and his dog chased a moose over a cliff, how Ethan the Giant killed two moose in the swamp with two consecutive shots from his rifle, managing to haul the moose home on his shoulders. I didn't get very far before Ethan the Boy was sound asleep. As I looked at the rough illustrations, I had an idea. Ethan the Giant would make a great subject for our Pumpkin People display.

Halloween was my favorite holiday as a kid. I loved everything about the season—hayrides, bonfires, apple cider, jack-o'-lanterns, and especially making a costume for trick-or-treating. There weren't many homes within walking distance of my grandparents' farm, but Granddad would drive me to a nearby development. I always came home with a decent haul of candy. Ethan hadn't mentioned Halloween. But I thought it best to check with Tessa before mentioning the subject.

"Calvin," I whispered. "Let's go for a walk. Come on."

He gave me a dubious look but his need to go out prevailed. We walked down the long hallway and down the far stairs leading to Cloverkist's main entrance. Outside, Cal jumped off the porch and headed for the shrubbery while I sat in one of the white wicker chairs. I lit a cigarette. The scent of burning wood from the fireplace chimney infused the cool air. The parking lot was nearly full, so both restaurant and pub must be packed. Balls to the wall, as Tessa said. The musicians had begun playing a traditional country tune on fiddle and guitar. Across the road the hillside cemetery was shrouded in dark shadows. Calvin returned, business done, eager to get back to his troubled young ward.

"Okay. Okay. Let me just finish my cigarette."

He gave a frustrated body shake and lay down at my feet. On my feet, to be exact, lest I forget he was ready to go in. It was hard to believe we'd arrived less than a week ago. We'd both fallen into regular routines. Calvin seemed more settled than me, which concerned me a bit. I had no timeline in mind for the future, had no idea how long we might stay and if—or when—we might leave. As far as Cal was concerned, we'd found a home. I was less certain. Amsterdam taught me the hard way that nothing was forever and to always expect the unexpected.

I flicked my cigarette butt into the dewy grass. Before I got up from the chair, Calvin was already waiting by the door. I let him in and he bounded up the stairs without waiting for me. He disappeared around the corner and down the hall. I hoped he wouldn't scare someone coming out from one of the rooms. It was almost nine, so most likely everyone was in the pub listening to the music. I'd check in on Ethan and have plenty of time to shower and change before meeting Gregor.

❖

Right on cue, my gentle Greek bear grunted and released me from his embrace, rolled over, and settled with his back to me.

Truth be told, I liked Gregor. A lot. Our evening together had been as enjoyable as it was surprising. He was funny and charming and didn't push when I avoided answering his questions about my years in Amsterdam. I didn't mention my relationship with Willy Hart since he might recognize the name, working in a major museum. Willy's death had been headline news in the art world and I wasn't ready to talk about him. I'd never be ready to talk about what happened afterward—not to Gregor, not to Tessa, not to anyone. It was easy enough to deflect the conversation back to him.

The music was better than expected, and the bartender under strict orders from Tessa that our drinks were on the house. Gregor kept ordering us pints of Guinness, which was stronger than I expected—I hadn't been drinking for months. By the time the duo finished playing and the pub began emptying, I was pleasantly tipsy. Tessa said good night an hour earlier, and only a few regulars and inn guests remained at the bar. Gregor left the bartender a hefty tip and we made our way to the door.

"Let's take a shortcut," I said, leading him through the darkened dining room and even darker kitchen. The door from the pantry into the Red Rum Room was locked, but Tessa had given me a full set of keys. We passed a couple of guests quietly talking in the Chandelier Room, and I turned to say good night at the foot of the tower stairs in front of his room.

Gregor had other plans.

"You said you would help with my fire," he said.

"Did I say that? Oh, yes. Room service." I didn't know why it struck me as funny, but I couldn't suppress a giggle. "Lead the way, sir."

Gregor unlocked his door and I followed him inside. The room was warm and toasty, the logs in his fireplace still glowing.

"Your fire seems to be doing just fine, sir. And so good night."

"Not that fire," he said, pulling me into a tight embrace.

Before I could respond, he kissed me and I kissed him back,

our hands were exploring and our clothes were falling and we were falling…into bed…into each other…touching each other, tasting each other…no words needed…pulling, pushing, holding tight…

I slipped out of Gregor's bed before memory turned to arousal. The moonlight was bright enough for me to find my clothes without difficulty. I pulled on my jeans, carrying the rest as I quietly left the room, closing the door softly behind me.

Cloverkist was perfectly still—*stil als een kist*, I couldn't help thinking in Dutch. Quiet as a coffin. The dimly lit stairs were covered in plush carpet, so I didn't make a sound as I climbed to the third floor. I fished the room key out of my pants pocket and unlocked the door. As I pushed it open, I heard, more than felt, the whoosh of flapping wings whiz past my ear. With a sharp intake of breath, I dropped my clothes, raising my hands instinctively to my hair, forgetting it was so closely cropped there was little to protect.

The bat's radar guided it up the stairwell into the observation tower before it swooped back down into the hallway where I stood frozen. The creature hovered above me for a moment, then flew across the landing and through the open door to Room Twelve. My senses recovered enough to dart over and pull the door shut, trapping the flying vermin inside. I heard a single piercing squeak, then nothing more.

My heart pounding, I picked up my clothes, entered my room, and flipped on the light switch. Nothing moved. I threw my stuff on a chair and peeked into the bathroom. Nothing. How had the little beast gotten in? The window was cracked open, but it was screened. Down the chimney? I hadn't used the fireplace in the room since I arrived. I'd have to warn Tessa in the morning. Maybe she'd want to call an exterminator, although I doubted there was much that could be done in a building this old. There must be dozens of hiding places a bat could call home.

I turned off the light, lay on the bed, and wrapped the comforter tightly around my body. A patch of light from the full moon rested on Willy's painting, which leaned against the wall, still carefully bubble-wrapped and covered in brown paper. Another secret to be kept—from Gregor, from Tessa, from everyone.

The beating of my heart may have eased, but the heartache lingered.

From the Diary of Corporal Anson Quimby
13th New Hampshire Infantry Regiment

October 1864

Travel worn and travel weary, we have at last arrived in Boston, where we will spend one night and continue by coach to Cloverkist come morning. Little did we know the journey would prove so long and fraught when, with such jubilation, 300 officers and men of the 13th and 10th N.H. boarded the train. As we marched to Getty's Station, thousands of cheering fellow soldiers lined the streets in a rousing, hat swinging show of support, as did near as many colored people, somehow cognizant of the urgent intent of our expedition. Ben and I reunited on the train, he having somehow secreted the two fugitive boys on board. How so he would not say, nor did I ask. But his spirits appeared less agitated than in the previous days, for which I was much relieved. At last the train departed, past midnight, and in the early morning hours reached Portsmouth. Again Ben disappeared from my side to find his boys, for that is how I think of them. On the dock he returned and huddled the clearly frightened fugitives among the soldiers, so as to escape notice, as we together embarked onto the steamer *Guide*. On the first day the sea was calm and smooth but during the night we encountered rough weather, which did slow our progress until a dense fog forced the *Guide* to a dead standstill in heavy rain. We lay at anchor all the following day. Some soldiers grumbled the Captain was a Democrat and would with purpose delay our arrival. As night fell, a few of our exasperated company threatened the Captain with a choice: steam ahead to Boston posthaste or be sent instead to Davy Jones's locker. Preferring Boston to a watery grave, he barked orders and the *Guide* began to move, just as a powerful wind arose and blew the blinding fog out to sea. Arriving in Boston two days late, some angry men fear they may lose all opportunity of voting. I think it not so. If the stagecoach carrying us North encounters no difficulty, we will arrive before the polls close, cast our ballots, and ensure our indomitable Leader the opportunity to settle this too bloody conflict. Not that Ben cares an iota, for his humane mission will have been accomplished. His fugitive boys will sure become Freedmen of New Hampshire.

Chapter Ten

I. Dekker

"Room Thirteen?" Tessa shook her head. "There is no Room Thirteen. Twelve rooms, that's all we have." She poured us each a cup of coffee and brought them to the table. "And if there was another room, I'd sure as hell call it something else."

I knew what she meant. Tessa wasn't the superstitious type. Not a woman who puts her trash in Dahmer bags or calls her reception lounge the Red Rum Room, in a macabre nod to *The Shining*. I hadn't made the connection when Ethan mentioned it on our Grand Tour. But now I couldn't shake the creepy image of that bloody knife-wielding little kid.

"I'm sure that's what he said. I asked him where he found the paintings. 'Room Thirteen,' he whispered. Then, wham! Out of nowhere, the massive meltdown. I thought I'd triggered some horrible memory."

"I'm sure it wasn't you," Tessa said. "I really thought he was getting better. When we came here he was happier than I'd ever seen him, smiling all the time, entertaining the guests, entertaining himself. But now...I don't know." She raised her shoulders in a half shrug. "Maybe moving here was a big mistake." She looked on the verge of tears.

Damn. I hadn't meant to upset her, certainly not first thing in the morning. She had enough going on, what with the inn full for Columbus

Day weekend and short-staffed to boot. I was supposed to lighten her load, not add to it. I wasn't sure what annoyed me most. Was it trying to get information about those damn paintings so I could impress Gregor, who I had no business whatsoever jumping into bed with so soon after we met? Sure, he was hot, but what got into me last night? Or trying to play Daddy to a weird ten-year-old when I know nothing about kids? For fuck's sake, Calvin had a better handle on him than I did. And who was his father anyway? It didn't feel like the right time to ask. And what right did I have to question anyone about anything when I was keeping so many secrets about my own sordid past? *Get a grip, Dekker!* Tessa sat across from me in pain, and all I did was think about myself?

What an asshole.

"I'm so glad you're here, Dekker. You're so good for Ethan. I don't know how I'd be coping with him if you hadn't shown up when you did."

"To be honest, I think Calvin is doing more for him than I am."

"Don't sell yourself short, Dekker." She smiled. Maybe she wouldn't cry after all. "You always did that at Camden. Let others take the credit when you did the work."

I had no idea what she was talking about. Nobody knew me in college. Not really. I didn't even know me. It wasn't until I met Willy in Amsterdam that anyone really saw me, understood me, allowed me to become—what? Who had I become? And with Willy gone, who was I now? I didn't know.

At that moment Ethan wandered into the kitchen, bleary-eyed and barely awake. Calvin followed him, giving me a sidelong glance before curling up in the corner and snapping at a big black fly buzzing around his head. The boy shuffled to the counter. He took a bowl and a box of cereal from the cabinet and brought them to the table. He stood motionless by his chair, looking like he might have fallen back to sleep. Tessa knew his morning routine. She lifted him into the chair and poured cereal into his bowl. Lucky Charms. As she went to the fridge for a carton of milk, he picked the green marshmallow bits out of the bowl and arranged them into lines on the table. Tessa waited until he was done, poured the milk, and gave him a spoon. He slowly began eating the cereal, but his eyes never left the clover-shaped pieces on the table.

Yup. He was one weird kid. Whatever his issues, they couldn't have anything to do with down-to-earth Tessa. Again, I wondered: who was his father?

II. CALVIN

backseat calvin
grumpy sitting watching / leaning ethan
dekker driving talking laughing
bigman laughing talking dekker / laughing hahaha

grumpy ethan sitting / leaning calvin
bigman laughing dekker laughing
licking kissing ethan smiling / laughing hahaha
ethan touching hugging calvin
ethan speaking soft&soft
love you calvin love you most
evermore&evermore

III. DEKKER

"Stop making me laugh," I said to Gregor. "I've got to concentrate on the road." The Jeep was handling the hair-raising turns down the mountain and through the Notch with ease. I was more concerned with leaf-peepers distracted by the views and drifting out of their lane. At least I didn't have to worry about moose along this stretch. Unyielding granite stone rose almost straight up on both sides of the road. I glanced in the rearview mirror to check on Ethan and Calvin. They were busy, as usual, exchanging secrets.

"How you guys doing back there?"

"We're fine," Ethan said. "But Calvin needs to pee." He giggled. "CALVIN NEEDS TO PEE."

"Well, Calvin will have to wait until we get someplace where we can stop." The driver ahead of us hit his brakes as we rounded another hairpin curve, and I was forced to do the same. Goddamn tourists.

"We can't be far from Hart's Location," said Gregor. "We can stop at Willey House."

Uh-oh. I knew what was coming next.

"That's odd," Gregor said. "Didn't you say you lived in Amsterdam for ten years? You must've heard of the artist Willy Hart? He was very well-known."

Jesus-fucking-Christ! What fresh hell was the universe tossing in my direction? I'd been so careful to avoid anything with Gregor that might bring up an association with Willy's name. And yet, in the middle of Bumfuck, New Hampshire—

"Willy House?" asked Ethan. "What's Willy House?" He giggled. "WILLY HOUSE."

"It's not spelled like that, you dirty-minded little bugger," Gregor scolded with a grin. That set Ethan off into howls of laughter. He was back to his mischievous ten-year-old self, and I was relieved for the distraction from the dangerous territory of my past life.

"WILLY HOUSE." He laughed so hard he could barely get the words out. "WHAT'S WILLY HOUSE?"

"The Willeys were early settlers here," Gregor explained. "A family of farmers who rented a house on the side of a mountain up ahead."

"Were there little Willys?" Ethan asked, setting him off again.

"Yes," Gregor continued. "There were five children, I believe. And a couple of farmhands. Anyway, there was a terrible drought one summer. This was a long time ago, in the 1820s, or thereabout."

"In Olden Days," said Ethan.

"Yes, in olden days. The land was bone dry when a torrential storm hit the mountain, flooded the dry riverbeds, and loosened the rocks and earth, causing a massive landslide. The Willey family heard it coming and ran from the house to where they thought they'd be safe. But they were wrong and they were all killed by the landslide."

"Even the children," Ethan whispered.

"Yes," Gregor mumbled, realizing too late the details might be too much for the boy. "Even the children. The saddest part is the Willey house was untouched. A large rock split the landslide in two—one down each side of the house. If they'd stayed put, they would have all survived."

"But they all died," Ethan intoned.

"Yes."

"Except the dog."

"What?"

"The dog didn't die."

"I don't know—"

"We know. The dog didn't die," Ethan demanded. "The dog stood guard. We know."

"I don't remember anything about a dog."

"THE DOG STOOD GUARD UNTIL RESCUE MEN CAME. THE DOG DIDN'T DIE. WE KNOW."

"For fuck's sake," I hissed at Gregor. The last thing we needed was a repeat of yesterday's meltdown. "Let him save the damn dog."

"Yes. Yes," he stammered. "I'm sure you're right. The dog didn't die."

"WE KNOW."

"Yes. Yes, apparently so."

Fortunately as we drove round the next bend, I saw a parking lot, next to what looked like a pond. It had wet dog written all over it. I pulled off the road, parked the Jeep, and felt a collective sigh of relief.

"Okay, Ethan," I said, making eye contact in the rearview mirror, "before we get out, put Calvin on his leash. It's on the floor by your feet." Calvin was already standing on the back seat, eager to jump out and explore.

"We don't need—" the boy started to say.

"I know. Calvin doesn't need to be on the leash at the inn. But this is a new place and he needs to know who's in charge. Remember what I told you? Who's the boss?"

"WE'RE THE BOSS," Ethan shouted happily.

"That's right. Calvin, sit," I commanded. "Hold your horses, we'll be out in a minute."

"Hold your horses, Calvin," Ethan said softly, attaching the leash to the metal ring on Calvin's collar.

"All set, Boss?" I asked.

"All set," said Ethan.

I opened my door and got out of the Jeep. Calvin would have normally squeezed between the front seats and followed me out. But now he simply sat next to the boy, almost patiently—his raised ears gave him away—until I opened the back door. I prepared for him to leap out, dragging Ethan with him headlong onto the pavement. Instead, Calvin gently hopped to the ground and waited for the boy to join him, tail wagging.

"Good boy," I said, and Calvin gave himself a big shake in response.

O ye of little faith.

"Take Calvin over by those trees at the edge of the parking lot," I said. "Looks like a good place for him. I'll be with you in a minute." Ethan nodded and the pair set off. "And no swimming!" I called after them. "Did you hear me?"

"No swimming, Calvin." Ethan nodded as they walked toward the trees.

Calvin allowed the boy to lead him, not tugging on the leash at all.

Who are you and what have you done with my dog?

"You're very good with him." Gregor had been watching, his muscled tattooed arms folded over the top of the Jeep. "You'd make a good Daddy." He winked.

"Don't." I glanced over to where Ethan and Calvin were walking along the edge of the woods, well out of earshot.

"Sorry," he said sheepishly. "I'm rotten with kids."

"Unless they like horror stories."

"Touché."

"But seriously, how did you even know about this place?"

"My research into the White Mountain School of Art, of course. The tragedy made headlines and Ethan Crawford—the guy Crawford Notch is named after—turned it into a popular disaster tourist destination. Writers and artists flocked to the site opportunistically using it to further their careers. Nathaniel Hawthorne wrote a short story about it. And Thomas Cole, founder of the Hudson River School, came and painted a landscape called *Distant View of the Slide That Destroyed the Willey Family*."

"That's pretty creepy." I looked across the road, goose bumps rising on my skin.

"Do you think? But inspired by him, other artists came to paint. Without the Willey House disaster there never would have been a White

Mountain School of Art—except for the occasional talented amateur like our Benjamin Chapman. Any luck on that front?"

"Not yet. I tried to bring up the paintings with Ethan and he went into meltdown mode. I'm not sure one had anything to do with the other but I'm afraid to broach the subject again—at least not right away." Ethan and Cal were walking along the edge of the water. Calvin stopped and looked up at the boy. Ethan nodded. Calvin bent his head and lapped up a long drink, without actually stepping into the water. Unbelievable.

"Shit. I just realized something." Sometimes I could be so thick. "Ethan's favorite stories are about Ethan, the Giant of the White Mountains."

"That would be Ethan Crawford," Gregor said, catching on.

"Of course it would. I bet that gift shop across the road will have some kind of souvenir related to Ethan the Giant, with which we might be able to bribe a ten-year-old."

"I like the way you think." Gregor smiled. "Though I must warn you, I'm extremely allergic to kitsch. Be ready to catch me if I faint." Another salacious wink.

"I'm sure you'll survive." I laughed and turned away, looking for Ethan.

The boy was crouched on a small sandy patch near the water, Calvin sitting by his side, watching attentively as he made marks in the sand with a stick.

"Hey, Ethan. Let's go look in the gift shop across the road."

No response. I looked at Gregor, shrugged, and walked across the dewy grass. As I approached, Ethan stood and stared directly at me, pointing the stick toward his marks in the sand with an infinitely forlorn expression on his face. I looked down and saw he had drawn a heart, above which he had written: WILLY.

The blood drained from my face. My knees weakened. I abruptly sat on the ground. I sensed more than saw Calvin come toward me, place a paw on my leg, and lick my face. I saw nothing but brash bold swaths of color filling the air and spiraling around me like a living, breathing, kaleidoscopic dreamscape—thalo green, burnt sienna, cadmium yellow, Tyrian purple, Venetian red. His colors. Willy's colors of me.

I heard a voice in the distance. Not his voice. A child's voice.

"It's a message."

And from a much greater distance, the softest of whispers like the gentle rustling of leaves.

If there is a way, I'll tell you.

CHAPTER ELEVEN

I. VALRAVEN

"My Granddaddy Rafferty was one of the founding members of the American Society of Dowsers," Duane told Valraven with pride, after having charted his family's dowsing lineage. He took another large bite out of his cheeseburger. The North Country lad's appetite had returned with a vengeance after his ordeal the day before. Valraven, on the other hand, picked at a rather unappetizing Cobb salad topped with too much Russian dressing. They sat in the booth of a small diner-style restaurant in Plymouth, New Hampshire.

They'd checked out of the Braintree motel, grabbing doughnuts and coffee to go before heading north in Duane's dilapidated truck. They stuck to state roads, since Duane didn't trust the temperamental condition of his rusty Tin Lizzie. And sure enough, the engine sputtered and died less than an hour outside Boston. Duane managed to pull off onto the narrow shoulder and spent another hour under the hood coaxing her back to life, voicing nonstop apologies.

Valraven didn't mind. He was in no particular hurry to get wherever they were going. He was convinced Duane was the ticket to his unknown destination. When Duane said he lived on the northernmost edge of the White Mountains, Valraven vaguely said that's where he was headed and could he hitch a ride? The unsuspecting young man was happy to oblige. He didn't even ask his new friend where exactly he was going, which was a relief, since Valraven had no idea. But he would know when he had arrived. Of that he was certain.

"Anyways," Duane continued after finishing his burger. "Granddaddy quit the Dowser Society over some kind of falling-out with the head honcho, a man named Ray Willey. He even wrote a book about modern dowsing, but Granddaddy said he was sick to death of that dang blasted engineer and his highfalutin ideas. I could see what he meant. Mr. Willey's book was all kinda technical for being about something that comes from the spirit. That's how my daddy described dowsing. 'Nobody knows how it works but that's no reason not to use it,' Daddy said. Thomas Edison said the same thing about electricity. If that was a good enough reason for Edison, it was good enough for us dowser folk, too." He took a sip of his iced tea.

"After Granddaddy passed, Daddy took me to a Dowser Society meeting at their Vermont headquarters. He said maybe it was time to reconnect but we never ended up going back. Anyways, this guy made a speech about a dowser called Springwater Bemas. In the first half of the 1800s he traveled around by horse and wagon and found dozens of springs all around Vermont—with just a hazel stick! He was like the Johnny Appleseed of dowsers, a real local hero. That made such a powerful impression on me—I must've been eleven or twelve—I wrote a report about him for school. The teacher made me read it out loud to the class and the kids all made fun of me, started calling me Dowser Duane. I didn't mind much. Folks laughed at Springwater Bemas, too, but he was the real deal. He had the gift."

Valraven didn't doubt it. Nor did he doubt Duane was also genuinely gifted.

"Anyways, now everybody calls me Dowser Duane. Don't get me wrong. I know I'm no Springwater Bemas. I don't do good with water. My specialty is findin' lost things—misplaced engagement rings, hidden wills, stuff like that. The more important it is, the more likely I am to find it. And then there's the cleansing with Jayceen. That's mainly her gig. I'm more of a wingman. Or was. Now she's gone, I don't know if I'll take those kind of jobs alone." A melancholy expression replaced his earlier cheerfulness.

"Can you make a living from dowsing?" asked Valraven, hoping to distract him.

"Hell, no," Duane said, shaking his head. "Dowsing is just a hobby. I'm a bladesmith. I forge knives." He paused, chewed on his lip, and stared out the window. Clearly, Duane had something more he wanted to say, but he was like a skittish colt. Valraven waited. He didn't want to spook him. Whatever it was would come out without pressuring him.

"Tarnation, Val!" Duane transitioned out of his trance state as effortlessly as he'd gone into it. "I been talkin' a blue streak and haven't let you get a word in edgewise."

"Not to worry." Valraven laughed. "Your life sounds a lot more interesting than mine."

"That can't be true. Heck, I spilled my whole life story like a kicked-over bucket of milk and I don't even know where you're from."

Valraven hesitated. He ordinarily didn't reveal himself to strangers. Doing so once had landed him in a world of hurt. But the current circumstances were far from normal. Someone was in mortal danger. *Save the only begotten son.* He believed RJ. Someone, somewhere, desperately needed his help. And Duane might be the one to take him there. To be fair, Duane could also use his help. Jayceen had probably been pretty much his only friend, outcasts laughed at and mocked. He needed to know he and his gift were not alone in the wilderness.

Before Valraven could figure out how to broach the subject of his own paranormal activities, a deathly calm descended on the restaurant. No clatter of cutlery, no banging of pans from the kitchen. Customers had stopped eating and the staff stood frozen mid-task like display mannequins. Everyone was listening to the radio.

"The Braintree Fire Department, joined by units from Boston and others in the vicinity, appear to have the blaze under control. A spokesperson told reporters that casualties appear to be high due to an event being held at the motel when the fire broke out. Cause of the fire is as yet unknown and a death toll has yet to be released. But one unidentified source on the scene is quoted as saying: 'The fire spread very quickly, trapping dozens of people inside. Bystanders could hear them screaming. It was horrible.' New Hampshire Public Radio will bring you more information on this breaking news story as it develops. But to recap, a tragic four-alarm fire this morning at Motel 6 in Braintree, Massachusetts, just outside Boston, appears to have claimed an unknown number of lives. We return you now to our regular programming..."

Hushed voices replaced the sound of the radio. New Englanders were no strangers to tragedy resulting in multiple deaths—fishing rigs lost at sea, hurricane-strength storms, flash floods—these were natural disasters, out of man's control. What people feared most was fire. Building codes and regulations meant they happened less often than in the past, but they were no less devastating. Valraven watched Duane carefully. The young man had turned a pale shade of gray and appeared to be holding his breath.

"The Dying Moon," he whispered. "That's what Mr. Masters called it. The Dying Moon. Do you think he…" His voice faded into the ether.

"Gone," Valraven said softly. "All gone."

"You can't know—"

"I know." He hated that he knew, so the words came out more forcefully than intended. "I'm sorry I do, but I know. Reg is gone. And he took everyone with him."

Duane didn't respond at first.

"You saved my life," Duane said. "If we hadn't met, if you hadn't chose me to be your partner, I would've been there. I would've died with all those people. You saved my life."

A tear rolled down his cheek.

Valraven felt a tinge of regret. There would not be a better time, whatever the consequences. He took a deep breath.

"I wasn't the one who saved your life. Your friend Jayceen saved your life."

"That's impossible. We buried Jayceen last week."

"I know," Valraven said. He kept it simple. "I met her yesterday at the motel. She was there, watching over you. She told me to get you the hell out of that place."

"I don't understand."

"You see, Duane, the thing is—I talk to the dead."

II. ETHAN

Bear Notch. Bear Mountain.

We are playing a Jeep Game. We look for Bear signs. Only signs that say Bear. We have two points. We saw Bear Notch first. One point. We saw Bear Mountain. Two points. Nobody else has points. Only we do. We see all the Bear signs first so we have all the points.

Bearfoot Motel. Gregor says. One point for me.

No fair. We weren't looking for motel signs. Just road signs.

NO FAIR.

Why? Gregor says. The sign said Bear.

Bearfoot.

Still. Gregor says. The sign said Bear. Why's that not fair?

Gregor rhymed. We laugh. Gregor laughs. Mom's Friend Dekker laughs. And Calvin laughs. We all laugh.

We can't think of a reason why No Fair.

Okay. We have two points. Gregor has one point. Fair and square.

We rhymed. Like Gregor. We like Gregor.

Bear Notch. Bear Mountain. Bearfoot Motel.

The Jeep slows down. Red lights flash and bells ring at a railroad crossing. That means we have to stop and wait for the train to pass. Toot. Toot. We hear the train chug-chug-chugging closer.

TOOT. TOOT.

The train engine is red like a fire truck, with white puffs of smoke coming out of its chimney. It looks like a train from Olden Days.

Must be one of those fall foliage excursions. Gregor says.

We have a secret with Gregor. He gave us a present at Willey House. A wooden Ethan the Giant carrying a bear across his shoulders. The bear is painted black. It's the cub Ethan the Giant brought home and made a pet. Like the story in our book. The wooden man is not tall like a real giant. Not as tall as Gregor. But Ethan the Giant is bigger than G.I. Joe.

At Willey House Mom's Friend Dekker stayed outside with Calvin. Calvin has a dangerous tail. Mom's Friend Dekker says.

We went inside with Gregor. Maybe they have a nice Christmas tree ornament. Gregor says. He sounds like he doesn't like Christmas tree ornaments. Willey House has lots more than Christmas tree ornaments.

Racks of picture postcards. Paperweight rocks and colored crystals. Old Man of the Mountain T-shirts, Old Man of the Mountain caps. Moose plates and mugs. Hunting knives, arrowheads, and dreamcatchers.

Kitsch for days. Gregor says. We don't know what that means.

Ethan the Giant is in the middle of a shelf of carved wood figures, mostly owls and bears.

Look who we have here. Gregor says. He lifts Ethan the Giant off the shelf and looks at him close. Not bad workmanship. Gregor says.

We want to hold Ethan the Giant. We want to bring Ethan the Giant home. It's not polite to ask for presents. Mom says.

I think I'd like to buy him. Gregor says. But where will I put him? I have too many things in my house already. Gregor squats down in front of us. I have an idea. Gregor says. You could keep him for me and I could see him next time I come to visit. Would that be okay?

We nod.

Don't show him to Jason or your mom until after I leave tomorrow. They might get mad at me for spending so much money on this beautiful piece of White Mountain artisanal handicraft. Gregor says.

We don't know what that means.

It'll be our little secret. Gregor says. Deal?

Deal.

TOOT TOOT. The train passes and disappears into the woods. The red lights stop flashing and the Jeep starts moving. Ethan the Giant is hidden in a bag under our seat.

Bear Road. Bear Creek. Bear Peak. Three in a row. We have five points. Gregor has one point. We are winning the game.

III. DEKKER

We couldn't have missed the road to Jackson if we tried. The Mad Hatter was hosting his tea party for Alice, White Rabbit, and Queen of Hearts on the front lawn of the corner house. The figures were more or less life-size—with pumpkins for heads, of course.

"Ethan, look out your window," I said. "It's Alice in Wonderland's tea party." I couldn't see the expression on his face but his funny high-pitched laugh resurfaced as we passed by the elaborate exhibit slowly before continuing toward the town.

"WE ARE THE PUMPKIN PEOPLE! WE ARE THE PUMPKIN PEOPLE!" Ethan chanted.

"Are you sure the flyer said 'Fun for *ALL* ages'?" Gregor asked, sotto voce.

"Cool your heels, Mr. Big City Curator," I said. "You know the old chestnut? You can take the boy out of the country…"

"But you can't take the country out of the boy," he finished in a singsong voice. "Yes, I'm familiar."

"Well, I'm here to tell you," I said with a slight twang. "Like it or not, this country boy is bound and determined to show you a good time today."

"You had me at *bound.*"

I shook my head. Incorrigible. Between him and Ethan, I had my hands full. But I was less worried about Ethan with Calvin close at hand.

"More Pumpkin People," Ethan said, pointing ahead of us between the front seats. "Stop. Stop. Stop. I want to see ALL the Pumpkin People."

"We're not going to miss any of the Pumpkin People," I reassured him. "Let me find a place to park and we'll walk around." In the rearview mirror, I saw Ethan whispering into Calvin's ear. I couldn't tell which was more eager to get out and explore.

A small stone bridge crossed over a swift-moving stream. To the right stood a box-shaped two-story white clapboard house with a steeply pitched roof, in typical New England style. A sign above the double front doors said *TOWN HALL, JACKSON, EST. 1800.* Behind the building I found a shady spot for the Jeep.

"On the leash, Calvin," I heard Ethan say without prompting, clipping it on Cal's collar again. The boy learned fast. I opened the back door to let them out.

"Let him walk through the trees along that stream before we get going," I told him. "We don't want Calvin peeing on the Pumpkin People."

Ethan giggled. "He won't pee on the Pumpkin People."

"He might pee on the Pumpkin People." More giggles. "Just keep an eye on him, okay?"

"Okay. Come on, Calvin. And no swimming." Off they went, giggling and tail wagging.

"It's extraordinary," Gregor said, scanning the horizon. I retrieved a knapsack with snacks, water bottles, and Calvin's bowl from the back of the Jeep. "The mountains almost completely surround the town. Whichever direction you look, the view is breathtaking. No wonder Jackson was the epicenter for the White Mountain painters."

"Hmm. Do I detect a hint of thank-you-for-asking-me-to-come-along?"

"Possibly." Gregor shrugged his broad shoulders. "We can thank each other later. I have a feeling your little plan may work out better than either of us imagined." He told me about the woodcarving and the secret deal he struck with Ethan. "I'll wager he's chomping at the bit to show it to you as soon as I'm out the door."

"You're still planning to leave in the morning?" I asked.

"As early as I can. I want to get a jump on the holiday traffic. And I can't wait to do some research based on what we've learned so far about Benjamin Chapman."

"But you'll come back next weekend?"

"Oh, yes," Gregor said with a glint in his eye. "I look forward to it. With any luck, we'll both have more information to share and a good reason to celebrate." He bumped his shoulder into mine as he started off toward Ethan and Calvin.

"Hold up," I said. "Is it too much to ask for a little discretion? We're in the sticks up here, not some gay bar in Boston." As if to underscore my point, a gust of wind blew through the trees and yellow leaves floated down around us. *The yellow afternoons of October.*

"Oh, I'm well aware of how red the necks are in North Country. Believe me," he said, a touch of anger in his voice. "Somehow I don't think that's what this is about at all. I'm going to take a stab here and say this is your run of the mill 'pretend you don't know me' morning-after routine. You're extremely difficult to read. Jason Dekker: Country Boy or International Man of Mystery? Last night you're all, 'Do you like me just for my paintings?' And this morning you tell me your lover was only one of the most important painters of the late twentieth century."

I'd told him about Willy by the river at the Willey House site. I didn't have much choice, collapsing the way I had. What happened there, anyway?

"Calvin peed on two trees and a rock." Ethan was back. "He won't pee on the Pumpkin People." Now I just had to get the ten-year-old to stop saying *pee* in every sentence.

"Okay, then," I said. "Let's go find some Pumpkin People!"

"WE ARE THE PUMPKIN PEOPLE! WE ARE THE PUMPKIN PEOPLE!"

Ethan marched toward Main Street with Calvin in tow. Gregor eyed me suspiciously but didn't say a word.

"I know I owe you an apology—or at least an explanation," I said. "We'll talk more later?"

"That's up to you," he said, clearly dubious.

I had no idea what we would talk about later but had dodged a bullet. We followed boy and dog into Jackson.

The late-afternoon sun cast long shadows across the town of Jackson. The crowd of visitors wandering up and down Main Street had thinned. I tried to imagine what the Pumpkin People would look like in the dusky twilight of early evening. No doubt creepier than in broad daylight. Some exhibits were tame enough for the smallest children: pumpkin-headed Fred and Wilma Flintstone in their stone-age car with Dino, elaborately designed with gourds as well; Babe the Pig and his barnyard friends in a creative array of pumpkin and gourd configurations. A couple of displays had a distinctly more adult flavor: a buxom pumpkin-breasted Pocahontas being wooed salaciously by Captain John Smith; three black-painted pumpkin bears helping themselves to beer in a camper's cooler. But the Halloween-themed installations were the most popular: white pumpkin skull heads pulling themselves out of graves; caped pumpkin vampires with flying pumpkin bats. Calvin barked his fool head off at a huge hairy-legged pumpkin-bodied spider crawling up the side of a house, until Ethan whispered in his ear and pulled him away.

Ethan's favorite Pumpkin People were the astronauts of Apollo 13, which Gregor said had been a big summer movie. Films hadn't been a high priority when I was homeless through the summer in Amsterdam. He also liked the white-sheeted white-faced pumpkin version of Casper the Friendly Ghost. He looked like any traditional Halloween ghost to me, but Ethan explained not all ghosts wanted to be friends with people—only ghosts like Casper.

Ethan was the only child left working on a long table outside a café, set up so kids could make Pumpkin People masks. He'd finished one, which he'd pushed up on top of his head. He was methodically coloring two more at the same time—one for me and one for Gregor, he said. We watched him from an outside café table, while Cal took the opportunity for a well-deserved rest to lie in the shade of a thick hedgerow.

Across the road, an exhibit by the Jackson Historical Society portrayed a pumpkin-headed artist at an easel dressed in nineteenth-century garb. He painted the same majestic mountain range we could see in the distance from where we were sitting. It reminded me of one of the Cloverkist paintings, the one that might have been done at Painter's Palette. In turn, it made me think of Benjamin Chapman's unusual gravestone marking. What had Ethan said later, at the Horse Cemetery?

Maybe that's why he's so angry.

I thought of the insistent loud knocking emanating from the Tower the day I arrived, the unruly incident in the kitchen with Dowser Duane, and my own inexplicable episodes in the laundry room and at Hart's Location. A quote attributed to Edgar Degas came to mind: "Art is not what you see, but what you make others see." What could the artist be trying to show me? And which artist?

"Gregor, I'm going to ask you a weird question," I said. "And no kidding around. I really need you to give me a serious answer."

"Fire away," he said, eyebrows raised.

"Do you believe in ghosts?"

IV. VALRAVEN

"A ghost train?" Duane asked, as they traveled north on Interstate 93. "Like in that movie *Ghostbusters*—the sequel, I mean—which I don't think was so funny as the first one."

Valraven laughed. On the rare occasions when he tried to explain what he did and how he discovered his calling, he always ran into the same brick wall of misunderstanding. People either saw it as some kind of religious or mystical experience—revelation from God or another so-called Supreme Being—or they simply reduced the concept to familiar folklore, as Duane had, despite his own numinous talent.

Valraven understood. The human mind has a natural desire to make relevant connections based on personal experiences, bringing order to the perceived chaos of the universe. He'd read countless books to try to understand more clearly what was happening to him and convince himself he wasn't losing his mind. No single source provided a full explanation. The work of Carl Jung provided psychological clues, as did the writing of Carlos Castaneda—if one read between the peyote-infused lines. He studied Catholic liturgy and Hindu reincarnation, Zen teachings and the sacred texts of Islam. Everything ultimately boiled down to what the Shaman had told him: *If you understand, things are just as they are. If you do not understand, things are just as they are.*

"You pretty much hit the nail on the head, Duane," Valraven replied. "A ghost train full of lost souls, stranded between this life and the next, reaching out to me, calling to me, begging me to help them cross over, and there was nothing I could do but oblige."

"But how did you know what to do?"

"I didn't, at first. There was a lot of trial and error in the early days, a lot of frustration. I mostly learned by doing. Some spirits required only a few soft words of gentle reassurance to coax them into the Light. Others dug in their spectral heels and refused to budge. A psychogenic kick in the ass might do the trick but I had to keep a watchful eye. An angry spirit can conjure a world of hurt and inflict severe damage, even on unsuspecting bystanders."

"Do you think that's what happened at the motel?" Duane asked in a small voice.

"Possibly." Valraven had no idea. He was certain Jayceen had nothing to do with it. Her abilities were haphazard, at best. It was more likely to do with that idiot Masters. No telling how many spirits he'd pissed off over the years.

"At the end of the day," said Valraven, "you do the best you can. Not so different, I'd imagine, from what you went through with dowsing."

"Maybe so," Duane said. "When I started out, it was like tiptoeing through a field of steamin' fresh cow pies each time I pointed a stick. You can't help but step smack into 'em until you get the hang of watching where you put your feet."

Valraven smiled. That was as good an explanation as anything he'd ever come up with, and Duane seemed content to leave it at that. They kept quiet for the next few miles, taking in the spectacular show Mother Nature put on each fall in New England. The colors burned brighter and with greater intensity than the foliage around Valraven's cabin in Maine. These mountains were higher, steeper, and more rugged.

"We're coming up on Franconia Notch," Duane said. "And the Old Man of the Mountain, pride and joy of New Hampshire. I'd stop but it's wicked busy this weekend. Cars parked every which way. You'll get a good enough view of him from the truck."

Valraven had seen the jagged granite profile before, but it was never less than awe-inspiring. Against the backdrop of threatening dark clouds creeping across the sky, the Old Man seemed to scowl. You didn't have to be psychic to feel the power of this place. Maybe not a major vortex, but the nearly vertical rock formations were ideal for electromagnetic energy. Valraven felt the faintest of vibrations move throughout his body. Native Americans would've called this "sacred ground." He didn't use words like *sacred* but knew they were getting close, close to whatever RJ presaged. After they passed the natural monument in reverential silence, Duane flipped on the directional signal.

"We could stay on the highway but I'd rather go this way. Prettier and less traffic, especially this time of year."

Navigating the sharp twists and turns with ease, Duane was clearly familiar with these backcountry roads. The old truck strained with exertion as it climbed a steep hill, creaking sighs of relief as it barreled down the other side. Duane had been a cautious driver at the start of their trip north but now was throwing caution to the wind. Valraven had no concern for his own life—he knew this was not his day to die—but he'd prefer they both arrived in one piece.

"This is Bethlehem," Duane said, easing up on the gas. "Highest town in the state, or so they say. Used to be quite the boomtown back in the late 1800s, on account of the low pollen count. Not so much anymore."

That was an understatement. A handful of still-extravagant summer cottages contrasted with large abandoned structures, once grand hotels. The few shops on Main Street all could use a decent sprucing up, as well as what was once an elegant old movie theater.

"Do you know why it's called Bethlehem?" Valraven asked. Could this possibly be home to *the only begotten son*? He didn't think so. Too obvious.

"Named on Christmas Day, they say. People still come from miles and miles to mail their Christmas cards from here, on account of the postmark." Duane pulled the truck into a parking spot by a small park on the far end of town. "You don't mind if we stop for a spell? I need a good stretch. I feel a cramp comin' on in my leg." He turned off the engine and they both got out of the vehicle. "Hey, I'm gonna sneak a piss over back of the bandstand. Won't be a jiffy." He hobbled across the overgrown lawn, strewn with fallen leaves, and disappeared into the bushes behind a small nineteenth-century-style gazebo.

Valraven felt the presence of a woman sitting on a bench along the edge of the sidewalk before he actually saw her. When he turned to face her, she was staring at him with her hands neatly folded in her lap. Of indeterminate age, as was so often the case with the dead, her thin white hair was pulled back in a bun. She wore a faded, almost colorless dress harkening back to the town's heyday.

"I know who you are," she said, in an accusing tone. "And I know why you're here."

"Then you have me at a disadvantage," Valraven said politely. "May I ask your name?"

"Lovina," she said softly. "Lovina Chase."

"That's a beautiful name." Valraven ventured a step closer.

"It's a movie star name," she fluttered. "I could've been a movie star. Everyone said so."

"But you never had the chance." A risky gambit but if it worked…

"I worked as an usher when the Colonial opened. *The Girl of the Golden West* starring Miss Mabel van Buren. What a picture! Mr. Big Shot told me I was prettier than Mabel van Buren. He said he could introduce me to his friends in Hollywood." She paused and looked over her shoulder, down the street toward the old theater. "Mr. Big Shot wasn't a very nice man. I ran out of the theater crying so hard I never did see that big black Cadillac come barreling toward me."

Sad as Lovina's story was, it was one of the most common ones Valraven heard. Hopes crushed by cruelty, dreams dashed by a sudden and most unexpected death. He sat on the bench next to Lovina, and he knew when she made no attempt to flee. She was ready. She only needed to be shown the Light. The air was already beginning to shimmer across the road.

"Look there," he whispered. "Do you see it, Lovina?"

"What is it?"

"Your spotlight. It's ready for you now."

"I'm gonna be in the pictures?" she asked, wide-eyed as any silent movie star.

Valraven willed her to rise and move toward the Light. Lovina floated away into the shimmering without ever looking back. And as the Light faded, Valraven heaved a deep sigh of relief. Even the easiest crossing took a toll on him.

"You did it, didn't you?" Duane's voice came from directly behind him. Valraven had no idea how long he had been standing there, or what he might have seen. But he knew he'd been played by the not-so-innocent dowser.

He was too tired to be angry.

"Duane Rafferty, were you testing me?"

"I'm sorry, Val," Duane said, full of sheepish contrition. He sat on the bench next to Valraven. "I had to know if all that guff you were talking was true or a load of bull crap."

"And so you led me to Lovina."

"Lovina? I never knew her name. I never seen her. But she's a local legend. Why, more car accidents happen at this intersection than anywhere in North Country. Bad ones—that killed people. A lot of people. If you got rid of that ornery ghost, you did us all one humongous favor."

"She's gone," he said. "But you only have my word for it. Where's your proof?"

Duane sighed. "I may not know what happened, but what kinda dowser would I be if I didn't sense the real McCoy when I'm sittin' right next to him? That's why there's someone I want you to meet."

Cloverkist was one of those blink-and-you'll-miss-it villages dotting rural New England.

"The inn is a couple miles up the hill," Duane said. *Up the hill* was an understatement. The road leveled off after the first steep incline where an auto-repair center, a liquor store, and a mini-mart passed for a strip mall. Up to a higher elevation and Valraven glimpsed a lake through the thick foliage, a roadside diner, and some run-down summer cabins. Still the road continued climbing past a few modest homes, then nothing but trees on both sides—yellow-leaf poplars and white birch intermingled among tall scraggly pines and lush evergreens—until Cloverkist Inn loomed into full view on the hill's high peak.

Valraven gasped. Duane had detailed a number of possibly paranormal events that had occurred at the inn but hadn't said anything about its striking appearance. The setting sun behind the Gothic Revival structure cast the sky with a pinkish hue, and the inn almost glowed in the otherworldly light. Though different from the shimmering Valraven had seen at the crossing over place in the desert, this location crackled with a similar intense magnetic energy. A threatening dark cloud above the tower heightened the overall effect, especially when a bolt of lightning flashed right on cue, followed by deep rolling thunder as they pulled into the nearly empty parking lot.

"Whopper of a storm comin'," Duane said, scanning the horizon as he hopped out of the truck. "If I keep the introductions to a quick howdy-do, maybe we can get to my digs before almighty hell breaks loose. I hate drivin' in the rain after dark."

As Valraven got out of the truck he noticed a small country cemetery across the road. Perfect. He didn't need the uncomfortable knot in the pit of his stomach to know this was the place he was meant to find. A powerful force was at work here. Though its purpose remained yet to be discovered, he felt its malevolence watching him, waiting for him to make the first move. Not tonight. He needed rest to restore his strength. There was indeed a storm coming, but the core of his being told him the weather was the least of his concerns.

Valraven followed Duane onto the porch, waving away a thick swarm of black flies. Inside the inn, a young woman and a large teenage boy, both in kitchen whites, blocked Valraven's view of another woman shouting at them.

"Shut everything the fuck down," she said. "Nobody is eating dinner here tonight, maybe never again unless we get this fucking mess sorted out. GO. NOW." The two employees rushed out through a side door. The woman leaned her elbows on the reception desk, hands over her face, but Valraven would have recognized her voice anywhere.

"Are you okay, Tessa?" Duane asked gently, approaching the desk. Tessa Bernstein raised her head. She was thinner and her auburn hair was shorter.

"Dowser Duane! Am I glad to see you," she said. "We are well and truly fucked. I mean, this thing has gone ape-shit biblical. Flies. Thousands upon thousands of flies. Coming in through the fireplaces in the tower rooms, coming in through the heating ducts in the new wing. The dining room is totally infested. Fucking bastard flies! Ugh! Half the guests left before dinner, the other half aren't back yet but won't stay the night. It's fucking disgusting. I sure as hell hope you learned some new tricks in Boston or we can all kiss Cloverkist goodbye."

Valraven stood by the door. Tessa Bernstein. What were the chances?

"I didn't really learn anything," Duane said. "But I met someone who I think might be able to help. Val, come on in. This is Tessa. She owns Cloverkist Inn."

Valraven took a step forward and stopped. Tessa Bernstein stared at him.

"Elliott?" she said, like she wasn't sure how to pronounce his name. His *former* name.

"Oh, no. Sorry," said Duane. "This is Val. Valraven, actually, but I call him Val. We met in Boston when—"

"What? NO!" Tessa Bernstein interrupted. "This is Drew fucking Smith fucking Elliott."

"I don't understand," said Duane, looking back and forth between them.

Before anyone could respond, the front door burst open. A small boy and two men stomped into the room wearing handmade brightly colored, grinning and grimacing jack-'o-lantern masks. A large white dog accompanied them.

"WE ARE THE PUMPKIN PEOPLE! WE ARE THE PUMPKIN PEOPLE!" they chanted in unison. Valraven, Dowser Duane, and Tessa Bernstein looked at them in silence. No one moved. The boy ran to Tessa, pushing the mask up on top of his head.

"What's wrong, Mom?" he asked. Tessa Bernstein said nothing.

The dog took a step toward Valraven, hackles raised, and growled. One of the men took off his mask and crouched by the dog, held him firmly by his collar.

"Calvin, shush," he said.

"Look who it is, Dekker," Tessa Bernstein said in a low monotone. "Look who dropped in to say hello. Drew fucking Smith fucking Elliott." She took the boy by the hand and rushed from the room, pulling him along with her. The dog barked once, Jason Dekker released him, and he followed close on the heels of mother and son.

The only begotten son?

The situation couldn't get any more bizarre unless the other masked man revealed himself to be their friend Maxwell Shelly. But Shelly was dead. He'd seen him on the Ghost Train. Sure enough, the tall man who also removed his mask was a stranger.

"Elliott," Jason Dekker said.

"Hello, Dekker. Long time no see."

"I don't understand," Dowser Duane said, shaking his head. "Do you all know each other?"

"We did," said Valraven, aka Drew Smith Elliott. "Once upon a time."

From the Diary of Corporal Anson Quimby
13th New Hampshire Infantry Regiment

October 1864

Our arduous journey, which has taken longer than was our original plan, has ended. Overcome with equal parts of exhaustion and elation, we at last reached our cherished Cloverkist in the dead of the night. The Concord coach from Boston did not fare so well, the roads being in such wretched condition. A wheel came loose and the subsequent crash did fright the horses and cause an axle to break. We were jolted and shaken but otherwise unhurt. It fills me with amazement still that those boys were able to hold tight and not be thrown from the rear outside seat. I cannot but think on the severity of Ben's reaction if either of them had come to harm. The driver could not say how long before repairs would render the coach roadworthy. And since we were but a few miles from our intended stop at the Mountain View Inn, we made the unequivocal decision to continue on foot. We are soldiers, after all, well accustomed to long marches, and under much harsher conditions than the brisk New Hampshire air of an early October evening, though 'twere a greater hardship on the young brothers. They hugged their light blankets tightly round their bodies, and Ben cajoled them with songs to lift their spirits. If only he could lift his own—for I could yet discern the profound sadness beneath his gentle demeanor, the breaking of his soldier's heart. Cloverkist was dark as we approached, save one dimly lit lantern on the porch, no doubt left burning at Mother's insistence, as a beacon in the night to guide us home. Ben and I slumped into the wicker chairs to catch our breath, but only for a moment. The boys stood shivering, cold to the bone, so we took the lantern and led them to the barn. It would provide enough warmth and comfort for the time being, until we found a better place to hide them. Father's hired hands are not known for their discretion, and one loose word could put us in danger of arrest. The harboring of a fugitive slave is still a crime in New Hampshire. The boys were content, wont as they were to such rough accommodation. But it was Cassie who did more to melt their fears and anxiousness than any words Ben or I might utter. Her new litter of sleeping puppies, nine that I could count, lit their innocent faces with smiles, the like of which I had not witnessed before, even as Cassie warned them with a soft growl to keep their distance. Once we had settled the boys in the loft, Ben and I returned to the house. Upstairs, my room was much as I had left it, with fresh linens on the double bed that proved unnecessary, for after we pulled off our boots, we stretched out on top of Mother's hand-sewn quilt without removing our jackets. Belike was Ben fast asleep before his head touched the pillow. I had the briefest time to consider the Battles that raged on without us, while we were fortunate enough to bask in the comforts of home, before I joined my friend in deepest slumber.

PART THREE: PUMPKIN PEOPLE

"I and this mystery here we stand."

—Walt Whitman

Excerpt from (entitled) a novel by Drew Smith Elliott

Nobody was supposed to die.

We were many things to many people. We were intelligent. We were curious. We were passionate. We were fearless. We were competitive. We were arrogant. We were self-assured, self-centered, self-absorbed. We were gifted. We were privileged. We were spoiled. We were offbeat, off-color, off-kilter. We took the road less traveled. We marched to a different drummer. We dreamed the impossible dream. We were tender. We were witty. We were cruel. We were attractive. We were narcissistic. We were duplicitous.

Most of all, we were young.

We were not killers.

Nobody was supposed to die.

We were the new Lost Generation, thrown together by chance, a roll of the dice, a spin of the wheel. The Fates determined our destiny. Snip. Snip. Snip. Snip. Snip. Three of us were assigned a suite together in coed housing. Two of us were placed in a room together in the men's dorm. We all met the day we arrived, equally eager for our adventures to begin. Bright-eyed and bushy-tailed babes in the wood. Literally. This was Vermont, after all. What were we thinking, we laughed and we laughed. We could have gone anywhere, we bragged and we bragged. We'd make it through. We had each other. Till death do us part.

Poor choice of words.

Nobody was supposed to die.

We were Landgrove College's bright shining stars of Comparative Studies, or as we preferred to call it, Comparative Life. Pick a card, any card. Pick another. The more random the better. Our classes were seminars, our teachers were advisors, the curriculum was our own. The Grove encouraged independent research and analysis, and we encouraged each other. We were bound for glory. We could not fail. But who were we, this merry band of academic outlaws?

<DRAMATIS PERSONAE NON GRATAE>

Beatrice Ginsburg, aka Queen Bee, undisputed leader of the pack from a wealthy family in New York, antithesis of the Jewish American Princess stereotype, which she repeatedly decried as misogynist and antisemitic, her striking natural beauty belied her fierce feminism, she never met a cause she didn't like and was not willing to fight for, she had but one weakness, one fatal flaw in her otherwise flawless character: her insatiable sexual desire and inexplicable love for—

Andrew Fitch Oliver, aka The Drone, typical New England White Anglo-Saxon Protestant, from the same mold as John F. Kennedy Jr. if John John had been a blue-eyed blond, intelligent with little interest in study, athletic with no interest in sports, generally detached politically and socially, but possessed of unerring psychological insight and ambivalent sexuality, often known to slip silently from Queen Bee's bed and tiptoe across the hall to join—

Samuel Lucas, aka Black Panther, tall, powerfully built, impossibly handsome African American from rural Georgia, neither superhero or revolutionary, though poster boy material as either, unapologetic self-professed flaming faggot, with a penchant for cross-dressing and a flair for creating carefully calculated but seemingly haphazard mayhem, his razor-sharp wit rarely missed its mark, particularly when aimed at an easy target like—

Walter Franklin, aka Lightning Rod, seriously studious, rarely seen far from his personal library cubicle, short and stout, hairless and bespectacled, with an off-the-charts intellect and eidetic memory, the group needs him more than he needs them and paradoxically the reverse is also true, from Utah so possibly Mormon but we dare not ask and curious speculation regarding his undergarments is neither confirmed nor denied by his roommate—

Carl Tucker, aka Friar Tuck, virginal Kansas farm boy, skinny as a fencepost, not so shy as diffident, not so quiet as introspective, ready to be coaxed from his shell, generous of spirit, accommodating to a fault, frequent mediator with an infectious grin and warm sense of humor, we know of his secret crush on The Drone (except Tuck himself) and we tacitly agree to keep the secret from him.

Now we have another secret to keep. And keep it we must, or inquiry will turn to inquisition. What's a little insignificant death between friends? We were not responsible. We say it again.

Nobody was supposed to die.

CHAPTER TWELVE

I. DEKKER

"What the hell, Elliot?" The question wasn't rhetorical, more the case of a total loss for words. True, I'd also shown up at Cloverkist out of the blue ten years after college. But I hadn't secretly written a satiric coming-of-age novel trashing my friends, watched it become a literary sensation during summer vacation, and not returned to school senior year to face the consequences. "Long time no see? Are you kidding me?"

"I'm sorry," Elliott said. "I didn't mean to sound so flip. I'm as shocked as you are. I met Duane in Boston and he—I mean, we—had this connection...and..." His voice faded away. "It's difficult to explain." He looked toward Dowser Duane, but he was peering out a window. The dark clouds were moving in fast. Gregor had nonchalantly taken a seat in the corner and watched with bemused interest.

"Look," Elliott started again. "I hitched a ride north with Duane. He thought I might be able to help with—whatever it was he'd been doing here at Cloverkist. Believe me, Dekker. I had no idea you and Bernstein owned the place when I agreed to come."

"Tessa and I don't—we're not—there is no me and Tessa," I sputtered. Ten years had melted away and I was a tongue-tied twenty-one year-old again. How could he still have that effect on me? "And she goes by Tessa up here, not Bernstein. At least that's her real name, not some bizarre alias. What's that about, Elliott?" I sounded more annoyed than I felt. I didn't know what I was feeling.

"I changed my name the day I burned all my books," Elliott said. "Every copy I owned."

"Oh," I said flatly. "How magnanimous of you. Let's just file that under Empty Gestures and call it even-steven. Hmm?" No one moved. No one breathed. I thought Elliott might take a swing at me. I might deserve it. A flash of lightning followed by a loud clap of thunder broke the standoff.

"We need to go, Val," Dowser Duane said in an urgent whisper. "This storm is practically on top of us. We can come back tomorrow and sort things out—if that's okay with you, Dekker?"

"Fine by me," I said, keeping my eyes on Elliott. "But call Tessa in the morning. She might have a thing or two to say about who does the sorting."

"Will do," Duane said, missing the point. He pulled Elliott by the arm hurriedly toward the door.

"Dekker." Elliott stopped in the doorway. "Tell Bernstein—I mean, Tessa—tell her I'm sorry if I—I didn't mean to upset—oh hell, tell her I said good night."

I said nothing as he walked out, took a deep breath, and turned to deal with Gregor.

"Bravo," he said, clapping his hands slowly.

"For what?"

"I'm not entirely sure, but I believe I just witnessed some Oscar-worthy performances."

I was in no mood for his sarcasm.

"Now, the little fellow must've been the ghost hunter you told me about."

"Not a ghost hunter—a dowser."

"You say potato, I say *potahto*." He shrugged. "And you and Tessa went to college with Elliott or Valraven or whatever his name is. But what I couldn't figure out: Who was he fucking? You? Tessa? Both of you?"

"Elliott and Tessa were a couple in college, yes. And I wasn't fucking anyone."

"Really?" He smirked.

"Look, Gregor, I don't want to talk about this right now. I'll explain in the morning before you go, all right?"

"No, not all right," he said peevishly. He stood and moved closer to me. "The book. You have to at least tell me about this tell-all book he wrote." His tone turned flirtatious again. "Are you in it?"

I regretted having sex with him last night. What had I been thinking?

"I'll give you the Reader's Digest condensed version in the morning—over coffee. I promise. But I want to check on Tessa—and Calvin." The last time Calvin had acted so aggressively toward someone, that someone had tried to kill me.

"Okay," he cooed. "I'll let you go." He leaned in to kiss me. I turned my head slightly, deflecting his lips to my cheek. He raised his eyebrows. "See you in the morning," he said, waving as he went out through the Chandelier Room. Allison and Storm emerged from the kitchen.

"All shut down?" I asked.

"What a clusterfuck," Allison muttered as they passed and left through the front door. She had no idea. I feared the worst was yet to come. I trudged upstairs and down the hall to Tessa's apartment. The door was ajar so I slipped in quietly without knocking. Calvin was sitting guard duty in front of Ethan's room. I could hear the boy telling his mom all about the Pumpkin People. I gestured for Calvin to come. He hesitated before heeding my command.

"Let's go outside," I said softly. He shook his body in assent, trotting out the door and down the hall ahead of me. I needed a few minutes to wrap my head around what had just happened. Calvin waited by the door and shot off the porch, heading for the shrubbery to take care of business. The impending thunderstorm had not yet unleashed the rain Dowser Duane had been so worried about.

Desperate for a cigarette, I pulled the pack from my pocket. One left, thank God. I lit it and inhaled deeply.

Drew fucking Smith fucking Elliott.

Hats off to Tessa for nailing the introduction. You had to love her way with words. Leaving the room like she had surprised me. She wasn't the type to avoid confrontation. Unless… Holy shit. How could I be such a dimwit? She wasn't running away from Elliott. She was protecting Ethan. Ten year-old Ethan. When was his birthday? When did we last see Elliott? That would've been May of '84. I tried to do the math. May to June, July, August… I counted off the months on my fingers. Nine months would mean February '85? If Ethan had turned ten in February... Holy shit. Could Ethan be Elliott's son? When did Tessa leave Camden? Wasn't it the end of October? How visible is a pregnancy at—what—five months? So she would have known... I counted backward. During the summer? Around the same time Elliott's book came out? Holy fucking shit.

There was no way Elliott could know. Ethan was small for his age and wasn't in the room long enough for Elliott to clock the possibility. He had somehow thought Tessa and I were a couple. Could he have forgotten the last time we spoke? What a mess. Gregor was not far off the mark.

I'd been in love with Elliott. Hopelessly, impossibly, in unspoken, unrequited love, almost since the day we met. Elliott had always known, long before I worked up the guts to tell him at the end of our junior year. His book must've been finished by then, but he could've gotten plenty of mileage out of my pathetic lovesickness. Why had I been spared the worst of Elliott's poison penmanship? The innocent Midwest farm boy in his story was the least memorable character, mostly notable for his lack of personality compared to the others.

I'd played the last time we talked over and over in my mind, that warm Vermont spring evening when I confessed my secret love.

"I'm flattered," he'd said with his gentle, ever-charming smile. "I'd be lucky to have a boyfriend like you. I'd be the happiest guy in the world if that could happen."

I knew what was coming. The inevitable *But*. I wanted to kiss him, silence him, prevent him from uttering that ubiquitous little word. I couldn't. I didn't. I was barely able to move, barely able to breathe.

The same way I felt when I saw him in the Red Rum Room.

"But it can't, won't, shouldn't happen," Elliott had said. "It's nothing to do with you, Dekker. It's me. I'm not the person you think I am. I don't know who I am. I have to figure out who I am, what I'm meant to be—or not to be."

We'd laughed, breaking the uncomfortable spell of our twilight-on-the-quad moment. God, such clichés. No wonder Elliott left it out of the book.

"Are we cool?" he had asked.

"Cool," I'd lied. A lie I'd never shared with anyone.

A low growl pulled me out of my reverie. Illuminated by the soft light coming through the sheer curtains on the bay window in Gregor's room, I saw Calvin standing at the top of the steps leading to the pool, covered for the season with a sheet of blue vinyl. I jumped off the porch to join Calvin, in case he'd spotted something threatening. I could not rule out the bear that had been dumpster diving behind the inn.

"What's up, Cal?"

He continued growling, adding a sort of whine. He was staring at the raised deck across the far end of the pool. Someone had moved the stone puppies onto the deck. Calvin was growling at those damn puppies again.

"Really, Calvin? You are one crazy dog. Come on, let's go find Ethan."

He turned tail and raced to the door, waiting impatiently for me to let him in. When I did, he went straight upstairs, slipping on the wooden floor as he sped around the corner and hightailing it down the hall. He could find his own way. I sat on one of the white wicker chairs and watched the lightning show above the tree line as fat drops of rain descended from the black clouds.

One thing still bugged me—one of many things. Elliott and Dowser Duane. Elliott said they met in Boston. Dowser Duane told Tessa he was going to Boston to attend some kind of psychic seminar. Elliott said they made a connection. Dowser Duane said Elliott could help him out with what was going on at Cloverkist. Had Elliott ditched his career as a best-selling novelist and gone paranormal? An unlikely scenario. More likely, he was in the process of collecting material for a new book and duped Dowser Duane into—what? It didn't make sense. I leaned back and listened to the rain pummeling the porch roof, obliterating other night sounds except for the occasional vehicle whooshing past on the slick asphalt. It did not obliterate thoughts of me whooshing away in my own vehicle.

Be careful what you whoosh for, the voice in my head mocked.

II. Calvin

guarding waiting / big moon fading
sensing danger / evermore&evermore
squirrels flying puppies laughing

badman coming more&more
watching ethan two boys sleeping
lookout dekker danger coming / evermore&evermore

III. DEKKER

As the thunderstorm raged into the night, it was still as a mausoleum inside Cloverkist. Tessa had been on the phone helping two unhappy couples find accommodations at a nearby motel when I passed through the reception area on my way upstairs. Gregor was the only guest staying the night. Even the flies were avoiding him.

The large six-paned window of my small top-floor Tower room was streaked with rain, giving the recurring flashes of lightning an eerie afterglow. I wondered if the Tower attracted more atmospheric electricity than the tall pines surrounding the inn. A tree across the road showed signs of a direct hit—its bark bore a deep wound down the entire length of the trunk. If Cloverkist had been standing nearly one hundred and fifty years, I didn't need to fear being struck by lightning.

I sat on the patchwork quilt–covered bed and looked at my prize possession, leaning against the wall, still safely secure in bubble wrap and brown paper. I hated the idea of parting with it, even temporarily. But necessity demanded it take a noble, if somewhat deceptive role in a plan I had up my sleeve. I wanted Gregor to leave the painting he had brought up here with me—at least until he returned next weekend. I needed to examine it more closely, see if there might not be some hidden clue to help understand what was going on when it was painted. I knew Gregor would be reluctant. But after the incident at Willey House, I'd told him just enough about my relationship with a certain Dutch artist to whet his appetite. So if I offered him the chance to take an original Willy Hart back to the museum for appraisal, potentially adding the painting to their collection, he might be persuaded. I'd wait until morning, adding pressure on him to make a quick decision. I'd apologize for acting so distant, tell him I couldn't wait until he returned so we had the chance to pick up where we left off.

Ugh. I hoped it didn't come to that.

I took a deep breath. If Dowser Duane was bringing Elliott back tomorrow morning, I needed to talk to Tessa. Whatever her feelings toward Elliott, we had to be on the same page regarding Ethan. She had to tell me the truth—whether she wanted to or not.

I made my way down the carpeted stairs silently, so Gregor wouldn't hear me. Maybe he was already sleeping. I noticed an unusual candle sconce on the wall by the door as I turned toward the Chandelier Room. I hadn't noted it before because the small tea candle hadn't been lit. Above the candle hung a large teardrop-shaped ornament of solid glass, which seemed to breathe in the candlelight and breathe it out, bathing the hall in soft wavering refracted light. The sconce looked old. I'd never seen anything like it.

A similar soft shimmering radiated from the Chandelier Room doorway. The source of the light was more mystifying. The electric chandelier had been replaced by a candlelit version. Delicate flames danced above my head almost as if unconnected to the candlewicks.

"Pretty, isn't it?" Tessa asked from an overstuffed easy chair in the corner. "Even if it's a little early for Christmas." She stared at the chandelier, mesmerized by the glimmering flames.

"Pretty, yes," I said cautiously. "Isn't it a little dangerous this time of year?"

"Don't be a party pooper, Dekker." Her voice sounded odd, not exactly her own. "Nothing to worry about. We're just having a little fun. We can be quite entertaining. Watch." She raised her hands and snapped her fingers. The flames brightened for a second, faded, and were gone, replaced by normal flame-shaped light bulbs.

"How did you…" I didn't know what to say. It was impossible. Beyond impossible.

"It's magic," Tessa said. She snapped her fingers and the flames returned. "See? We can do magic." She snapped again and they disappeared. Snap. Flames. Snap. Gone. Snap. Flames. Snap. Gone.

"Tessa, stop. You're freaking me out."

She threw her head back and laughed. Not a Tessa laugh. An Ethan laugh. Each of the candle flames flashed for an instant before sputtering out like Fourth of July sparklers. The electric chandelier returned to normal. Tessa looked at me.

"He's gone," she said, with a trace of sadness. "I think you scared him away, Dekker."

"Scared who away?"

"I honestly don't know. I wish I did. Hasn't he introduced himself to you? He was here the day you arrived, knocking on the banister, scaring the girls down the stairs. It would've been funny if one of them hadn't gotten hurt. I think that's what he intended. I don't know why he's become so aggressive. But I'm scared, Dekker. What if he tries to hurt Ethan?"

"Wait, wait, wait, wait, wait," I interrupted. "You're talking about—a ghost?"

"Yes," she said. "He was harmless when we first got here. He'd play little tricks or move things around, like a friendly poltergeist, I guess. The whistling in the kitchen, but for some reason I don't think that's him. I'd hear him at night, footsteps in the hall getting louder as he approached the apartment. I'd open the door and no one was there. Not that I could see. But then I'd hear the footsteps again, slowly fading away back down the hall. He never seemed to mean us any harm." Her face darkened. "Something changed. He became angry. And now this." She gestured toward the chandelier. "Is he playing with us? Or warning us?"

Maybe this was not the best time to broach the subject of Ethan and Elliott. But would there ever be a good time? Probably not. I had to tread carefully or risk her wrath.

Maybe if I eased into it from another direction...

"When did Dowser Duane come into the picture?" I asked casually.

"Soon after we moved in," she said. "He showed up one day and offered to do a cleansing. Everything seemed to calm down after he and Jayceen burned sage and scattered salt and chanted their way through the place."

"Last time he tried that," I said, "he told me he was in over his head."

"And that's why he went to that seminar thing in Boston," Tessa added. "To see if he could find some help after Jayceen—oh God. Jayceen. I forgot about Jayceen. Do you think—"

"I don't know what to think," I said. "About anything. But while he was in Boston...well, that's where he met Elliott. And Dowser Duane seems to think Elliott might be able to help him out. He wants to come back tomorrow. I told him he needed to call you in the morning—to make sure it's okay."

Tessa said nothing. Her thunderous silence spoke volumes.

She rose from her chair and cocked her head, as if considering the appropriate reply.

"Tomorrow, huh?" she mused. "What might be a good time for them to come tomorrow? Hmm. I know. How about when hell freezes over?"

It was now or never.

"Because Elliott is Ethan's father?" I hoped the question sounded casual.

"You mean, *biological* father?" Tessa said. "Of course he is. Who else? Whatever you or anyone else at Camden thought, I wasn't sleeping around."

"I didn't think that," I protested. Tessa gave me a look. "Well, maybe a little. But why keep it such a big secret?"

"What secret? You never asked. I assumed you were smart enough to figure it out and didn't mention it because—oh, I don't know." She shook her head and smiled. "Because you're that kind of guy."

I rolled my eyes and we both laughed. I sensed an opening to press the more important issue at hand.

"Then why are you so dead set against Elliott coming back here to check things out?"

"I don't want to risk him seeing Ethan and putting two and two together," she said. "Plus, I haven't been entirely honest with Ethan about his father. I'll cope with that eventually, but now is not the time."

"Isn't it possible that keeping him away might be more likely to raise suspicions?" I asked.

"You're probably right. He's an asshole but not stupid." She sighed. "Okay. Tell them to come. I'll take Ethan to Littleton for the day and you can deal with Elliott and Dowser Duane. But promise they'll be gone by dinnertime."

"No problem. And if he asks about your obvious anger seeing him last night?"

"Tell him it's all about the fucking book," she said. "That should play nicely into his gargantuan ego. And not a word to him about Ethan or I swear I'll have your balls for breakfast." She made a scissors gesture with her fingers as she turned to leave. "Good night, Dekker."

I trudged up the stairs to my room, keeping a watchful eye out for bats. Maybe the rain lulled them to sleep under the eaves. I hoped the percussive tattoo would do the same for me.

Too exhausted to undress and too agitated to sleep, I lay down on the bed. Dammit, Dekker, what is your problem? All things considered, the conversation with Tessa had gone better than I could have hoped. As for the creepiness with the chandelier, it must have been some kind of shared delusion. Tessa's conviction the illusion was real made her capable of making me believe it. *Folie à deux* was the psychiatric term. It's how Willy used to jokingly describe our relationship. "Madness for two," he'd say, like he was requesting a table at a restaurant. It always made me laugh—until Willy got sick and began exhibiting actual psychotic behavior. Not so funny anymore.

Memories of Willy brought me back to the cryptic message Ethan had written in the sand at Crawford Notch. Easily explained, if thought about logically. The boy had simply misspelled the Willey family's surname and had drawn a heart to express his sadness for their tragedy. Nothing more. Certainly not Willy Hart reaching out to me from beyond the grave.

Maybe I was more suggestible than I wanted to believe.

Chapter Thirteen

I. Valraven/Elliott

Valraven sat in Duane's kitchen, waiting for the coffee to percolate on the white enamel stove. The appliances and furnishings looked like they were from the 50s, probably the last time the kitchen had been refitted. The Rafferty homestead was a traditional New England saltbox house with dark weathered cedar shake shingles, and a garage at the end of the long driveway. Occasional mailboxes along the way were the only visible signs of neighbors, their houses set deep in the woods like Duane's. People who lived on Faraway Road took their right to privacy seriously, something Valraven understood and respected.

They'd arrived the evening before as fat drops of rain began to fall. Duane offered to rustle up something to eat, but neither were hungry. He showed Valraven up to a room above the kitchen with a simple single bed where he could "bunk for the night." It was said politely, of course, but Valraven had the distinct feeling that the sooner he was gone, the better. As he had tossed his small knapsack on the bed, he remembered the one change of clothes inside was as grimy and sweat-stained as what he was wearing. He asked Duane if he had a washing machine he could throw everything into overnight. It was on the side porch off the kitchen. Duane also gave him a threadbare robe, several sizes too large for him. It had probably once belonged to the young man's father—or maybe Granddaddy Rafferty. Valraven thanked him and Duane said he'd put the clothes in the dryer first thing in the morning. He planned to get up early and finish off a set of knives he'd been working on for Tessa. Duane pointed out the bathroom down the hall, bid a quick good night, and left Valraven alone. He stripped, pulled on the bathrobe, and gathered the small armload of clothes to take downstairs. The first wave of exhaustion hit when he started the washing machine, intensifying with each step he took back up the stairs. He slipped between the cool sheets. The insistent drumming of the rain on the roof finished him off in seconds.

A solid night's sleep, clean clothes, and the smell of fresh coffee revitalized him. He heard the faint high-pitched sound of metal on stone coming from the garage. Duane sharpening his blades. He decided to bring him a cup of coffee to maybe smooth over the vague sense of unease he'd picked up on last night. He filled two mugs.

Outside, the sun was breaking through the treetops. The air was cooler, damper, after the severe storm. The yard was littered with leaves and small branches pummeled and ripped loose by the heavy rain and strong winds. This was the beginning of the end of the fall foliage season. It was almost mid-October, the first snowfall not far off. Winters always arrived early in New England. He wanted to be back at his cabin in Maine before that happened.

The wide double doors were both open. Duane had his back to him, wearing both headphones and protective goggles as he bent intently over a workbench at the far end of the garage. Sparks flew as a knife touched the grinding wheel, after which he honed the blade in a rhythmic motion back and forth on a flat rectangular stone. A large anvil sat on the floor in front of a forge, generating a surprising amount of heat that could be felt from the doorway. One garage wall was lined with neat rows of hammers, long-handled tongs, pliers, chisels, and other implements Valraven couldn't name. It was the other wall that caught his attention. A vast arrangement of antique axes, ax heads, sickles, scythes, sharp hooks, pitchforks, a rusty scimitar, and other unidentifiable tools carefully mounted or hung from the ceiling. A variety of old, different sized mason jars sat on the sill of a narrow horizontal window at eye level. They contained small animal skulls and bones, speckled birds' eggs, and dried reptilian remains. Several snakeskins were draped on what might've been a hat rack.

An unsettling collection.

"I like old stuff."

Valraven jumped, hot coffee sloshing over the edge of the mugs. He somehow managed not to drop either.

"Jesus, Duane!"

"I'm sorry, Val," he said with a grin. "I didn't mean to startle you. Let me take one of those." He reached for a mug.

They stood together in the garage, avoiding eye contact, drinking coffee without speaking.

"Quite a setup you have here," Valraven finally said, looking around. "I'm not sure what I expected, but certainly not a full-fledged blacksmith shop."

"Oh, it's hardly that," Duane said, blushing. "I barely have what I need to hammer out a halfway decent blade, carve it a workable handle, stitch up a leather sheath, and call it a knife."

"I think you're being modest. I watched you work for a bit. You look like you know what you're doing. Another skill passed down from your daddy?"

"Not so much. Not like dowsing." He paused, shuffling his feet on the hard-packed dirt floor. "Granddaddy gave me a folding pocketknife when I was just a little kid. He said it may not look like much but I had to treat it with respect. 'Every knife has a story,' he said. And I was the one responsible for whether that story had a good ending or a bad ending. I carried that knife in my pocket everywhere until…I don't know. I lost track of it somehow. After Granddaddy passed, I looked high and low for that knife. I broke so many willow rods across my knee, gettin' so god-awful frustrated 'cause no amount of dowsing could help me find that damn knife. Sometimes…a thing just don't want to be found." He heaved a big sigh, shook his head, and continued. "Anyways. Daddy took me to the Lancaster Fair over Labor Day weekend and some guy was doing a bladesmithing demonstration and I thought, I could do that. Like a hobby. Something that was just mine. I could be the beginning of a knife's story, even if I never found out how the story ended." He shrugged. "So I just started learning stuff, trial and error—mostly error. The thing is, once I got good enough, turned out there were a lot of folks in North Country wantin' custom knives. So my hobby kinda turned into a business." He smiled. "Dang it, Val. I don't know how you get me chatterin' like a chipmunk, the way you do."

"You know, Duane, Val—Valraven—is not my real name."

"I sorta figured that out right off the bat," he said shyly.

"Did you now?"

"Yeah. It sounded made up. Don't get me wrong," he added quickly. "I'm not sayin' nothin' against it. People have lots of good reasons for changing their names. I'd just as soon keep calling you Val, if you don't mind."

"I don't mind."

"Good. Now if you'll excuse me, I wanna put a last spit and polish on these knives for Tessa, so we can bring 'em when we go back to Cloverkist. I called her already this morning and she said drop by after lunch. She's gotta take Ethan to a doctor appointment but she'll leave all the keys with Dekker."

"Is her boy sick?"

"She didn't exactly say and I didn't ask. I hope not. Ethan's a good kid, even if he has some dark clouds following him around." Duane returned to his workbench without elaborating.

Valraven took the mugs back to the kitchen, rinsing them out in the sink. He wondered if the doctor's appointment was a ploy to avoid seeing him. He wouldn't be surprised. Tessa had every right to be furious with him for the way he'd treated her—and not just in the book. *Drew fucking Smith fucking Elliott.* He needed to talk to her, try to explain—explain what? Where to even begin?

The book started as a few random jottings, humorous sketches of him and his classmates, the kind of thing they'd read out loud and have a good laugh—when he was ready to show them. When had it turned into a dark secret? When the tone changed from mildly sardonic to viciously satiric? When his cast of characters turned into ridiculous caricatures?

On a whim, he submitted a proposal and a few chapters to an agent in New York, a woman who had gone to school with his mother. After that, everything happened so quickly, it seemed a blur. The interest of a top publisher, a hefty advance, late-night phone calls with an editor, furtive meetings in the city. Evasive answers turned to full-fledged lies. A marketing guru said release it *while still at Camden*—capitalize on the literary *wunderkind* angle. Deadlines came fast and furious; he could barely keep up, let alone think about possible repercussions. Hollywood might option it. A rising director called it the perfect vehicle for his hot young brat pack—whatever that was. Suddenly everyone wanted a piece of *Drew fucking Smith fucking Elliott.* The *New York Times* and *Interview* Magazine wanted exclusive pre-publication access. Were they fucking serious? He wanted to pull the plug on the whole thing. No can do, boy. Contracts signed; careers at stake. Calm down. Take a breath. Finish the term, they said. Take your exams, they said. Details can wait, they said. So he did what they said and said nothing.

To anyone.

He'd wanted to tell them, especially Bernstein. She'd understand. Fuck the nondisclosure agreement. She was his best friend. She knew him better than anyone. She saw past his façade. She'd find a way out of the shit storm, guide him through it. But he'd said nothing. And when the semester ended, he was terrified. No matter what happened with the book, he wouldn't return to Camden. He found the cabin on a lake in Maine, used the advance to pay for it in cash, and disappeared to his own Faraway Road.

II. ETHAN

We look out the window and watch Mom's Friend Dekker help Gregor the Giant load a large package wrapped in brown paper into the car. Calvin watches with us.

It's okay. We whisper in Calvin's ear. Mom's Friend Dekker isn't going with Gregor the Giant. Calvin knows.

We watch Gregor the Giant give Mom's Friend Dekker a big bear hug. Mom's Friend Dekker doesn't hug back. Calvin growls. Gregor the Giant gets in his car and drives away.

We sit on the window seat and count to ten. Our knees bounce up and down, up and down.

Why are our knees bouncing up and down?

We have to wait.

Why we have to wait?

We have to wait for Mom's Friend Dekker.

Why we have to wait for him?

Gregor the Giant said.

What he said?

IT'S A SECRET. WE HAVE TO WAIT.

What's that, Ethan? Mom asks from the kitchen. Mom is making coffee.

MAYBE YOUR FRIEND DEKKER WANTS COFFEE TOO.

Okay. Why don't you go ask him? And you don't need to yell. Mom says.

Let's go, Calvin. We run out of our room and through the kitchen. No running, Ethan. Mom says.

We walk fast out the door. We walk fast down the hall. We walk fast down the stairs. We walk fast through the Chandelier Room. We start upstairs. Calvin won't come with us.

Calvin, come.

Calvin sits. That means NO.

We climb the stairs fast and knock on Mom's Friend Dekker's door.

Mom made coffee.

Why, thank you, Ethan. Tell her I'll be right down. Mom's Friend Dekker says.

We want him to come now but we don't say. It's not polite. Mom says. We go back down the stairs. Calvin waits. He wags his tail.

Calvin, come.

At the front door, Calvin stops and shakes. He wants to pee. We open the door. Calvin runs to the bushes. He pees and kicks his legs. He barks twice at the stone puppies and runs back to the porch. Mom's Friend Dekker waits in the doorway.

Calvin had to pee.

We raise our leg and pretend pee. Mom's Friend Dekker laughs.

Okay, but next time wait for me to let him out. I have to keep an eye on that dog when he pees. Mom's Friend Dekker says with a funny wink.

We giggle and go upstairs to the apartment. Mom sits at the kitchen table with two cups of coffee. We march off to our room. Gregor the Giant's secret lies hidden under our bunk beds. Nobody saw us put it there except Calvin and the fish in the aquarium. We made them promise not to tell. We know how to keep secrets.

III. DEKKER

"What's up with him?" I asked Tessa.

"I was hoping you might know," she said, offering me a cup of coffee. "He's been acting weird since he woke up—weirder than usual, I mean. Did he behave himself yesterday? Last night he told me all about the Pumpkin People. He had a blast. But he's famous for leaving out details he thinks will upset me. Anything like the candy shop incident?"

"Nope. Nothing like that. We had a great day." I decided not to mention the stop at Willey House. Ethan and I were of one mind when it came to keeping certain details to ourselves.

"And did you see Gregor off this morning?" she asked with raised eyebrows.

Before I could respond, Ethan emerged from his room. He was holding the carved wood figure Gregor bought the boy.

"Look, Mom. Ethan the Giant." He held it out proudly.

"May I see?" asked Tessa, with a sideward glance toward me speaking volumes. Ethan handed her the woodcarving tentatively, like he was afraid he might never get it back. She examined it closely. I had the feeling she was looking for a price sticker and hoped Gregor had been smart enough to remove it. The craftsmanship was first-rate, but the piece had been seriously overpriced.

"He's very handsome," Tessa said. "But, Ethan…"

"He wasn't a present," Ethan added quickly. "We're taking care of him until Gregor the—until Mr. Gregor comes back. We swear. He's not a present. Mr. Gregor says."

Ethan looked like he might burst into tears. I wanted to help him out but I wasn't supposed to be in on Gregor and Ethan's secret. She handed Ethan the Giant back to the boy.

"If Mr. Gregor asked you to keep him until he returns," Tessa said, eyes darting between Ethan and me, "then I guess it's okay. He reminds me of your story. Did Mr. Gregor say it was all right if you played with him?" Ethan nodded vigorously. "Well, be careful. You wouldn't want to damage him before Mr. Gregor comes back, right?" Ethan shook his head. "Good boy. Can I have a hug?" She reached out and he threw his arms around her. Another meltdown avoided. Tessa still looked at me suspiciously. I wasn't off the hook yet.

"You know, Ethan," she said, redirecting her attention to the boy.

"It might be nice to do something special for Mr. Gregor to thank him for entrusting you with Ethan the Giant."

"Like what?"

"Hmm. I'm not sure." She smiled. Butter wouldn't melt, as my grandmother used to say. "Any ideas, Dekker? You know him better than we do."

"Um. Let me think." I paused. The last time I'd broached the subject hadn't gone well, to say the least. But Ethan was in good spirits at the moment. It was worth another shot.

"Well, Gregor is really interested in those paintings you found." *Gently, Dekker.* "In Room Thirteen? He'd love to see if there were more."

"No more pictures. Just frames and stuff. From Olden Days," Ethan said calmly.

"There might be something else he could use for his research," I said. "It might not seem important but it could be a clue. We could surprise Gregor with it when he comes back. We could take a look just to see?"

The boy tilted his head one way, then the other, considering the possibility.

"Okay," he said. "We'll show you." He started for the door.

"Ethan," Tessa stopped him. "Show Dekker where it is and come right back. We have to leave for Littleton soon."

"Okay," he repeated. "DEKKER, COME," he said as he left the apartment.

"ETHAN, DON'T BE RUDE," Tessa shouted after him.

"It's all right," I said. "He's imitating how I talk to Calvin." Tessa didn't look convinced. "Calvin, come. See?"

Calvin scooted out the door to catch up with Ethan. I followed, before Tessa had a chance to say anything else.

Calvin stubbornly refused to go up the tower staircase, as usual. I found Ethan standing in the middle of the top-floor landing between Room Eleven, where I stayed, and Room Twelve across the hall. Between the two rooms was the door to the lookout turret. Maybe he called that Room Thirteen? Bookshelves lined the walls and a small desk had been custom-made to fit under the narrow stairs, leading to the uppermost windows and their panoramic views. I remembered finding the Ouija board the young maids had abandoned here. The limited floor space showed no signs of clutter or space for the "frames and stuff" Ethan mentioned.

"So, where's this mysterious Room Thirteen?" I asked, trying— and failing—to sound casual. Ethan raised his arm slowly and pointed to Room Twelve. "Unless you see something I don't, I could swear there's a 12 on that door, Ethan."

He gave me the kind of look all kids use when an adult says something stupid. There was a peculiar darkness in his gaze. If he was deliberately trying to freak me out, he succeeded.

He took two steps toward the door and reached for the knob. He turned it slowly and pushed the door open. The hinges creaked. Ethan entered the room and I watched from the doorway. The only window faced north. I could vaguely see the red barn theater through sheer lace curtains. Diffused light added to the room's gloom factor, another reason I'd chosen to stay across the landing.

Ethan ran his right hand along the molding above the darkly varnished wood wainscoting that wrapped around the walls. In his left hand he held Ethan the Giant tightly against his chest, as if for protection. Halfway along the wall, Ethan stopped. Using two fingers, he pushed against the molding, and an entire panel of the wainscoting popped open like the lower half of a Dutch door. It must have been hinged on the inside because there was no visible hardware.

"Room Thirteen," Ethan said softly, backing away from the secret door in the wall.

"I'll be damned," I said under my breath, pulling the panel open and ducking my head inside. It was more of a crawl space than an actual room, although it would seem bigger to a small ten-year-old. Someone shorter than me might stand against the near wall but the roof angled sharply to the floor, so the navigable space was less than two yards wide. It was dark, dusty, and smelled of old timber. In the shadows at one end I could see the pile of empty picture frames and items more difficult to identify; on the other side, an old trunk sat against the wall. That looked promising, but I didn't see a key in the lock. Attached to the slanted ceiling ahead of me was an ancient light fixture with a bare bulb and pull chain. Unlikely it would still work, but I reached for it anyway.

"ETHAN."

I jumped, my head connecting soundly and painfully with the solid frame of the low door. *Goddamnit, Tessa.*

"GET DOWN HERE. WE HAVE TO GO."

"We have to go," Ethan said, disappearing. I could already feel a good-sized bump rising on the back of my skull, but no sign of blood.

"DEKKER. WHAT DO YOU WANT TO DO WITH CALVIN? I'M NOT TAKING HIM TO LITTLETON."

"I'LL BE RIGHT DOWN." Shit. My head started pounding. This was not how I wanted to begin the day. I'd have to be on my toes with Elliott. But at least I'd discovered where Ethan had found the paintings. Other treasures Room Thirteen might contain had to wait.

"DEKKER, COME."

I didn't know if Tessa was joking, but I trotted down the stairs with my tail between my legs.

From the Diary of Corporal Anson Quimby
13th New Hampshire Infantry Regiment

October 1864

A furlough of fourteen days, including two sea voyages, subject to stormy weather and rough seas, and therefore delays beyond our control, all for the glorious right of Suffrage, does now appear too brief to fully cleanse the noxious scent of gunpowder from so deep within our lungs. If we miss departure of the *Guide* in Boston to return unto the dismal swamps and pestiferous forests of Virginia, the godforsaken blood-soaked battlefields, which have cost so many stalwart Patriots their lives, most sure shall we be promptly put under arrest for absence without leave, even when we could in no way avoid it. Is it madness to risk my career for the sake of my dear friend, who I fear will not survive yet more atrocities such as we have witnessed till now? Every morning Ben walks the rock labyrinth, head held high, back straight, shoulders square, much improved in appearance and weight. The War seems but a distant memory to him now. 'Twas Uncle Phineas who constructed the labyrinth in the field behind Cloverkist, during an extended leave from his mesmerist shows. He told Mother walking the labyrinth would improve her delicate health and do wondrous good for her soul. This displeased Father, who never had appreciated his brother's preoccupation with the spiritual world, and said so at every opportunity, until he at last drove Uncle Phineas away. I was but too young to understand the full nature of their rift. But I see full well the benefit my friend derives from the daily exercise and thoughtful meditation. Ben has also returned to his paints and brushes, filling canvas after canvas with colorful landscapes and barnyard scenes, remarkable in their detail and their lifelike imitations. Every day he embarks with Moze and Doxey, who carry his easel and artist box, to some new location, and every night he continues to work on the pictures by gaslight, in a corner of the barn he has arranged as a studio. A kind of frenzy overtakes him when he is painting, which causes me some concern. Last night he asked if I would sit for a picture, one as like he had not tried before. I am reluctant to refuse his request, for I do not want to hinder his improvement, both of his physical and mental state. As for our young fugitives, we take care to keep them out of sight of passersby. By day, Ben keeps them close at hand, and by night, they sleep in cramped but not uncomfortable quarters in the Tower, above the kitchen, where they often help our Cook, who has a fondness in her generous heart for them.

CHAPTER FOURTEEN

I. VALRAVEN/ELLIOTT

Valraven watched from the loading dock as Duane, Dekker, and the dog headed down toward the labyrinth and beyond. After a cursory orientation tour of Cloverkist, inside and out, Valraven asked if they wouldn't mind leaving him alone for an hour or two. He needed to focus his attention without their preconceived impressions. On the one hand, Dowser Duane had both Tessa's reported experiences and his own, which combined to form his version of what was happening; on the other, Dekker's obvious cynicism was an equally unhelpful distraction. Not to mention his dog's aggressive stance toward Valraven. Animals, in general—and dogs, in particular—had a sixth sense when it came to the spirit world.

But this unprovoked animosity felt personal.

The other reason he wanted to be left on his own required a more complex explanation, if it could be explained at all. Duane thought of him as Valraven or Val, while to Dekker he was still Elliott—an identity he'd abandoned long ago. Elliott had never been party to the spirit world. The return of Elliott wouldn't necessarily diminish Valraven's powers. But the dual personas potentially could become entangled and create confusion at a time when focus was important. Was Elliott's past with Dekker and Bernstein connected to what was going on at Cloverkist? If so, he would deal with those complications when they arose. With so many disparate elements converging in the same place, at the same time, there was always the chance of getting lost in the chaos, unable to solve anything.

Worse, it could prove dangerous.

One thing Valraven knew with certainty. Cloverkist stood at the center of a strong vibrational field. Not as powerful as the vortex in the Southwestern desert or other spiritual locations he'd visited. But an undeniable, deeply rooted confluence of forces was at play around the inn. He had sensed them before he saw the rock labyrinth and remembered the petroglyph of the figure holding a spiral. He stared into the trees, saw the roughly carved lines on the wall anew, and remembered the snarling canine beast at the figure's feet. Without a doubt, this was where he'd been sent. Now to figure out why.

Easier said than done.

He jumped off the loading dock and walked behind the inn toward the old red barn summer theater next door. The windows were covered over with plywood panels also painted red. Each had a vertical and horizontal white stripe like a cross. Energy emanating from the barn pulled him closer. The closer he got, the warmer the afternoon sun felt on his back. Except it wasn't only his back. The air around him was becoming more heated than the low autumn sun accounted for. He reached out to touch the rough-hewn double doors. He knew before his fingers touched the wood that it was hot, hot like it might spontaneously combust. No sign of fire; no scent of smoke. He stepped back from the building. With each step, the air temperature dropped. He'd never experienced anything like this. Clearly, the barn was a relevant factor in what was going on at Cloverkist.

He headed around the end of the inn where Bernstein's apartment occupied the second floor. *Drew fucking Smith fucking Elliott.* On reflection, he was glad Bernstein arranged to be away while he was here. When Dekker and Duane walked him through her private quarters, he'd sensed nothing more than a minimal magnetic hum, emanating from the boy's room. Children sometimes attracted benign spirits who pulled mischievous pranks or lulled them to sleep.

Save the only begotten son.

Could that be the boy? Perhaps. But Dekker was an only child— and an orphan to boot. Duane hadn't mentioned siblings. Too many possibilities. No need to revisit the apartment. He was searching for a stronger presence.

And there they were, sitting just off the shoulder of the road. The two red foxes watched him from tall dry grass. *Volpes volpes.* Most people would think it mad to believe the pair traveled across almost the entire country and managed to precede him. He was relieved to see his faithful guides. He made silent contact with them. They stood, turned, and disappeared up the hill between the gravestones. Crossing the parking lot, he waited for a couple of cars to pass before jogging across the road.

The grave markers were old and weatherworn. He guessed no one had been buried here in decades. With no restless spirits to be seen or heard, he wondered why the foxes had directed his attention to the peaceful graveyard. He trudged up the hill and stood above the few rows of graves, facing the inn. He noticed a distinct chill in the air, cooler than in the morning. Again, a common cemetery phenomenon, but the psychic energy field—more electric than magnetic—was as present on the hillside as he'd felt near the barn.

The significance hit like a thunderbolt. The Barn. The Labyrinth. The Cemetery. Connecting these three vibrational locations formed a triangle, and smack in the center stood Cloverkist Inn. His thoughts raced. The Tower. Add its peaked roof to the equation and you had a triangular pyramid. A tetrahedron. First of the five Platonic Solid Shapes, representing the element of fire and containing great power to link the physical and spiritual worlds. Energies directed from the three corner points—Barn, Labyrinth, Cemetery—into the top of the pyramid—Tower—could create limitless healing capabilities, per psychic lore.

Unless something—or someone—was either blocking or tapping into it for purposes other than good.

❖

The front doors were locked, so Valraven walked around back to the loading dock. As he passed the covered pool he felt hackles on his neck rise, an odd sensation—more canine than human. He pulled himself up onto the loading dock and walked through the kitchen. The new set of sharp knives Duane fashioned for Tessa were laid out on the counter. He paused when he got to the staircase. Through Room One's open door he saw the painting that art guy brought up from Boston, leaning against the wall atop a bureau. Dekker thought the picture of the nude man looking out the bay window could be a significant clue, but Valraven wasn't convinced. He climbed the staircase to the third floor and continued up the steep narrow stairs leading to the lookout tower. The window at the top of the stairs faced the cemetery. The south-facing window provided a picturesque view of the blue-tinted White Mountains. He could see down to the labyrinth from the west window. The fourth window faced the barn, but that wasn't what caught Valraven's attention.

A slender young man sat perched atop the tallest of several square brick chimneys, staring off into the distance. He wore battered boots, threadbare trousers, some kind of paint-spattered smock or apron, and an old military-style cap. Civil War, maybe? He turned his head slowly, making direct eye contact with Valraven. His deep-set eyes widened in surprise when he realized he could be seen.

POOF.

And he was gone.

II. CALVIN

one boy jumping / calvin jumping / two
     boys jumping more&more
one boy running / calvin running / two boys running more&more
hiding seeking finding barking
two boys laughing / calvin wagging
evermore&evermore

III. DEKKER

"Mom. Can we take Calvin to play in the maze?"

"If it's okay with Dekker." They looked at me for permission. I nodded and Ethan took off at a run, Calvin at his side.

"BUT ONLY ROUND THE MAZE," Tessa shouted. "DON'T WANDER OFF. DINNER WILL BE READY SOON!"

"WE WON'T WANDER," Ethan yelled over his shoulder, disappearing behind the pool.

"Quite the reunion," Tessa said, getting bags of groceries from the back of her SUV. "You'd think we'd been gone a month, not an afternoon."

"Calvin was very annoyed with me when I said he had to stay."

"Annoyed with me, you mean," Tessa said.

"Oh, no. I always get the blame. He lay on the porch pouting the whole time we showed Elliott around."

"Grab the rest of those groceries," she said, ignoring Elliott's visit.

"Sure. Inn kitchen or your kitchen?"

"All mine. The inn kitchen is closed until further notice," she said. The front door slammed behind her.

One thing hadn't changed. Tessa Bernstein was the most obstinate person I'd ever met. Wasn't she the least bit interested in what Elliott discovered? Not that I'd be able to explain it. Yes, he'd seen something but didn't want to elaborate until he was certain of the significance. He'd launched into some psychobabble song and dance about electric or magnetic vibrations and solid geometric shapes with Cloverkist in the center. Something about a vortex and cave drawings he'd seen somewhere else. I couldn't make sense of it, although Duane seemed to follow his confusing rant with interest. Maybe he just pretended to understand. He was completely under Elliott's spell. I knew that look.

I spent three years at Camden with that stupid look on my face.

Ethan's distant laughter carried along a chilly late afternoon breeze. The storm had left fallen leaves and cooler temperatures in its wake. The autumn colors were losing their vibrancy and too soon winter would descend on North Country. I grabbed the remaining bags of groceries from the back of the SUV, pulled the rear door shut, and brought them inside. My steps on the hardwood floorboards echoed as I walked down the long empty hallway past the vacant rooms. Without the buzz of guests and staff, the inn felt smaller and darker, more claustrophobic. Eager for the light and warmth of Tessa's apartment, I picked up my pace.

I set the bags on the kitchen table. She busied herself putting away groceries, closing cabinets and drawers with more force than necessary. Was she annoyed with me or with the situation in general? To break the awkward silence, I opened Calvin's bag of dog food and poured kibble into his bowl. He'd moved in full-time with Ethan. Tessa put two pots of water on the stove to boil.

"What's for dinner?" I asked. I had a feeling I wasn't invited.

"Mac and cheese—from a box—and frozen green peas—also from a box. Not the most nutritious meal. But I just don't have the energy for a mealtime battle of wills. Don't judge me, Ethan likes this shit."

"I didn't say a word," I said. "I like mac and cheese."

"Oh." Tessa turned to me. "Were you planning to eat with us? I assumed you would've made plans to meet your old college buddy for dinner. Have a laugh about old times. Old friends."

"Whoa, Tessa." The general annoyance *did* include me. I tried to stay calm. "Nobody's having a laugh at your expense. And you say that as if I had something to do with Elliott being here. You know I didn't. You asked me to have him gone by the time you got back. I did. You told me not to say anything about Ethan. I didn't. I don't understand why you're so pissed off at me."

"Jesus, Dekker," she sighed, shaking her head slowly. "I'm not pissed off at you. I'm pissed off at the whole fucking universe. I came here for a fresh start and everything was great at the beginning. I didn't know what the hell I was doing and I figured it out. Like I always have. Like I did at Camden, until I couldn't anymore and I went home to live with my family. That was fine until Ethan was born and they started driving me nuts. I held it together until my inheritance kicked in and headed west to Colorado. A single mom and her kindergarten kid against the world. We were nailing it, until the shit hit the fan with the PTA and I ran again. So here I am. We survived the crazy busy summer. We won over most of the crazy local bigots. We made friends with the crazy restless spirits. Or at least I thought we had, until a month ago when the crazy wasn't funny anymore and you showed up and everything got worse and Drew fucking Smith fucking Elliott appears out of nowhere and I want to scream because I feel like I'm right back where I started and this is not how my fucking life was supposed to turn out."

I didn't know what to say. Ethan and Calvin burst through the door.

"WE'RE HUNGRY," he said, laughing.

"Oh, we're hungry, are we?" Tessa transitioned back to fun-loving mom instantly. "All I have to do is add macaroni to this pot of boiling water, green peas to this pot of boiling water, and dinner will be ready in a jiffy."

"MAC AND CHEESE AND PEAS."

"Indeed," Tessa said. Her smile turned into a concerned frown. "But where's Ethan the Giant?"

Ethan's mouth opened, but he said nothing.

"Did Ethan the Giant stay in the car?" Tessa asked.

Ethan hung his head, muttering something under his breath.

"I'm sorry. I didn't hear you."

"We left him at the maze."

"Well, I don't think Ethan the Giant wants to spend all night out in the maze, do you?"

Ethan shook his head without looking up.

"I think someone whose responsibility it was to take care of Ethan the Giant should run outside and bring him in before something terrible happens to him."

Boy and dog slunk out of the room. The patter of six feet picked up speed and ran down the hall.

"You're terrifying," I said, adding quickly, "A terrifyingly fantastic mom."

"Ethan and I understand each other—most of the time. It's a high wire act. That's why Elliott mustn't know."

"About that..." I started. "Elliott says he thinks he can help but he needs to spend more time here."

"No."

"Maybe just one or two nights, he said."

"Absolutely not."

"He could stay in the room across the landing from mine. He wouldn't have to come anywhere near your apartment."

Tessa started to laugh.

"You're so transparent, Dekker, I can see right through you. We want the exact opposite. You want to rekindle your long-lost first love."

"What?"

She was laughing harder. "Do you think we didn't know? Everyone knew you were in love with Elliott from the day you met him. Nobody wanted to mention it, so we watched and we waited. You still haven't gotten over him, have you?"

"I don't know what you're talking about."

"I always wondered why you were such a minor character in the book. So many missed comic opportunities with the virginal lovelorn farm boy. Maybe the feelings were reciprocated. Maybe that was Elliott's secret. The Drone was a big closet case."

"You're not making any sense."

"I think I'm making a lot of sense. I think you arranged this whole coincidental meeting. Did you track him down, Dekker? Did you arrange to meet here? Did you tell him I owned Cloverkist? How many secrets are you juggling in hopes of finally getting to suck Drew fucking Smith fucking Elliott's cock?"

I couldn't respond. I headed for the door.

"I don't want him back here, Dekker. NOT FOR ANOTHER MINUTE."

I walked down the hall in a daze, her voice ringing in my ears. I almost didn't see Ethan and Calvin when we met halfway. He held up the woodcarving for me to see.

"We found Ethan the Giant. Nothing terrible happened."

"That's good," I said. Something terrible *had* happened, something I couldn't explain to him. "Enjoy your mac and cheese and peas. And, Calvin, dinner's in your bowl."

"MAC AND CHEESE AND PEAS. MAC AND CHEESE AND PEAS," he chanted, marching down the hall.

Calvin stood still for a moment, looking up at me. I bent down and gave him a quick cuddle.

"Go on, now. I'll be okay." He didn't look convinced. "Go." And he did.

To be honest, I wasn't entirely convinced. How much of what Tessa said was true?

CHAPTER FIFTEEN

I. DEKKER

I called Dowser Duane first thing in the morning, telling him we have to hold off on Elliott coming back to the inn. I didn't say why.

I didn't have to.

"Just as well. We ain't goin' nowhere today," he told me. "Last night, damned if we didn't hit a deer. I saw the light reflect off her eyes but before I even touched the brake, she jumped out right in front of us. Dead before she hit the road, and my truck's smashed up pretty bad. Val helped me lug the carcass onto the bed of the truck and somehow I got her started up again. We barely made it home but that truck is dead as that doe now."

"You brought the deer home?"

"Yup. Val helped me field dress her and we hung her up to drain. Tell Tessa we'll have a heap of venison steaks later if she wants. And I'll save some bones for Calvin, too."

I told him I'd relay the message and get back in touch tomorrow. At least I'd been spared the gory details of field dressing a deer before having a cup of coffee. The aroma of fresh brew pulled me into the kitchen once I hung up the phone. I poured a mug full and leaned against the counter.

I wanted a cigarette but I'd left them upstairs. There was probably a pack in the glove compartment of the Jeep, but I didn't feel like looking for them. More pressing issues were on my mind. I'd gone to sleep last night pondering what Tessa'd said, waking up with the same thoughts whirling around in my mind.

Of course I hadn't gotten in touch with Elliott and arranged to meet him at Cloverkist. I hadn't thought about him in years. Yes, I'd asked Jefferson if he knew what became of our most famous classmate. He didn't know. No one did. The consensus was drugs were involved. But Jefferson and I had never seen Elliott do drugs—and Jefferson had been his roommate. But neither of us had the slightest inkling he'd been writing a book, either. "Who knows what other secrets he was keeping?" Jefferson had shrugged.

Indeed. Elliott had always been secretive about his comparative studies. Had he been dabbling in the spiritual world at Camden?

Apparently I had no talent for secrets. *Everybody knew...you never got over him...you still haven't.*

No. Tessa was wrong about that, too. It took a while, but I *did* get over him. I forgot him once I met Willy. Why did Tessa's accusations send me into such a tailspin? I was just as shocked as she'd been to see him again after ten years. Ten years that looked good on him. Was that what set Tessa off? Yes, Elliott was hot.

This was getting me nowhere fast. I had a few other important things to deal with that did not have to do with my screwed up sex life. I wanted to investigate Room Thirteen but that had to wait. I'd promised Ethan we'd turn Ethan the Giant into one of the Pumpkin People. Ethan would be busy with his homeschool work until lunch. The pumpkins we bought on the way back from Jackson were still in the back of the Jeep. As I went outside to get them, I said a little prayer inspired by the Charlie Brown comics of my own childhood.

Please, Great Pumpkin. If you exist, help me find a way to not disappoint this little boy. Why did I promise him we could make Ethan the Giant climb the Tower?

Drenched in sweat, by noon I had gathered all the bits and pieces I could think of and was ready—I hoped—to build a giant. Everything was laid out on the square patch of grass in front of the Tower. I found two ladders behind the inn: a regular straight ladder and a taller A-frame ladder with an extension. That was my *Eureka!* moment, when I saw how the whole thing could come together.

Thank you, Great Pumpkin.

I retrieved a roll of Dahmer bags from the laundry room, a length of clothesline, and a package of clothespins. I discovered a plastic storage container full of hideous brown and green plaid curtains in the linen closet, obviously destined for the dumpster. I took a couple of flattened cardboard boxes from the loading dock, where I also found a shovel and a toolbox, complete with hammer and nails, a staple gun, gaffer's tape, a roll of wire, and a ball of twine. From the kitchen I borrowed a heavy pair of scissors, a sharp knife, and a black Magic Marker, which reminded me I had black shoe polish in my room.

I took a quick look into Room Thirteen while upstairs. I grabbed a dusty old moth-eaten lampshade with remnants of fringe. Though I was eager to conduct a thorough investigation of Ethan's secret hideaway, it could wait. Last but not least, I took two of the highchairs for babies or toddlers, stacked in a corner of the Hunt Room. These items joined the four huge pumpkins, lined up on the side porch. I only needed three. Nice to have a spare in case of an accident, though. The extra one could be carved into a jack-o'-lantern when we got closer to Halloween.

After a quick cigarette, I mapped out the basic structure. I set up the A-frame ladder flat against the windowless front side of the Tower, raising the extension ladder in the center to a total height of about twelve feet. The proportions looked right, so I climbed the ladder and tied the length of clothesline to a rung near the top. I scrambled back down, took the shovel, and marked the placement of the ladder's feet. I wanted to sink them into the dirt a few inches so the ladder would be stable. I stood under the ladder, laid it on the ground, and dug the four holes.

Before raising the ladder back into position, I had to figure out a few measurements. I estimated how many Dahmer bags I needed for the trousers and how to lay out the curtains to make a shirt. I needed to mark the pumpkin that would sit atop of the extended part of the ladder. I brought the largest one over, placing it on its side next to the top of the ladder. The pumpkin's diameter was wide enough to accommodate the two carved holes needed to secure it. I made sure the balance was right so the weight of the pumpkin wouldn't pull the whole structure down. To be on the safe side, I decided to attach the ladder to the side of the building. Gaffer tape and a staple gun might do the trick. The rest I'd play by ear.

All I needed was the help and imagination of one small boy.

II. ETHAN

Mom comes down the stairs. We tell her to stop.

Before we go outside you have to close your eyes.

What's all this about, Ethan? Mom says.

It's a surprise.

I don't like surprises, Ethan. You know that. Mom says.

It's a good surprise. Sometimes surprises are good and sometimes they are not. We worked hard to make a good surprise. Mom's Friend Dekker said we did a good job. He said we have artistic talent. We don't know what that means. We smiled and said thank you. Always be polite. Mom says.

MOM, PLEASE. YOU HAVE TO CLOSE YOUR EYES OR IT WON'T BE A SURPRISE.

OKAY. Mom says. Mom closes her eyes tight. We stick our tongue out at her to check. She doesn't see us. Or else we'd be in big trouble.

We take her hand and open the front door.

Keep your eyes closed.

I am. Mom says.

We lead her outside onto the porch. We lead her to the corner.

Careful. One step, two steps down. Keep your eyes closed. We're almost there.

We lead her a few steps toward the bushes for the best view.

Mom's Friend Dekker is on his knees waving his arms in the air and pretending to be scared. Calvin gives him a funny look but we try not to laugh. We let go of Mom's hand and get on our knees with Mom's Friend Dekker. We pretend to be scared, too. Everyone will be scared of Ethan the Pumpkin Head Giant.

All ready, Mom?

Ready as I'll ever be. Mom says.

ONE. TWO. THREE. OPEN YOUR EYES.

AAAAAAAAAARRRRRGH. Mom's Friend Dekker screams.

AAAAAAAAAARRRRRGH. We scream.

AAAAAAAAAARRRRRGH. Mom screams.

Calvin is barking at everyone screaming. We roll on the grass screaming and laughing and screaming and laughing more and more. Mom is laughing, too.

Did we surprise you?

Surprise me? You terrified me. Mom says. Or your giant terrified me, I should say.

He's Ethan the Pumpkin Head Giant. A good surprise.

Ethan the Pumpkin Head Giant is absolutely amazing. Mom says. She takes a closer look and shakes her head. Dekker, where did you— how did you—

We helped.

He sure did. He was responsible for the important parts. Mom's Friend Dekker says.

We made his pumpkin boots black with shoe polish. We cut the cardboard for his hands. We used the Magic Marker to paint the face on his pumpkin head. Dekker put his lampshade hat on top because we couldn't reach. The fringe is his hair.

Well, you both did a fantastic job. Mom says. You really are the Pumpkin People. She winks.

WE ARE THE PUMPKIN PEOPLE. WE ARE THE PUMPKIN PEOPLE. We sing and we jump. We do a silly dance. Calvin jumps and wags his tail. Mom and Mom's Friend Dekker laugh. We all hold hands and sing and dance together.

WE ARE THE PUMPKIN PEOPLE. WE ARE THE PUMPKIN PEOPLE.

III. DEKKER

Once I'd tidied the yard and returned the leftover materials and tools to where I'd found them, I could finally get to my other project. Room Thirteen. Tessa said we could all go to the Dairy Bar for ice cream. She was extending an olive branch. I thanked her, saying I wanted to take a little nap after I finished cleaning up. Did she mind taking Calvin with them? I slipped Ethan a five-dollar bill and told him Cal would love a kiddie-size soft vanilla cone.

I retrieved a hammer, a screwdriver, and a heavy-duty flashlight before putting the toolbox away. I didn't need anything else for a minor case of breaking and entering that old chest.

I opened the low door. A dank, musty smell filled my nostrils, much stronger than before. I gagged, thinking about a century's worth of bat guano. As I suspected, the light fixture didn't work—either the bulb had blown or the wiring had been chewed up by rats and other vermin. Fortunately, the flashlight worked not only for light but for clearing away the myriad ancient cobwebs crisscrossing the raw timber beams. When I finished searching the space, I'd need a long hot shower.

The trunk was locked and there was no key. I tried pulling it toward the door, thinking it would be easier to open if I moved it out of the claustrophobic crawl space and into Room Twelve. But it wouldn't budge, like it had been nailed to the floorboards. Why would someone do that? I had to sit and work on the lock where it was. I grabbed the screwdriver and inserted the flat tip between the metal and the wood to pry it loose. Maybe being so old, the whole thing would simply crumble. No such luck. Back then things were made to last. I'd wanted to do as little damage as possible, but no one would be the wiser if I took more drastic measures. Placing the flashlight on the floor, I held the screwdriver in my left hand, picked up the hammer with my right, and began bashing away at the lock. After a few minutes, my shoulders and arms ached. I tried to stretch but there wasn't enough room. I paused before trying again. In frustration I slammed the hammer against the lock with all my strength. Nothing. In the silence, I heard a soft *pop.* I raised the lid like the chest had never been locked at all.

Using the flashlight, I looked inside. There wasn't much to see. I pulled out a folded rough blanket, a few pieces of clothing—possibly a Civil War uniform—and a cap that looked familiar. Otherwise, the trunk was empty. No paintings, no treasures, no clues, no nothing. Damn. It didn't make sense. Why go through all the trouble to lug a heavy chest up three flights of stairs, stow it in a secret attic crawl space, nail it to the floor, for fuck's sake, lock it, and throw away the key?

Just to hide a few articles of clothing?

Look again. The softest whisper of air tickled my ear. *Look again.*

I looked inside the trunk again. Something was wrong. The chest was lined with brown paper. I examined the chest. The dimensions seemed wrong. The inside was not as deep as the outside of the trunk. A false bottom? I began ripping the paper lining out. The glue was old, so it didn't take long to reveal a hardboard panel, wedged into the bottom. I picked up the screwdriver and pried it loose.

Yes. Beneath the false bottom was a box, also wrapped in brown paper. I gingerly lifted the package out. It was heavy. My body tingled. I didn't want to open it in the dark of the crawl space. Cautiously, I carried my newfound treasure out of Room Thirteen and into the light.

From the Diary of Corporal Anson Quimby
13th New Hampshire Infantry Regiment

October 1864

I wrote a letter to Miss Sarah Low, the nurse from Dover who was so generous of spirit during my recovery in Washington. I cannot but think it too bold, and yet she is never far from my thoughts since first we met these many weeks ago. I began to be troubled that she may ask of me and hear perchance some idle gossip or rumor regarding my absence, though I fear this may be but wishful thinking on my part. I desired to inform her, or so I wrote, of my delayed return to the Regiment. I expounded little, only to say my friend was in a poorly condition and feared he might worsen should he undertake the long journey, even as he would not see me depart alone. It pained me to be untruthful to her, but the complexities of our predicament are too difficult to put into words. Now the letter is sent, it is too late for regrets. As regards Ben, he wanted to visit his mother. I hoped seeing her would bring him some cheer, but she was much distraught by his ill health and beseeched me not to let her dear sweet Benjamin return to that bloody conflict, lest she lose him, her only son, for all Creation. I assured her I would not, for she would accept no other reply, even as I knew the extreme danger of doing so. For if I returned without him, questions would surely be raised, and I fear a warrant would be issued for his immediate arrest and imprisonment, as befits any deserter. And I have grave concern such severe punishment would serve him no better than the battlefield. Best we remain together, until I can muster some better solution. Back at Cloverkist, I relented and posed for the picture he was eager to begin work on. He asked me to sit in the bay window of the sitting room, in a relaxed fashion, and look out toward Possum Pond. And so I did for an hour or more as he sketched in silence. I had thought he would use his paints but he said he must let his pencil have free rein to capture what he called the essence of the vision in his head. In the end, he filled several sheets with what looked to me to be random arms and legs, hands and heads, bearing no relation one to another, as well as numerous framed landscapes with little or no resemblance to what I saw through the window. Why he should need me to sit for those sketches, I could not understand. I have no knowledge of the workings of an artist. I only know the feverish process served to calm my friend in a way that I was unable to accomplish. When he was done, he rolled the sheets together in his arms and rushed out of the room, presumably to his studio in the barn, where overnight he would turn them into a painting fit for hanging on a wall, or were he not pleased with the result, better fit for the fire.

CHAPTER SIXTEEN

I. DEKKER

Gently, I set the package on the bed in Room Twelve and knelt beside it to examine it more closely. The plain brown paper looked the same as the chest's lining. I unwrapped the package with greater care, delicately unfolding each flap to not to tear the brittle paper.

I wasn't expecting to find a massive antique Bible.

It looked like the one Van Gogh painted, belonging to his clergyman father. Done shortly after the man's death, Vincent had paired the open Bible with Zola's *The Joy of Life*. Never underestimate the depth of an artist's daddy issues. Like the Dutch family Bible, the one before me was leatherbound but more elaborate, with ornate embossed patterns on the cover, shiny gilt-edged pages, and a decorative bronze clasp holding it shut.

Why would someone go to such great lengths to hide a family Bible? I couldn't imagine nineteenth-century New Hampshire was a hotbed of religious intolerance. Bibles often contained ancestry information, a family tree. Maybe scrutiny of the family's lineage would reveal skeletons in the closet? Even if it had nothing to do with the paintings, I was eager to investigate further. But there was a catch.

Literally.

The attractive bronze clasp had been crudely but securely soldered shut, making it impossible to open the Bible. A secret definitely lurked within its pages. But I didn't want to cause even minimal damage to such a beautiful antique. It might be worth a great deal—secrets or not. That's when I heard Tessa scream my name.

❖

When I reached the apartment, Tessa stood in the middle of the smoky kitchen, holding a fire extinguisher. Something had been on fire.

"In there," she said weakly, motioning toward Ethan's room.

I stepped inside. The room was full of thicker, more acrid smoke. The source was clear. Fire extinguisher foam was dissipating, leaving trails of wet streaks down the wall below the singed wooden frame. The thin paper of the grave rubbing had burned completely, leaving no trace of Benjamin Chapman's death marker.

Only a blackened spot on the wall remained.

"What happened?" I asked Tessa.

"You tell me," she said. "I was fixing dinner and Ethan was playing with Calvin. At least, that's what I thought until he raised his voice, like he was arguing with someone. 'We can't,' he said. 'We have to,' he said. Back and forth, back and forth, louder and louder. He started to shout, 'NO. NO. NO.' Calvin began barking. I shouted, 'Knock it off in there.' And then it got quiet. Too quiet. I looked in and Ethan was just standing in the middle of the room, staring at the rubbing, which was smoking. All of a sudden it burst into flame like—what do you call it? Spontaneous combustion? I pulled Ethan out of the room, told him to take Calvin and wait for me outside, and grabbed the fire extinguisher. That's when I called you. What the hell is going on?"

I glanced out the window. Ethan was looking up at me. He was sitting on the ground, one arm around Calvin's neck and holding Ethan the Giant in his other hand. I waved and he waved back. I opened the window.

"Everything's okay. I'll be right down. Just wait there, okay?"

"WE'LL JUST WAIT HERE. OKAY?" He threw his head back and laughed.

I gave him a thumbs-up and turned back to Tessa.

"I'm as confused as you are. I keep trying to connect the dots, see the big picture. But none of it makes sense. What if there's no picture to see? What if all the pieces belong to different puzzles that got all mixed up in the same box?"

Tessa simply stared at me.

"Okay," I said, inhaling deeply. "Let's take this one step at a time. You said the rubbing burst into flame when you went into the room. Right?"

"Yes," she said. "But what if I hadn't been so close? What if I'd been in the laundry room or something? Ethan could've been—I swear to Christ, if anything happens to my son, I will burn this fucking place down myself."

"Whoa, take it easy. Nothing's going to happen to Ethan. We need to focus. Could this be somehow related to what happened the other night? In the Chandelier Room?"

She looked at me blankly.

"You know. That stunt with the chandelier? Flames. Light bulbs. Flames. Light bulbs."

"What are you talking about?"

"Come on, Tessa. You know." I snapped my fingers, imitating what she'd done.

"Jesus, Dekker. I'm losing my freaking mind here and I need you to be the normal one. So please, don't mock me or whatever it is you're doing. It's not helping."

Perhaps not *folie à deux* after all. Madness for one?

"Get him back here," Tessa said in a low voice.

"Dowser Duane?"

"No, not Dowser Duane. He's a sweet kid and I've let him do his thing, but seriously?" She shook her head. "Not very effective. I mean Elliott. You said he thinks he can help? So let him try. Let him stay the night, a week, I don't care, as long as he fixes this. Let's see if he's capable of doing one decent thing in his fucked-up life. And, Dekker. Do me a favor?"

"Anything," I said.

"Take Ethan down to Granny's for a toasted cheese sandwich. I want to get this place aired out before the stink soaks into the timber. I'll let him sleep with me tonight. Deal with clearing up his room in the morning."

"Sure. I'll take him."

"And, Dekker?"
"Yes?"
"What I said still goes. Not a word to Elliott or..." She mimed scissors.
"Gotcha."

II. CALVIN

watching ethan silent sleeping
tessa tensing tossing sleeping
calvin watching both protecting
burnman come&gone
waiting watching never sleeping
and another never sleeping
both protecting ever silent
burnman come&gone

CHAPTER SEVENTEEN

I. VALRAVEN/ELLIOTT

Valraven watched Duane, hunched over his workbench. Dekker paced around the garage. Dekker called early to say Tessa relented—a telling word choice—and they should return to Cloverkist soon. When Duane explained his truck was still in the shop, Dekker drove over to pick them up. He also had a more mechanical problem Duane might be able to solve, something to do with a jammed lock. Duane told him to bring it over and gave him what sounded like complicated directions. Sure enough, it took Dekker considerably longer to reach Faraway Road than his rides with Duane.

"Dammit, Dowser Duane," Dekker said upon arrival. "Could you live any deeper in the sticks?"

"Are you kidding?" Duane laughed. "This is downright suburban compared to where my Uncle Jacob lives. He built a place way up yonder beyond the ridgeline at the end of an old logging skidder road. The perfect spot to train his hounds. He's the finest tracker in North Country."

"Tracker?" Valraven asked.

"Yessireebob. His dogs will hunt down a wounded deer or moose or even bear for miles until they find 'em. And Jacob finishes 'em off for no extra charge. We get a lot of flatlander hunters up here who don't know shit about tracking, pardon my French." He actually blushed. "Now where's that book? Bring it on in and we'll have a little look-see."

Dekker retrieved a package from the back seat of his Jeep and laid it on the workbench, where he unwrapped it reverentially. Valraven understood why when the contents were revealed. The Bible shimmered amid the much humbler items around it. A strikingly beautiful objet d'art, at least nineteenth century, and in perfect condition. One didn't have to be religious to appreciate the high level of craftsmanship that had gone into its creation.

Dekker pointed out the brass clasp holding the Bible closed. Duane examined it and shook his head.

"I don't know, Dekker. It looks pretty messed up. I'm not sure reverse soldering will work on this old hasp. It'd be a lot easier to pull out two of these little pins attaching it to the covers."

"Oh." Dekker bit his lip. "I don't want to damage the covers if at all possible. Could we at least try to do it some other way?"

"I'll give it a go," Duane said after a brief think.

As Duane gathered the tools he'd need and started working on the clasp, Valraven coaxed Dekker to tell him where he had found it and why he thought it might be significant. Though reluctant, Dekker told him about finding the trunk in a storage space and discovering the false bottom where the Bible had been hidden. What secrets it might hold or why they might be important, Dekker honestly didn't know or was being deliberately reticent. Valraven didn't push too hard. He wanted to get back to Cloverkist first.

"Bingo!" Duane shouted. Dekker rushed to his side. "Your Bible is ready to open. I jus' wanna wait for the metal to cool down and check if the clasp will still click closed and open again. But I think it's good to go."

"Dowser Duane, you're a genius!" Dekker said, reaching for the Bible. But Duane stopped him.

"No. I fixed the clasp. But someone went through a heap of trouble to seal it shut. I don't know why and I don't need to know. Leastways not now. Not here."

"Pandora's Box," Valraven said. Duane nodded.

"Something like that. A spell of darkness passed over me while I was working on it." He looked at Dekker. "I'd just as soon you opened it elsewhere." He tinkered with the clasp for a moment before handing the Bible to Dekker. "You take care now." He headed out of the garage.

"I'll swing by and see how you're doin' when my truck is fixed," he said, not looking back.

❖

Dekker backed the Jeep out of Duane's driveway and onto Faraway Road. Valraven sensed Dekker was annoyed, but he understood Duane's reluctance to have anything more to do with the antique Bible. He wondered if he could help Dekker understand. It wasn't long before Dekker gave him the opening he had waited for.

"You know, I like Duane and all but he's weird."

"How so?" Valraven asked.

"Come on, Elliott. Pandora's Box? Really?" He snickered. "As if opening a book was going to release a host of evil spirits intent on destroying mankind? Seriously. I took the same Greek mythology course you did. Remember?"

He did but didn't want to get sidetracked by that memory.

"It's more complicated for Duane. Duane is an empath. He's keenly aware of other people's emotional states."

"I know what empathy is, Elliott."

"Being empathic is slightly different, more intuitive. In Duane's case it extends beyond individuals. He can sense psychic energies from objects as well—a rarer gift."

"I'm not sure I'd call soaking up someone else's emotional baggage a gift. More like a curse."

"A gift often feels like a curse, Dekker. I know from experience."

Valraven willed Dekker to ask the next question. If Dekker believed he could tease out his old friend's story, maybe he would open up in return. Valraven knew Dekker was holding back. Dekker had information Valraven needed, but it had to be given freely. The goings on at Cloverkist undoubtedly involved them both. Why else the significant alignment of their arrivals? *Volpes volpes.* It might take both of them to defeat whatever entity was pulling the psychic strings. The young man he'd seen sitting on the chimneytop was the most likely candidate. But who was he? What did he want?

"Just to be clear," Dekker said, his voice tight. "When you say 'gift' you're not talking about some generational hand-me-down like

Duane's dowser DNA. I assume you mean your own—I don't even know what to call it. Epiphany? Manifestation? Some late-twentieth-century New Age variation on The Great Awakening? WHOA!"

He slammed on the brakes, stopping just short of hitting a moose standing in the road. The massive animal looked in their direction, stamped its hooves, and emitted a hoarse bellow before lumbering off into the woods. Dekker pulled over, switched off the ignition, and turned to Valraven.

"Okay. You've got my attention now. Tell me your story."

Not exactly the question he had expected; more a demand than a request. And yet the belligerent tone indicated a high degree of skepticism toward anything Valraven would say. He needed Dekker to understand, and he needed him to listen.

"I saw Shelly," he began.

"I wondered if he might have managed to track you down before he died," Dekker said.

"No. He didn't. I saw him after—after he died."

"You went to his funeral?" Dekker looked confused.

"No. Nothing like that." Trying to explain events in the metaphysical realm left Valraven struggling in the best of circumstances. He'd started out on the wrong foot with Dekker and now had to backtrack.

"Let me try another way—and hold off on your questions until I'm through. Okay?"

Dekker shrugged.

"So, before the book came out I moved to this secluded cabin in Maine. Middle of nowhere; totally off the grid. I didn't even read about all the hoopla until later—much later. I just hiked around the lake, sat and stared across the water, tried clearing my head of everything. On good days, I thought I might be getting somewhere by doing nothing, going nowhere. Anyway, in the fall—past peak—I start having this dream. At least, I thought it's a dream. I was standing near what look like abandoned railway tracks, coming right out of the woods and across a rusty trestle over a lake or a wide river, fading into the mist before they get to the other side. Other people are around but everyone looks a bit uneasy; no one knows why we're there. A loud blast signals the train's approach. It bursts through the trees and speeds past us. We see the passengers, hands pressed against the windows, screaming, screaming for help. Some turn away, others watch as the train disappears into the thick fog. I closed my eyes for only a second and when I open them, I'm back at the cabin and the sun is rising. The same thing happens every night. Less people show up to watch, and more turn away, as the train disappears with a growing number of passengers, mostly young men, pale, thin, and frightened. I want to help but I don't know how. One night I'm at the tracks alone and I hear the train's whistle and yell as it passes, 'What can I do?' Someone yells back, 'Stop this motherfucking train!' I recognize that voice. It's Shelly. I catch a glimpse of him as the train heads into the all-consuming mist and I knew he was dead. They were all dead. Souls trapped on a train to nowhere. The next night I know what to do. I stood on the tracks, legs spread, arms open wide, and I waited for the train. It came hurtling out of the forest. I waved my arms and screamed, 'Stop!' It didn't stop. It passed through my physical body, train and passengers. I felt every one of them passing through me, screaming, and when the last car of the train passed my body, Shelly was left standing before me, laughing. 'Elliott, you always gotta do things the hard way.' And somehow I mustered the energy to laugh with him."

"Shelly said that?" Dekker asked in a low voice. Valraven nodded. "I can hear him saying it, laughing the whole thing off like it's some cosmic joke. I miss Shelly."

"It wasn't all fun and games," Valraven said. "Shelly had a great deal to teach me and didn't have much time. He explained how so many young men were dying, so quickly, so unprepared, with so few guides to help them cross over. All one had to do was answer the call and the rest of the pieces would fall into place. Shelly said a soft word, a light touch, or sometimes a gentle human hug was all a soul needed to find the path and see the welcoming White Light. Could it really be so simple, I wondered. 'Most times,' Shelly said. 'But you'll have practice enough before the hard cases come knocking on your door. Most times it's no more difficult than a goodbye kiss.' He smiled, brushed his finger along my cheek, and with a wink he disappeared."

"Huh. That's it?" Dekker asked. He didn't sound convinced.

"That's how it began. Yes."

"And when you roll out this story, is it always Shelly? Or do you choose someone else so it always has that personal touch?"

"I don't 'roll out' my story very often," Valraven said, keeping a lid on his temper. "When I do, it's always Shelly because that's who was there. Believe me or don't, but spare me the sarcasm."

Dekker started the Jeep and pulled back onto the road without another word.

Valraven felt a tingling sensation in his palms. He glanced down and saw a faint redness. Nothing serious. Although the conversation had not gone as well as he'd hoped it would, he was certain Dekker needed to know the basic truths—maybe more. That could wait until he'd digested what he'd already heard and was receptive to further information. But not long.

Valraven had a feeling time was running out.

II. DEKKER

I had to give Elliott credit. He was a hell of a storyteller. For a while he had me in the palm of his hand, right there in the forest by the train tracks, waiting for his mysterious ghost train. Shit. I was ready to hop on board. Then he took it that step too far, like always, and threw in all that stuff with Shelly. Why? Why turn it into something personal? Same as that stupid novel—a perfectly good story idea, used like a weapon to eviscerate his friends, people he'd at least pretended to care about. Maybe that was the key. He didn't care about anyone but himself. Tessa had said the same thing. Elliott was a classic sociopath—intelligent, manipulative, and dangerous. And this sociopath sat in the seat next to me as I drove him back to where I lived. Sound familiar?

It's not déjà vu if it really happened before.

Driving always relaxed me. Even doing only twenty miles per hour on narrow twisty roads cutting through a colorful canopy of trees. The tension eased out, my breathing slowed, and my anger dissipated.

Elliott wasn't evil. Elliott was an asshole. He didn't care if anyone else believed in his so-called gift. Did what I thought matter as long as Elliott believed? Given half a chance, Tessa would believe him. Tessa had asked me to bring him back in case he had the power to protect her boy. That was the bottom line—keeping Ethan safe. It's what Elliott would want, too, if he knew the truth about his son.

I felt uncomfortable even thinking that. Could he read my mind?

Did telepathy go hand in hand with helping dead souls cross over? Better focus my thoughts elsewhere. I knew things that might be helpful for Elliott. I wasn't sure why I'd been keeping them from him.

"Benjamin Chapman," I said, breaking the silence. "If there's a ghost who's been haunting Cloverkist, I think he's an artist named Benjamin Chapman. He may have been killed in the Civil War. I'm not so clear on that."

I told Elliott about Ethan's gravestone rubbing, and what the boy later said at the Horse Cemetery. *Maybe that's why he's so angry.* I told him about the paintings—the one Gregor brought to the inn and the ones Ethan found in Room Thirteen.

"We haven't figured out yet how all of this fits together," I explained. "Or why one painting got separated from the others. Maybe none of it has anything to do with what's happening at Cloverkist. But there's another reason why we think Benjamin Chapman might be behind it all." I told him about the grave rubbing bursting into flame.

"And this happened yesterday?" Elliott asked.

"Yes. That's when Tessa got worried and asked me to bring you back."

"You said the boy found the paintings. The boy chose which gravestone to do the rubbing. Am I right?"

"Yes."

"Whether he knows it or not, the boy is a conduit. He's made some kind of contact with this Benjamin Chapman fellow. I need to talk to the boy."

I should've seen that coming a mile away. Of course Elliott wanted to talk to Ethan. Of course Tessa would never allow Ethan to talk to Elliott. Dekker would be stuck in the middle, as usual—unless I could arrange an "accidental" meeting between Ethan and Elliott. Maybe at Room Thirteen? Tessa rarely went up in the Tower. It might work.

"Wow. That's impressive," Elliott said.

It took me a second to realize he wasn't prying into my thoughts but referring to Ethan the Pumpkin Head Giant. I had to agree as I pulled into the parking lot. With the plaid curtain shirt billowing slightly in the breeze, it almost looked like he was breathing. Even in broad daylight, he gave me a serious case of the creeps.

❖

I installed Elliott in Room One, having changed my mind about putting him upstairs across the hall from me. I checked in with Calvin, patiently waiting for Ethan to finish his lessons. Elliott wanted to take a shower and Calvin wasn't ready for a walk, so I had a few minutes to settle onto my bed with the Bible. I removed the brown paper wrapping, set it aside, and paused for a moment to admire the hefty book's elegant beauty. I ran two fingers along the smooth gilt-edged pages.

I opened the Quimby Family Bible—that was the name inscribed on the brown leather cover. The front endpapers were illustrated with a simply drawn tree, with many intertwined branches filled with names going back generations. The Quimbys' ancestral past didn't interest me so much as the last name in the family line: *Corporal Anson Quimby, born 21st of March 1840.* His military rank had been added at a later date, in different ink. Given the date of birth, he was probably a Civil War soldier. There was no death date, indicating he was probably not a war casualty. The missing date also pointed to the corporal as the probable suspect who'd gone to such great lengths to hide the Bible. But why?

I turned the page and found an engraving depicting King David spying on the bathing Bathsheba. It was an odd choice for the frontispiece of a Bible. The lurid picture surely wasn't reason enough to out-and-out banish the Holy Book. On the title page, block letters read "The Self-interpreting Bible by the Rev. John Brown." The old Civil War marching song popped into my head. *John Brown's body lies a-mouldering in the grave...* I doubted it was the same John Brown, but it made my flesh crawl. *His soul is marching on!*

I closed the Bible and put it on the bed. I stood up, giving myself a good Calvin shake to get the song out of my mind. More than a little spooked, like I wasn't alone in the room. What had Dowser Duane said? Something about darkness passing over him when he was working on the locked clasp? Ridiculous. This was just an old book, hidden away for some unknown reason that probably had nothing to do with anything happening now.

Why was I not convinced?

I looked back at the Bible and noticed something I hadn't seen before. A sliver of something purple peeked out between the pages close to the binding. I knelt by the bed to get a closer look. The tail end of a ribbon bookmark, marking a relevant Bible verse. I took the piece of ribbon tightly between my thumb and forefinger. Gently, slowly, I pulled it toward the middle of the book. I lost my grip as the ribbon started to disappear between the gilt-edged pages. I opened the Bible to where I thought was the right place. No ribbon. I turned a few more pages, and a few more. I still saw the tiny edge of the bookmark sticking out, so I turned a few more pages. And there it was—the Bible's secret. Not a particular passage of scripture. Quite the opposite.

What I found was a whole lot of missing scripture.

The middle of the pages had been cut away to form a neat rectangular compartment within the Bible, containing something wrapped in yellowed cloth. A handkerchief? The initials A.Q. were delicately embroidered in the center. Anson Quimby. Who else? Heart pounding, holding my breath, I pulled the object from its hiding place. I sat on the floor, untied the rough string wrapped around the object, and let the handkerchief fall into my lap.

I thought it was another book at first, brown leather covers like the Bible but softer, thinner, and without any engraved designs. It was more like some kind of wallet. It held a fair number of folded papers filled with neat handwritten lines. I assumed they were letters, but realized it was a diary, Corporal Anson Quimby's diary, dated June 1864, the same year on the paintings.

The same year Benjamin Chapman died.

I nearly jumped out of my skin when I heard the creak of a hinge. I looked over and saw the door slowly opening.

"Elliott?"

I closed the folder, quickly slid it under the bed, and closed the Bible. I wasn't ready to share my discovery yet. I stumbled toward the door. When I opened it, I saw the landing was empty. Across the hall, the door to Room Twelve was slightly ajar. I heard a faint rustling from inside. Had Ethan finished his schoolwork and come up to play in Room Thirteen again?

I crossed the hall and listened at the door. Nothing. I pushed it open. The entry to the crawl space was not closed shut as I had left it. I pulled the low door open and stuck my head inside. Nothing moved among the dim shadows.

"Ethan?" I said softly. Not a sound. To my right I saw that the soldier uniform and cap still rested on the floor next to the trunk where I'd left them. I heard a barely perceptible flutter and felt the graze of a bat's wing on my cheek as it flew past my face and out through the door. I gasped, and again, my skull connected with the hard wood doorframe. I saw stars before they disappeared into blackness.

III. VALRAVEN/ELLIOTT

Valraven wrapped a large soft towel around his waist and emerged from the steamy heat of the bathroom into the warmth of the main room. Lighting a fire before taking a shower had been a good idea. Maybe it was time he broke down and installed a water heater in his cabin. Living off the grid was one thing, but why deprive himself of hot running water? It was such a good remedy for clearing the confusion in his head.

He grasped the poker hanging on the side of the black wrought-iron firewood rack and stoked the burning embers. Sparks danced and disappeared up into the chimney as he added logs to the flames. A roaring fire this early in the season—not to mention in the middle of the afternoon—seemed indulgent. But the temperature inside Cloverkist felt colder than outside—not unusual considering the astral factors currently at play.

Valraven crossed the room and sat on the cushioned window seat, leaning back against the smooth wood trim. He closed his eyes, feeling the dappled afternoon sunlight play on his face, and opened his mind to the free-flowing melodies of Bach's *The Well-Tempered Clavier*. He didn't need his vintage recordings of João Carlos Martins on piano. He'd been listening to them before he was born. While pregnant, his mother attended a concert of the young Brazilian at Carnegie Hall. They'd become the musical accompaniment to his childhood. He could recall them at will—especially the fugues, their simplicity entwined in complex contrapuntal voices.

He often summoned them when faced with a challenging task. The music focused him, freed him from the distracting noise of the everyday world and everyday complications. The music might help him untangle the multitude of threads converging on Cloverkist from so many different places in space and time.

Save the only begotten son.

Interpreting even seemingly direct messages from spirits was never easy. He remembered the two messenger spirits that appeared to him in the Southwest, pointing him in this direction. Assistant Surgeon RJ Sibald had been more talkative, but his chatter was the forlorn self-pitying variety. Or was it? What had he said about the soldier he couldn't help? The one brought to him by a friend? The meeting had taken too much out of him to remember it with any clarity. And Duane's friend at Motel 6—he wouldn't forget her any time soon. But her role didn't seem connected to the rest of the story, certainly not with the spirit he had seen so briefly sitting atop the chimney. The artist?

The timeless preludes and fugues continued casting their musical spell over Valraven. He set the spirits aside for a moment to focus on the living, the players assembled at Cloverkist, setting the stage for whatever was about to happen. Bernstein arrived first with her son. Her only son? Dekker said she'd bought the inn and taken up residence before summer. He didn't say from where or why. Did that matter? Duane said he'd dropped by not long after her arrival to welcome the newcomers and offer his dowsing services. He said stories of Cloverkist Inn being haunted circulated for years. The sound of footsteps, unexplained knocking, or whistling in the kitchen—all benign stuff. A simple cleansing always helped. But when summer turned to fall, the paranormal activity took on a more pernicious quality. What caused the escalation, which started before Dekker showed up?

Valraven didn't believe in coincidences. The unplanned reunion with his two college friends had to be significant. Yet nothing came to mind, nothing that made sense. They had both been in love with him when he left Camden without explanation. What could that have to do with Cloverkist?

What was he missing?

The painting. That museum curator brought the painting home, in a sense. The painting by the young artist buried in the cemetery across the road, the young artist he'd spotted from the Tower. The painting of a naked young man who sat in the window seat where Valraven was sitting. Who was the young man in the painting?

"Anson."

Valraven turned, startled by the whispered voice. Dekker stood in the doorway, a lopsided grin contrasting with the fire reflected in his eyes.

"Jesus, Dekker! Maybe knock, next time?"

"Corporal Anson Quimby." Dekker tipped the vintage military style cap atop his head.

"Corporal who?"

"Anson Quimby. The figure in the painting," Dekker said, with a sly wink.

Valraven hadn't voiced his question aloud. Had he?

"The resemblance is uncanny." Dekker crossed the room unsteadily, like he'd been drinking. He removed the cap and placed it on Valraven's head. "Almost perfect." Cupping Valraven's chin with one hand and the back of his neck with the other, Dekker angled his face toward the window, fingers cold as a corpse. Dekker wasn't playing games. This was someone else, someone inhabiting Dekker's mind and body. The artist? Who else? Clearly, a powerful entity. Spirit possession was a rare phenomenon, not to be taken lightly. Forcing it out against its will could be dangerous for Dekker. Best to play along.

The intruder took a few steps backward, feeling comfortable in Dekker's skin. Valraven watched as the spirit of the dead artist surveyed the scene he had painted so many years ago. A mixture of emotions flickered across his face, melancholy to puzzlement to anger.

The room temperature dropped, despite the fire still crackling in the hearth. Valraven felt too exposed, sitting in the window with just a towel wrapped around his waist, the dead artist staring at him without seeming to see him. He rose carefully off the seat and spoke in a soft voice.

"Getting a little chilly in here, Dekker," Valraven said. "Let me get dressed and we can talk more. We have a lot of catching up to do."

He moved toward the bathroom but with unexpected agility, the spirit darted across the room and blocked his way.

"What's your hurry, soldier?" The lascivious tone was unmistakable, the attempt at a grin menacing. Tugging the towel with considerable force, he spun Valraven around and snapped the towel in the air like a whip. Before Valraven regained his balance, he was being flung naked onto the bed. Dekker's body landed on top of him. Ice-cold hands pinned his wrists to the mattress. Such was the spirit's emotional fury, he had difficulty maintaining control of Dekker's facial features.

"Why?" the spirit screeched, his fetid breath filling Valraven's nostrils. "Why did you have to kill me?" Using his feet, the dead artist spread Valraven's legs apart, ground his hips into Valraven's crotch, dry-humping him. No amount of twisting or turning could release Valraven from the deathly grip. The spirit let go of Valraven's wrists, grabbed his hair with both hands, and pushed their mouths together, forcing a long frozen tongue between Valraven's lips and down his throat, blocking his ability to breathe.

There was nothing for Valraven to do but use force, dangerous as it was. He summoned all his psychic strength and blasted the spirit with a nonverbal scream.

GET OUT! he commanded. *GET OUT OF DEKKER THIS INSTANT OR I WILL SEND YOU DOWN TO THE FIRES OF HELL TO BURN FOR ETERNITY!*

Spirits usually responded to such threats. The dead artist was no exception. Valraven felt Dekker's weight lift into the air above him and he rolled out from under his friend's body. He sensed more than saw the spirit disengage from the corporeal plane into a diaphanous ectoplasmic state. The ghostly substance disappeared into the fireplace and up the flue, leaving an angry sputter of sparks in its wake.

Dekker fell face first to the bed with a heavy thud. Valraven turned him on his back. Dekker was not breathing. Valraven pushed firmly on the middle of his chest half a dozen times with no response. He took a deep breath, pinched Dekker's nose, and tried mouth-to-mouth resuscitation.

Still no response.

"Come on, Dekker. Breathe." He continued chest compressions. He took another deep breath and blew air forcefully into Dekker's mouth. Nothing. Valraven was about to try again when Dekker coughed weakly. His eyelids fluttered, opened, and he smiled.

"If we're going do this right, shouldn't we both be naked?"

IV. DEKKER

With the inn closed for the time being, Tessa and the staff had pretty much cleared the walk-in of perishable food, so there wasn't a great deal of choice. I found a rasher of bacon, eggs, butter, cheese, potatoes, and onions—enough for a simple omelet and some home fries. I lit the burner under a large cast iron skillet, threw in some butter, and pulled a knife from the magnetic strip on the wall. I grabbed a cutting board and small metal bowl from under the counter. I gave the potatoes a quick scrub in the sink and was about to start slicing them when I heard a loud bark from the dining room. Calvin bolted in through the doorway, tail wagging, and greeted me with a nose placed firmly into my crotch.

"Hey, buddy, I missed you, too."

Ethan burst into the kitchen.

"Calvin wants to go to the maze with us."

"Oh, he does, does he?"

"He does," Ethan said, giggling.

"What are we burning today?" Tessa asked from the doorway. The butter in the pan had turned brown and was starting to smoke.

"Oh, shit." I grabbed the pan, dropping it when it burned my hand. "Shit. Shit. Shit. Shit."

"Mom's Friend Dekker sweared," said Ethan, still giggling.

"Run your hand under cold water," Tessa said.

"Of course," I said. "I'm such an idiot. I'm sorry."

"No problem," said Tessa. "What were you planning to do?"

"Rustle up an omelet and home fries for me and Elliott. We had quite the afternoon, which I'll tell you about later." I glanced toward Ethan.

"How about this for a deal? I'll do the cooking and you take Ethan and Calvin out to the maze for half an hour."

"That's a deal I can live with—if you don't mind cooking for us."

"Get out of here. And do me a favor. Tire them out."

"Mom's Friend Dekker will tire us out," said Ethan. "Calvin, come."

I started following them out through the loading dock but stopped at the door. Tessa was unrolling the leather case of new kitchen knives. She pulled the longest knife from its sheath and turned it so light reflected off the shiny blade.

"Dowser Duane," I said. "A man of many talents."

"Yes," she said softly, never taking her eyes off the knife. "Looks sharp enough to cut bone."

❖

"Today we did social studies. We like social studies." Ethan was in a talkative mood. He and Calvin marched through the maze, taking turns leading.

"I'm surprised you like social studies," I said. "I thought social studies was boring."

"Oh, no! Mom always makes social studies fun. Today we learned about jack-o'-lanterns."

"Really? That doesn't sound like anything I learned in social studies."

"Yes. When the Irish ran out of French fries to eat, they came across the sea to America. Nobody liked them because they were always hungry. The Irish made jack-o'-lanterns out of pumpkins because the turnips were too small. People thought they were funny so they liked the Irish then."

An interesting perspective on famine and immigration.

"What did turnips have to do with jack-o'-lanterns?"

Ethan gave me an exasperated look.

"Now pay attention," he said, imitating his mother. "There might be a pop quiz. Back in Irish Olden Days, there was a lazy blacksmith named Stingy Jack, who drank too much and stole people's money. So the devil decided it was time for him to die. When the devil came to take him down to the fires of hell, Stingy Jack tricked the devil." He paused, eyes widened for dramatic effect. "So he couldn't go to heaven because he was a bad man. He couldn't go to hell because even the devil can't break a promise. So he put a burning piece of coal inside a turnip and wandered the Irish land forever. The end."

"I still don't get it. Why a turnip?"

"BECAUSE IN OLDEN DAYS THE IRISH DIDN'T HAVE ANY PUMPKINS!"

I was beginning to see signs of a meltdown early enough to prevent them from happening.

"Well, I'm sure glad they found those pumpkins here. Otherwise, we'd have to call big Ethan out front the Turnip Head Giant." Ethan rolled his eyes.

"ETHAN! DEKKER!" Tessa shouted from the loading dock. "COME INSIDE. NOW!"

Ethan quick-marched up the stone steps toward the inn, Calvin at his heels. As I started to follow them, Calvin stopped, turned, and looked up at the only Room One window facing the back. Hackles raised, he emitted a low growl. Elliott stood at the window, gazing down at us with an odd expression. I waved, but he didn't notice. I couldn't see what captured his attention. I tapped Calvin to get him moving and he responded with an uncharacteristic short angry bark at me before running to catch up with Ethan.

It dawned on me I would be in more trouble with Calvin than with Tessa if I let Elliott anywhere near the boy.

From the Diary of Corporal Anson Quimby
13th New Hampshire Infantry Regiment

October 1864

I am in such unbridled Turmoil, I know not where to turn. I fear my simple belief unfounded, that Ben suffered only the trauma of War, dire though the condition may be, one from which he would eventually make a steady recovery and return to his robust self. His latest actions find purchase beyond the realm of what one doctor called the result of "long-continued overexertion, with deficiency of rest." To be most clear: he has reached a stage I can only describe as nothing less than bald-faced, full-fledged Lunacy. I should never have indulged his mad fancy for me to sit for that damnable picture. And were more proof required, the overly dramatic arrangement he attended to for the unveiling, as he called it. He sent Moze and Doxey to accompany me to the studio. Before we stepped inside the barn, one of the boys gave me a bandana, instructing me to wear it as a blindfold. With some reluctance, I did so, and the boys led me inside. When they let go my hands and scurried away, Ben stood close in front of me and took my face in his hands and kissed me full on the lips, in such a way as no two men should do. I pulled away as he lifted the blindfold from my eyes. The picture sat on an easel, unframed but for the soft light of a lamp that illuminated it, the rest of the barn in darkness. By the Lord, I thought myself dreaming as I stared aghast at the ungodly image before me, the image of a man sitting in the bay window of the sitting room, a perfect facsimile of the manner in which I had sat, except for the man being naked as the day we are born, a Union cap perched on his head. I knew not what eldritch magic possessed him to paint such a picture. Even now am I loath to remember the words I spoke, or attempted to speak, so did my rage increase with each inflammatory incitement. Ben knelt beside me, clung to me, implored me to see beauty in the love he had worked so tirelessly to portray. I threw him off and demanded he destroy the abomination so no other eyes should ever rest upon it, or behold a righteous Judgment descended on him. I stormed out of the barn, past the two boys cowering in a corner, still shouting oaths, arms flailing like a moonstruck scarecrow in the field. I will write no more about the incident, and even now I pray these pages never be read by any living soul, such is the abject humiliation that enshrouds the very depth of my being. God help Benjamin Chapman, for much as I have attempted to do so, I must accept the utmost conclusion that I cannot.

CHAPTER EIGHTEEN

I. DEKKER

"Get back up here as soon as you can and bring everything you've got about the painting and the White Mountain School." I stood in the Red Rum Room talking to Gregor in Boston. I called him as soon as I'd woken up and dressed.

"Fine. Make copies. And if you can't cancel your meeting this afternoon, drive up first thing tomorrow. That'll give you time to find whatever you can on nineteenth-century figurative male nudes. Thomas Eakins and anyone else you can think of. If this diary is authenticated, we've maybe happened on a great discovery about early American art."

Gregor asked if he should bring Willy's painting back with him. I told him it was probably safer at the museum. We'd deal with that later.

"I miss you," Gregor said softly, as I hung up. I'd have to nip that in the bud, especially if we were going to work together on a paper.

This was going to make one hell of a story for the art history world.

I made a pot of coffee, thinking about all the pieces falling into place. I wasn't sure what to believe about my alleged attack on Elliott. Spirit possession? I had no memory how I got from my room upstairs to Room One, or the unsettling events Elliott described. Waking up in his bed with him hovering over me naked was something I might've experienced during my hard-drinking days in Amsterdam. And sleeping with Gregor? Could that have been another instance of Benjamin Chapman inhabiting my mind?

When I'd brought Elliott the light supper Tessa prepared for us, he was still looking out the window. He spoke without turning.

"Who was the Black boy with Ethan?"

I froze, holding the two plates. "Who was the who?"

"Ethan must have mentioned him," Elliott said. "They appear to be good friends."

"Tessa said he had an imaginary friend, but what makes you think he's Black?"

"I saw him. He's anything but imaginary. From his clothing, I'd say he died a long time ago."

"A child ghost? Like Casper?" I laughed, setting the plates on the window seat.

"Why not?" Elliott turned to me. "Children die and their spirits move on—or not—same as adults. I have a strong feeling he's a protector spirit, watching over Ethan, much like your dog. The question is who or what are they protecting him from?"

"Benjamin Chapman," I said, more statement than question.

"A likely candidate," Elliott said. "But it doesn't have to be someone dead."

"Come with me. There's something I think you should see." I led Elliott across the hall and through the Chandelier Room. I avoided the kitchen, in case Tessa was still clearing up. I peeked through the kitchen doorway, relieved to see Tessa was gone. Enough for one day that she'd made supper for Elliott. Baby steps.

"Look at this."

Elliott joined me in front of the painting with two boys playing in a barn. He stared at the canvas as I switched on the lights.

"That's him," Elliott said, pointing to one of the boys. "Ethan's protector spirit."

The two boys did appear to be dark-skinned. No way did it explain how Elliott could know such a thing.

"Be as skeptical as you like, Dekker, but that's the boy I saw outside with Ethan. And that's the child I need to talk with—not Ethan. He probably knows very little, if anything, about what's going on. This boy has spent a long, long time at Cloverkist and I'm sure he knows a great deal. Can I get him to tell me?"

"Room Thirteen," I said. "That's where you'd most likely find Casper, the friendly spirit."

Elliott smiled. "Not a bad idea. We'll make a believer out of you yet, Dekker."

Elliott said he wanted to eat and turn in early to get a good night's sleep. He said he'd need all his strength to deal with what was to come. I didn't ask any questions. I took my own food upstairs, eager to read pages of Corporal Quimby's diary. I hadn't been disappointed.

I poured a cup of coffee. Elliott would probably want some, but I'd yet to hear any sign of life from Room One. I also needed time to decide how much I should tell Elliott of what I'd learned from the diary so far. Keeping secrets at this point might be counterproductive, but the two boys in the painting must be the fugitives Anson and Benjamin smuggled to New Hampshire. If Elliott was right, one of those boys had died and been hanging out at Cloverkist ever since. Moze or Doxey? Did it matter? I wanted to hear what Elliott discovered when he attempted contact with the spirit child. The less information I gave him in advance, the more I might trust what he learned.

I took my coffee out to the porch for a smoke. A thick fog hung in the damp morning air, obscuring anything beyond the Jeep in the parking lot—including the creepy old cemetery across the road. I remembered a book we'd all read at Camden. *Cloud-Hidden, Whereabouts Unknown.* It was a bunch of metaphysical crap, easy to buy into at that age. Maybe Elliott had taken it more seriously than the rest of us.

My coffee had gone cold. I'd thrown on a hooded sweatshirt but the mountain air was colder than anticipated. I could see my breath, and it wasn't the cigarette smoke. I'd need my leather jacket to take Calvin for a walk. I took a last drag, crushed the butt into the retro ashtray standing by the door, and went inside.

I'd missed Calvin's company as he'd spent more and more time with Ethan. His somewhat aggressive show of affection in the kitchen indicated maybe he felt the same. A long walk while Ethan did his schoolwork would do us both a world of good.

II. CALVIN

waking watching waiting dekker
knowing dekker coming
wagging walking sniffing sitting

knowing dekker coming
waiting dekker more&more

two boys sleeping restless dreaming
calming two boys sleeping
calming watching waiting dekker
hearing dekker coming
standing wagging more&more

III. DEKKER

I knocked lightly on the door to Tessa's apartment and opened it a crack. Calvin's nose appeared, pushing the door open, jumping up on me.

"Hey, Calvin! Nice to see you, too." He slobbered dog kisses under my chin.

"He knew you were coming," Tessa said. "He's been waiting by the door for at least ten minutes. How do they know?"

"All dogs are psychics. Calvin, hold your horses. We'll go out in Two Minutes." I held up two fingers. "Two Minutes. Wait here while I talk to Tessa." He heaved a dramatic sigh and curled himself down in the middle of the doorway, in case I tried to leave without him.

"I don't know about psychic," Tessa said. "But he's the smartest dog I've ever met."

"Tell me about it. You'll be interested to know he has a lower opinion of Elliott than you do."

"Dekker, I'm sorry. I don't know where all this is coming from. It's been ten years, for fuck's sake. And some of the things I said to you..." She shook her head in dismay.

"Hey, you didn't say anything I didn't deserve. Same goes for Elliott. But that's not what I wanted to talk to you about. Do you have more of that coffee?"

"Of course." She poured me a cup and topped off her own. I draped my jacket on the back of a chair, and we sat together at the kitchen table. The door to Ethan's room was closed. I assumed he was still asleep.

"Elliott thinks there are at least two ghosts haunting Cloverkist."

"Jesus fucking Christ! Two?" Tessa laughed.

"One he said is a child spirit. A young boy."

"Oh my God. Ethan's invisible friend?"

"Um...possibly?"

"Is he dangerous? Does he want to hurt Ethan?"

"No. Elliott says he's a protector spirit, keeping Ethan safe."

"Safe from what?"

"Maybe from the other spirit. The artist. Benjamin Chapman."

"Chapman?" Tessa looked confused. "The name on the gravestone rubbing? That burst into flame?"

"One and the same. Or so Elliott thinks."

"And he's dangerous? To who? To Ethan? Why?"

"We're still trying to...to work all that out but..." I took a deep breath and gave her an abbreviated version of my "spirit possession" and waking up in Elliott's bed with him giving me mouth-to-mouth resuscitation. "Anyway, that's Elliott's story and he's sticking to it."

"Why was he naked?" she asked.

"I don't know why. I...I didn't ask," I stammered. "I was kind of distracted by the whole, you know, possession...thing." She smirked at me. "Give it a rest, Bernstein."

"Just yanking your chain."

"Thanks. What I really wanted to ask—when did Ethan start speaking in first person plural?"

Tessa thought for a moment. "After we moved to Cloverkist," she said. "That's right. Never in Colorado, I'm sure of that."

"And his imaginary friend. Does he have a name?"

"Moose," Tessa said. "Ethan muttered it as he was falling asleep your first night here. You asked me about it. Remember?"

"Right. Moose." Moose...Moze. Too close to be coincidental. "Could it be Moze?"

"I suppose so," Tessa said. "Is that the spirit child's name? How does Elliott know that? Has he spoken to him?"

Goddammit. I didn't want to tell Tessa about the diary yet. With his usual impeccable timing, Calvin yawned an audible admonition signaling Two Minutes were up.

"Look, Tessa," I said, grabbing my jacket and heading for the door. "It's like we have all these pieces but none fit together yet, and we don't have a box with a picture on the cover to help us. But we'll get there. Despite what you think of Elliott, I think he's going to find out what's going on and make things right once and for all. Hang in there and trust us."

"Thank you, Dekker. Tell Elliott whatever he needs, just ask. I don't give a shit about our past." She shrugged. "I do believe he can help us. I do. Now get out of here. Both of you."

Calvin trotted off down the hall, expressing his need to go out with an impatient bark when I got to the front door. I didn't check on Elliott since I'd slipped a note under his door before going up to see Tessa.

Out with Calvin. Coffee in kitchen. Help yourself.

Calvin jumped off the porch and rushed to the shrubbery, raising his leg high and making a big show of relieving himself. I pulled on my jacket and zipped it up against the crisp air. I'd forgotten Calvin's leash but we didn't need it. The mist was dissipating. We could take the well-marked trail behind Cloverkist Ethan had shown us, down past Painter's Palette and along Possum Pond to Granny Stalbird's. I'd order breakfast to take back for Elliott. I was in the mood for American-style waffles and bacon with maple syrup.

I started down the stone steps when I realized Calvin wasn't following me. I looked around. He stood by the Cloverkist Inn sign, looking across the road toward the cemetery intently.

"Calvin, come on. We're going this way."

Cal gave me a glance, shook himself, and continued staring in the direction he wanted us to go. It was a habit I'd let him develop in Amsterdam, deciding which park he wanted to explore on any given walk. It was impossible to change his mind once he'd made it up.

Who's the Alpha?

Fine. There were several houses tucked back along the other side of the road down the hill toward Granny's. Whether there was a trail through the woods behind them or not, I didn't think we could get lost. Especially if we stayed within earshot of road traffic. At this hour large logging trucks making a fair amount of noise chugging up the steep hill were the only vehicles.

I trudged through the parking lot, empty except for my Jeep and Tessa's car. Odd that Elliott didn't have his own vehicle. A lot about Elliott was odd. I joined Calvin and we crossed the road. He showed no interest in scenting the cemetery's long dead, choosing to walk along the perimeter fence. I regretted giving in to his demand. My chosen walk was mostly downhill. Calvin's choice meant trekking uphill before coming across a trail that might lead us down to Granny's. Calvin seemed to know exactly where he wanted to go. He barked at me to hurry up, darted between two tall fir trees, and disappeared into the woods.

"Hey, Calvin, wait up!" I didn't expect he'd go far without keeping me in sight but I wasn't sure he could resist chasing off after a rabbit or a deer. And what might happen if that bear was still in the neighborhood? I moved fast as I could. When I stopped to catch my breath between the two trees, I saw Calvin patiently waiting for me in the middle of a well-worn path.

"Good boy," I gasped. It was enough for Cal to turn and lead us on, head high and tail wagging. He knew exactly where he was going. At least he continued at a slower tempo, stopping here and there to investigate an interesting scent.

Once my heart rate returned to normal, I began enjoying the beauty of the fall foliage among the pockets of mist still settled in the woods. Although the storm of a few days ago had blown many branches bare of their leaves, hardier varieties still sported shades of red, orange and yellow, contrasting with the abundant dark green conifers. The freshness of pine perfumed the air. The trail was soft, covered with dry needles and fallen leaves.

Elliott had revealed little about his life. A cabin in Maine, the discovery of his so-called gift, the burning of his books—not much to account for the ten years since we'd seen each other. Could royalties from book sales keep him flush enough not to have to work? I knew he'd grown up in a wealthy New York City family. Maybe an inheritance he lived on? But no relationships? No friends? Was he an actual hermit living all these years alone in the woods?

But how much had I told anyone about my ten years in Amsterdam? My relationship with Willy? My close encounter with a serial killer? Elliott and I were not that different. In college we'd been polar opposites. What brought him to Cloverkist? I didn't buy into the coincidental meeting with Dowser Duane in Boston. I'd managed to track down Tessa. Couldn't he have? Maybe I was the one he had tracked down. I hadn't considered that. What could he possibly want from either of us? Unless…did he somehow know Ethan was his son? If so, Elliott was one hell of an actor. He hadn't shown the slightest hint he knew he was the boy's father.

None of which had anything to do with the supernatural shenanigans going on at Cloverkist, why Dowser Duane had brought Elliott here to do whatever it was that Elliott did. Maybe I was wrong about withholding information in the diary from him. The more he knew, maybe the sooner things could get back to normal. That would be better for Tessa, Ethan, and everyone involved.

We could deal with the personal shit later—if we had to.

I was so wrapped up in my thoughts I hadn't paid attention to where Calvin was taking us. I stopped dead in my tracks. I was in the middle of a clearing, and not a natural one. Directly in front of me stood a tall, curved stone staircase, built over three arches. The stairs led nowhere, literally disappearing into clouds. There were partial remains of walls and a few square columns, some of the stonework overgrown with thick ivy or covered in moss and lichen, but most rocks were bare of any vegetation. Had this once been someone's home, it would have been a private castle. More likely it was a folly, an ornamental mock-Gothic ruin popular in the nineteenth century. Maybe it was on property once belonging to Cloverkist. I thought of the labyrinth behind the inn. This spot had the same enchanted, magical feeling—even more so, with the pockets of mist hanging in the air.

The kind of place that would spark a ten-year-old boy's imagination.

A glint of sunlight reflected off a cellophane wrapper from a package of peanut butter crackers. Ethan's favorite snack. Had Calvin been here with Ethan? Tessa would shit a brick if he'd strayed this far from the inn on his own. I'd have a talk with Ethan before saying anything to Tessa.

My stomach growled. I'd forgotten all about waffles and bacon. I didn't trust Calvin to find the shortest route through the woods to Granny Stalbird's. Better retrace our steps back to the inn and drive down.

"You hungry, Cal? How about we go back and get some breakfast?" He barked his approval. Off he went the way we came, as if that had been the plan all along.

IV. VALRAVEN/ELLIOTT

Valraven savored the last bite of waffle, followed by the last strip of crispy bacon—a far cry from his usual morning handful of dry granola and nuts. When Dekker arrived with the food, he'd said breakfast was a specialty of the nearby diner, and he wasn't wrong. Comfort food indeed, nourishing the body and warming the soul. Over the last years, Valraven had grown unaccustomed to being treated with kindness and generosity. Dekker refused to let Valraven pay for the meal, adding Tessa didn't want anything for the room, either.

Dekker told him about his discovery of the diary hidden in the Bible that Duane had helped unlock. It confirmed what they had pieced together so far, as well as what Valraven had learned from the Civil War medic RJ. The two soldiers had been boyhood friends and showed courage bringing the young fugitive brothers with them to New Hampshire. The artist did show signs of extreme post-traumatic stress disorder.

Did the soldier kill his artist friend? If so, under what circumstances? How did the boy die? At the same time? Was his death related in some way to the murder of the artist? How had he died? And when? The actual date could be important. Valraven had a feeling the anniversary was soon, hence the recent escalation in paranormal activity.

Dekker went back to his room to finish reading the diary, to see what else he could learn. Valraven also wanted to read it, but could wait. He knew enough to make contact with the spirit boy, Moze. He'd spend time today in the room next to the crawl space Ethan called Room Thirteen. They'd probably met there. Hadn't Dekker said it was where Ethan found the Chapman paintings, the ones in the dining room? But not the crucial picture, the nude soldier sitting in the window, which he'd inadvertently recreated. How had that work been separated from the others? Valraven believed the return of the painting to its place of origin had been an inciting event.

Valraven gathered together the dirty plates. The least he could do was take them back to the kitchen and wash them. Both hands full, opening the door was a bit tricky and he almost lost his grip on the dishes. He regained his balance, backing slowly out of the room, just as Tessa came down the stairs laden with an armful of crumpled bed linen. They collided. Tessa screamed, plates and cutlery clattering to the carpet, bedspreads and pillowcases scattering over the hallway.

"Jesus Christ, Elliott! You scared me half to death!"

"Sorry, Bernstein," Valraven said. "I didn't hear you coming down the stairs."

She sat on the carpeted steps, breathing heavily. "You could've given me a heart attack."

"At the ripe old age of thirty-three? I doubt that."

"Speak for yourself, old man," she snapped back. "I'm still thirty-two for another month."

They spontaneously burst into laughter. Ten years melted away in a heartbeat and Valraven saw the young woman he had fallen for in college—the rebellious beauty determined to change the world. Would they have stayed together if Valraven—no, *Elliott*—had not staged his disappearing act?

Valraven moved to pick up the dishes but Bernstein—no, *Tessa*—stopped him.

"Leave it," she said. "Sit here with me for a minute." She patted the step next to her. He did and she leaned her head against his shoulder. "Don't get the wrong idea. I'm still pissed at you. I know it's ridiculous after all this time."

"You have every right to be angry," he said. "I was an asshole to leave Camden like I did, without a word to anyone. You—especially you—deserved better."

"I thought so at the time, but it wasn't long before I turned it around and began wondering what I'd done to drive you away. I didn't want anyone to know how I felt, so I kept it all inside, letting the pressure build until I was ready to explode. I became an absolute bitch after you left. Ask Dekker. He can tell you."

"I don't think he'd tell tales out of school."

She smiled. "You're probably right, but he's not a naïve farm boy anymore. I think Dekker's been through the wringer more than he lets on. Maybe more than any of us. Well, except for Shelly, who had to go and die. Always the fucking drama queen."

"Harsh," Elliott said softly.

"I know," Tessa sighed. "I'm a horrible person. You should hear what I say about people I hate."

"I think I have," Elliott said. Again, they laughed. Valraven had many questions, but Elliott was reluctant to ask. He didn't want this moment ending just yet. Did Bernstein feel the same way?

"Well, this fly-infested laundry isn't going to wash itself." She pulled on a sheet draping the newel post like a skinny Halloween ghost.

"Let me give you a hand." Elliott collected bed linen, handing it to Bernstein. None of the plates he'd dropped had broken. He picked them up and followed Bernstein through the lounge. The chandelier flickered as they passed beneath it.

"Looks like you have a dodgy electrical connection," he said. "You should have that looked at."

"I'll add it to the list. Right now, I'm worried about more than that freaky chandelier." As if in answer, the lights flashed again, but Bernstein was already on her way to the kitchen and didn't notice. Maybe the problem was not electrical. Valraven knew of spirits who manifested through electricity.

He hurried into the kitchen and set the plates and cups on the counter near a large industrial dishwasher. Bernstein stepped down into the laundry room and started loading two washing machines. Elliott sat on the steps, watching. He remembered asking her once to do a load of laundry for him at Camden, a mistake he'd never repeated. "Do I look like your fucking maid?" she'd replied.

"So you've been running this place all by yourself?"

"Yup. It's a lot of work but I like being my own boss. I found a great chef, Allison, who's become a good friend. The rest of the staff—well, they're a work in progress. Not all of us have fat royalty checks to support us while we wander around communing with the dead. Some people have to earn a living."

A minefield of space still existed between them. He'd have to tread more carefully.

"Dekker says you may actually have met our disruptive spirit," Tessa said. "So how does that work? Do you figure out what he wants and send him on his merry way? I mean, don't get me wrong. I'm not a skeptic like Dekker. I know the ghost is real. I've even talked to it, and sometimes he seems to listen. I just don't understand what you think you can do to get rid of him."

Bernstein and Elliott were slipping away, as Tessa directed her questions to Valraven.

"Each case has its own set of unique circumstances," he explained.

"But all spirits crave the same thing, whether they know it or not. Peace. A release from whatever holds them here, preventing them from moving on into the Light. Eternal rest. I'm not sure yet what ties this spirit to Cloverkist—he and the child spirit Dekker may have mentioned. The child appears to be benign, the other is the obvious threat. He's crafty and angry and his powers are strengthening. My hope is to use the child to get to the man."

"You don't mean Ethan."

"No, no. The child spirit, Ethan's imaginary friend," Valraven assured her. Concern for her son was etched on her face. It was the only reason she'd allowed Dekker to bring him back to Cloverkist. Valraven didn't want to disappoint her.

Elliott did not want to disappoint her again.

"On my journey here, I met a spirit in Arlington Cemetery who pointed me in the right direction. He'd been a Civil War medic who'd crossed paths with the New Hampshire soldiers. His last words to me were 'save the only begotten son.' Who did he mean? Since being here, I've assumed he must've been referring to our troubled spirit—not the child, who apparently had a brother. But then I wondered, could it be Dekker? I remembered he was an only child, orphaned very young. And yet I'm not convinced he's the one who needs saving...which leaves only one other possibility."

Tessa's face turned pale.

"I've no desire to pry. I wouldn't ask if I didn't think the information might help me break whatever has chained this spirit."

"That's an interesting way to frame it," Tessa said with a smile. "Ask your fucking question, Elliott, but don't blame me if you don't like the answer." The harshness in her voice was unmistakable.

"Does Ethan have or has he ever had a sibling?"

"Not to my knowledge," Tessa said. "But you'd know better than I."

"What do you mean?" Valraven asked, confused.

"Give me a break, Elliott. Dekker must've told you by now. He couldn't keep a secret to save his soul. Are you going to make me say it out loud? Ethan is *your* son, you fucking idiot!"

"I'm...Ethan's father?"

"No. You're not his father," Tessa said. "You've never been his father. You're nothing more than an anonymous sperm donor and don't you fucking forget it."

The cruelty in her tone shocked Valraven. Did he deserve it? A pang of anger crept into his mixed emotions.

"Is that what you'll tell him when he asks about me?"

"I don't need to. I already told him you were dead."

Valraven flinched. Tessa smiled and brushed past him up the steps. She froze. Valraven turned to see what stopped her. The boy was standing in the kitchen doorway, eyes wide, the dog at his side. A single tear rolled down his son's cheek. Ethan bolted out of the kitchen, the dog following. Elliott looked up at Bernstein. She hadn't moved a muscle.

A single tear rolled down her cheek, as well.

From the Diary of Corporal Anson Quimby
13th New Hampshire Infantry Regiment

December 1864

Sarah has banished me to the quietude of my study, while she enlists the assistance of Mother and Cook to decorate Cloverkist for the festive season, as she is determined to bring more than a modicum of cheer to our household, which she herself has supplied these past six weeks since her arrival. I have never dared ask how she came to hear of my desperate condition, nor what provoked her to embark on the perilous journey here, to sit steadfastly by my bed and tend my wounds. Her gentle kindness knows no bounds. Belike 'twas Sarah who removed the four pictures from the parlor, Ben's gift to Mother, and stowed them away out of sight, I know not where. I cannot but express my enduring gratitude. I pray my courage fails me not that I may ask her hand in holy matrimony on the eve of the New Year, and disfigured though I am, I pray she will accept my humble offering. I only wish Benjamin were here to share in our felicity. He was most undeserving of such torment, which drove him to deadly distraction. The tragedy of his horrific death haunts my dreams and oft I awake in the bleak darkness of night, screaming in unspeakable dread and profound sadness. I am wracked with thoughts that in some way I am responsible, and suffer near to unbearable anguish, if it be true. When Ben burst red-faced into my study and demanded I return his painting, in faith, I had no notion of what he spoke. He called me a damned thief, and accused me of stealing his picture, the one I had beseeched him to destroy. I told him he was a fool to think I should stoop so low as to misappropriate his worthless artistry. He stormed out of the room, hurling epithets so vile I am loath to commit them to paper. With profane oaths of my own, I followed him out of the house and across the yard, where the first snow of the season had started to fall. He strode forthwith to his studio and began to toss stacks upon stacks of his pictures, some finished, some not, into a pile on the earthen floor, all the while raging as a man possessed. Once the last picture had been added to the heap, Ben seized a lantern from his worktable and glared at me, eyes ablaze. Worthless, he said. All worthless. With great force, he smashed the lantern onto the pile of pictures, where it burst into flames, which snaked across the canvases, igniting the painted surfaces, as Ben laughed like a lunatic. Seeing nothing at hand to douse the fire, I grabbed a pitchfork and attempted to disperse the burning pyre, but Ben pulled me back. Sparks ascended toward the loft full of dry hay. Ben held me tight as I tried to wrestle free, to no avail. I saw our dog, Cassie, emerge from the shadows with a pup in her mouth and carry it outside. Even the dog had more common sense than my deranged friend. Flames darted up the wooden walls and acrid smoke filled the air, choking us. I saw the boy, Moze, run past with an armful of puppies. With the last of my waning strength, I pulled myself away from Ben, who struck out at me blindly with his fists. Amidst the crackling flames, a loud crack sounded from above and flaming debris rained down on us from the loft, catching fire to my clothes. I could think of nothing more than to run outside and roll in the new-fallen snow to quench the flames. And I remember nothing more, until awakening in my bed, swathed in bandages from head to toe. I know not what compels me to compose these last pages, knowing full well they will be hidden away, never to be seen while I still breathe. And yet, the writing may grant some respite from the fateful events I fear will haunt my thoughts for the rest of my days. I can write no more. My fingers ache. No more than my heart...

PART FOUR: Æ

"And I will show that whatever happens to anybody it may be turn'd to
beautiful results,
And I will show that nothing can happen more beautiful than death."

—Walt Whitman

CHAPTER NINETEEN

I. VALRAVEN/ELLIOTT

Lying on the bare mattress in Room Twelve, Valraven had a clear view of the entrance to the crawl space behind the wall. He'd left the low door open a bit, as an invitation, in case the child-spirit was shy about meeting strangers. His eyes had adjusted to the darkness several hours ago and he'd yet to see the slightest sign of movement. Staying awake all night wasn't uncommon for him—he did most of his work at night—but keeping his mind clear was more difficult than usual. He hadn't spoken to Tessa since Ethan had overheard their conversation. He'd have to wait to find out the boy's reaction to the revelation his father was alive. He'd talked to Dekker, who'd told him the tragic end to the story found in the final pages of the diary. Valraven thought meeting Moze might result in a more complete, up-to-date view of what Benjamin Chapman had up his sleeve for later this day—Friday the 13th, the day he'd died in 1864.

Valraven closed his eyes for a moment. Unsure how much time had passed, he opened them again. He was no longer lying down. He sat cross-legged with his back against the wooden headboard. At the other end of the bed, Moze sat facing him in the exact same position.

Valraven raised his hand in silent greeting. Moze mirrored the gesture. He wanted to give the boy a chance to speak first, to not frighten him away. Valraven smiled. The serious expression on the young spirit's face did not change.

"You're too growed up to play games," Moze said, crossing his arms across his chest.

"Grown-ups like to play sometimes, too," Valraven said. The boy looked unconvinced.

"You're not the one with the dog," the boy said.

"No. The dog belongs to Ethan's friend Dekker."

"We like dogs. We tried to save the puppies from the fire but we couldn't save them all." Moze frowned. He may have died young but he was old enough to understand he was no longer among the living.

"Trying to rescue the puppies was very brave," said Valraven.

The boy shrugged.

"What kind of games do you like to play?" Valraven changed the subject.

"We like to play hide 'n seek. We're good at hiding. We know all the best places to hide."

"I'll bet you do," Valraven said. "I'm not a good seeker. Any other games you like?"

"We like the labyrinth. We always end up in the middle. Every time. And we like to play in the Fairy Forest but sometimes it's too far away. It hurts our head and we have to come back."

"Back to Cloverkist?" The boy nodded. Like the spirit on the road in Bethlehem, the child was tethered to this location, which meant the same was likely true for Benjamin Chapman.

"Did you have other friends before Ethan?"

"No one special. A little girl came once but she got ascared and ran away."

"That must be lonely." Moze shrugged again. "Do you ever play with Benjamin?"

The boy shook his head violently, hugging himself tight. "No. No. No. No. No. No. No. Mister Benjamin don't like to play games. Mister Benjamin likes to scare people. Knocking. Smashing. Throwing. Burning. Mister Benjamin used to be nice to us but after...after... after he always angry. So angry and so mean. We're ascared of Mister Benjamin now. That's why we stick together. The dog don't like Mister Benjamin. He growls him away. We like the dog."

Dekker had mentioned how Ethan and Calvin bonded instantly, how the dog rarely left the boy's side. In Native American folklore, white dogs were attributed with special powers. Based on their initial meeting, Calvin didn't like Valraven either.

"He's a good dog to keep you safe," he said, trying to calm the boy, who seemed to grow agitated. "But do you have any idea what Mister Benjamin wants to do? Does he want to hurt someone at Cloverkist? Is he trying to scare someone away?"

"Can't tell," said Moze, eyes darting around the room. "Mustn't tell. He'll punish us."

"How will he punish you?"

"He'll send us down into the forever darkness." The child spirit shivered uncontrollably, his form beginning to fade.

"I won't let him do that. I can help you, I promise. He won't send you down to the forever darkness. But please tell me. What does he want?"

"To burn it down, burn it all down, into the forever darkness, forever and forevermore."

Moze dissipated, leaving only a slight indentation on the mattress where he'd been sitting. If what the boy said was true, Cloverkist was in grave danger.

II. CALVIN

watching waiting two boys talking
whisper whisper more&more
one boy standing fisting madness
one boy sitting tearing sadness
two boys clinging holding tight
whisper whisper more&more

III. DEKKER

The door to Room Twelve was ajar, so I looked inside to see if Elliott was still there. No sign of him. He must've gone downstairs to his room. Eager to know whether he'd succeeded in summoning Moze, and what he learned, I didn't want to wake him. Tempted as I was to call Gregor again and update him on what I'd discovered in the last diary pages, he might already be on his way back from Boston. I had to be patient. I wanted to talk with Tessa, but Elliott suggested it would be smart to give her some space. She'd told him about being Ethan's father. He seemed shell-shocked by the news and reluctant to discuss it. I've been in some crazy situations, but discovering I'd been a dad for ten years?

I went back to my room, took the painting from the dresser, and sat on my bed with it. My first impression was much the same as Gregor's—a well-painted, if somewhat naïve study by a talented, inexperienced artist. The details of the room around the edge of the picture were roughly sketched in, using impressionist strokes. Chapman had focused his attention on the nude figure and the light pouring across it through the window. Now knowing the story behind it, I viewed the painting differently. I saw Chapman's feverish determination to capture his love for his friend—the casual pose, the jaunty angle of the soldier's cap. I imagined how nervous he must have been to show it to his friend at last.

The diary left no doubt to the horrified response of Corporal Quimby. The work's innovation meant nothing to him, nor the modesty provided by the raised knee. All he saw on the canvas was a naked representation of his body and the humiliating abomination of his friend's desire. His reaction must have devastated Benjamin, already on shaky territory in the mental health department.

One thing the diary didn't shed any light on was the provenance of the painting. Corporal Quimby denied Chapman's allegation of stealing the painting. There was no evidence to suggest he had lied. Could Chapman have hidden it himself and forgotten, in his emotionally fraught state? Why wasn't it destroyed in the barn fire with the rest of his work? How did this painting survive? Who'd sent it to the museum? Maybe we'd never know. Some mysteries remained unsolved.

Another lesson I'd learned back in Amsterdam.

I set the picture back on the dresser when I heard Tessa yelling for Ethan outside. From the window I saw her on the raised deck at the end of the covered swimming pool, screaming his name in the direction of the labyrinth, her voice panicked. She disappeared through the gate at a run. Something was wrong. She shouted to me from the bottom of the stairway.

"DEKKER, ARE ETHAN AND CALVIN UP THERE WITH YOU?"

"NO," I shouted back, bounding down the stairs at a breakneck pace. She pounded her fists on the door to Room One.

"ELLIOTT! IS ETHAN WITH YOU?"

Bleary-eyed, Elliott opened the door, shaking his head.

"Of course not," he said. "Why would he be?"

"Tessa, calm down. What's going on?" I asked.

"What's going on? I'll tell you what the fuck's going on—Ethan and Calvin are gone!"

CHAPTER TWENTY

I. ETHAN

We stop at the Fairy Forest for a rest.

We are not tired but we have to save our energy.

It is hard to climb the mountain all the way to the top. Dowser Duane says. You can see forever in all directions. You can see Father Rock. Dowser Duane says. With a wink. That means he is pulling our leg.

Dowser Duane showed us the Fairy Forest. We must not come here alone. Dowser Duane says. We are not alone. Calvin is with us. Calvin likes the Fairy Forest.

We sit on a stone wall across from the magic castle with the stairs that lead to nowhere. We open our knapsack, take out Ethan the Giant, and lay him on the wall beside us.

Snack time. Peanut butter crackers. Our favorite.

We took ten packs. It will be a long hike.

Be prepared. The Boy Scout motto. We are too young for Boy Scouts. Mom says. We can still Be Prepared. We wear our red hooded sweatshirt because it is cold in the morning.

It will get colder up the mountain. We know because in Science we learned about Mount Washington, the coldest mountain in the world.

We put a long warm scarf in our knapsack for later. Be Prepared.

We only eat one peanut butter cracker. One for us and one for Calvin. He likes peanut butter crackers. He licks the orange crumbs off his mouth.

We save the rest for later. Some for eating. Some for tracking.

Hansel and Gretel left breadcrumbs in the woods to find their way home. They did not know the birds would eat all the breadcrumbs and they would get lost.

We are smart. Smarter than Hansel and Gretel.

We will smush a peanut butter cracker on the back of a tree. White birch. So we can find our way home through the woods.

Brush the crumbs off your sweatshirt. Mom says.

Time to go. We have to go up the mountain and back down before it gets dark.

Mom will be mad.

We know. We are mad, too.

Never tell a lie. Mom says. Mom told us a lie.

We will ask Father Rock what we should do.

Father Rock knows the answer to all questions. Dowser Duane says.

We gotta go back.

No. We are climbing the mountain.

We can't go so far away. We got to say goodbye.

We will come back.

We might be gone.

We don't know what that means.

We put Ethan the Giant back in our knapsack and pull our arms through the straps.

Calvin, come.

The deer path is the best way to go. Dowser Duane says.

The deer know the easiest way to climb the mountain. We will go up and up and up to the top until we can see Father Rock.

II. DEKKER

Calming Tessa down was no small feat. Hysteria wasn't helpful. I told her Calvin would never lead Ethan into danger and would keep him safe. Elliott called Dowser Duane, who said he'd get in touch with his Uncle Jacob, the tracker. He told Elliott we should have a piece of Ethan's clothing ready so the hounds could get his scent.

"Oh, Jesus," Tessa moaned, as she ran off to Ethan's room.

Elliott and I stood by the reception desk. Dark clouds had moved in, casting shadows in the room. I switched on the lights, which didn't relieve the gloom. Elliott started pacing, swinging his arms in circles by his sides.

"If anything happens to him, Tessa will kill me," he said. "We can't just stand here waiting for some backwoods tracker. You know the kid. Do you have any idea where he might've gone?"

"I barely know him," I protested.

"Think, Dekker. Think."

"Okay. Okay. We took a hike down behind the inn to Possum Pond. There was this rock formation he showed me. Painter's Palette. It's in one of the Chapman paintings in the dining room. But I don't know why he'd go there."

"Where did the hike end?" Elliott asked.

"At Granny Stalbird's, the diner where I got you breakfast."

"I hardly think the kid went out for waffles and bacon, do you? Think again, Dekker."

"I'm trying." The labyrinth didn't have any places to hide. The cemetery across the road? Ethan would have heard Tessa calling him, but I could imagine him leaning against the back of a gravestone, hiding out—and it hit me.

"The folly!"

"The what?"

"Back behind the graveyard, a trail leads to what looks like an old ruined castle—a folly, one of those nineteenth-century affectations. Calvin led me to it."

"The Fairy Forest," Tessa said. She stood in the doorway holding a T-shirt I recognized as one of Ethan's favorites. "Dowser Duane takes him there to play sometimes. He knows he's not to go there alone."

"But he's not alone," Elliott said softly. "He's with Moze."

"You said he wouldn't hurt Ethan," Tessa said. "You said he was some kind of protector spirit."

"I still believe that, but from the boy's perspective, he's not alone. Dekker, grab your jacket and let's go find this Fairy Forest folly. It's as good a place to start as any."

"I'm going with you," Tessa said.

"No," Elliott said gently. "You need to stay here in case Ethan

comes home." He hesitated. "And wait for the tracker to get here."
Tessa's face was heartbreaking.

I dashed upstairs as Elliott ducked into his room. When I got back,
Tessa was slumped in a chair in the corner, breathing into Ethan's shirt.
I knelt beside her.

"Try to stay calm. We'll find him. Remember, Elliott's got this
psychic thing going for us. It can't hurt, right?"

Tessa did not respond.

Elliott returned, a determined look on his face. "Let's go," he said.
We went out to the porch.

Dowser Duane pulled into the parking lot. Snow started falling in
big fluffy flakes, dusting the ground. Dowser Duane got out of his truck
and looked skyward.

"Looks like we're fixin' to have our first blizzard of the season.
Don't you worry none. A little snow's gonna make no nevermind to
Uncle Jacob's hounds. They're used to trackin' in all weather. But if
you boys are headed out, you might consider scarves and headgear."

I didn't need to be psychic to know an early snowstorm was the
last thing we needed to find Ethan and Calvin.

CHAPTER TWENTY-ONE

I. ETHAN & CALVIN

Snowflakes tickle our nose. We try not to sneeze.
We stand like a statue. Not moving. Calvin, too.
The bear is not moving. Just looking at us.
A cub but not a baby anymore. Bigger than Calvin.
We wonder if Mama Bear is nearby. We do not want to meet her.
Calvin growls, soft and low.
Hush, Calvin.

standing watching hackles rising
scenting danger wild&wild
no one moving silence holding
danger staring eye&eye

We have a peanut butter cracker in our sweatshirt pocket.
Do bears like peanut butter crackers? Bears like garbage. Maybe
they like peanut butter crackers, too.
We slowly pull the peanut butter cracker out of our pocket.
The cub sniffs the air. He looks hungry.

We throw the peanut butter cracker to him. He backs up and sits down.

standing ready watching waiting
danger sniffing cookie treat
scenting something stronger wilder
tensing growling holding ground

❖

The cub is sniffing the peanut butter cracker when Mama Bear crashes through the trees.
Mama Bear is huge like Ethan the Giant. Mama Bear stands tall on her back legs.
We are very small. We are afraid.
Calvin is not afraid.

❖

barking snarling threatening danger
danger roaring danger warning
danger swiping bigpaws closer
danger moving close&close
dodging darting forward backward
barking danger more&more

❖

The cub runs away behind Mama Bear into the woods. Mama Bear shows her claws and roars loud at us.
Calvin keeps barking. He runs back and forth.
Mama Bear does not know which way to look.
Calvin stays between us and Mama Bear.
Mama Bear lowers her front paws to the ground and twists her head and roars again.
Calvin crouches and jumps toward Mama Bear.
Mama Bear swats Calvin away with her huge paw.

Calvin squeals, runs back, and stands beside us. We see blood on his ear.

Mama Bear sniffs the peanut butter cracker. She picks it up with her tongue and pops it into her mouth. She chews it like Calvin. Mama Bear looks around for Baby Bear. She gives Calvin a long stare and a quiet roar. She turns around, poops on the ground, and goes back into the woods to find Baby Bear.

We take a deep breath and smell the stinky poop.

Calvin sniffs the stinky poop, raises his leg, and pees on it.

Good boy, Calvin.

We give Calvin a hug.

Calvin gives us a paw. He wants a peanut butter cracker, too.

II. DEKKER

Getting to what Tessa called the Fairy Forest was no problem. But I had no clue which direction to go from there. The temperature had dropped. Snow was beginning to stick to the ground, erasing any minimal traces Ethan and Calvin might have left behind. Elliott scanned the woods surrounding the clearing and found what he thought might be a trail. It all looked the same to me, so I let him take the lead.

"Keep your eyes peeled for anything out of the ordinary," he'd said as we headed into the woods. I may have grown up in the country but had never been much of a hiker. I couldn't help noticing this trail was taking us gradually upward.

Every so often, Elliott paused, looking around carefully before continuing. I didn't know what he expected to find. All I could see were trees, thick bushy evergreens mixed in with tall trunks of other varieties. Trees, trees, and more trees. Nothing to confirm Ethan and Calvin might have taken this path. I was starting to think we should turn back and wait for the tracker, when Elliott stopped again. He turned to me and pointed to a white birch tree beside the trail.

"What?" I said. "Oh, wow. Another tree."

"Take a closer look," he smiled.

Adhered to the trunk was a square orange cracker. Ethan must have licked the peanut butter to soften it and stick his favorite treat to the bark.

"Clever boy," Elliott said.

"At least we know we're headed in the right direction," I said. "But we have no idea how far ahead of us he might be. Or where he thinks he's going. And this snow is not letting up."

"Let's get a move on," Elliott said.

We set off at a quicker pace than we'd been walking so far. I hoped Ethan had been as smart about dressing warm enough for this change in the weather. A bitter wind gusted fiercely, the snow blowing in all directions. Maybe he'd found a sheltered spot to huddle with Calvin and wait out the blizzard. The trail got steeper, more difficult. Surely the boy wouldn't be going as fast as us? I wasn't sure how much longer we could keep up this pace.

We found another orange cracker marker. It hadn't stayed glued to the bark, but since we knew to look, we saw traces on the tree and found the cracker on the ground. We pushed on, coming upon another clearing in the woods. The snow was falling so heavily now our visibility was no more than a few feet before us. I almost bumped into Elliott when he stopped and pointed to a pile of animal shit. It couldn't have been there long.

"Bear scat," Elliott said.

"Fucking hell. Bear? Are you sure?"

Elliott nodded. "Afraid so."

"Shouldn't they be in hibernation by now?" I asked.

Elliott shrugged.

Black bears don't normally attack unless threatened or to protect their cubs. I didn't think Calvin would confront a bear. He'd faced a dangerous beast with murderous intent in the past and managed to be smart, keeping himself from getting hurt. But if he was protecting Ethan, I couldn't predict what he might do.

"Where do we go from here?" I said. "I can't even tell what direction we're headed anymore, can you?" It couldn't be much past noon. Between the cloud cover and the blizzard, the pale light of day seemed to darken by the minute.

"I'm going to try something," Elliott said. "Something that worked once when I was caught in a thick fog. I've never tried it with snow but the same principle should apply."

`What are you talking about?" I asked.

"Stand back and give me some space," he said. "I'm going to go into a trance state. I might need a little nudge to get out of it, so try not to freak out, Dekker. Think of it as a party trick."

I backed a few steps away, watching while Elliott closed his eyes and raised his arms. He swayed a bit and brought his hands together palm to palm. He rolled his hands so they were back to back and began moving them apart, slowly. I felt the air change, almost a quivering. The snowfall undulated and shifted, making cloudlike shapes moving in the air around us. I realized the snow was no longer falling on us, and visibility increased. Elliott was parting the snow!

Within a few minutes, I could see the mountain beyond the trees, a massive slab of rock towering straight up several hundred feet. Sweat dripped from Elliot's brow despite the cold. I remembered he'd said something about a nudge. I tapped him lightly on the shoulder.

"Elliott?"

He opened his eyes and shook his head.

"Thanks, Dekker. For a moment there I thought I might've gone too deep. It's a difficult thing to control. Did it do any good?"

"Jesus, Elliott. Look!" I pointed toward the mountain. Snow continued falling on either side of us, and the way forward was free and clear. "How did you do that?"

Elliott stared upward. I followed his gaze. On a ledge at the top of the rock face, a tiny figure in a red hooded sweatshirt sat next to a white shadow—Ethan and Calvin.

III. VALRAVEN/ELLIOTT

Climbing the steep embankment off to the side of the vertical rock face had been rough going. There might have been an easier way up, but Valraven didn't want to waste time searching for it. Dekker struggled most. The treads on his fancy boots weren't designed for hiking or climbing. He'd lose his footing on a loose rock or grab the wrong branch and slide backward. Valraven had to give him a hand more than once. They were nearly to the summit when Dekker slipped again.

"SONUVABITCH!"

"Dekker, are you okay?"

"I twisted my damn ankle. It hurts like a motherfucker."

Valraven didn't want to stop, not when they were so close. "Can you put any weight on it?"

"Barely," he whined. "You keep going. I'll be right behind you. Just get Ethan off that ledge."

Valraven didn't hesitate. He reached the top with a few more careful steps.

A large flat rock shelf separated him from the boy. He'd apparently not heard Dekker scream in pain. Ethan sat with the dog on the edge of the precipice, staring over the treetops. Valraven approached quietly. A fall from this height would be fatal.

As he came up behind them, the dog uttered a soft growl. Valraven sat on the opposite side of the boy and the dog quieted. Ethan held a carved wooden figure in his hands.

"Do you mind if I sit with you?"

Ethan shrugged.

"Who's your little friend?"

"Ethan the Giant. He keeps us safe."

"Well, he's done a good job. You're a long way from home. Your mom is worried. That's why her friend Dekker and I came looking for you."

"Where is Mom's Friend Dekker?"

"He's on his way. He hurt his ankle but he'll be okay. How about you? Are you okay?"

Ethan shrugged and sighed.

"Dowser Duane said if we climbed to the top of the mountain we could ask Father Rock any question we want. Father Rock knows the answers to all questions."

"Have you asked Father Rock a question?"

"We can't ask him if we can't see him," the boy said, exasperated.

"Maybe you don't have to see him to ask a question. Maybe you could just think it."

"Like a prayer?"

"Kind of like a prayer, yes."

"Okay." Ethan closed his eyes tight and scrunched up his face in concentration. When he opened his eyes, Ethan slid back from the edge and got to his feet. "Time for us to go home."

"Hey, Ethan," Dekker said, hobbling toward them.

"We climbed the mountain with Calvin," Ethan said, full with pride.

"You certainly did." Dekker laughed. "Elliott and I climbed it after you, but you climbed it first. You're the Number One Explorer."

"We can see the inn from here," Ethan said, pointing across the treetops. "Uh-oh. Fire."

Valraven and Dekker both turned to where the boy pointed. In the distance, a vague outline of the inn was visible through the falling snow. Blue flames danced atop the tower, the chimney, and the rooftop.

"Ethan, could you take Calvin over to those trees and maybe find Dekker a stick he can use for a cane so we can get him down off this mountain?"

"I don't need a cane, I need a ski lift," Dekker said. Valraven shot him a look. "But sure, a cane would help a lot."

"Calvin, come," Ethan said. They marched off together toward the tree line.

"Elliott, what the hell—"

"Dekker, listen to me. It's Chapman. Moze said he wants to burn Cloverkist to the ground. We'll never get back in time. There's only one way I can think of to save Bernstein. I have to fight him spirit to spirit." He pulled a thick envelope from his jacket pocket and pushed it into Dekker's hands. "This is for Bernstein. Tell her I'm sorry." He pulled Dekker close, hugged him tightly, and whispered in his ear, "I love you, Dekker. I always have. Take care of my son."

Before Dekker could respond, Valraven broke their embrace and without another word leapt off the ledge. The last thing he heard was Dekker's scream.

"NOOOOOOOOOOOOOOOOOOOOOOOOooooooooooooooooooo—"

CHAPTER TWENTY-TWO

I. VALRAVEN

In helping the dead cross over into the Light, Valraven never considered the act of dying, how it felt the moment one's soul left its body. He had never seen anyone die. And he had no time to think about it in the few seconds before he hit the ground. He focused every fiber of his being on Cloverkist and the necessity to materialize there, to do battle against the forces of evil wrought by the misguided machinations of Benjamin Chapman.

He had no memory of the violent impact, which would have crushed skull and bones, burst arteries and organs, sucked air from lungs, and shattered consciousness into a million pieces. When something akin to awareness returned, he had no sense of how much time or space had passed, no sense of his physical being, barely a sense of being at all. The particles of cognizance he recognized as his own floated in an unending sea of white. Not the white of the Light, but a more delicate crystallization of white. Snow. He remembered snow. His transmigration into spirit form was happening during a snowstorm, the same snowstorm. Immediate or not, his death had not traveled far in time.

What happened next was impossible to comprehend. He felt a powerful surge of energy, and the particles belonging to him began swirling in the air as one, like a murmuration of starlings creating moving shapes against the sky. In sudden darkness, he found himself in the cemetery across the road from Cloverkist, almost whole again, standing on the grave of Benjamin Chapman.

Valraven watched a car pull into the parking lot. A large man got out, popped the trunk, and moved to the rear of the vehicle. Suddenly the air filled with peals of demonic laughter, coming from the giant pumpkin-head figure attached to the side of the inn. The man looked up in time to see the grotesque creature pull free from whatever moored it to the wall. In awkward jagged movements, it staggered toward the man, who was frozen in shock and disbelief. The pumpkin-head monster reached out with its huge inflated mitt-like hands, grabbed the man, and tossed him into the air like a rag doll. He landed with a dull thud on the swimming pool cover. The two stone puppy statues appeared to leap from the deck on top of him, ripping the vinyl cover from its ties, enshrouding the man, who sank to the bottom of the pool. The pumpkin-head automaton shrieked in laughter again before exploding in a blaze of blue pyrotechnics, strewing the lawn with shredded body parts and smashed pumpkins.

Valraven could only watch in horror. He was not yet strong enough to do anything to help the drowning man, who must be Dekker's art curator from Boston. More to the point, he was unable to move at all. He needed to be inside Cloverkist to help Tessa, but his feet remained securely rooted to the ground.

Moze materialized beside him. Valraven realized he had not seen the spirit child with Ethan on the mountain. Was it too distant from Cloverkist? Or had he stayed behind with good cause? Did he know more than he was letting on? Moze romped in and out amongst the gravestones, like he was inviting Valraven to join the game.

I can't seem to get my legs working. Telepathy seemed the way to go since he had no control of his facial structure.

We don't move with our legs. We think move. We don't know how to explain it better.

Like a prayer... Valraven thought.

Yes. Moze disappeared.

Easier said than done. Valraven could not summon the energy he had used when alive to assist a spirit's journey or part the falling snow. Something altogether different seemed required. How to tap into it? He remembered Ethan's scrunched-up little face on the ledge. Could it be as simple as a boy asking Father Rock a question? An image came to mind—Tessa in the Chandelier Room—and like a soft breeze rustling the autumn leaves, he was transported there.

Tessa stood beneath the blazing chandelier, fueled more by flame than electricity. The crystal pendants trembled and shook, gently at first but with increasing violence. Valraven gave her a slight psychic nudge, which pushed her with great force through the doorway into the reception room. He did not yet control his abilities. Tessa looked back, a puzzled expression on her face, as the chandelier fell to the floor with a deafening crash on the spot where she had been standing. Tiny flames danced among the scattered pieces of glass, casting sharp prisms of blinding light that bounced off the walls and ceiling.

Tessa dashed through the pantry to the kitchen. Valraven followed her, taking a shortcut through the wall. He was getting the hang of this noncorporeal existence. She was filling a bucket with water, to douse the phantom flames in the Chandelier Room. She didn't see what was happening behind her, but Valraven could. The leather case holding the set of knives handcrafted by Duane unrolled on the counter. Each knife slipped out of its sleeve, hung suspended in midair—clearly Benjamin Chapman at work.

Valraven saw no other sign of his presence.

Tessa turned with the bucket full of water, saw the knives, and screamed. She dropped the bucket, spilling the water, which turned a menacing dark red as it spread across the floor. When she started to step carefully toward the loading dock, the knives began spinning in a circular motion. She lost her footing on the slippery wet floor and fell. The same demonic laughter Valraven heard outside filled the kitchen. Chapman appeared, juggling the knives with horrific glee. Tessa crawled to the door and pulled herself up, her hair and clothes covered in what looked like blood. One by one, the knives propelled through the air toward Tessa. She screamed as each knife pierced her clothing, pinning her to the door. It barely mattered that none of the blades touched her skin.

"YOU FUCKING ASSHOLE! I'D KILL YOU IF YOU WEREN'T ALREADY DEAD," Tessa shouted at the top of her lungs. "WHAT DO YOU FUCKING WANT FROM ME?"

Benjamin Chapman ignored her and smirked at Valraven.

"Having difficulty protecting your sweetheart?" Chapman crooned with unveiled disdain. "If this was your scheme to eliminate me, you must needs have not considered how ungainly we are when first we pass into the afterlife. Your ill-advised desire to safeguard Cloverkist is no match for my potent power to destroy it. Come. I will show you."

Chapman whisked his way up the flue of the chimney above the stove, pulling Valraven after him. Valraven allowed himself to be led, knowing his strength was gaining as each minute ticked by. He hoped he could keep this fact from Chapman. He had ended his life with a courage of conviction Chapman would never understand. Valraven had gotten off to a shaky start, but his determination to overcome Chapman knew no bounds.

Benjamin Chapman and Valraven alighted on the angular rooftop of Cloverkist. Snow continued falling and the wind howled around them. The weather was no concern to the two spirits. Valraven was not sure how but was convinced he would recognize the right moment to strike.

"The mystery to me is why you are here at all," Chapman said. "You have no vested interest in Cloverkist. You only discovered your sweetheart—or should I say *two* sweethearts were in attendance once you arrived. What forces brought you here? Surely not that inept little weasel Dowser Duane."

Valraven had been waiting for the chance of direct communication with the spirit.

"I was directed here by two messenger spirits—a soldier and a fireman in life. I believe you knew them," Valraven said.

"Perhaps," Chapman said. "What did they want?"

"They wanted me to help you."

"Help me? HELP ME?" Chapman roared. "THE ONE WHO MURDERED ME WANTS TO HELP ME? YOU ARE SORELY MISLED, MY UNFORTUNATE FRIEND. YOUR DEATH HAS BEEN IN VAIN!"

Chapman raised his left arm to the heavens and caught a spiraling ball of fire in his hand. *The man with the spiral.* The petroglyph Valraven had seen in the desert.

"Be careful with that fireball," Valraven said. "You may not be able to control where it ends up."

"You doubt my ability? Choose a spot."

Valraven scanned the landscape behind the inn.

"A perfect target," he said, pointing. "How close can you get to the center of the labyrinth?"

"Pshaw," Chapman sputtered. "Mere child's play." He leapt to the top of the lookout tower, the powerful point Valraven calculated as the peak of the tetrahedron. Chapman lobbed the ball of fire over his head. It landed with an explosive crash in the exact center, annihilating the altar rock into a million shards. The fireball burned bright for a few moments before extinguishing itself, leaving an ugly black hole in the ground.

"ENOUGH GAMES! Tell me why Cloverkist should not be next." Another spiral of fire appeared in his hand, plucked from the bolt of lightning flashing from the clouds.

"Because you are mistaken," Valraven said. "You were not murdered by your friend. It was an accident. Anson tried to save you but to no avail. He never meant you harm. You have harbored this hatred against him for years without cause. Anson cared for you more than you know."

"You dare use his name against me?"

"Not against you. Never against you. Anson loved you, Benjamin."

"LIAR! LIAR! WHAT'S GOOD FOR THE LIAR? BRIMSTONE AND FIRE!"

As Chapman began hurling the fireball at Cloverkist, Valraven summoned all his energy and directed it toward the burning spiral. It hovered in the air, growing larger, spinning faster, capturing Chapman in its turbulent maelstrom, before following the same trajectory as the first, dragging the unsuspecting spirit with it. The air filled with his apoplectic shrieking, but not for long. Benjamin Chapman vanished in the second violent impact. When the smoke cleared, there was no remaining evidence he had ever existed.

Valraven had made a terrible error in judgment. He did not intend Chapman to be taken with the fireball. He had inadvertently sent the disconsolate spirit Down, down to the place for souls incapable of redemption, down to the place Moze called the forever darkness. It was not the eternal fate Benjamin Chapman deserved. Was the mistake irreversible? He had never attempted to save a spirit who had been sent Down. If he tried, he could also be trapped there. He had no choice. He imitated Chapman's leap to the lookout tower's powerful peak and willed all the energy he could muster into the smoking black hole at the center of the labyrinth.

The word *darkness* did not come close to describe the deep black nothingness. No sight. No sound. Noiselessness. Nothing to touch, to taste, to smell. A void below vaster than the universe above. Down. With only his intuition to guide him, Valraven impelled his energy down, down, down, reaching out for Chapman, only Chapman. He sensed the slightest brush against the fingertips, but the presence slipped away. Chapman? Valraven reached down deeper, deeper, deeper. Down. He was gripped by a clawing sensation, digging sharpness into him, wrapping its limbs around him, strangling him. Chapman? He could not change the direction in which his energy pushed him, nor could he untangle the energy seizing him, pulling him, tearing him apart. Never had the impulse to scream *help* been so strong. With no vocal cords to scream, no one to scream to, he was alone in the blackness of Down, where he would spend the rest of eternity.

And yet…

He was not alone. He perceived the existence of another spirit. And another. And another. They hovered around him, enveloped him, became one with him. Was that RJ…and Jayceen…and Lovina? The souls he had most recently helped into the White Light. Could they be joining forces to help him, to wrest him from the darkness, to save him? Was that brave young Moze, as well? Taking his hand in his, pulling him up, up, up. He wished he could hug the boy. He must work as hard as they to rise from Down. Rise. Rise. Rise.

The quartet of spirits surrounded him in the labyrinth. He stood in the center of the black hole in the ground, cradling the spirit of Benjamin Chapman.

"Pleasure to be of service," said the Civil War medic.

"What Duane woulda wanted," the North Country witch added.

"It was like being in a movie," said the pretty usherette.

Before Valraven could find the words to express his gratitude, one by one they disappeared peacefully into the Light. Once they were gone, Valraven looked at the broken spirit in his arms. Benjamin opened his eyes and looked up at Valraven. The healing had begun. Valraven lifted the artist into the air and his spirit floated upward into the Light.

"Time for us to go, too," Moze said, shyly. He held out his hand. Valraven hesitated before taking the boy's hand in his. The White Light shimmered before them. He had done all he could for his friends, for his son. He wished he had done more, but...

Regrets were for the living, not the dead.

CHAPTER TWENTY-THREE

I. DEKKER

"There goes one," Ethan said with excitement. "Did you see it, Mom?"

"I did," said Tessa. "That was a good one."

A late-night picnic was Ethan's idea. We'd spread blankets on the lawn behind Cloverkist so we could lie back and watch the Orionids put on a show. Tessa and I shared one blanket, Ethan and Dowser Duane shared another. Calvin lay on the grass, Blue Bear between his paws, expressing no interest in shooting stars. A week after the blizzard the October weather returned to normal—warm afternoons and chilly evenings. We all wore hooded sweatshirts with scarves wrapped around our necks to witness the meteor shower on a clear starry night.

"Dowser Duane, can you tell it again?" Ethan asked.

"Oh, Ethan, no," Tessa said. "He must be tired of telling that story."

"No, ma'am," Dowser Duane said. "My great-granddaddy used to tell it to my granddaddy, and Granddaddy told it to my daddy, so now it's my turn to tell Ethan. Way back in the winter of 1817, New Hampshire got hit with a terrible snowstorm. Thunder, lightning, the whole shebang."

"Not ordinary lightning," Ethan chimed in.

"No, indeedy! St. Elmo's fire, they call it. The electrical field created a luminous plasma that made it look like fire had spread over the rooftops of houses and barns, chimneys and silos, and even—"

"EVEN COW HORNS!" That was Ethan's favorite part. He and Dowser Duane had a good laugh about that every time.

Of course, St. Elmo's fire explained what Elliott and I saw from the mountain. Cloverkist hadn't been in flames. A meteorological illusion had been the cause of Elliott's death. How does a psychic get something like that so wrong? Maybe he knew his time was up. The envelope he'd handed me to give to Tessa was a will of sorts—instructions for the property in Maine, his book royalties, and everything else in his estate placed in a trust fund for Ethan.

If only we'd waited for the tracker to show up, we'd have known Dowser Duane had stayed behind to keep an eye on Tessa. A good thing he did, since he saved Gregor from drowning in the pool. We still don't know exactly what happened. Gregor was too shaken to talk about it. Dowser Duane had a half-baked theory about lightning striking Ethan the Pumpkin Head Giant and knocking Gregor off his feet. Was that what crashed the chandelier and left a black burned-out hole in the labyrinth? And in all that chaos, what possessed Tessa to throw Dowser Duane's knives at the loading dock door?

"There goes one," Ethan said, pointing to the sky.

Gregor returned to Boston the day after the blizzard and his "accident." I did show him Corporal Anson Quimby's diary, identifying the soldier as the subject in the painting. But our hearts weren't in the right place to discuss it further. We needed time to reassess what we wanted—in art and life. As for the Willy Hart painting, I told him the museum could consider it an indefinite loan. It would be selfish to hold on to such a masterpiece, not sharing it with the world. I could find the tender solace it had provided elsewhere.

All I had to do was look around me.

"I think it's about time we pack it in and go to bed," Tessa suggested.

"One more?" Ethan pleaded. "I want to see one more meteor." He giggled. "I made a rhyme. One more meteor. One more meteor." Dowser Duane and I joined the chant and Tessa relented. How could she resist?

We received permission from the town to bury Elliott in the cemetery across the road. His family in New York hadn't heard from him in ten years and they weren't the forgiving kind. A granite gravestone marks the spot, with a traditional nineteenth-century engraving:

DREW SMITH ELLIOTT
BORN 1962
DIED Æ 33 YEARS

In the aftermath of that tragic day, I couldn't stop thinking Elliott had died for no reason. Had he achieved what he'd set out to accomplish—banishing the ghosts of Cloverkist "spirit to spirit"? Tessa believed he did. We'd lingered in the cemetery after the small graveside service, while Dowser Duane took Ethan and Calvin on a walk to the Fairy Forest.

"What makes you so certain?" I'd asked her.

She thought for a moment before answering. "When that chandelier nearly fell on my head, someone—or something—pushed me out of the way. The same asshole spirit that was always messing with me. Or so I thought." Her eyes had a faraway look, as if she was seeing it happen again. "But in the kitchen, there were two presences—one trying to kill me and another who…wasn't. It's hard to explain. After you told me what Elliott said—about fighting spirit to spirit—the other presence had to be Elliott."

"Kind of a leap, don't you think?"

"Maybe." Tessa smiled. "But don't tell me you're a stranger to leaps of faith, Dekker."

"Touché."

She was right, as usual. She had no way of knowing some of my leaps had been blunders. Elliott may not have made a true believer out of me, but I could no longer say I didn't believe in things I couldn't see.

Tessa seemed genuinely happy when I told her I'd like to stick around for a while and help get the inn up and running again. There was more to it, of course. At Cloverkist, I found something I never realized had been missing from my life for far too long—a family.

"I see another one!" Ethan exclaimed. The meteor was so bright no one could miss it. Even Calvin gave it a bark.

Ethan had stopped speaking in first person plural since his hike up the mountain. Tessa noticed it first. We weren't sure why but thought it best not to ask. Tessa said he was becoming the happy little boy he'd been when they first moved to Cloverkist.

I did ask him about his friend, Moze.

"He's gone," Ethan said, with an enigmatic smile. Case closed. The bond between him and Calvin remained the same. Nothing gets between a boy and his dog.

II. CALVIN

watching waiting one boy laughing
one boy happy / one boy gone
calvin&dekker&ethan&tessa
evermore&evermore

1939

When Doxey looked in the mirror he saw an old man. He did not understand. He did not look in the mirror much these days. He lay in bed looking at the ceiling. Sometimes he had help to sit in his chair. Not so much these days.

Doxey was tired. Sometimes he slept all day. He was having a good spell today. Maybe he would ask Nurse to help him sit in his chair. He pushed the button so Nurse would come. There was something he wanted to tell Nurse but he always forgot. Not today. Today he remembered.

"How's our Fireman doing?" Nurse always called him Fireman, even though he had been Fire Chief. No nevermind. Doxey liked Nurse.

"Behind my chair." Doxey had trouble putting a sentence together sometimes.

"You want to sit in your chair today? Well, okay." Nurse started to help him out of bed.

"Behind my chair. The picture."

"Yes, your nasty old picture is still behind your chair. All wrapped up like always. You ever gonna look at that picture?"

Doxey shook his head. He never wanted to see the picture again. He wished he could tell Nurse the story of the picture. How the Corporal and Mister Benjamin argued about the picture. How he stole the picture so they would stay friends. So Moze and Doxey would never have to go back to the cotton fields. Doxey did not have the words to tell Nurse the story. They were stuck in his head.

"The picture gallery."

"Whatcha saying, Fireman? Sometimes you are a hard man to understand. Like my husband." Nurse laughed. She was always laughing. Doxey needed her to understand.

"Send…the picture…to the picture…gallery." If Doxey spoke real slow maybe Nurse would understand.

"Do you still wanna sit in your chair or are you gonna be a chatterbox today?"

"No chair." Doxey was too tired. He needed to try one more time. "The picture…"

"You still on about that picture? What are we supposed to do with that nasty old picture after you're gone, Fireman? Toss it in the trash, I expect."

Doxey shook his head again. "To…picture…gallery…"

"You want us to send it to some picture gallery? And who's supposed to pay the postage? Shall we just take it out of your account?" Nurse laughed again.

"Yes, please." Nurse was still laughing.

"Okay, Fireman, we'll deduct it from your account." Nurse laughed her way out.

Did Doxey have an account? He didn't know. But he hoped Nurse understood. All these years gone, mayhaps someone at the gallery would like Mr. Benjamin's picture.

Doxey closed his eyes. Moze waited for him in the darkness. Like as always.

About the Author

David Swatling was a 2015 Lambda Literary Award finalist for his debut thriller *Calvin's Head*. He grew up in rural New York, studied theater at Syracuse University, and pursued an acting career on both coasts—before moving to Amsterdam in 1985. He produced arts and culture programs for Radio Netherlands Worldwide and is a three-time winner of the NLGJA Excellence in Journalism Award, among other international honors. He wrote for Amsterdam's first gay weekly *Trash in the Streets* and hosted *Alien*, a local gay radio show.

His short story "Poets' Walk" appears in Volume One of *Chase the Moon: The Magazine of Misfit Stories*. He has also contributed articles and interviews for numerous online publications, including *The Big Thrill*, *Chelsea Station*, and *Gay Star News*. He continues to blog about the arts and LGBTQ issues, from Amsterdam and elsewhere. Visit his website at http://davidswatling.com.

David can be contacted at dswatling@gmail.com.

Books Available From Bold Strokes Books

Corpus Calvin by David Swatling. Cloverkist Inn may be haunted, but a ghost materializes from Jason Dekker's past and Calvin's canine instinct kicks in to protect a young boy from mortal danger. (978-1-62639-428-5)

Calvin's Head by David Swatling. Jason Dekker and his dog, Calvin, are homeless in Amsterdam when they stumble on the victim of a grisly murder—and become targets for the calculating killer, Gadget. (978-1-62639-193-2)

Murder at Union Station by David S. Pederson. Private Detective Mason Adler struggles to determine who killed a woman found in a trunk without getting himself killed in the process. (978-1-63679-269-9)

A Champion for Tinker Creek by D.C. Robeline. Lyle James has rescued his dad's auto repair business, but when city hall condemns his neighborhood, Lyle learns only trusting will save his life and help him find love. (978-1-63679-213-2)

Heckin' Lewd: Trans and Nonbinary Erotica, edited by Mx. Nillin Lore. If you want smutty, fearless, gender diverse erotica written by affirming own-voices folks who get it, then this is the book you've been looking for! (978-1-63679-240-8)

Inherit the Lightning by Bud Gundy. Darcy O'Brien and his sisters learn they are about to inherit an immense fortune, but a family mystery about to unravel after seventy years threatens to destroy everything. (978-1-63679-199-9)

Pursued: Lillian's Story by Felice Picano. Fleeing a disastrous marriage to the Lord Exchequer of England, Lillian of Ravenglass reveals an incident-filled, often bizarre, tale of great wealth and power, perfidy, and betrayal. (978-1-63679-197-5)

Murder on Monte Vista by David S. Pederson. Private Detective Mason Adler's angst at turning fifty is forgotten when his "birthday present," the handsome, young Henry Bowtrickle, turns up dead, and it's up to Mason to figure out who did it, and why. (978-1-63679-124-1)

Three Left Turns to Nowhere by Jeffrey Ricker, J. Marshall Freeman & 'Nathan Burgoine. Three strangers heading to a convention in Toronto are stranded in rural Ontario, where a small town with a subtle kind of magic leads each to discover what he's been searching for. (978-1-63679-050-3)

One Verse Multi by Sander Santiago. Life was good: promotion, friends, falling in love, discovering that the multi-verse is on a fast track to collision—wait, what? Good thing Martin King works for a company that can fix the problem, right...um...right? (978-1-63679-069-5)

Fresh Grave in Grand Canyon by Lee Patton. The age-old Grand Canyon becomes more and more ominous as a group of volunteers fight to survive alone in nature and uncover a murderer among them. (978-1-63679-047-3)

Loyalty, Love & Vermouth by Eric Peterson. A comic valentine to a gay man's family of choice, including the ones with cold noses and four paws. (978-1-63555-997-2)

Bury Me in Shadows by Greg Herren. College student Jake Chapman is forced to spend the summer at his dying grandmother's home and soon finds danger from long-buried family secrets. (978-1-63555-993-4)

A Different Man by Andrew L. Huerta. This diverse collection of stories chronicling the challenges of gay life at various ages shines a light on the progress made and the progress still to come. (978-1-63555-977-4)

Busy Ain't the Half of It by Frederick Smith and Chaz Lamar Cruz. Elijah and Justin seek happily-ever-afters in LA, but are they too busy to notice happiness when it's there? (978-1-63555-944-6)

Pursuit: A Victorian Entertainment by Felice Picano. An intelligent, handsome, ruthlessly ambitious young man who rose from the slums to become the right-hand man of the Lord Exchequer of England will stop at nothing as he pursues his Lord's vanished wife across Continental Europe. (978-1-63555-870-8)

Best of the Wrong Reasons by Sander Santiago. For Fin Ness and Orion Starr, it takes a funeral to remind them that love is worth living for. (978-1-63555-867-8)

Coming to Life on South High by Lee Patton. Twenty-one-year-old gay virgin Gabe Rafferty's first adult decade unfolds as an unpredictable journey into sex, love, and livelihood. (978-1-63555-906-4)

Death's Prelude by David S. Pederson. In this prequel to the Detective Heath Barrington Mystery series, Heath discovers that first love changes you forever and drives you to become the person you're destined to be. (978-1-63555-786-2)

His Brother's Viscount by Stephanie Lake. Hector Somerville wants to rekindle his illicit love affair with Viscount Wentworth, but he must overcome one problem: Wentworth still loves Hector's brother. (978-1-63555-805-0)

The Dubious Gift of Dragon Blood by J. Marshall Freeman. One day Crispin is a lonely high school student—the next he is fighting a war in a land ruled by dragons, his otherworldly boyfriend at his side. (978-1-63555-725-1)

Quake City by St John Karp. Can Andre find his best friend Amy before the night devolves into a nightmare of broken hearts, malevolent drag queens, and spontaneous human combustion? Or has it always happened this way, every night, at Aunty Bob's Quake City Club? (978-1-63555-723-7)

Every Summer Day by Lee Patton. Meant to celebrate every summer day, Luke's journal instead chronicles a love affair as fast-moving and possibly as fatal as his brother's brain tumor. (978-1-63555-706-0)

Everyday People by Louis Barr. When film star Diana Danning hires private eye Clint Steele to find her son, Clint turns to his former West Point barracks mate, and ex-buddy with benefits, Mars Hauser to lend his cyber espionage and digital black ops skills to the case. (978-1-63555-698-8)

Royal Street Reveillon by Greg Herren. In this Scotty Bradley mystery, someone is killing the stars of a reality show, and it's up to Scotty Bradley and the boys to find out who. (978-1-63555-545-5)

Accidental Prophet by Bud Gundy. Days after his grandmother dies, Drew Morten learns his true identity and finds himself racing against time to save civilization from the apocalypse. (978-1-63555-452-6)

Counting for Thunder by Phillip Irwin Cooper. A struggling actor returns to the Deep South to manage a family crisis but finds love and ultimately his own voice as his mother is regaining hers for possibly the last time. (978-1-63555-450-2)

Of Echoes Born by 'Nathan Burgoine. A collection of queer fantasy short stories set in Canada from Lambda Literary Award finalist 'Nathan Burgoine. (978-1-63555-096-2)